Peaceful

C000151771

Chosen Voyage
Book 1

C. G. Lail

Prologue

↔

The *greatest* King, the one who had ruled over the Kingdom for eight incredible years, was mad. Furious, in fact. Zami wasn't sure why she was even surprised. He was rarely *not* angry.

Perhaps had she not been training, in a course designed by The Majesty himself, she might've heard the furious yelling reverberating through the dark, cold halls of the palace. But alas, as always, she *was* training, and she was only made aware of the fact her father was angry when she heard a commotion from the doorway. Elios, her mentor and closest friend, came sweeping into the room, white robe billowing behind him, and bespectacled eyes wide with fear.

He was quick to apologize though, when Zami, who had been distracted by his entrance, was whacked upside the head by one of her sparring partners. The trainer, who despite muttering an apology as well, didn't really look all that sorry due to the blows she had been delivering up until the interruption.

"*Yes?*" She inquired, snatching the ice pack he held out to her, once he had drug her all the way to his lab. He had the decency to look abashed as he shuffled his feet, pushing up his glasses.

"Uh, well um...", he mumbled. She raised her eyebrow at his hesitancy, and he cleared his throat before spitting out the rest of his ridiculous question. "Don't you think it's time, you know... you told him?"

She rolled her eyes and dropped the ice pack on his desk, turning to leave. "If that's what you brought me here to ask, I'm going in to take my leave now."

"Zami!" He squeaked and she sighed at the concern in his voice. She knew he was only trying to take care of her, but she was done being babied. She'd *been* done for the past eight years.

"I already told you, Elios." She remarked, pivoting to face him again. "I don't care how temperamental and insufferable he gets. I'm *not* letting him use me as a weapon."

"He's going to use you as a weapon either way!" Elios cried, sweeping his hands out. "Isn't it better to just give in now and save yourself the suffering when he *does* find out?"

She pursed her lips and turned her head away so he couldn't see the hesitation in her eyes. "I don't care if it'll make him hate me more. He already hates me. What matters is that right now, at least, I can save all the lives that would be lost should I tell him. I'm past thinking of the future for our King, Elios. You know that." She gave him a pointed look and he ducked his head. He had argued with her about this almost every day, and her answer hadn't changed. Not for the years that he'd been asking.

"The King's mad, Zami." Elios finally said. "They still can't find *him*. It's like he's just disappeared."

She rolled her eyes and rubbed her jaw, wincing at the soreness. "Doesn't matter to me. It's their problem if they can't find some guy they've been chasing for forever." He went quiet after that and Zami let out a breath, rubbing her forehead.

"Listen, Elios." He looked up and she held his gaze. "I only have so much power." She remarked, and his eyes dropped a bit. "There's no winning this war. Not when there's no such thing as a correct outcome. No matter what I do, this war is going to be bloody and long and horrible for everyone. The only thing I can trust is that it'll be over one day." With that, she turned again. This time she was just heading out the door when he responded, voice soft.

"Think of yourself for once, Zami. *For* yourself. Please."

She frowned and closed the door. For a long second, she leaned back against it, staring at her feet. She didn't trust herself enough to know what to do. She didn't have anything to believe in when it came to war. Not when either outcome meant misery on her part. It didn't matter anyway, she supposed, straightening up and starting towards her corridors. It wasn't like she was going to last all that long here. No assassin lasted long enough to see the end of their cause.

Footsteps interrupted her thoughts, and a voice cut through the air, frantic and harsh compared to the relative silence she was accustomed to near her rooms

"The King is calling for you!" She froze on the spot. That couldn't mean anything good. It never meant anything good. But she nodded slightly to show that she had heard the Page, and then slowly turned around, making her way back down the hallway.

The short walk to the throne room was enough time for a chill to set in her bones, and for her palms to become sweaty with fear. The dank, shallow walls of the castle never felt as suffocating as when she was being summoned. Her heart never pounded so dangerously fast in her chest.

Why are you so scared? She berated herself. She wished she were braver. She wished she were stronger. She wished she weren't his daughter. But as the yells got louder, reverberating through the halls, she knew she was a goner.

She mentally listed everything she'd done, trying to remember what she could have forgotten. But there was nothing. Not that that was rare. He often was mad for any random reason *but* her behavior

Her panicked rationalization was interrupted by a guard swinging the door open and nodding his head into the hall. The hall overlook on the Kingdom Damrion should've been pretty. It had an open view on to a beach and a peek of lush forest land to each side of the castle. But the cloud of misery that hung in the air, no matter where you traveled in the land, ruined the image. *Or perhaps*, she mused, amusing herself, *it's just him.*

"Kid." Her head shot up and she realized she had made it to the end of the hall. Her father sat on the throne as always, eyebrow creased. But not with concern about her, or anyone he *should* care about. He was concerned about the fact that he couldn't manage to track down, and kill, the only person destined to keep him from ruling until he died of ripe old age.

"You know how hard I've been trying for this." He remarked smoothly, and she hesitantly nodded. He seemed pleased enough with that response and continued. "Now, I've come to one conclusion through these past years." Some annoyance that hadn't previously been in his voice began to seep into it. "That somehow, no one, despite their supposed expertise, has been able to find this *hero*." She swallowed at his words, keeping her eyes dead set on her feet.

Why is he telling me this? She fretted. *What is he planning?*

"So. I've decided that I've been holding off from using the right person all along." Her head shot up and her heart seemed to come to a complete stop. "Because even if your magic isn't working yet, you still have it in your blood." She let out a relieved breath and ducked her head back down to let him finish his speech. At least he didn't know.

"Zami." She stiffened at the pure, malicious intent in his voice. "I have a mission for you."

Chapter 1

↔

Ray woke up with a groan, hand swinging out to slam the button on his alarm. He'd never been someone to despise mornings that much, but given how late he had stayed up last night fretting about today, he was in rare form.

Slipping on clothes and fixing his hair had never felt quite like a chore as it did at that moment, hands fumbling to button jeans and smooth his shirt. It took far too long for him to wobble down the stairs, where he stopped as his Aunt Laurel looked up from the stove.

"Ray, sweetie, you're a mess." She observed. He grumbled at that, aware that she was referring to the unrest in his slightly disheveled form, and the tightness of his lips. He didn't think she had a right to judge though, because the shadows under her eyes revealed that today hadn't come easy for her either.

"Thanks." He mumbled, shoveling food onto a plate as well as he could with his sweaty hands.

Dew, his other aunt, stalked into the kitchen, stretching her arms with a cheeky grin. Based on her tank top and the sheen of sweat against her skin he fathomed she had gone out running.

"Dig in hotshot. You'll need your energy to save the world." He rolled his eyes but returned a smile as she ruffled his hair.

He plopped on the couch with a sigh, leaning his head back to stare out the glass door into the backyard. Birds chirped from the trees, and the chimes Laurel had hung up all those years ago hummed a melody supporting that of the animals. The peacefulness of it all reassured him. Just because things would change, didn't mean everything was changing for the worse.

"Get your fill sleepyhead, remember Ray is leaving today." The weight on the couch shifted as his bed-headed mess of a brother flopped down, lips curled in a pout that was no doubt because of his brother's imminent departure. Ray smiled at him, not at all affected by the half glare he received in return.

"You ready for your big future, mister prophecy?" Dew asked as she leaned over the back of the couch.

"I don't know." He responded, poking at his pancakes, stomach too knotted with anticipation for food to be alluring. "It depends on the future I suppose. If it's crappy, I figure it won't be very exciting." He yelped as she playfully punched his arm, eyebrow crooked in exasperation.

"Heroes shouldn't have that type of attitude." She retorted.

"Well excuse me!" He snarked, stabbing a piece of pancake. "Have you ever been a hero?"

"And that's exactly what I'm talking about." She said smugly, snatching his plate and hustling into the kitchen.

"Hey I wasn't done with th..." He started, only to be interrupted.

"No time, you have to get ready!" Laurel said, pulling him off the couch and shoving him to the stairs. He let out an exasperated sigh as he made his way back upstairs to brush his teeth and slip on his shoes.

He'd been preparing for this moment since he had found out what he was capable of months ago, and he'd been vibrating with excitement just days prior. Yet now, as he stood there, facing the inevitable, he couldn't help but feel a little sad and uncertain. It had been obvious, the moment he'd agreed to join the rebellion, that there would be no easy-going life any longer. That knowledge didn't make it any easier to swallow.

"Ray! Get your world-saving butt down here! They're here!" He jumped up, grabbing his jacket and taking the stairs three at a time, only slowing to pull it on when he was completely downstairs. Standing at the door was a woman who looked so much like his mother, it made him catch his breath. Red hair, held together in a braid, fell over her shoulder and sparkling green eyes stared back at him from above lightly freckled cheeks.

"I'm Sylvia." She offered, shaking hands with his Aunts. At their looks, he hurried forward, clearing his throat and holding his hand out.

"Ray." Sylvia nodded, smiling widely. Her grip was startlingly hard and he held back a wince.

"Are you ready? We're ecstatic to have you join."

He swallowed and nodded. "Yeah, thanks." He rubbed his neck, slightly unsure of what to say. "I think...." He turned to receive a big hug from both his aunts, bombarding him with cautions and reminders. He couldn't help but chuckle at their concern, hugging them back before pulling back to ruffle his brother's hair.

"Be good for them, 'kay?" He said, smiling down at the unhappy face.

"Am I not always?" Blaze retorted, though his voice shook just enough to indicate exactly how upset he was.

"Yeah, whatever, dork." He responded, taking him by his shoulders and pulling him into a hug. Blaze's complaining didn't at all convince any of them, especially when it was accompanied by tears.

With a pat on his shoulder, he pulled away and said one last farewell before stepping out the door with Sylvia.

The first minutes were spent in complete silence before he realized they were just walking down the street, and he turned to Sylvia to ask where exactly they were going.

"Ah," she cut in before he could ask. "You'll see." He shut his mouth and turned away. Sure enough, only a minute later she turned sharply around a corner he had never even bothered looking at in all the days he had passed it, and stopped right before a dead end.

He watched in awe as the air began to shift, revealing a swirl of reds and yellows that just hung in the air. The air was hazy around it, too blurry to truly feel real.

"What are you waiting for?" Sylvia asked, and if he wasn't imagining it there was a hint of mischief in her voice. "Step in." He swallowed a snarky comment, about how it'd been a while since he'd seen a space warp, and slipped inside, skin tingling at the strange sensation.

The feeling was similar to that of a roller coaster, including the drop of his stomach and the tingle of his skin. It wasn't the most pleasant thing he had experienced, and when he stepped out it took him a moment to figure out where he was. Quickly though, as he gained his bearing, the uneasiness was gone, replaced with wide-eyed shock.

Soaring canopies blocked the sky far above them, supported by enormous redwood trees that curved in unnatural ways to shield every part of the settlement beneath them. Branches curved to create bridges with other branches, on which breathtaking wooden structures sat, bustling with people of all shapes and sizes. He saw people with the strangest colored hair, wearing things from robes to ripped jeans. *No wonder the motto of the rebellion was "all are welcome,"* he thought, peering around in wonder.

"Never seen something quite like it before?" Sylvia asked from beside him, nudging his arm.

"I'm a country boy. I think it's safe to say I couldn't imagine something like this if I tried." He managed to get out, taking in the rays of sunshine filtering through the leaves.

Technology had grown and evolved over the past decades to fill in the spaces basic magic didn't quite cover. He'd grown up most of his life in a town where technology had been much more prominent than magic. So being here, in a place where magic was quite literally hanging in the air, left him slightly breathless with excitement.

Sylvia laughed, patting his shoulder.

"That's fair." She called out to a dude nearby with soft eyes and a gentle smile. His skin seemed to catch every bit of sunlight as he walked towards them, then bowed deeply to Sylvia.

"Thank you, Cole, there's no need for that, though." He stood up straight and Ray swallowed. That was one *big* dude.

"Do you have any clue where Strike and Blu are?" Sylvia asked, and the boy shook his head.

"I couldn't be sure ma'am, but they're probably either in the pavilion or training." There was something very grounded in his movements, something soothing about his voice. Ray was struck with the realization that this was what being around *magic* was like. It was marvelous.

Sylvia sighed, rubbing her temple. "Of course. Thank you Cole." Cole bowed his head again and then shuffled away, people scattering to stay out of his way. Sylvia didn't speak immediately, but when she did, she sounded like an exasperated mother.

"Come, Ray, I have two people for you to meet. I figured Blu and Strike are the best fit for helping you get used to it here." He followed her through a tunnel dug in a tree and around a cabin, taking in the smell of grass and earth. "They can be a bit much sometimes, but..." Sylvia stopped in front of a large pavilion, peeking around before turning the other way and walking in the opposite direction. "They do know what they're doing." She paused to think for a moment before adding, "Most of the time."

He tried to ignore the last part and instead focused on where they were going. Near the far corner of the settlement to his right stood a large rocky hill with a neat tunnel dug in the center. Kids bustled in and out of it, the occasional one looking slightly frayed or wet. He followed her into the opening, only half-listening to her explanation on the importance of training while you were still young, and observed each person walking down the tunnel.

His attention was quickly diverted, however, by what the tunnel led into. A large soaring cavern echoed with shouting and yelling from many figures below them. A dirt track surrounded the perimeter, and most of the space was a grassy field just below them, filled with kids fighting. The feeling of magic lay heavy in the air, a feeling he wasn't accustomed to. Most of the kids in his town didn't have magic, and those that did have it, didn't seem all that interested in applying it to anything other than small pranks and such.

Sylvia didn't leave him long to stare though, but just slid down the steep decline into the pit where kids were fighting. Feeling a little awkward, he planted his feet and slid down as well, surprised when he landed on his feet. He ducked under a stray fireball, waving back at a shout of apology. He didn't mind the idea of being pummeled by magic, it was pretty enough to look at.

He stopped to see who Sylvia was waiting for, watching from beside her as two boys tumbled with one another. He could only make out a head of bright blue hair and another of dark hair as one of them yelped. It ended pretty quickly with the blue-haired one standing over the other, who was on the ground rubbing his head with a pout.

The one standing that he figured was Blu, for obvious reasons, laughed and held out his hand, pulling up the other, Strike, he guessed.

"Come on bro, you were closer that time!" Blu exclaimed, brushing off a startlingly bright pair of skinny jeans.

"Face it, Blu. I'm not going to be able to beat you without magic." Strike grumbled, crossing his arms. Strike was tall and gangly, donning a thin pair of glasses that perched on his nose and with dark curly hair that fell into his bright eyes. Blu was around a head shorter, but the amount of energy in even his still figure was enough to rival a racing motor. He had a bright smile, blue hair, and bright jeans that were almost as loud as he was. They looked almost comical together.

Sylvia cleared her throat and they turned, eyes falling on him. "Blu, Strike, meet Ray."

Blu smiled brightly, holding out his hand. "I'm Strike." Ray frowned, and the real Strike smacked Blu on the head. Blu pouted, rubbing his head. "Fine, yeah okay, I'm Blu." Ray bit back a smile and shook his hand.

"Strike." Strike sighed loudly, shaking his hand as Sylvia reprimanded Blu.

"You do that every time! Stop confusing new kids!"

"It's just too funny!" Blu complained, waving his hands around wildly. "Can you blame me? Their faces are priceless!"

Sylvia sighed again. "Just show Ray around, okay? Strike, you have permission to smack Blu if he's acting stupid." She walked away, shaking her head slightly, and Blu sniffed loudly, brushing off his sleeves.

"I feel bad for her. Too old to enjoy anything."

"I HEARD THAT!"

Blu snorted but quickly straightened up, sending Strike a look. "You wouldn't smack me for telling jokes, would you?"

Strike shrugged, pushing past him. "Only if I feel like it."

↔

"OW! Strike, that's like the seventh time today!"

"There wouldn't be a seventh time if you would just shut your trap."

Ray chuckled as Blu and Strike bickered, poking at his food. They were by far some of the most interesting people he'd ever met in his life, but he wouldn't change them for a moment. They'd enthusiastically shown him the whole place, not without a few smacks and arguments, and now he sat with them, as Blu complained loudly over dinner.

"Strikeyyyy, you're so mean to me." Strike snorted, ignoring Blu and shoveling lettuce into his mouth. Blu leaned forward and Ray perked up, leaning in to hear what he was going to say.

"If you're gonna date someone, don't date someone like him." He let out a yelp as Strike flicked his ear, sitting up and rubbing it with a frown.

"Don't talk crap about your boyfriend when he's right next to you." Strike stated, smiling slightly.

"Awww, you're smiling! You really do love meeeee." Blu exclaimed, flopping down so he was laying across Strike's lap.

Strike frowned distastefully at his lap, poking what Ray assumed was Blu's nose. "I won't for much longer if you keep being such a dork."

Ray snorted when he saw Blu's arms flail from where he was sitting, poking Strike's nose back.

"Aww come on. You love my dorkiness!" Strike rolled his eyes but didn't argue, instead, stabbing a potato with his fork. A few seconds later Blu sat up, hair slightly disheveled.

"Hey Ray, what's it like being a hero?" Blu leaned forward, blinking expectedly at him.

He raised an eyebrow at him, setting down his fork. "Well, I'm not really a hero, at least not yet." He informed the boy, smirking at the look on Blu's face.

"Good point. What's it like knowing you're gonna' be a hero?" Now Strike was looking up too, although less enthusiastically than Blu.

"Kinda stale." He responded honestly, rolling his shoulder. He hadn't really done anything in his whole fifteen years of being the person in the prophecy. People tended to make way more of a big deal out of it than necessary.

"Aw come on man, you can't just leave it at that!"

Ray stood up, grabbing his plate and saluting at them. "Actually I kinda' can." He heard the shuffling of both of the others getting up and waited for a moment. Sure enough, only a second later Blu was bounding up beside him, Strike at his shoulder.

"What about fame? The glory? The swooning ladies all over such a majestic man?"

Ray couldn't help but laugh and nudge the other slightly. "You've watched too much TV." Blu gave him a wide grin.

"Everyone getting along?" He turned to see Sylvia standing behind them, hand on her hip.

"Yup." Blu chirped. Sylvia gave him a look and Ray turned away to hide a grin.

"Right," Sylvia remarked, giving Blu a surprisingly affectionate pat on the head. "Well don't stay up too late. We're planning a lot for tomorrow." Ray nodded, trying to wipe the smirk off his face. They all watched as she walked away, initiating conversation with a tall girl sitting at the tables.

"Right man, imma' go to sleep," Blu exclaimed, grabbing Strike's hand and bounding off in the opposite direction. Ray smiled as they disappeared in the distance and made his way to the room they had shown him, staring out the window for a considerable amount of time before actually slipping into bed. He fell asleep to the sounds of people bustling around, and the thought of where he was going to be headed in a couple of days.

↔

Zami stalked through the forest silently, unsure where she was going. It was an eerie place to be, especially when you were alone.

Her father hadn't given her much in the way of directions, only the *extremely* useful advice that she was clever, and it was her future.

So here she was, walking through a very dark, very big forest without the slightest clue of where she was meant to go.

She stopped at a particular ray of sunlight, holding out her hand to feel the warmth of the sun. Breathing out slowly, she closed her eyes, trying to think of what she was going to do. She had never been out of the castle like this, and she couldn't come back as a failure, so the only answer was to finish the mission. It was just one person, she just had to kill *one* person. Yes, it was a particularly important person, but it was still *just* a person.

Opening her eyes she began to pull her hand away, only stopping when a whisper of an idea began to plague her mind. She peered contemplatively at the pale light. If she could feel the sunlight in her palm, perhaps she could feel similar types of power through her magic.

Glancing around to make sure she wasn't in any danger, she closed her eyes again, this time reaching past the feeling of warmth to something *else*. There was something there, a bigger source that fed on all this sunlight, a connection. With no fear whatsoever, she tapped into it, trying to grasp onto some part of it.

And almost immediately she let go with a yelp, trying to stem the burning that was growing in her chest. Taking gasping breaths, she clutched the skin over her sternum, wanting to stop the burning somehow. It took several minutes until it faded and she opened her eyes, blinking spots out of her vision. It figured that to do this mission against her will, she would have to get hurt in the process.

It took her a couple of minutes to build the courage to try again, this time promising to herself that she would push past it. With a shaky breath, she closed her eyes, attempting to find the connection again. It came quickly, and just as last time she reached out to grab it, trying to ignore the burning spreading from her core. It stung her skin and she resisted the urge to itch it, as she focused all her attention on her task.

The relief came all at once, as soon as she felt the connection latch back onto her as well. Her eyes shot open in surprise when she realized she could feel someone, a few emotions that hadn't been there before, not super noticeable if you didn't think about it. And to her excitement, she could feel where the other person was, the connection growing stronger every time she stepped towards her right.

With newfound enthusiasm, she began to follow the pull, ignoring everything in her way.

She didn't know exactly how long she ended up following it, but it was long enough that her legs started to ache and her throat was dry from lack of water. When she finally looked up, she noticed the sky was dark, and she could feel the connection weaken slightly. Making up her mind to rest, she plopped down against a tree, picking anxiously at her thumbnail.

Tomorrow she was going to go through with the mission, and live with the fact that she had killed someone, and there was nothing she could do to make it better.

Feeling conflicted, she pressed her finger to her sternum, internally apologizing to the person on the other side of the connection. The person had family, friends; heck, they were supposed to save the whole freaking world! And *she* was going to ruin that all.

With a sick feeling settling in her stomach, she leaned her head against the tree, staring at the night sky between the trees. She fell asleep thinking of what was going to happen tomorrow, and wondering how in the world she was going to live with herself afterwards.

Chapter 2

Ray could hardly sleep that night, his mind wandering amongst the possibilities of the future. He was too pumped up about finally being in the rebellion, where he would finally be able to do something meaningful with his magic.

He sat up on the bed with a sigh, deciding he might as well get up if he couldn't sleep longer. Based on the number of people wandering around it was early morning, and to his disappointment Strike and Blu didn't seem to be up yet. So he was left on his own, sitting on a bench and wondering if there was anything he could do. Normally he'd play with his brother or work on studying, but here there was no school and no brother.

Pulling this jacket tighter around him he stood and began walking around, taking in every detail of the buildings around him. He guessed they must've been there for a while considering the amount and size of some of them. Certainly no one had any time to build recently.

He turned around when he heard a yell from a kid, and watched as a little boy grabbed the hand of a much older one, dragging him out to see something. It was only when he glanced around that he noticed the emptiness of the street and the eerie silence of the alley he had turned into.

Uncertainty built in his gut and without further thought, he quickly turned to leave the alley. In that instant he felt something slam hard into the side of his head and stumbled backwards. Seeing double, he ducked as fast as he could, registering something whisking just past where his head would have been only a second ago.

He shot back up and attempted to ignore the stinging of his temple as he wildly glanced around, eyes wide with shock. Nothing like this had ever happened to him before, and as he waited hesitantly with bated breath he found himself mildly confused.

If this was an assassination attempt, why was it happening early in the morning instead of late at night? And where in the world *was* the assassin?

Despite his uncertainty, he didn't let his guard down as he slowly backed up a bit. He slowly realized that someone was playing with him, and waited with his heart thumping dangerously loud. He furrowed his eyebrows.

Whoever had attacked him was waiting, he knew they were. He could feel eyes on him, cold and calculating, even though he couldn't see them. They were baiting him, testing him, trying to figure him out. They wanted him to play into their hands.

Which could only mean that whoever this was, they didn't know him all that well. They were making tactics up on the fly, based on how he was acting.

He turned his back on where he felt the watcher and ignored the prickling in his skin. He had to play this wisely if he wanted to survive. Combat training alone wouldn't save him from a seasoned assassin.

He was well aware of the feeling that his survival could be short-lived, but that didn't keep him from a sigh of relief at a tangible shift of the tension the air. The assassin hadn't been expecting him to simply begin to walk away so soon after the first hit, and if he made it into a common area, their shot was gone.

Of course, he didn't plan to go somewhere far, and he knew the person he could sense following wouldn't let him. So, he simply took a few steps at a time, eyes searching his periphery. Just then he sensed movement and didn't waste a second before he lifted an arm and casting his magic before him. As usual, he couldn't tell if it had gotten any brighter, but when the attacker froze, he knew the blinding light was working.

The assassin's face was shaded by a hood, and clothes too dark and loose to tell anything other than size a head shorter than him, but he didn't have time to act on that new information as they started running toward him.

No way, he thought, and had barely a moment to process the fact they'd so easily shrugged off his magic because they were nearly on top of him already.

A shoulder shoved hard into his torso, which tore him from his shock in time to block a swinging fist with his arm, then twist around to grab their arm. A little gasp made him pause before a knee was shoving into his stomach, making him wince and step back as he blinked through the pain. Whoever they were, there was no way they were human. No one could hit that hard and accurately purely as a reflex.

Quickly he was dodging another pass at him, and with determination, he shoved his shoulder into the attacker hard enough for the other to stumble. In fights like these, he wasn't ashamed to use size and strength to his advantage. He'd always been more strong than agile, which meant a lot of hard-learned tactics to avoid getting knocked over easily at the beginning by someone smaller and faster. Like said assassin now.

A flash of metal left him ducking rapidly with strained breath under a swinging knife, then recovering to kick at the other's legs. They didn't collapse as he'd prayed they would, but they did buckle and that was enough time for him to lunge forward and grabbing at their wrists. He jerked at the one with the knife and squeezed, pushing it away from him.

For a second he was worried that it hadn't worked, because the knife wasn't moving, but then with almost a surprised squeak the attacker jerked their wrist involuntarily and the knife went clattering to the ground.

He pushed them back and heard a crack as the attacker's head hit the brick of the building behind them. Ray was about to resume fighting before the assassin could gain the advantage again, but he froze when their hood fell back and he met a girl's wide, bright eyes full of shock, and something else he couldn't quite place.

"You're *good.*" It was a breathy comment, one that surprised him so much he was caught off guard. Apparently, she was surprised as well, because she wasn't moving from her place, hood pooled between her neck and the wall, and shoulders hunched. She cocked her head and he blinked.

"Am I supposed to respond to that, because I'm kinda weirded out right now", Ray croaked out.

She looked a bit taken aback at that response. "Aren't we suppose to be doing something?" She asked, almost nonchalantly.

He raised an eyebrow. "If you mean attempting to commit manslaughter yeah."

She narrowed her eyes. "You sound peeved."

"Oh gee, do I?"

Ray paused when he heard his name called out.

"Ray, where in the world did you go?" He straightened up at Sylvia's voice and turned to find her, only realizing his mistake seconds too late. Faster than should be humanly possible, the girl had the knife in her hand again, and he froze in shock as metal pressed harshly against the skin of his throat.

Sylvia's voice halted abruptly as she turned the corner and her eyes met his with something akin to bewilderment. He could understand why, however, considering the scene she'd stumbled upon right in the settlement.

For a long moment, the only sound in the air was his labored breathing and the slightly hitched breaths of the girl beside him.

In all the stories he'd heard and books he'd read, the person with the knife to their throat would come up with some heroic plan, which ended with cheers and the attacker successfully arrested. But having a real knife pressed to his neck didn't help his thinking process much. In all honesty, the only thing he could focus on at that moment was the cold knife pressed against his skin and the hand flat against his shoulder.

"Ray, stay calm," Sylvia warned, clearly trying to think of something.

"Am I not?" He asked back, swallowing roughly and instantly regretting it when he felt the knife dig further into his skin.

"Listen to me," Sylvia said, eyes focused on the spot behind his shoulder. "You're young, Ray is young, and you have a choice just like he does. Don't throw away your future like this."

The girl didn't respond, though he took it as a good sign that she hadn't pressed the knife any harder.

"There are so many people that need him right now; if you were to kill him there'd be chaos!" It was clear Sylvia was on the edge of hysteria and it wasn't hard to see why. He had just come here, as a symbol of hope for everyone around him, and now he was under the whim of this girl and the slightest flick of her wrist while there wasn't a thing Sylvia could do about it. It was probably infuriating, not to mention a bit scary for him.

"Put the knife down, please." The knife shifted slightly and his breath caught until he realized her hand was shaking slightly.

"I can't." Her voice was fairly steady, but there was something else laced deeply in there, which for some reason he could feel. He recalled the look in her eyes only moments ago, the shock and *hesitance* in her expression. And at that moment he knew that she wasn't going to move that knife any closer to him. She couldn't.

So without further thought, he reached up and grabbed the hand holding the knife, pulling it as far away from him as he could and whacking it back, wincing when he heard the thud.

Surprisingly she was still standing, though she looked a little wobbly. And she didn't even attempt to pick up the knife again, rather she avoided his gaze as Sylvia ran up to her and grabbed her wrists.

The next few minutes passed by quickly, as a guard came to yank the girl away, Sylvia ran over and gave him a worried hug, several people were yelling, and things seemed overall in chaos.

Then before he knew it he was sitting on a bed with an ice pack up to his head (props to Sylvia) and a guard at his door (also thanks to Sylvia). Only a few minutes later Blu and Strike walked in, Blu considerably peppy for what had just happened.

"Wow! Only your second day here and you nearly died! I think that's a record!"

"Thanks for the sympathy." He breathed out, rubbing his neck.

"Oh come on man, what happened? What do they look like? Are they…"

"Blu." Strike interrupted, sending a look to the other. "Give him a moment."

Ray gave him a thankful nod. "It's okay, I'm mostly just confused." Blu hopped onto the bed, crossing his legs and blinking at him, which caused Strike to let out an exasperated sigh. "Fine," Ray sighed, rolling his eyes, though he didn't mind at all having them both there. "I woke up early, so I decided just to take a walk around."

"You mean, you're the most important asset to this war and you decided to take walk off by yourself." Blu corrected, narrowing his eyes at him.

"Okay, maybe. But to be fair this is supposed to be a safe place and I'm probably the most capable of protecting myself."

Blu seemed to consider that for a moment before nodding. "Yeah, I suppose that makes sense." He waved his hand. "Go on."

"Well," He swallowed. "It kind of just happened…"

Chapter 3

↔

Zami growled as she pressed a loose fist against the wall, leaning over to stare at the ground. She was furious, absolutely steaming. But not because she had failed, not because she had been hit, no, she was angry because of her father. He had told her that the person she was after was vile, a pig who used his fame for his own good. And it had turned out it was an innocent boy her own age?

She punched the wall and whipped around to pace the room, chewing on her thumbnail. Her head pounded from where he had hit her and her stomach still occasionally stung, reminding her of her defeat.

Why had she hesitated? Why did she listen to that lady and freeze?

Because she hadn't wanted to kill anyone, because she couldn't kill anyone. And maybe, she had simply been hesitating because she wanted to have an excuse to not hurt him. The only problem was....what now? She couldn't just escape and go back to her dad without proof that she had done her job, and who knows what they would do to her here. She had tried to murder their hero, for god's sake!

Feeling torn she dropped to the floor and pushed herself to sit against the wall, wrapping her arms around her knees and pressing them to her chest. Why couldn't she do anything right? No wonder her dad hadn't sent her on any missions before this; she was an utter failure and a complete disaster.

They had brought her down a level into the ground, where it seemed she was the only person being held. Which could be good, or really, really bad. The only sound was her breathing and the tap of her foot against the cement. They hadn't posted a guard outside her cell, but she figured there must've been a couple outside the entrance of the dungeon.

Anxiety welled in her chest as the minutes passed, each one marking a minute less before she found out what they planned to do with her. She could only hope that being young and independent might help lean them into her favor, though she wasn't sure they were going to stand it anyway, considering who her target had been.

She chose to level a long glare at the opposite wall rather than punching something again.

What had she been expecting? To kill someone and then leave like it was nothing? Ignore the family and friends that would be devastated, the everlasting effect on the world?

A commotion outside caused her gaze to wander, watching as a woman walked through the door and opened her cell with a key. Zami didn't move, instead just watching as she closed the cell behind her and walked in, taking a seat on the ledge for a bed.

At first, she attempted to stay composed, blatantly ignoring the woman's stare that felt like it could see her soul. But after at least ten minutes of trying to avoid it, she gave in to the discomfort and looked up. The eyes that were staring back at her made her freeze. They weren't particularly unusually colored, although a pretty shade of green, but they stopped her every thought, froze all her inhibitions on the spot. They didn't make her feel unsettled or scared, but there was something there that made her realize that she had no choice in this, what this woman says, goes. She wasn't going to make the calls herself, they had the power here, this *woman* had the power.

Zami coughed, ducking her head and trying to calm her nerves before she noticed. The number one rule about being imprisoned was to never let the people who did it think you're lower than them. But she was most definitely far lower than this woman sitting in front of her. She didn't need a crown of gold or silky long robes to prove her authority.

"It's alright to be nervous."

Her head shot up and she met the gaze of the other again for a long moment before she pulled away and glanced in the other direction. "I'm not..."

"Nervous? Well, that's my mistake dear, I just figured that you might be." The silence stretched out between them, her heart beating loud enough for probably anyone in a ten-mile radius to hear.

"No-no you're right. I am." She amended, refusing to look up. "But, can you blame me?" She gestured half-heartedly to everything around her.

"Of course, a lot has happened on this day. Too fast for most minds to process in that same time."

Zami risked a glance up, finding that her eyes weren't filled with any hostility or hate, just understanding, a deep understanding that only someone who had been through hell itself would have.

"Yeah-yeah I guess it has." She answered, feeling a little more relaxed than before.

"So, young one, do you have a name?"

Zami was far beyond her ability to even try and compose herself at the moment, so she just let herself follow the lead of the other. "Zami."

"And how old might you be, Zami?"

"Fourteen."

The woman nodded, eyes sparkling with something that hadn't been there before. "Good. Please, can you tell me why you're here now?"

Perhaps it was the calmness of which the words were spoken or the ringing in her head, but Zami felt unusually relaxed at that moment, letting her foot stop its repetitive tapping and her shoulders slump.

"I just uh, I was sent to try and kill him. I didn't want to, I don't want to, but I couldn't argue and now I'm here and I don't know what's happening." She blurted out, blinking at how honest she had been.

"That's what I thought, thank you." The woman stood up and reached out as if to pat her shoulder, but then decided against it. "Get some rest, you have a long path ahead of you." Then she was gone, leaving confusion and the scent of earth in her wake.

Shaking her head she leaned her head back against the wall and stared at the ceiling. Hopefully, a long path meant a long life rather than the dirt path on the way to be executed.

Zami woke up the next morning with a pounding in her head and a cramp in her neck. She frowned at where she supposed the wall would probably be, not willing to open her eyes just yet.

"You know there's a bed... right?" She couldn't help but let out a startled yelp as she opened her eyes, flailing to not fall over as she remembered the events from the day before. And to her absolute confusion, the person talking to her was none other than the prophecy kid, Ray.

He blinked at her from outside the bars, and she couldn't really muster up enough hate to scowl at him so she just sighed, standing up on slightly shaky legs. Without looking at him she responded.

"Duh, I just like floors a ton more. More back support, ya know?"

"I can't really tell if you're being sarcastic or not but given the fact that you're you, I'm gonna say that's a yes." She turned and raised an eyebrow at him as he leaned against the bars. "And I can't say I do."

"Well, that's a shame. Maybe you should try it, you know just switch places with me for a night?"

"You know, I think I'm gonna pass on that one. My back's plenty supported already."

"Ah, that's too bad. Had to try though, life's rough down here in the deep darkness of the dark."

"I'm shaking." He responded, shaking a key in his hand. "Lucky for you you're coming out."

"Oh yay!" She brushed off her shirt and then frowned at him after a second. "Though, last time I checked you weren't a prison guard."

He looked up from where he was unlocking the door and shrugged. "Nah they just shoved me down here and said to get you. Probably a test of some sort."

"You know you probably shouldn't be warning me if something's a test against me."

"Oh no." He said, straightening up as the door swung open. "You can't tell anyone, I'll be executed." With a wink he strutted away, whistling as he twirled the key ring around his finger. Feeling a little bit giddy she stepped out of the cell, following him through the tunnel and up a couple of steps. He pushed the door open in front of him and light flooded the dimly lit room, causing her to hiss slightly.

"What, are you a vampire?"

This time she did glare at him, though it didn't seem to have much of an effect. "Well some of us don't have stupid sun powers."

He turned at her words, giving her her first real look at him. Blonde hair fell in slight waves to his eyes which were a startling shade of blue and his lips were curled into a permanent crooked smile.

"What, you jealous?" He asked, tilting his head just enough for her to catch the teasing sparkle in his eyes.

She scoffed, crossing her arms. "You wish."

He chuckled, running his hand through his hair and gesturing her out the door while holding it open. "Assassins first."

She rolled her eyes and pushed past him, making sure to hit his shoulder with hers. He didn't seem perturbed though, just closing the door behind him and sidling up beside her again.

She began to zone in the short walk to wherever it was they were going, trying to think of what she was supposed to be doing. Yeah, she was supposed to be heading back to the castle right now, guilty conscience intact, but she was kind of okay with being where she was right then.

A hand grabbing her arm jerked her away from her thoughts and she looked up in confusion at the boy beside her.

"You know for an assassin you're kinda clumsy." He noted as she realized she had been about to smack face-first into a door.

"I was just testing your reflexes." She shot back, heart still pounding from the close call.

"Well if you're gonna be doing that you better hope I'm fast." He responded, letting go of her arm with a smirk.

"If you really look at it, I'm just helping you." She said, trying to look innocent. "Practice is the key to success."

Ray raised his eyebrow at her, crossing his arms against his chest. "Yeah well, you're gonna get *real* good at smacking into doors if I'm not there."

"Well then you better be there." She grabbed the door handle and yanked it open, staring at him with a grin. "Assassin stoppers first."

"As in I stopped you from killing me or stopped you from breaking your face?"

"Whichever one you'd like." He shrugged and walked through, seemingly happy with the response.

When she walked through the door she froze. Nearly a dozen hard-faced people sat in a narrow U, the dimly lit room casting harsh shadows across their faces. The room seemed to be set up solely on activating one's nerves, forcing them to walk by every single person in the room before coming to the necessary spot. The redhead from before sat to the left of the center, and a woman Zami didn't recognize sat in the middle, gaze set on her.

"You gonna move or....." Ray whispered out of the corner of his mouth.

"Shut up." She murmured, narrowing her eyes at him.

"I'm just saying." He whispered back, lifting his hands slightly in surrender. She swallowed, risking a look forward and then freezing. Every single eye was on her, all startling just as the woman yesterday.

"Do they choose these people on a level of intimidation?" She whispered aggressively, feeling very small under all the gazes. Ray didn't seem to mind, just stuffing his hands in his pockets and leaning over to whisper back.

"I don't know, probably."

"You're a real help."

"I try."

"Zami and Ray." They both jumped in surprise and immediately turned to look at the redhead who was raising her eyebrow as if to ask "Really?"

"What? I mean uh... yeah?" Ray scratched the back of his neck and she focused her gaze on the wall, trying to act as nonchalant as possible.

"You realize what we're here for, right?" Zami nodded quickly, biting her lip to keep from grinning. She had a feeling that if these people thought she was smiling, she would be marked off as a psycho, which wouldn't fit very well on her personnel record.

"Yeah of course sir... I mean, ma'am." She stumbled out, mentally slapping herself. The lady stared at her for a long time, making her shift slightly.

"Right. I'm Sylvia, please come forward." She gestured to the spot in the middle of the room and Zami sent a look to Ray who urged her forward with his eyes. Resisting the urge to stick her tongue out at him she stalked forward, trying to look as confident as possible.

Walking by the row of people on either side of her was the most nerve-wracking experience of her life, and that was saying a lot. By the time she stepped to the spot in front of the lady, she felt ready to curl up in a ball and cry from how much her knees and hands were shaking. She gripped her hands behind her in an attempt to stop the trembling and dug the tip of her shoe into the other heel, trying to meet the eyes of the woman and failing.

"So, Zami, you're aware you've been charged for attempt of murder?" She nodded, rocking on her toes.

"Yeeeaaaah."

"And that we take that very seriously?"

"Mmhhhhmmmm."

"And your target was one of the most important people on our side."

"Yuuuuup."

"And that we're going to completely forget that you ever did it?"

"Yup." Zami froze, processing what was said. "Wait, what?" Sylvia stood, holding a folder in her hand and meeting her eyes.

"This is all the information written in your file." Then her hand lit on fire and Zami jumped, watching in shock as the file burnt into ashes in the woman's hand.

"Wh... why... huh?" She asked in disbelief, eyes following the smoke trailing up to the ceiling.

"Well we figured, since it wasn't your choice, and it didn't do too much harm, we could just, you know," she studied her fingertips as if she were talking about what she had for breakfast. "Forget it."

"But like..." she flung her hands in the direction of the previously intact paper. "Why?" Her voice unintentionally raised a couple of octaves as she spoke, too surprised to pay any attention to it. The lady raised her neat eyebrows and tilted her head.

"Do you not think that's fair? Because we can always just..."

"Nonono, I appreciate it a lot." Zami hurried to say. "I..."

"Well then, let's get you out of here!" Before she knew what was happening the lady was pushing her out of the door with a smile and shouting at Ray to do something before she was standing outside, staring at the house across the way.

After a long moment, she turned around and blinked at the closed door, scratching the back of her head. A moment later it opened and Ray was walking out, looking about as confused as she felt.

He opened his mouth as if to say something, but a loud yell came from a couple of yards away.

Two boys came bounding up their way. Well, more like one of them was bounding, and dragging the other along, who looked considerably less enthusiastic. If she were to describe the excited one as a single word, it'd be *loud*.

Not just because he spoke loudly, but because of the offensively neon blue hair falling across his brow and the blindingly wide smile that seemed permanently written on his face. Along with the bright jeans and sparkling eyes he made for a... remarkable individual.

The boy next to him looked a lot less remarkable, which here, actually made him stand out even more than the blue-haired one, what with his dark hair and striking eyes as he straightened up from being pulled, fixing his jacket.

"What happened with the trial? That went awfully quick" Zami shifted slightly, risking a glance at Ray who turned out to be looking at her too.

"Um, I guess it went fairly well." He trailed out, eyes still on her.

"So are they getting executed, or what?" The blue-haired one asked, looking a little confused.

"Nah," His gaze trailed across her face for a long moment before he continued. "Thankfully no one's getting executed." She bit her lip and turned away to hide a little grin.

"Then where's the assassin?" The boy looked around as if said assassin was right in front of him, which she was.

"That'd be me," She said with a smirk, raising her hand slightly. The look on his face was worth every bit of their attempt at straight faces.

"You were the one who tried to kill him?" He asked in surprise, looking more shocked than scared.

"Yup." Then to her surprise, he held a hand out with a blinding smile.

"I'm Blu, nice to meet ya'." She snorted and shook his hand, avoiding looking at Ray because she knew that would make her laugh.

"Zami, it's a pleasure." She stated, trying to remain serious.

"Any assassin of Ray's is an assassin of mine." Blu seemed to contemplate that for a moment. "You know what? Forget what I just said."

"Yeah, this one's annoying enough on his own." She noted matter-of-a-factly, thrusting her thumb in Ray's direction.

"Hey!" Ray complained.

"I'm just saying!" She said, pursing her lips. "That most victims don't fight back after the first hit to the head."

"That's only slightly disturbing." He muttered.

"Really?" Blu asked. The boy next to him sighed, smacking his forehead with his hand. She nodded, completely serious.

"Yeah."

Blu elbowed the boy beside him, giving him a devilish grin. "Come on Strike, you get to meet a real-life assassin and you're gonna let it pass you by?"

"Yes," Strike responded, crossing his arms.

"Killjoy." Blu pouted.

"Moron." Strike retorted.

"Dummy."

"Funny. I don't remember being the one who said any assassin of Ray's was an assassin of mine."

"That was an accident, bro."

"An accident that could kill you."

"Oh, don't be so uptight." Blu slapped Strike's shoulder and Strike stumbled slightly. "You're not a target!" Strike huffed, brushing off his sleeve.

"Yeah well, you need someone to have some common sense for you."

"And I'm still alive, so clearly you're doing fine," Blu remarked, leaning his elbow on Strike's shoulder. Which was kind of ridiculous considering it took more effort than it would've to just stand normally. Strike rolled his eyes but didn't shove Blu off of him.

"Right... um..." Ray trailed off, looking understandably confused.

"What are you kids doing still here?" Zami whipped around to see Sylvia frowning at them.

"Umm..." She started, unsure what to say.

"We were just gonna show good old Zami where the training course is!" Blu said, smiling brightly and throwing his arms around hers and Ray's shoulders. "Right?"

"Yeah." She said at the same time Ray asked,

"We were?" She reached over and smacked his shoulder, which made him jump. "I mean, we were."

"Well then you better get going," Sylvia said, with what looked like a small grin. "One might think you were getting into trouble."

"Oh no, never. Not me." She responded, shaking her head. Sylvia raised her eyebrow but slipped back in the door without a word.

"She's all bark and no bite; she's probably the softest person you'll ever meet. Other than Ray of course." Blu informed.

"Aw, the prophecy kid's a softy?" She cooed with a grin at said prophecy kid. Ray stuck his tongue out at her as Blu pulled them both away from the door.

"Let's go! I wanna see Zami beat up Ray!"

Chapter 4

↔

Ray woke up the next morning with sore calves and a bruised shoulder. Maybe it hadn't been a good idea to spar with an assassin, though having her around was nice. He liked the way she talked and joked, he liked how much her eyes sparkled in the light and her wild grins. Overall, she was quite nice to be around.

He had to admit it was a bit odd how quickly everyone looked past her attempt on his life only a day prior, but if they trusted her, he was convinced he could as well. There was something very obviously *right* about her being there, even in the way that she arrived. He had a feeling there was something else involved in why Oak, the rebellion leader, trusted Zami. Oak had a way of telling who they needed on their side.

Rubbing his eyes, he stumbled into the open pavilion, plopping across from Blu and Strike. Blu was trying to get Strike to eat a spoonful of oatmeal and Strike was ducking his head, giggling madly. Ray couldn't help but smile when Blu shoved the spoon into the corner of Strike's mouth and a chunk of it smeared on his face, Strike frowning at him, though his eyes were still smiling. Blu laughed, poking his cheek.

"Aw! So cute!" Strike sighed, grabbing Blu's hand away from his face.

"I'd be more careful if I was you. I have a fork and I'm not afraid to use it."

"You wouldn't attack your handsome boyfriend!"

"Oh yes, I would."

"Strikeeeeee," Blu complained, pouting. Strike sighed, setting the fork down and wiping his face with a napkin before turning back to Blu and leaning over to whisper something in his ear. Whatever he said made Blu perk up and his eyes sparkle dangerously.

"Really?" He asked, looking at Strike as if he were bestowing the greatest gift on him.

"Really." Strike said, giving a rare, shy smile.

Ray jumped when someone sat down next to him, relaxing when he realized who it was. Which was kind of counterintuitive, considering recent events. Zami stole the apple in front of him, twirling it on her finger, but not making any attempt to eat it.

"Are they conspiring to kill us?" She whispered at him, blinking her pretty eyes.

"Nah," he whispered back, leaning a little closer. "Just flirting madly." She nodded at that, turning to look at him.

"You sore?" She teased, glancing at him through her lashes.

"In your dreams." He retorted, snatching the apple back and biting into it.

"Yes, please." She replied, sending him a wink that made him choke on the apple.

"You okay dude?" Blu asked, finally noticing that they were there. Ray just ducked his head, trying to catch his breath.

"Zami!" He heard Blu exclaim. "You can't kill him until he saves the world."

"Whoops," Zami responded, and he could almost hear her grin. He sat up and sent her a half-hearted glare, deciding against trying to eat while she was there.

"You're impossible."

"Well, you better get used to it." She replied, examining her nails.

"So do you know what you're gonna do with your life now that you have some freedom?" Blu asked Zami, reaching his arm below the table to grab something.

"I don't know," Zami drawled. "There's just *so many* possibilities." She finished sarcastically as Ray realized Blu had been grabbing Strike's hand. Strike didn't even seem affected, just poking at his oatmeal with his free hand.

A yell kept Blu from responding and they looked around to see everyone standing up and staring at the far side of the base. Only when people started running in the direction of the yelling did Ray stand up, sharing a concerned look with the others. In a moment he found himself running towards the yelling, hearing Blu asking someone nearby what was going by.

"They don't know either." Blu breathed out as they stopped behind the crowd of people. Ray peered over the crowd's heads, trying to figure out what all the commotion was about.

All at once, people began to part around him, and after a moment he realized they were moving away from Zami too. Leaning against Oak, the rebellion leader, was a man he guessed to be her husband, with similar silver hair and bright eyes. But there was something wrong with his eyes as he looked up, smoke curling through the air, surrounding him and Oak.

"*It's you.*" He rasped out and Ray turned around, confused. Zami was the only one standing within his gaze but she looked equally puzzled.

"Zami," Oak said. "Come here, please." Zami sent him a slightly worried look before walking forward and stopping in front of the man. He stared at her for a long moment before reaching up with a trembling hand and taking her hand.

"*You're the other one. Show them.*"

Zami was frozen on the spot, but Ray wasn't sure whether it was from fear or because she understand what the man wanted. Or possibly both.

But everyone's attention shifted as the man collapsed and Zami reached forward to help catch him, hoisting his arm over her shoulder. Oak sent Ray a "get over here" look as they passed, and with a shrug at Blu and Strike he followed her, slipping into her place to take the man's other arm. She sent him a thankful nod and he followed her down the path, having a silent conversation with Zami about what had just happened.

What was that about? He mouthed, gesturing at Oak and then the man in their arms.

Her eyes told him that she had not a clue, and he looked up as Oak opened a door, gesturing them in. With one final look at Zami, he walked through the door, settling the man onto the couch.

"Sorry about that, I suppose neither of you knows he has a habit of passing out after doing magic." Oak calmly pulled a blanket out of a nearby drawer and laid it across the man, as if spewing out nonsense and passing out was an everyday occurrence. Considering what Ray had learned the past few days, he found that he wouldn't be surprised if it was.

Oak continued, "Do you have any idea what he meant by 'it's you', Zami?" She asked and he also glanced over at Zami. She looked as if considering saying something, picking at her sleeve. But after a moment she shook her head.

"Okay, well you two get back to your day; remember, we may be in a war, but that doesn't mean you aren't kids. Do something fun, go on a date, just don't kill anyone." She sent a look to Zami. "That includes each other."

He nodded and sent a concerned look as Zami walked out, leaving without a word. When he looked at Oak she just shrugged sadly.

"We'll find whatever we need to in due time." She waved a dishtowel at his face. "Now shoo, unless you want to do some dishes."

He shooed.

Catching up with Zami, who was standing with Blu and Strike, he caught a snippet of conversation.

"...passed out." Blu finished saying and Zami nodded in response to something. "So you don't have any clue what he was talking about ?" Zami shook her head, eyes looking slightly downcast.

"Well, what're we supposed to do now?" Ray shrugged, not sure.

"We can always go to the training arena." Strike suggested, and Ray briefly wondered if that were the only thing people did around here. He hurried to respond, however, hoping to cheer up Zami a little bit.

"Sure, as long as I don't have to spar Zami again." He teased, glancing down at Zami. She sent him a halfhearted smile.

"Yeah, whatever." He followed Blu and Strike to the arena, watching their playful shoving and bickering with a smile.

Then someone bumped harshly into his shoulder just as they were entering the tunnel, and he turned in surprise to see Zami, holding her hands out to steady herself, and the figures of a group of teens running away in the distance. It wasn't all that unusual for people to bump into others here, but what was unusual was the way the air seemed to chill a dozen degrees and the shadows seemed to sharpen. He was confused at the terrified expression on Zami's face until he realized his power was acting up along with whatever was causing this chill. Normally he'd be able to feel if he was using magic, but here it was just flowing out, without him willing it.

"Um, you guys?" Blu asked, looking between the two of them in confusion.

Ray just stared at Zami, connecting his unintentional magical reaction to what Oak's husband had said.

"You're…" He began, faltering at the fear in her eyes.

"What is going on…" Sylvia stepped into the tunnel around a group of people who had started to gather, staring at the bright light penetrating the air and the deep shadows that seemed to fight against it. Sylvia took one long look until she reached the same conclusion he had.

"You're the other one in the prophecy." She stated, and a hush fell over the group. Zami looked like she was having a hard time breathing, and with every passing second, the light seemed to dim. His power had dissipated quickly after he had managed to get a grip on it, but she didn't seem to be having the same control.

When he met her eyes, he froze at the sheer amount of uncertainty and unbridled fear in them, sending a clear message that she had not a clue what she was supposed to do. Before he could try and figure out what to do himself, darkness shrouded the tunnel, leaving everyone shouting in confusion.

He heard Sylvia and Blu yelling his and Zami's names, but he didn't attempt to respond, just trying to squint through the dark before remembering that he had magic of his own.

Without a second thought, he pushed out a burst of light, which he probably should've controlled a little better, but he was under a lot of stress at that moment so it kind of just came out. To his surprise there was a considerable amount of resistance that he hadn't ever experienced before, a barrier to work through.

But eventually, the resistance cracked and with a gasp, everything went back to normal. For a long moment, it was completely silent before people started chatting and shouting, curious about what just happened.

"What was that, dude?" Blu asked amongst all the yelling, and Ray just shrugged helplessly, looking around for the source of it all. But not much to his surprise, she was nowhere to be seen.

"Where's Zami?" Strike asked, looking around as well. He felt Sylvia's hand on his shoulder as she located them, and turned to see her expression. She looked surprisingly ecstatic.

"We've gotta go find her." She said, glancing around as well.

"Wait a moment. Hold up." Blu exclaimed, stopping them in their tracks. "What was that?"

"Isn't it obvious?" Sylvia said excitedly. "We've found Ray's other half!"

Chapter 5

↔

Zami glared at the ground as she stalked out of the tunnel, crossing her arms tight across her chest. Right, just when everything was turning up better, her stupid magic had to get in the way. It wasn't like anything could just let her be happy or anything, no of course not.

She knew she should've waited to see how people reacted, but her instincts had kicked in, and before thinking she had to get away from everyone.

Her head spun as she slipped into one of the narrower alleys in between several cabins, and pressed her back to the wood with a shaky breath. The feel of the rough material beneath her fingertips calmed her nerves, and slowly she felt her heartbeat slow to normal, dissipating most of the panic in her chest. Right as she began to wonder what she was going to do, warning bells sounded in her head. She wasn't sure how, or why, but she could *feel* something was wrong with Ray.

Unsure what she was doing, she slipped back out of the alley and sprinted in the direction of the tunnel, forgetting every bit of common sense she had. She made it back in record time, skidding to a stop right as he and Sylvia walked out the tunnel, Sylvia saying something that was making him frown in confusion.

She didn't even process them noticing her there and Sylvia calling her name, but instead, was absorbed in trying to figure out what was wrong, what *felt* wrong. There wasn't anyone near them, no spots suitable for a sniper or ambush, no particularly dangerous-looking anything.

"Zami?" Sylvia asked, stepping closer to her and reaching out a hand. Zami pulled back a bit and immediately felt badly at the hurt on Sylvia's face.

"Yeah?" She responded, ducking her head from view.

"Why didn't you tell us?"

She shrugged, pulling at a piece of hair that had come undone. "I guess I uh... wanted to just..." *Be normal. Feel normal.* Her brain supplied, but she didn't say anything, just left it at that.

Then her ears perked up and she straightened up, picking up on a weird rumbling sound. Her body moved faster than her mind, registering the sound of rocks shifting and crumbling, and shutting her eyes tight, she tackled Ray as hard as she could, causing him to stumble forward with a yelp. Her eyes shot back open just in time to see the daylight cut out and hear an earth-shaking crash. Dust billowed up and she coughed, trying to figure out what had happened.

"Hey, you alright?", Ray asked while choking a bit.

She blinked at him, finally piecing it together. The reason she had thought he was in trouble was the sensation of some magic force building up. The same force that made the roof crumble just above him; the only thing keeping him from becoming a squashed sunshine-boy being her trained instincts.

She couldn't help but laugh, staring in shock at the slightly dusty, but intact boy before her. Only a couple of days before she had attempted to kill him, and now she was trying her best to save his life? What was even going on anymore?

"Yeah, I'm fine." She answered, grinning. "You?"

"Yeah." He answered, sounding slightly breathless. She glanced around, taking in the large wall of rock behind her, leveling up with the wall next to the tunnel, leaving only a jagged opening to her right. A little trickle of light shone through it, paired with the yells of Sylvia and someone else.

"We're fine!" She shouted back, hoping they could hear her. After some shuffling, she caught a glimpse of red hair through the small opening, and then Sylvia was speaking.

"Sit tight, Oak's coming." They both acknowledged this, but as soon as Sylvia left, Zami snorted, trying not to giggle.

"I'm not so convinced you're all right," Ray said, leaning against the wall and raising his eyebrow at her.

"Depends on your definition of *all right*." She said, dusting off her boots. "If you mean physically, yeah."

This time Ray chuckled, standing up straight from the wall, and to her surprise, poking her forehead. She let out a little yelp, trying to keep upright from the wave of dizziness that rushed through her.

"Don't even think you're that." He commanded with a smile.

"Hey!" She complained, reaching out to poke him as payback. "You should know, you don't poke a lady!"

"Oooooh, is that what you are?" He asked, ducking when she went to smack him.

"You're really mean, for a hero!" She remarked with a pout.

"Says the girl who was trying to slap the hero!"

"Says the hero who deserved to be slapped!"

He huffed, crossing his arms. "I don't deserve to be slapped!"

"Tell that to the *lady*." She muttered, narrowing her eyes at him.

"Try not to kill each other in there!" Sylvia called, making both of them jump in surprise.

"Whatever are you talking about?" She asked, throwing her arm across Ray's shoulder. "We're besties already."

Ray nodded, completely serious. "Yeah, bro's, homies, broskis." Zami could tell Sylvia was giving them her 'are you serious' look even though she couldn't see it.

"Right. Well try to get comfy, this might take a little while. But not too comfy, we can't afford any prophecy babies running around right now." Zami could feel her face flush red and she turned away, coughing violently into her elbow in surprise.

"Sylvia!" Ray said, aghast. Sylvia didn't respond.

She couldn't help but giggle at his cute reaction, glancing up to meet his eyes. "You intimidated, sunshine?"

He scoffed, turning away. "Never."

She jumped again at a large scraping sound, followed by a number of yells. The rock shifted slightly sideways and forwards, which meant towards her. She hurried to take a step to the opposing wall, swallowing hard.

"Seems like you're pretty intimidated, though," Ray noted and she leveled a glare at him. But his point was only proven further when she stumbled a few more steps at another loud scrape. She started to point her finger at him and hit his chest, stopping when she realized how much closer he was. Heart pounding, she looked away, a snarky retort caught in her throat.

"Cat got your tongue?" He teased, giving her a grin that made her heartbeat rise even higher.

"Be quiet!" She squeaked, shoving him away, which didn't work well since he was already right up against the wall.

He nodded, miming zipping up his lips and throwing the key away, a wild grin still on his face. She sighed, rolling her eyes and internally yelling at her heart to get back in her chest.

The next few minutes were spent in silence, her avoiding looking at him and trying to think and failing, and him just standing there, staying quiet.

"Why didn't you say anything?"

She looked up, taking in his completely serious expression and curious eyes. "I uh, mostly didn't even really think about it. Magic's never been a big part of my life."

"And the other part?"

She ducked her head, biting her lip. "I kind of just wanted..."

"To have a normal life?"

She nodded, frowning at him. "How'd you..."

"I used to wish I was normal." He said, sounding perfectly at home with saying such a thing.

"And now?"

He hummed, and a smile took over his face as he met her eyes with something that made her heart stop. "I enjoy not being it."

She startled when the rock shifted loudly, leaving light flooding in from the opening which had widened considerably. Sparing one more glance at Ray, she shoved him in the direction of the opening, hiding her face from him.

Soon, she stepped into the light and proceeded to be tackled by a loud, fretting Sylvia. She laughed as Sylvia hugged them both, muttering words about "stupid rocks" and "I'm gonna' kill whoever did this" which made her heart warm slightly. The fact that Sylvia was so worried about the both of them, despite Zami's original mission, made her slightly giddy and light-headed. Or maybe that was the aching in her head.

Hands pressed against her back, gently pushing her away with a chuckle.

"Where..." she began, turning to frown at Ray. He gave her a gentle smile, continuing his pushing.

"You need to rest, you look like you're gonna fall over."

"I always look like imma' about to fall over." She pointed out. It was true, but only because she rarely got good rest. Which she supposed, didn't much help her point.

"Don't care." He said and she found herself standing in front of a cabin. "See ya' soon." He saluted and turned around the corner, leaving her standing there alone. She sighed, sticking her tongue out at him and stumbling into the same room she had fallen asleep in the night before. She hopped around, pulling off her boots and jacket before laying down. The moment her head hit the pillow, she was fast asleep.

The next morning she woke up feeling strangely calm. The light was filtering through the window, settling warmly on her face and she felt as if she was sinking into the sheets. Rubbing her eyes she propped herself up on her elbow, looking to see what time it was.

2:30 pm

She sat up in surprise blinking at the closed door. Why hadn't anyone gotten her up? Oh god, she was going to be in so much trouble.

It was only when she was halfway through pulling on her boots that she remembered where she was. Her dad couldn't get mad at her, because he wasn't even here! Feeling giddy, she finished tying up her laces, grabbed her jacket, and stepped out of the door. For some reason, the sight of people bustling around yelling and laughing made her heart thump, and the sounds of everyone going about their normal day caused something to ping in her chest. Yes, this was much better than anything she'd ever experienced.

With a bounce in her step, she searched for the others, knowing they wouldn't be in the pavilion at this time, so she decided to attempt the training arena. Ignoring any weird looks she got, she made her way down through the tunnel and stepped out into the open space. She spotted them almost immediately, standing on the field area closest to the opening. They didn't look to be doing much, Blu waving his hands wildly about something, Strike rubbing his temple, and Ray nodding along. Although she could only see the back of his head, she could tell he was smirking, trying to remain serious.

Strike noticed her first, and soon after, Blu did too. She grinned as she sidled up beside an unsuspecting Ray, who in turn jumped slightly at her presence. He blinked widely at her for a long moment before his surprise faded into a teasing smile.

"She finally rises." He joked, smiling softly at her.

"Of course, I need all my energy to beat the crap out of y'all." She responded, wiggling her eyebrows at them.

"Oh yeah, Sylvia needed to talk to us once you were up." Strike said, pushing his glasses up his nose.

She winced, wondering if the morning, or rather, afternoon, was going to turn unpleasant as they turned back towards the tunnel.

"Don't worry dude. Probably just need to remind us that we still need to like, learn a bunch of stuff or something." Blu informed, taking bubbly strides.

"Probably because someone hasn't been doing their schoolwork," Strike muttered as she and Ray both snorted in amusement.

"I don't know what you're talking about, my love. You would never betray me, would you?" Blu asked very pointedly, slipping his arm through Strike's. Strike shook his head, face serious.

"No, never." He said, swinging his arm slightly. Blu narrowed his eyes slightly, but didn't say anything, just continued with his normal bouncy steps.

Zami followed them out of the tunnel and to a building right next to the same one she had been judged at the other day. When Blu knocked, it swung open to reveal Sylvia, whose face brightened up considerably when she saw who it was.

"Come in!" She called, turning around and leading them into a living room. Several couches and recliners surrounded a fireplace, which she figured was mostly used for guests, considering Sylvia's magic powers. The paned window in the wall allowed sunlight to filter in, warming the room and brightening it considerably.

Sylvia's eyes seemed to bite into her soul as she walked in, and she ducked slightly behind Ray. She settled for sitting on one of the recliners after the others sat on a couch, and she nervously settled, not used to being in another person's house. Sylvia stood in front of them, gaze unwavering from her eyes. Zami swallowed nervously as she began to speak.

"I figure all of you know about the prophecy, right?" Zami nodded along with the others, wondering where this was going.

"And you know it hints that when the sun and moon magic wielders path's cross, that's the time when we must arise?" Again, Zami nodded.

"We've decided that this is the time to do something. So you four are leaving tomorrow for Zamoth, where we intend for you to find out where to look for the first desirable." Zami froze, mind on overdrive. They wanted her to go on a mission. Which would determine the future of the rebellion. With the guy she had tried to murder just a few days ago.

"You know what the desirables are, right?" Zami nodded again, swallowing her doubts. The desirables were artifacts of magic; strong magic created by the last pair of sun and moon power wielders. That had been the reason the war had been so devastating, so costly, so bloody. They had found a way to combine the elements with their own powers, and created the single deadliest weapon in the world. How they had done it, nobody knew, but the magic took the form of whatever you desired the most with your heart and soul, and beyond the reason of logic or the fabric of reality itself, you would be granted that desire. Now that weapon was broken into four pieces, pieces that were hidden far away from each other.

"Wait, you want us to find something that no one has been able to find in nearly fifty years?" Blu asked, sounding slightly skeptical.

Sylvia sighed, rubbing her eyes. "We know it's a long shot, but we have a clue where to start. We just got intel from our agent in Zamoth that a prophet has information on where the first desirable might be." She gestured to her and Ray.

"And with both of you finally here with the rebellion, it may be our opening to beat the King."

Zami froze at that. Beat her father. They wanted to beat her father, the all-powerful tyrant who could do whatever he pleased without any consequences. Or at least any consequences that he cared about.

"All right!" She agreed enthusiastically. More than anything in the world she wished her father was dead. Then she frowned at herself. Man, that sounded messed up.

"Are you sure? This is a big decision to make, there are a lot of risks..."

"One-hundred percent. When are we leaving again?" She asked, standing up. Sylvia laughed and Zami furrowed her eyebrows in confusion. "What?"

"I just thought you would be the last one to agree." Sylvia stated sardonically.

Zami gaped at her, offended. "Never! I go with the flow." She responded cooly, flipping her hair over her shoulder.

"Right. Well that's nice..." Sylvia said, sounding amused. "How about you go with the flow and get something to eat with the others so you don't fall flat on your face?"

Zami hadn't realized how hungry she was until food had been mentioned, and didn't even argue. But as she began to follow the others out of the room, she was stopped by Sylvia, who peered at her with wide, curious eyes.

"Oak said she felt something when she saw you," Sylvia remarked and Zami furrowed her eyebrows, unsure of what she was leading to. "She said there's something in you that we *need*. We're putting all of our trust in you. Please do not break it."

She was a little surprised at how forthright Sylvia was. And a little bit conflicted that the only reason she had been let off so easy had been someone's gut feeling. Nevertheless, she nodded. She was finally getting a chance to change everything. Finally getting a second life to make up for all that she had done. She wouldn't just *waste* it.

The next few hours passed quickly, eating, listening to Sylvia's directions about where they were going and her cautions on what to avoid. By that evening she was restless with excitement for the next day.

"Remember what I said, try not to draw attention to yourself. That area's very unused to just see kids wandering around on their own." Zami nodded, smacking her thigh to stop her leg from shaking. Sylvia gave her a weird look but didn't say anything. "Okay, you four, rest up. I want all of you back *alive.*"

"Okay *mom,*" Blu remarked, receiving a smack to the back of his head. Zami giggled as they stood up, making their way to bed with a considerable amount of bickering. That night she fell asleep with her stomach bubbling in excitement.

Armed with water, food, and sarcasm, Zami watched Blu and Strike say goodbye to a group of people who were talking very animatedly about their future. Ray was standing beside her bouncing slightly on the balls of his feet.

"Calm down. Why are you so excited?"

"The adventure! How could you not be!" She rolled her eyes, but before she could tease him about being so childish, Sylvia stalked up to then, a sly grin on her face.

"I believe I have something of yours that you will enjoy having back." She said, and Zami lit up at the knives she was holding out.

"Thank you!"

The moment they were tucked safely in their sheaths, a sense of security enveloped her. The weight was comforting, and she felt some of the tension leave her shoulders. Soon after, Strike and Blu made their way back to them, Blu with his startling smile and Strike looking exasperated but pleased.

"Come on, the portals don't stay open forever!" Sylvia exclaimed, gesturing them towards a big tree on the far side of the base. People hustled in and out of portals located around the area, carrying weapons and food, among other things.

Zami stared at the one they were walking towards, blinking at the bright swirl of colors. "How does this even work?" She asked, watching uncertainly as it shifted slightly in the air.

"Well, we can't completely explain the mechanism behind it, but we know how to set the place. Anyone who's used a portal to one place in the past, opens that location up for anyone who needs to get there in the future." Sylvia replied.

"How'd you get this one?" Blu asked.

Sylvia glanced at Ray before answering. "From the last time your parents used it... to come here." Sylvia gestured at Ray, who looked a little paler than normal, swallowing roughly. "Well come on, in you go. I'm not coming with you, but Ray knows the way." They had decided since Ray's house was in the right direction, they would start their travels there. Also he could say goodbye to his family before they left. It felt odd that she was about to meet the family of the boy she had previously tried to kill, but she supposed there wasn't a better time than the present. *Plus*, she thought guiltily, perhaps *they won't know*.

She followed the others into the portal, clutching her stomach in surprise when it lurched violently. When she stumbled out of the portal, she frowned at the others, miffed that she hadn't been warned.

"No way, you're motion sick!" Blu exclaimed and Zami made a mental note to slap him later when no one else was watching.

"No." She said, swallowing back her nausea. "I'm not." She watched in disbelief as Ray reached out and poked her forehead *again* and her vision doubled.

"Yes. You are." He said and if she hadn't felt so pathetically weak she would've smacked him.

"Everyone has their flaws." She mumbled, rubbing her temple.

"Such as an assassin who gets motion sick?" Blu asked.

She lifted her finger and pointed at him. "Shut up." Blu avoided meeting her eyes, just holding his hands up innocently and turning to follow Ray down the alley and onto the road. She narrowed her eyes at their backs but trailed behind them, breathing in the fresh air.

Every house had huge lawns and tall, healthy trees, their bushes bursting with colorful flowers. She figured it must have been a fairly small-knit community, as everyone they passed seemed to know Ray, including a couple of kids his age, a couple walking their dog, and an elderly woman watering her flowers. She wondered what it would've been like knowing so many people and having them genuinely *like* you simply because they could.

She stopped abruptly as they came up to a house that looked like every other, two stories, neutral paint and tiling, a bright lawn. Ray waltzed up to the door and knocked, stuffing his hands in his pockets. She listened as a kid yelled something and a woman yelled something back, before the door swung open wildly to reveal a kind-eyed woman wearing a flowered apron, and a kid around ten with startlingly bright red hair and a face full of freckles.

She giggled when the woman attacked Ray, squeezing him hard and running her hands through his hair.

"We missed you so much!" She exclaimed, tilting her head up at him and lightly brushing hair from his eyes.

"I was only gone a few days," Ray said, looking a little red. The boy was still standing there, pushing thick glasses up his small nose and staring at each of them in turn.

"That doesn't matter Ray! It feels like it's been a century!" She bustled back inside, gesturing for them to come in and closing the door behind them. "Now, who might these lovely people be?" Zami was amused by her use of the word *lovely,* considering who exactly she was dealing with.

"I'm Blu!" Blu chirped. The woman shook his hand with a bright smile.

"I'm Laurel, Ray's Aunt."

"Strike." Strike said, giving a little wave.

"Zami." She offered, holding her hand out and shaking the woman's hand.

Laurel looked pleased as she shook her hand, flexing her hand slightly afterward. "Strong grip. I like that." Zami grinned, trying not to preen at the praise. Usually, people didn't appreciate her strong grip because they were too busy sulking after she beat them up. "Now, are you going to explain what you're doing here?" Laurel's face changed suddenly as she turned to Ray. "You didn't get kicked out, did you? I told you that snarky attitude would get you in trouble!" Zami giggled along with Blu, as Ray held his hands up in surrender.

"No! We came to say bye, we're heading off to Zamoth."

Laurel looked confused. "Why Zamoth?"

Ray swallowed, catching her eyes. "They've found information on the first desirable."

Laurel was frozen for a long moment, processing the information. "You mean to tell me you're already on the way to find the desirables?" Ray nodded and Laurel's eyes dropped.

"Well, you all rest for a bit and I'll make an early lunch to celebrate your visit. I'm sure Dew can take an afternoon off work to come home." Ray started to argue, but Laurel shook her head, pushing him towards the couch.

"She'll want to, Ray." Ray nodded and Zami sent him a concerned look as Laurel disappeared into the kitchen.

Ray turned to the kid, raising his eyebrow. "There a reason you aren't at school?"

The kid pushed his glasses up with a huff. "I'm sick." Ray gave him a look. "It was a field trip day! You know how much I hate field trips!" He looked worried that Ray was gonna' be mad but Ray just smiled, patting the couch beside him.

"I know. As long as you got your work done." The boy shuffled to the couch, plopping down next to Ray who ruffled his head. "This is my dork brother, Blaze." Blaze pushed Ray's hands away, but as soon as Ray pulled them away, grabbed them again, gripping them as if they were a lifeline. Zami smiled, feeling a little sad at the sight and ignoring Blu's blathering and the others' responses.

She missed her mom. A lot. It hadn't affected her that much in a while, but seeing Blu and Strike, and then Ray and his Aunt and brother, seemed to dig it out of the ground, flinging the feeling back at her with the force of a bullet.

The sound of the door opening disturbed her thoughts, and she looked up just in time to see a brunette woman storming in, dropping a bag on the floor and crossing her arms at Ray. Ray rolled his eyes but stood up, walking over to hug her. Her hugs looked a lot more bone-crunching than Laurel's, and she held back a laugh at Ray's wince.

They introduced themselves again and were greeted in turn by Dew, then somehow only a few minutes later, Zami found herself standing at a sink, given the chore of peeling potatoes. Leaning over to Strike, who was cleaning lettuce on the other side, she whispered,

"How do you peel potatoes?"

He gaped at her, hands still buried in the leaves. "You don't know how to peel potatoes?"

She frowned at his shock, crossing her arms against her chest. "I can't say I was taught very many domestic skills. The last time I saw a kitchen was when I was five."

Strike looked thoroughly offended, rinsing his hands from the lettuce and reaching over to grab a peeler. "Watch. Observe." She watched, impressed, as he managed to flick his wrist in just the right way to peel the potato in less than a minute, without peeling any of his skin. When he finished and held out the peeler, she swallowed, staring at the potatoes. It took some coaching to get the right form, and even then it took nearly four minutes for her to peel one, and nearly a finger or two along with it. As she sucked on a cut on her forefinger, Strike raised his eyebrow at her, drying his arms with a dishtowel.

"You'd think with those knife skills you have, you'd be better with a peeler." She pouted at him, staring at the next one with narrow, but determined eyes. If she knew one thing above all, it was that she was *not* going to be bested by a vegetable.

Chapter 6

Ray glanced over and grinned, watching as Zami attempted to peel the potatoes. He had never seen her so focused before, eyebrows scrunched and sticking her tongue out as she made another pass at the vegetable. It was adorable.

"Funny, she can nearly chop your head off, but can't peel a potato, huh?" He turned in surprise to see Dew leaning against the fridge across the stove from where he was standing, stirring the stew.

"You know about that?" He squeaked, swallowing roughly.

"Of course, Sylvia told us all about what happened," Laurel replied, coming up beside Dew and leaning onto her shoulder.

"Right," he said, focusing his eyes on the stew.

"She is cute, though."

"Aunt Dew!" He exclaimed, head shooting up, and then relaxing in relief when Zami didn't seem to have heard her.

"Yeah, a really strong grip too." He smacked his forehead at his Aunt's gossiping, feeling his face turn red.

"She is quite small though, you sure she's eating right?"

Ray looked up and narrowed his eyes. "I've known her for two days. How would I know?"

"She could just be genetically petite." Laurel offered and he sighed, turning to them. They both just looked at him innocently, acting as if they hadn't been purposely drawing his attention to the girl across the room.

"Aren't you more worried about... you know..." He waved his free hand to allude to the whole assassination attempt and such. Laurel shrugged and Dew gave him an evil grin.

"We like a strong independent woman."

He raised an eyebrow. "So you aren't worried about her killing any of us? Cause she kinda' always looks like she's five minutes away from that."

They blinked at each other before turning back, looking at him as if he were crazy for thinking such a thing. "Nah. We can tell she's way more innocent than people say."

"Yeah. Plus, she's basically destined to kill you or die herself either way."

"Why not have the fun of anticipation while you can?"

"And she's technically your soulmate."

He flushed at that and quickly looked away, well aware of the things they were saying and their credibility. That didn't mean he was used to them being said out loud.

He'd been aware of his *destiny* for as long as they'd known he was who he was. He knew what was supposed to happen, and the significance of the girl only a few feet away.

"Oh, we'll watch the stew!" Dew finally exclaimed, and he startled as the spoon was yanked from his grip and he was being shoved away. "You go help her with the potatoes! Show her what a good wife you would make!" He choked on air, ducking his head to try and catch his breath as he stumbled over to Zami.

"You okay there, sunshine?" Zami inquired. He nodded, not trusting his voice just yet and straightened up to grab another peeler and fresh potato. To his surprise, that was the last one, and only a minute later they finished and he brought the peeled ones to his Aunts. When he stepped up beside Laurel, who was drying her hands on a towel, she gave him a devilish grin, flipping her hair over her shoulder.

"Excitement of anticipation, eh?" He sputtered as she strutted away and then whipped around to level a glare at his Aunts. They coincidentally were facing the other way. He sighed and shook his head, running his hands through his hair.

A couple of minutes later he was carrying a bowl full of steaming soup to the table outside, dodging Blu's swinging arms as he set it down on the table, letting out a breath he didn't know he had been holding. Eventually, everyone managed to get seated, and much to his skepticism that it was accidental, Zami ended up between him and his Aunts, which for some reason caused his Aunts to avoid his eyes when he glanced at them.

When they were all settled, Dew stood up, holding her water glass in the air. "To our heroes for risking everything, for everyone."

He laughed, standing up and clinking glasses with everyone else, heart warm at the smiles on everyone's faces.

Lunch passed peacefully, with a lot of joking and the occasional suggestive comment, mostly by his Aunts and Blu, who seemed to fuel one another. It was fine though, at least until they began to pry.

"So Zami, where did you grow up?" Dew asked and Ray froze, unsure how she would answer that.

"Um, well, I was born in Velian but we moved to Damrion when I was like five." The table went mostly silent, and the fact that Zami had lived in the worst place to be in the world for so long was suddenly so real.

"Have you ever met the Dark King?" Blaze blurted out to Ray's horror and to his Aunts admonishing "Blaze!", but Zami, to his surprise, smiled.

"Yeah, I have." She said which made him freeze yet again, on the spot.

"You met the Dark King! Like the horrible, child slaughterer, 'kill your family' guy? And survived!" Blu exclaimed, voicing the thoughts in all their minds.

Zami looked amused, running her hand over her wrist. He raised an eyebrow at the action but passed it as a habit and shifted his gaze to the fork he was flipping around his fingers.

"Um... yeah? And he doesn't kill everyone he meets." She seemed to think a moment before shrugging. "Just most."

"Wow, he must've really liked you," Blu remarked. Ray peered over in time to see a flash of something odd on her face before it was covered by her normal smirk.

"Yeah... I guess." A heavy silence took over the table for a long time, the only sounds being the clanking of utensils and shifting of chairs. He was thankful for Dew's social skills when she spoke.

"Well, I think everyone's very glad that you decided to join the rebellion. That place isn't anywhere for a kid to be." Dew said with a smile.

Zami laughed, which made his heart do a little cartwheel in his chest. "Yeah, well I'm glad to be here too. Although I have to give some credit to the dork who has too hard of a head to get hurt."

Ray pouted her way, trying to be mad and failing. "You're very welcome, for being too cool to die." She snorted and he bit back a smile, focusing back on his food. And all at once, the tension was gone and they were back to the chatter the way it had previously been.

Later as he was cleaning plates in the sink, Blaze sidled up beside him, fiddling with his fingers.

"You know, with walking and only short breaks plus sleep it'll take close to three days to get to Zamoth, and even then it may take weeks to finally find who you're looking for," he stated all in one quick breath.

Ray set down the plate and dried his hands, holding his arms out. His brother swallowed deeply before stepping into the hug.

"I promise I'll come back safe, 'kay?" I can't promise how long it'll take, but I'll come back." Blaze nodded and Ray could feel the poorly concealed shaking. "Blaze, it's okay to be worried or sad. You know that." Blaze nodded again, but this time he let out a little cry and Ray felt his heart throb as he held him.

He didn't try to make any promises he couldn't keep, that everything would be fine, or he wouldn't get hurt. Those were bound to happen. So he just held his brother as he cried, feeling undeniably guilty. This was exactly how they'd lost his sister and parents, walking out the door to help the rebellion. It wasn't fair to Blaze to do this. It wasn't fair to his Aunts. But he couldn't just *not* do anything, he was *supposed* to do something. And to be completely honest, he wanted revenge. No, he didn't want to cut off anyone's heads or hurt people. The revenge he wanted was to show everyone that their side could win this, and still come out as the good guys. That you didn't need to hurt people to be powerful.

They left not long after noon, starting the trek to Zamoth with his heart slightly heavier than before. It hadn't seemed that real before, but now that they were walking through the wild desert on a dirt path, on their way to find an artifact that was extremely dangerous, it became all too real.

He had never been a fan of the heat, ironic as that was given where he lived, so the moment he felt sweat start dripping down his back, he decided he didn't like having to be a hero *at all*. The others didn't seem too enthusiastic about the blistering heat either, and very few words were exchanged through the course of the rest of the day, everyone too focused on staying in motion. Occasionally, a gust of wind would swish by and blow dirt up into their eyes and mouths, leaving a gritty feeling under their teeth, and they had already given up keeping any dirt out of their shoes. Overall, it wasn't the most pleasant of situations.

They all let out relieved sighs when the sky darkened, cooling the air and relieving their eyes from the brightness of the sun. It was nearly midnight by the time they decided to settle, and Ray plopped down on a rock as he watched Blu unsuccessfully kick the dirt out of his way for a sleeping area

"You would think saving the world would be a little more... glorious," Blu said, poking at a cactus.

Strike swatted his hand away, rolling his eyes. "You don't just poke a cactus, Blu!"

"What?" He complained, pushing Strike's hand away. "I've never seen one like this!"

Strike smacked his forehead. "So your immediate reaction is to get stabbed by it?"

Blu nodded vigorously. "You never know, maybe it grants infinite wisdom!" He turned back to the cactus, poking it again.

"I don't think even infinite wisdom could help you," Zami muttered from where she was still standing.

"Hey! Rude!"

"Sorry," Zami said, not looking sorry at all. He watched as she slipped off her jacket and laid it on a rock before sitting back. At their looks, she frowned.

"What? My shirt is black, that doesn't go very well with dirt." Ray hid a grin as he slid to the ground, back against his rock. "You guys go to sleep, I'll take first watch." She said, pulling out one of her knives and beginning to scrape the dirt off her boots.

He was going to argue, but she was holding a sharp object and he really didn't want to test her limits. So he bunched his own jacket behind his head and closed his eyes, wondering how long it would be before he could fall asleep.

Ray woke up before the sun had completely risen, so the air was still slightly chilly and he could see a long distance through the crystal clear air. He sat up and rubbed his eyes, slowly realizing that Blu and Strike were both asleep and Zami was still up, now flipping her knife like it was a pencil.

"You know that's dangerous, right?" He asked, feeling slightly scared for her fingers.

She just gave him a wicked grin and switched hands. "That's the point."

He sighed at her, leaning on one of his hands. "Did you get *any* sleep last night?"

She shrugged, slipping her knife into its sheath and sitting up completely, shifting her bright eyes to him. "I got plenty before we left." He opened his mouth to say something but she shushed him. "I can live with very little sleep, sunshine. And I'm not the one that's supposed to save the world." He shut his mouth and crossed his arms, raising his eyebrow at her. She ignored his look, instead seemingly becoming very, very interested in her knee.

"Do you think there's going to be any actual... danger in Zamoth?" He asked, wanting to hear someone else's thoughts. Blaze's concern had been etched into his mind.

"I think there's no way we're going to get past with no trouble at all." She shared truthfully, not meeting his eyes. "But, I think we'll be able to handle it just fine." She gave him a genuine smile before standing up. "Let's get these dorks up, hopefully, we can reach the forest before it gets too hot again." He grinned and stood, watching as she nudged Blu with the tip of her foot. Blu woke up easily, then reached over to wake Strike, who looked a little more perturbed at being woken up. But after everyone was fully awake, it barely took a minute before they could begin walking again, this time with more enthusiasm since it was cooler.

And of course, Blu decided that they must have something to entertain them on the way.

"Ray, would you rather switch powers with Zami or keep your own?"

Ray frowned at Blu. "Really?"

"I'm curious."

"Well, I'd have to say keep. Not because there's anything wrong with your powers." He added, with a glance at Zami. "But, no offense, a lot of people seem to hate you for it." He said, thinking back to all the sour looks she had gotten in the rebel camp.

"No offense taken," Zami said. "And they have a reason, I mean one of us is supposed to destroy the world, and not only was it the dark girl last time, but I also look a lot more destruction-y than you do." Ray contemplated that reasoning as Blu spoke up again.

"Hey Zami, would you rather take back all the people you've killed, but have succeeded in killing Ray, or have everything the way it is now?"

"Now." She said without hesitance. The rest of them froze, trying to process what she just said. Her face broke into a grin as they gaped at her, confused. "I've never killed anyone guys." If anything, that just confused them more.

"What, but why..." Blu started.

"Ray was my first mission. Guess I failed pretty badly, huh?" Ray suddenly felt newfound respect for the girl in front of him who looked undeniably pleased with the information she'd just shared.

"I mean, I just, you know, failed to kill said subject." She began to count on her fingers. "Got imprisoned for not killing said subject, then befriended said subject, joined the rebellion, and am now currently helping said subject with finding what the King wants most before the rebellion gets it. So... yeah.", as she ticked off finger number five.

"Well, that's a plot twist if I've ever heard one." Blu joked, relieving any tension in the air as they walked. "What's next, the King's your dad?" Ray must've imagined seeing the shock on her face, because she was laughing only a second later.

"What? No, that'd be crazy!" She said, waving her hand in the air. Ray chuckled along with the others, though the way she reacted now had his fullest attention. As Blu continued to ask questions, which became dumber and dumber as they went on, they passed through some hills into a scrubby grass area, the forest came closer and closer, and the gangly branches seemed to grab at them, beckoning them forward.

They stepped into the cool shade of the trees right as the sun reached overhead, marking midday. As they stopped for a moment to breathe, Zami's eyes were flicking around the area, and she frowned, looking skeptically at the trees.

"What's wrong?" Ray asked, looking up as well and frowning when all he saw was the sunlit branches above their heads.

"It's just... I vaguely remember reading about something dangerous in this forest."

He raised his eyebrow at her, crossing his arms. "Vaguely?"

She dropped her gaze to his and gave him a little shrug, bringing her hands up. "Um, yeah, dork." He sighed as she turned away, equally impressed and concerned about her level of snarkiness.

"Wait, so like, what danger level?" Blu asked, holding out his hands and gesturing one at a time. "Like, accidentally drinking orange juice after brushing your teeth or like, I forgot to set my alarm and now I'm an hour and twenty-six minutes late to school." They all stared at him, exasperated. "What?" He said, taking in each of their expressions.

"Which one is supposed to be the dangerous one?" Zami questioned, tilting her head at him.

After a long moment of thinking, Blu looked up. "You know, I guess it could go either way."

"That's cause none of them are dangerous," Ray said, highly amused.

"Ah," Blu corrected, holding up a finger. "Unless you have a really mean teacher."

Ray rolled his eyes and readjusted the strap of his bag. "Yeah okay. How about we just avoid orange juice and mean teachers altogether?" The others nodded and Blu sighed.

"That's fair." With a chuckle, Ray followed them through the forest, occasionally glancing back. He really hoped Zami remembered wrongly.

By the time the sky had been fully sheathed in darkness, even Blu was running out of games to play, leaving them in a sort of stillness that the darkness amplified. The only sounds, besides the leaves crunching beneath their feet, were a loud cricket and the sound of water running in a nearby river.

Ray figured this would've been a place that someone would paint; the moonlight highlighting the forest floor, peeking through the canopy. Moss covered every rock and tree in sight, hanging vines swaying from branches in the wind. A breeze chilled his face and he reached to brush his hair out of his eyes, catching a glimpse of Strike doing the same.

It was a weird feeling, one he had never experienced before. Unlike other awkward silences that surrounded groups of teens who barely knew each other, with this group it wasn't weird or uncomfortable. Each was too wrapped up with their own thoughts and the surrounding forest to mind each other.

With a glance at Zami, he took in the slight droop of her shoulders and hazy expression, and stopped. The others seemed to get his drift and dropped their bags, although they didn't look quite as wobbly as Zami. He gave her a look when she hadn't made a move to rest, and she stuck her tongue out at him, dropping to the ground in a way that he figured only she would be able to do gracefully.

He watched as she leaned back against a tree, pulling her knees up to her chest and resting her head on her arms.

"I'll stay up!" Blu chirped, plopping down against a tree across from her and holding his hands out as if to meditate. "I have a feeling we won't be needing a windstorm any time soon, so you should rest." Ray rolled his eyes at Blu's antics but sat down, leaning on his hand. He had a feeling he wouldn't be able to fall asleep anytime soon, so he just stared at the trees, thinking about his brother.

He hoped that no one bothered Blaze at school while he was gone; his brother had never been the social type. He preferred to spend his time reading and playing with dogs in the park.

A rustling in the bushes caught his attention and his head shot up, meeting Blu's equally alert eyes. He could see Zami and Strike straightening up out of the corner of his eye as he strained his ears to hear anything else. Several minutes passed without any further movement, and slowly they all relaxed again. He sighed and rubbed his eyes. They were just tense from their unfamiliar surroundings, that was all.

Laying down, he attempted to calm his beating heart, closing his eyes. Slowly he fell asleep, listening to the quiet noises of the forest.

The next morning he woke up with a stinging headache, every sound around him sending a new wave of pain through his head. Stupid people grumbling and ridiculously loud waterfalls... wait, people? His eyes shot open, the bright light causing his head to pound harder.

When the spots in his vision cleared, he was left staring at what looked like a camp, with strange creatures wandering around and gargling at each other in a language he didn't understand. Dark horns jutted at odd angles from their deformed faces, some on the chin or forehead. Their mouths were marked with darkly stained teeth that looked a little *too* sharp for his liking. They hobbled around on two legs, but their arms swung wildly as if boneless and he saw multiple creatures picking things up with their oddly large feet. Oily rags hung from their crooked shoulders and stopped at knobby knees, ratty hair matted across their heads. He stared in shock as they moved around, disappearing into little open tents supported by stakes with animal carvings, and jostling around a large bonfire.

Slowly grasping on to where he was, he registered the ropes that dug into his arms and chest, pressing his back against the rough bark of the tree behind him. Swallowing roughly, he turned his head as much as possible, relief fluttering in his chest when he recognized a blue head of hair to his right and Strike's dark hair to his left. He figured and hoped Zami was on the other side, and sighed, turning his head back to look at the creatures.

So they were tied to a tree, somewhere in the forest, surrounded by a bunch of weird-looking beasts that he figured weren't just going to invite them to tea. Great.

"Please tell me I'm dreaming," Strike muttered from beside him, having just come to consciousness.

"I'm afraid not." He said, voice coming out slightly hoarse from dryness and lack of speaking, for who knew how long.

"Well, I guess Zami's 'vague' memory was right." Strike sighed loudly.

"What the Wazzocks?" Blu swore, twisting his head in a way that made his shoulder shove hard into Ray's. "I have a feeling this isn't Zamoth for some reason." He noted, stopping his wiggling.

"No dur." He heard Zami say from the other side of the tree, sounding positively miffed.

"Well *sorry*." Blu snarked out. "Not all of us are quite as observant as you, miss *I almost killed the prophecy hero and then not two days later became friends with him.*"

Zami scoffed loudly. "It's not my fault I actually plan to *do* something with my life!"

This time Blu was the one who scoffed and Ray felt the ropes jerk slightly. "*Excuse me*! I *was* planning on doing something with my life until *you* popped up and started all the drama!"

"I did not!" Zami exclaimed. "Maybe I should've gone for you instead, then there would be a lot less talking going on!"

"Oh, that's a good plan." Blu snarked. "Kill the small gay dude who's trying to keep the conversation lively!"

"Oh, is that what you call it? Well..."

"Guys." Strike cut in, sounding exasperated. "We're all on the same side, remember? How about we focus on *not* getting killed and then you can deal with your differences? Have a thumb war or something?" He heard Blu and Zami both huff and sighed, though he was highly amused.

"So, uh, anyone know what these things are?" He whisper-yelled out of the corner of his mouth, not wanting to draw attention to them. Well, anymore, at least.

"Harpals, I believe." Strike said, turning his head slightly. "They live as nomads in jungles and forest regions. Usually, they live in groups of around twenty or thirty, with a few alpha males. They speak in grunts that indicate their emotions, which makes it one of the only languages you can't learn to speak." If his head didn't hurt, Ray would've turned to stare, but instead he settled for gaping in the general direction of Strike.

"And you know all this why?" He squeaked.

"In case of something like what's happening right now, happens." Strike said matter-of-factly.

"Right, 'cause it's a common occurrence to get captured by weird nomad troll-looking things." Zami snapped, sounding less than enthusiastic about their current predicament.

"Well, clearly it's more common than you realize." Strike said, getting sassier and sassier with every word.

"Right, any idea how we can get out?" Ray asked before any of them exploded.

"Easy, just throw your sunshine at them. Boom. No more Harpals" Blu said.

This time Ray couldn't help but roll his eyes. "*Without* any of us getting hurt?" He responded, glancing at the sharp teeth in the animals' mouths. Before Strike or anyone else could answer, a group of about four harpals began to hobble towards them, trading loud grunts.

"Uh-oh." Blu amended lamely.

"I *really* hope you don't plan on those being your last words," Ray said, feeling more and more nervous as the harpals got closer. "Cause that's kinda' lame."

"Says the guy whose last words might be 'that's kinda' lame.'"

Ray jumped when something sharp poked his side and nearly let out a very uncharacteristic whimper, when he realized one Harpal was gnawing at the ropes beside him. Technically, he could use his power, or lash out. But not only was there the chance he would accidentally hurt one of the others, he really didn't want to hurt the little dudes. They were just living their life. Plus, who knew, maybe they were sun-absorbent, and attacking them would make them double in size. He mused over that thought as the ropes fell away and his arm was grabbed by the same Harpal.

Sharp nails dug into his skin as it twisted his arm around to tie it to his other hand with surprising grace for such a stout, knobby little thing. To his side, he could see both Blu and Strike having the same done to them, and he guessed on the other side of the tree, so was Zami.

A jerk on his arm caused him to stumble forward, barely righting himself since he didn't have his arms out to steady himself. With a shaky breath, he watched the Harpal loop a rope around him and then through his hands, then disappear behind him to do it to the others as well. It was a highly intelligent design, which kept each person in line unless they wanted to pull everyone over all at once. *Great*, he thought, *not just strong unknown creatures. Strong and smart.*

He considered looking over his shoulder to check on the others as they pulled the rope, leading them through the little camp, but he decided against it when he realized how rocky the ground was and how un-heroic it would be to fall flat on your face because you weren't paying attention.

Harpals stared and garbled at them as they passed, looking excited. He hoped they got excited because they liked letting people go. Though, he figured, that probably wouldn't happen.

Only when he was yanked to a stop near a tent and the harpal tied the rope to a thick stake and hobbled off, did he finally risk taking a look back. Everyone looked intact, though a little annoyed. Well, that was an understatement; Zami was practically streaming.

"So are we going to do something, or wait around to be eaten?" Blu asked, from behind him as the others huddled closer, the rope being loose enough to do so.

"I say we sacrifice the slowest, and make a run for it," Zami said, in a completely serious tone.

"Hey!" Strike exclaimed, furrowing his eyebrows at her. She shrugged nonchalantly and looked away, biting her lip in innocence. Ray glanced at the harpals and did a double-take when he realized they were gesturing to them and the fire, some tying up a big stake in the center of it. They stepped in the coals as if they were normal rocks, garbling continuously, the fire flicking at their knees and feet. However, what worried him more was the obvious spit they were tying up.

"Um, guys. What are they doing?" He asked nervously.

"Oh, probably preparing to eat us." Strike said as if he were suggesting a solution to a math equation.

"Eat what, now?" Zami asked, voice cracking slightly.

Strike frowned and looked between them. "I thought you knew?"

"No!" Blu squealed. "We did not!"

"But you said..."

"That was a joke, man! A joke!" Blu jerked his hands as if trying to gesture and in result nearly pulling Strike over.

"Well, how was I supposed to know that!" Strike said, glaring at Blu, who stuck his tongue out at him.

"Intuition?" Zami suggested, looking more exasperated than concerned. "Because none of us even know what in the ever-living world a Harpal is?"

"I just told you, they're no..."

"Strike!" Blu said. "Not helping!"

"Um, just a heads up, they're coming this way." Ray cut in, trying to will the creatures wandering towards them away.

"Well, what are we going to do?" Blu asked, speaking even more quickly than normal.

"Try to stay standing," Zami said, eyes focused on the harpals by the fire. Before he could ask what that incredibly ominous statement meant, he was being jerked towards the bonfire as harpals began to assemble, making loud noises that sounded a lot like cheering. He could feel the heat of the flames as he was pulled closer, and internally, began to freak out. In only about four steps he would be *in* the fire. Without further thought, he grasped his magic, preparing to fight with it. However, before he could act, the rope jerked backward and he stumbled to keep his footing.

He looked up just in time to see sharp talons swiping right at his face and he yelped, ducking as fast as possible. Behind him, he could hear Blu startle and the rope gave another sharp tug. This time, he wasn't quite as lucky and he found himself on the ground, Blu's foot close to his shoulder.

A hand grabbing his pulled him out from his shock, and he realized with surprise that his hands were free. He looked up to see Zami turning just in time to kick at a harpal. Without hesitation, he pulled himself up and pushed a harpal away from Blu, who was also standing up, though with the assistance of a few colorful terms.

The harpals snarled, though they had backed up, none approaching them again. Zami's back was pressed to his, and he stared out at the creatures who were gaining confidence by the second, edging closer and closer. He attempted to reach his magic again, but Zami elbowed him.

"Magic doesn't work with them here for some reason." She stumbled out, voice getting a little smaller every moment. He sighed inwardly and swallowed, glancing at Blu and Strike who were right next to them. That wasn't good.

"On my count, run. We'll meet up at Zamoth." Zami called and Ray bunched his fists, watching as the harpals came closer and closer.

"Three."

"Two."

"One."

Ray ducked under a swipe and lashed out, giving up on not hurting them. He ran wildly, unable to glance back before he broke into the forest, weaving through the trees. His legs moving on their own, he wasn't aware how long he had been running, but only when he realized he could only hear his own panting breath did he stop. Leaning forward on his knees, he took a gasping breath, trying to calm his pounding heart.

When he regained his lung capacity, he looked up, taking in the dark forest and the eerie silence of it all. Swallowing roughly he glanced up, trying to figure out which way he was going. The sun had been in the direction they needed to go in the early afternoon the day before, and he guessed it must be around that same time, so he followed it, taking large strides to calm his nerves. He hoped that the others were on their way as well.

Chapter 7

↔

Zami cursed as she stepped wrong and felt her ankle wobble under her, shooting pain up her leg. *Curse my weak joints,* she thought angrily, trying to shake it off and continue on. But of course, that was impossible, and she found herself slowing down, hobbling on one leg. She whipped around to see a small group of harpals breaking through the brush, hissing at her. It figured they would go after her.

"Oh come on!" She shouted at them, trying to wave them away. "Go bother someone who has more meat on their bones! All three of those dudes are bigger than me! Shoo!" When they only hobbled closer, growling at her, she grumbled in disbelief. Turning around she attempted to take another step and nearly fell, her ankle giving under her. With a glare at it, she wildly searched her mind for an idea.

As they got closer and closer, a memory flashed in her brain from back in training years ago; how she had been forced to climb a smooth, vertical wall. It had been a horrendous task, and by the time she did manage to get to the top, she had sported several rather attractive bruises.

She eyed the trees in appreciation before stumbling over to one and reaching up to try and grab the lowest branch. When her fingers didn't connect with anything, her heart gave a dangerous thud in her chest and she gasped, jumping and landing on her ankle with a spike of pain that made her eyes water. With a wince, she jumped again, grasping at the rough bark, and only just managing to pull her legs out of the way as one of the harpals attacked. Its rough nails caught her boot and she jerked it up before it could get a solid grip.

Grasping at the branch, she froze, unable to move any further. If she stood up to grab the branch above her, she risked falling right into the creatures, and without magic and with her cursed ankle, fighting was out of the question. So that left only one thing. Waiting.

Fear kept her strong enough to hold onto the branch, even though she desperately wanted to rest. For at least an hour, the only thing she was focused on were the creatures below her, who didn't seem to be giving up any time soon. By the time a second hour passed, her arms and legs were tired of clinging and her ankle was sending vicious throbs up her leg. The mix of the harpals' yells and her own pounding heart made her head throb unpleasantly, and there was a sour taste in her mouth.

She wondered if any of the creatures had chased the others, and if so whether they were in a similar situation as her. Which in retrospect, was very unlikely.

"Hey, y'all?" She asked the harpals, who looked up at her and began to growl again. "I know I must look delectable to you, but have you ever thought of the consequences of eating meat? How many germs are probably stewing inside of me right now? You should consider going vegetarian, it's really a much healthier lifestyle choice." The harpals just blinked their beady eyes at her.

"Fine." She said, deciding to take a different approach. "How 'bout you let me off this once? Not every fourteen-year-old girl is forced to help save the world you know. Though, I suppose it's nice having such a cute boy near you all the time. I wouldn't blame you for wanting to eat him. He has nice bone structure." The harpals still just blinked at her, unmoving, and she groaned, slamming her forehead into the branch.

"I give up. Life's too hard. Can I resign?" Of course, no one was there to respond, so she was left staring at the creatures, who didn't seem to understand a single thing that came out of her mouth. Feeling dejected, she shifted, giving up on being afraid, and sat up, pressing her back into the trunk of the tree. She hooked her uninjured ankle along the bottom of the branch in case she got off balance.

Uncomfortable with the silence, she hummed under her breath, habitually breathing out the tune of the lullaby her mom used to sing her. She chewed on her thumbnail and grabbed onto the fabric of her jacket with the other arm, desiring to bring her knees up to her chest, but unable to do so for balance. So instead her leg began to shake against the branch, thumping her thigh into the rough bark. She tried to push away the swelling anxiety in her stomach, but it rose anyway and she felt her breathing pitch slightly as she began to uncontrollably shake.

You're not alone. They're just across the forest, probably perfectly fine. The harpals will leave eventually and you'll find the others. They're okay, you're okay. She chanted the mantra in her head, squeezing her eyes shut. *Stop panicking, you're such a wimp. You couldn't even finish a mission that your dad sent you on. Why do you think you'll be able to do this? Remember, you're destined to fail. You can't do anything about it.* Her thoughts began to fade into her father's voice, edging at her heart.

"Worthless. Pathetic. That's what you are. Can't even do one thing right. Just like your mother." She attempted to drown out her thoughts out with plans for the future, hopeful plans. But that was when she realized she had never even thought about the future. She supposed she had been too busy trying to survive at the moment, to think what might happen if she was without such harsh boundaries.

When she opened her eyes, she realized it had gotten significantly darker, and the harpals were gone, nowhere in sight. Feeling slightly shaky, she glanced around multiple times before grabbing the branch and sliding down to the ground, wincing when she set weight on her left foot.

It was eerily silent as she set off in the direction she believed Zamoth would be, limping slightly. She knew that it would normally take about two hours to get there, based on her knowledge of where she was, but with her ankle, she was guessing much longer than that. Gripping her sleeves, she shuffled in the leaves, heart-pounding ridiculously loud in her ears. She shivered in the chill air, trying to ignore the goosebumps spreading across her arms.

The trees passed by slowly and leaves crunched underneath her feet, disrupting the silence of the forest.

So I can beat up four men without getting a cut, but I nearly broke my ankle running. What a lovely set of events.

Okay. She was grumpy. But that was fair, considering she was alone, in the dark, her ankle was stinging and she hadn't even been supposed to be going on this adventure in the first place.

The moment she felt a raindrop on the top of her head she froze, clenching her fists. Sure enough, more followed and in only about five minutes it was completely pouring, so loud she couldn't hear her voice when she called out. The rain fogged her vision, leaving the surrounding area even darker than before, branches swinging everywhere. She was going to scream.

With an unhappy snarl, she stormed through the storm, too pissed to care about being cold. Maybe it was a good thing she was alone because otherwise, her knife might have ended up somewhere rather unpleasant.

Stupid rain. Stupid harpals. Stupid boys and their prophecies and light powers. In retrospect, her anger probably wasn't a good thing, but she probably wouldn't have made it through the storm if she hadn't been fueled by spite.

The weather would *not* get the best of her. And neither would lame destiny.

So she trudged through the muddy forest floor, dodging swinging branches and pushing her soaked hair from her face. Eventually, the cold began to get to her, chilling her to the bone and plastering her clothes unpleasantly against her skin. Gritting her teeth, she slashed past the branches in front of her, trying to mentally calculate how far she had walked. Slowly the throbbing in her ankle had subsided, only occasionally sending small sparks of pain through her leg. That meant she began to walk faster and faster, fueled by her annoyance and the cold, and eventually she found herself at the edge of the forest, staring at a fog-covered town.

Remembering what she said back with the harpals, she squinted, searching for any sign of the others. Only a few minutes later did she remember that she had a much easier way to locate Ray and reached for the pressure in her sternum. *Worry.*

That confused her. Why would he be worried? Were Blu or Strike hurt? Feeling a little worried herself, she followed the feeling, hovering just inside the forest, on the edge of the trees.

Eventually, she could make out three figures, standing under a large tree, looking soaked to the bone. She couldn't help the grin that spread across her face as she made her way towards them, all annoyance gone, replaced with determination. They had gotten through the first task, mostly unharmed, and safe. When she got close enough to see them and slipped up beside them she laughed. Strike had removed his glasses, for obvious reasons, and all of them looked a little miffed with their hair plastered to their faces and clothes soaking wet.

"What, d-d-don't like the rain?" She teased, though her teeth were chattering a little too much to speak properly.

"Hahaha," Blu remarked, holding his arms out and shaking them off as if that was going to dislodge any water. She looked over in time for her heart to skip a beat as Ray smoothed his hair back from his forehead, water dripping from his eyelashes as he met her eyes.

"Slow runner?" He teased back, humor still intact.

She swallowed and glanced away, trying to ignore the fluttering in her stomach. "Harpals don't understand plain language."

He raised an eyebrow at her. "You tried to speak to them?"

She scoffed, feeling slightly flustered. "I was surprised!"

"I'm sure."

"Hey dudes, I mean I'm always one for some playful flirting, but I'd prefer it to not be in the middle of the rain," Blu said, looking very displeased.

"Well, I mean, we could always risk waltzing unannounced into a town that's nicknamed after its phantom streets in the middle of a rainstorm," Zami suggested, unsuccessfully wringing the water out of her hair.

"Right. We probably shouldn't do that." Ray said and Blu sighed.

"Fine." Zami grinned as Blu plopped down under the tree and began attempting to fix his soaking hair.

"Oh don't be a baby. You won't melt." She teased, leaning against the tree, though she stayed standing.

"You might." He observed and she shot him a warning glare, though it didn't have any real venom behind it.

"So do we have a plan for waltzing into Zamoth or are we just going to assume everything will go all right?" Strike asked, looking unperturbed by the rain.

"I don't know." She answered, brain too cloudy to think properly.

"I think that's a sign that you need to sleep," Ray remarked.

She rolled her eyes at him, though she knew he was right. "You sure this time I won't wake up tied to a tree?" She asked, sliding to the ground next to Blu.

"Can't promise anything," Ray said, and she grinned at the ground, water dripping down her face. A warm shoulder pressed to hers, shocking her into looking up at Ray, who was giving her a sideways glance that just looked like trouble. "At least know if you're tied to a tree, we'll be there with you."

She laughed, sinking into the warmth spreading from her shoulder from his touch. Maybe it was a good thing to be with a boy with light powers after all. To her right, she registered the gentle brush of Blu's shoulder as well, as they huddled against the trunk, Strike on the other side of him.

As the rain poured down, she listened to their playful conversations, not feeling any necessity to talk or think. So she just breathed, smelling the rain and earth, and feeling the chill that was slowly leaving her bones, replaced by a comfortable warmth.

Hours must have passed, her slipping in and out of sleep, sometimes just half paying attention to what was being said. When the voices did finally start to clear enough for her to hear, she realized the rain was gone, leaving the pale, just rising sun, filtered softly in the air. The trees still dripped, the ground moist underneath them, and the air held a fuzzy, clean quality that only occurred after a rainstorm. She found herself wondering if there may be a rainbow, then frowning at the childishness of the thought.

When something shifted under her head, she was left confused, only then to register that she was laying her head on none other than Ray's shoulder. *Oh.* She thought, heart thumping unnecessarily loud in her chest. *Okay, don't freak out. Be smooth. Natural.*

Swallowing nervously, she observed the feeling of leather pressed to the side of her face, along with the gentle vibrations of his voice through his arm. Well, she kinda' liked it, she wasn't going to lie. And she was only going to live once, so why not just go with the flow?

So, closing her eyes again, she relaxed her shoulders and sunk into the feeling, ignoring any anxious thoughts clouding her mind. *Not today, world.*

"Prophets normally hang in churches, right?" Blu asked. Ray did what she assumed was nodding as he answered.

"I think so."

"My guess is it's going to be one of the best-preserved buildings in the area since religion is so important to them. That means we should hypothetically not draw any attention to ourselves by slipping in during service." Strike informed.

"The only problem is, when's service?" She questioned, sitting up and rubbing her eyes.

"Well, normally there are two different services held two hours or more apart in the morning, and an evening one for after work hours and school," Blu said. If it had been Strike, or even Ray sharing that information, she wouldn't have been all that surprised, but as Blu talked she stared at him, confused. When he looked up and saw her and Ray's looks he shrugged, turning away. "My parents are very religious." She stared at him for another long moment before tearing her gaze away.

"Right, well it's fairly early, so we should be able to make a morning service," Ray stated, leaning back to the tree, seemingly unbothered by Blu's unusual claim.

"Let's get a little closer." She offered, standing up and brushing off her legs. Her ankle barely hurt any longer, which somewhat surprised her. She had never been one to heal quickly, even after simple injuries. "That way we can see when people start leaving their houses." She finished, shaking her head to try and avoid getting distracted. If everything unusual caused her to contemplate existence, there wouldn't be much prophecy fulfillment getting done.

The others nodded and rose, rolling their shoulders and rubbing their necks. She snorted and turned away, a little bounce in her step as she made the small trek into the bushes at the edge of the town.

She decided against sitting again, and instead leaned against a small tree that was positioned so no one would even spare it a glance, but she could see everything. Now that all the fog had lifted, she was able to make out the broken shutters, moldy walls, and caving roofs, along with the few haggard looking people bustling around.

Most seemed to be scooping water from a well in the center of the village, others walking into stores and putting up the 'Open' signs. The rain had left a ditch of water on either side of the main street, puddles next to houses, and the road looked distastefully muddy.

Great, more mud. At the end of this, she was sure her boots would look more like she had spent all her time stuck in quicksand rather than trying to save the world. Which really wouldn't be that weird considering her luck.

"You think they have any good food?" Blu asked.

She looked at him in exasperation and sighed. "We have plenty of food, Blu." She said, highly amused.

Blu frowned. "I know... it's just..." he sighed dreamily. "Cheese."

Strike looked horrified as he turned to Blu. "You're lactose intolerant!"

"Oh yeah... I forgot about that."

Strike smacked his forehead. "You've been lactose intolerant since you were five!"

Blu shrugged. "It's an honest mistake bro. Sometimes I forget." Strike looked close to smacking his head against the nearest tree until he passed out before Ray spoke up.

"I mean, I forgot I was allergic to honey, until Aunt Dew walked into the kitchen and freaked out cause I was eating honey bread."

Zami stared at him in shock. "You mean the world's greatest hero, the one who's supposed to save the world, can be killed by some honey?"

Ray shrugged. "Well, I haven't died yet, sooooo..."

This time it was her who smacked her forehead in disbelief. "You two!" She exclaimed, sharing an exasperated look with Strike.

"What? You can't tell me you guys aren't allergic to anything. I know for a fact Strike can't even touch wool without getting all itchy!" Blu exclaimed, pouting slightly.   She snorted at Strike. "You're allergic to wool?" She asked in disbelief, giggling.   Strike frowned and crossed his arms. "I'm not allergic to it, it just irritates my skin!" That just made her laugh harder, doubling over.

"Okay, Miss assassin, you can't be immune to everything. Give it up." She looked up to see all of them narrowing their eyes at her, Ray doing the little 'give it here' gesture.

"The only thing I'm allergic to is imperfection." She snarked, slapping Strike's hand in a high five and flipping her hair over her shoulder. "Now, let's get going, my sensitive friends! I haven't gone to church in years!"

Strike's theory had been correct; it was nearly effortless to slip into the crowd of people entering the building. They did stand out some, however, as everyone here had a sort of drab look to them, with no smiles, even the kids. So between Blu's sparkling smile, and Strike's and Ray's height (since most of the people were hunched permanently, leaving them around Blu's height), they got several glances. Though, to her relief, everyone seemed inclined to not get involved, so they were mostly ignored. A couple of little kids kept on glancing at them curiously, but their parents just yanked them away.

The church was indeed well taken care of, with polished statues of their god and shining pews inside. Banners and more depictions of their god covered the walls, a naga of some sort, with a long green tail and dark skin, covered in golden robes.

"They worship part of the Da'raom?" Blu whispered as they slid into one of the rows.

"Yeah, they're a part of the kingdom now," Strike murmured back. The Da'raom was one of the biggest kingdoms in the world, with many millions of citizens and a strong army. It catered mostly to unusual creatures, including half-humans and users of forbidden magic. It was currently the only major kingdom that had chosen to remain neutral, which she remembered from how pissed her father had been. That had been a rough day.

"I wish they'd just join the rebellion." Blu sighed heavily, crossing his legs.

"As long as they don't join the Dark King, I'm happy," Ray remarked.

"They'll have to join sides eventually." She said, picking at her sheath. "The Dark King is ruthless; no one will be able to just remain neutral." The others looked concerned at that, sharing looks before turning back to look at her.

"You think he'll be able to convince them?" Blu asked.

She shrugged. "He can be awfully convincing."

Chapter 8

↔

Ray watched as people settled into the rows, chattering among themselves with considerably disinterested expressions. Blu was whispering something to Strike on his left, and he smiled when Strike let out a barking laugh, eyes crinkling as he listened to Blu. Zami was slumped in the seat to his right, examining her nails as if something interesting was going to come out of them. She had her left leg kicked up at her right knee, swinging her combat boot back and forth.

"You might not wanna flash those around." He whispered pointedly, gesturing to the very, *very* noticeable knives strapped to her thighs. Everyone here was fairly chill, but he wasn't about to risk it.

"Aw, I forgot about those." She responded, glancing down as if she had never seen them before.

"And we want everyone else to forget about them too." He said, raising his eyebrow at her.

She sighed and rolled her eyes but grabbed her bag and swung it onto her lap, subtly slipping them into the bag. "Is it not normal to bring knives to church?" She asked innocently, hugging her bag to her chest, over her now knife-free legs.

"Only if it's secretly a cult." He murmured as she shifted slightly, arm brushing his. To his surprise she didn't pull it away, leaning into him just a little.

"Isn't that what church is?" She questioned, blinking at him.

He chuckled, leaning over a little since people around them were quieting. "Depends which side of the door you're on." She giggled slightly and he looked up in time to see a man rushing to the podium, looking slightly disheveled. Tousled brown hair hung in his eyes and dark green robes several sizes too big hung off of him, nearly making a train like a dress behind him.

He looked sort of nervous and overall not very imposing, but the moment he spoke, Ray understood why he was the minister. His voice was enchanting, not particularly strong or harmonious in any way, but captivating. The minister didn't pause in his words; didn't stutter or hesitate. The moment he stepped onto that podium, all eyes were on him, everyone stopped talking.

"That has to be him," Zami murmured in his ear. He nodded, speechless. They sat and listened as he spoke, telling a story about the Renma, their god. Ray hadn't been born into a particularly religious family; sure they occasionally went to church, but it had stopped after his parents died. He wasn't even sure what he believed in; he just kind of floated around the topic. It didn't bother him or interest him in any way, so he had never put the effort into making up his mind. Now, he felt himself question his beliefs a little.

The man's voice echoed around the walls, bouncing off the domed ceiling, and dug itself into his brain, triggering endless trains of thoughts in his mind. Great, like he needed something else to think about.

The time passed smoothly, the minister's voice lulling him into a sort of trance, where he was listening but not fully aware. Before he knew it, everyone was standing up and filing out the door, looking considerably more alive than they had before. Religion was the only thing that these people had, the only thing to brighten their days and fill their hearts with hope.

An elbow nudging his ribs made him look up, registering the empty church, other than them and the prophet, with Zami gesturing to the man still standing at the podium. Nodding at her, he nudged Blu and stood, holding out a hand for her. She took it and stood up, Blu and Strike doing the same beside him. Feeling a little nervous, they made their way down the aisle.

The man only looked up when they made it to the pedestal, giving them a big smile and setting down the book he was flipping through.

"Ah, yes. I know who you are, come with me." Ray sent a look to Zami, who looked just as disturbed as him, while the man stalked away, out a door in the back. With a shrug he followed, the others close behind.

The door led into a ridiculously long, narrow hall with bare walls and a tiled floor. At the end stood a single door, which the prophet opened up and strode through without pausing. With a glance at Zami, who just shrugged, he followed the man, staring at the new room as he entered in a mix of shock and amusement.

Racks and tables were spread around the room in no particular order, stacked high in a seemingly never-ending bounty of various books, papers, and knickknacks. The clutter made the room seem smaller to the eye, with the only open space being a few feet around a table to their right. Even the ground was stacked with weird objects, which were stacked upon dusty boxes and broken side tables. Somehow, vines seemed to grow across all of the walls and up the legs of the tables, covering the sides of the racks. He walked over to a vine, running his hand over it. How did he keep real plants underground without light?

"Ah!"

Ray nearly jumped out of his skin as the prophet slapped a hand on his shoulder. "You noticed my grapes!"

Grapes. This man was growing grapevines in an underground room. Of course he was.

"Did you know that you can live off of grapes, added with a few other vitamins?"

Before Ray could respond, the prophet whipped around, sliding rapidly across the floor. Then he was saying something wacky to Blu, who looked like he was about to explode, holding in laughter. He had to admit that although this was all weird, it was also quite comical in a way.

A glance at Zami confirmed the fact that she was also highly amused by this place. She seemed extremely focused on a particular grapevine, a grin on her face as she stared at it. He made his way over to her to ask what she thought of the place, but as soon as he started to talk she jumped straight up, whipping around with a hand held over her heart.

Raising an eyebrow at her, he watched as she took a deep, faltering breath. She was normally so on guard, he wouldn't ever be able to scare her like that.

"Ray! You nearly gave me a heart attack!"

He felt a grin spread across his face. "Sorry." She sighed, turning back to the shelves. He leaned over her shoulder.

"Whatcha' lookin' at?"

"I don't know, something just kinda' feels familiar here."

He studied her face as she squinted at one of the grapevines. She reached forward, poking a grape and quickly withdrawing her hand as if it was going to hurt her.

After a moment she leaned back, giving him a quizzical look. He snorted. Then she gestured for him to lean forward and he did. She whispered into his ear.

"This place is wack, I don't like it."

He gave a nod of confirmation, tilting his head so he could whisper back. "Agreed. I wouldn't take anything he says too seriously unless we're sure we want to risk it." She nodded just as the prophet spoke up, sounding far too excited for the circumstances.

"Now, let's talk." Ray turned to see the prophet standing in the center of the room gesturing to a group of chairs scattered amongst the crowded area. After they all settled into chairs, the prophet began with his legs crossed and hands behind his head.

"I know why you're here." A moment of silence. Ray glanced at Zami who met his eyes with equal wariness. "I can give you what you need. But," the way he smiled made Ray shiver. "I have a favor to ask. He didn't wait for them to say a thing before he continued.

"I need an... item from someone."

"Why can't you just get it?" Ray asked, unable to help his curiosity.

"I have my reasons." His eyes flickered across their faces.

"What's the item?" Ray questioned.

"The item could be anything." Ray stared at him. How were they supposed to know what to look for if it literally could be *anything?*

"You'll know it when you see it." Ray stared incredulously at him. That instruction was helpful.

"I'll give you directions to get started. All you need to do is find the object, bring it to me, and I'll give you the information you need."

Ray hated how simple that sounded. Yet, as he looked to the others, they were all nodding, reminding him that they didn't have much of a say in the matter. "Okay."

The prophet smiled, popping up from his chair. "Wonderful!" He exclaimed, walking to one of the shelves, rustling around seemingly looking for something. After a minute he exclaimed in triumph. In his hands was a map, a crumpled sheet of paper with winding lines and scribbled labels on it. Walking back over, he shoved it into Ray's chest.

"This gives you everything you need." Then the prophet walked back to his rolling chair, plopping down and sliding across the floor a few feet. "I would hurry, you have six days, or," he smiled wickedly, "deal's off."

Of course it was. Why wouldn't it be?

They said their goodbyes, then he followed Blu and Strike as they made their way back down the hall, Zami right behind him. Maybe it wouldn't be as bad as he thought it would. It was just a simple mission, what could go wrong?

A lot. That was the answer. It seemed people were far more interested in them after they stepped out of the church, eyes following their backs as they moved. At first, it wasn't a big problem, just a lot of attention. But then right as they were about to disappear back into the woods, a voice stopped them in their tracks.

"Now, what might several young kids be doing about at this time in the morning? Where are your parents?" He turned around to see a squat man in uniform, a sheriff's badge on his front pocket. Ray was frozen, trying to come up with something to say, an excuse as to why four kids that didn't live there had just attended church and then started to leave. Apparently, this lack of response confirmed the man's belief that they were up to no good.

"I'm going to need you four to come with me until your parents come. We can't afford any trouble." Ray inwardly sighed. That was one thing about being young, no one just trusted you walking around. The others looked equally annoyed but didn't argue. They all knew that it was a bad idea to argue with someone in a position of authority.

The sheriff's office was a small, dark blue building that was fairly well taken care of, the small front step swept clean of any dirt and the shutters wiped clean. The officer opened the door and ushered them inside, pointing them to a row of seats at the back of the room. There was only one detainment cell in view, and in it sat a boy who looked around eighteen or so, with messy brown hair that needed a trim. He didn't even look up when they came in, just continued slouching in his seat, legs crossed and staring blankly at the floor.

"Ignore that one, he's all trouble." The sheriff said, giving them each a stern look. "As long as you don't cause any trouble, you can sit and wait for a guardian to come and I won't put you in there with him." He turned to look at Zami who seemed to be contemplating something. "What's up with you?" He snarled and Ray furrowed his eyebrows at the rudeness in his voice. It seemed Zami knew what to say though, as always.

"I just remembered I left my necklace in the church." She replied shakily, and Ray startled at the panic in her voice.

The officer frowned. "So what?"

"It's all I have left of my mother, sir." She explained, voice edging on panic. The officer looked startled too, but after a moment he was turning Zami around and leading her out the door.

"I'll come with you to retrieve it." He sent a glare back at them, and Ray's hands twitched when the officer's hand slid to the curve of her waist. Only when

Ray saw Zami peer back and wink at them did he realize she was faking it, and let out a breath, settling back in the chair.

"I swear to god if he tries anything on her..." Blu snarled. Ray nodded, flexing his fingers as he stared at the door. He trusted and respected her too much to just foil her plan without a thought, but his nerves were still on edge.

"I wouldn't trust him either. That man's scum if there ever was." Ray turned to the boy in the cell who was now looking up at them. Ray assumed his eyes were on them, but he couldn't really tell from underneath his flop of hair. "My name is Nick. My friends call me Nick. If I had any, that is."

"I'm Blu and that's Ray and Strike." Nick raised his eyebrow as Blu spoke, gesturing to each of them in turn.

"Ah, Blu, what a fitting name," Nick stated, standing up and brushing off his shorts. He wore loose khaki shorts that fell past his knees and a big red shirt with a dragon on it under a grey sweatshirt. "Let me guess, the sheriff just picked on you for no real reason?" Ray nodded and the boy continued. "He does that so he can get credit for doing his job, even though he doesn't do anything to help with real crime out here."

"Ugh." Blu groaned. "What a weirdo." Nick nodded, stretching his arms.

"Did he pull that on you?" Ray asked curiously.

Nick leaned against the bars casually. "Nah, this is like my second home. I come here to protest the kingdom's lack of support in the war and always get thrown in here." He gripped a bar on either side of him and pulled them apart effortlessly, stepping out and bending them back into shape. "They can't contain me though." Ray laughed in shock at the smooth show of strength.

"No wonder!" That's amazing dude!" Blu exclaimed, inspecting the bars. When the door opened again Ray whipped around, met with the sight of Zami looking a little too pleased with herself. She lifted her hand and shook a little slip of paper.

"You'd never believe it, you guys!" She exclaimed, faking shock. "We can go!" Ray raised an eyebrow at Zami but she just grinned, holding the door open, Nick waving goodbye to them as he also disappeared.

"What happened?" Ray asked, amused and impressed.

"He got a taste of his own medicine. He won't be tormenting any more kids. *Ever.*" Zami sounded so intimidating *he* almost wanted to confess any little sin and let the police take *him* away.

"Remind me not to mess with you." He stated.

She giggled and shoved his shoulder. "Come on! Let's go get the prophet his 'object'." He rolled his eyes and followed her, Blu and Strike murmuring amongst themselves.

When they were about two minutes into the forest he pulled out the map, not wanting to be close enough to town to run into more trouble.

"Where are we supposed to go?" Blu questioned.

He frowned, triple-checking before answering. "The... forest."

Ray flicked a card through his index finger and thumb, sliding it across his palm in a way that made it seem to disappear. He had subconsciously been doing it for nearly half an hour now, and his fingers were starting to tire a little. It turned out it had been a good idea to bring cards, as they had ended up playing every time they stopped for the night and had trouble falling asleep, which was fairly often.

A couple of feet away, Blu was snoring loudly enough to wake the dead. Strike was still awake, sitting on a nearby stump quietly, and Zami, despite her previous complaints, was sound asleep.

Slipping the cards into his pocket, he stood up and made his way over to Strike, plopping down beside him.

Neither of them said anything for a while, just reveled in the silence of the forest. Well, as silent as it could be, with Blu's snoring. The wind tousled his hair, and he felt an unusual breeze across his forehead that would normally be covered by his bangs. There was something peaceful about the stillness of the world at that point. He didn't know how long this would last, so he drank in everything around him. The overwhelming smell of pine and fresh water from a nearby creek tickled his nose. The breeze slightly chilled his skin, and he was suddenly hyper-aware of everything; the way the wood felt underneath his palms and the sound of the wind rustling the leaves. He could even hear the small breaths Zami was taking, along with the gentle exhalations coming from her nose.

"We'll be there in only two days." Strike informed him. Ray glanced at Strike, who had his eyes focused on Blu's sleeping form, fingers playing with his hoodie string.

"Yeah, hopefully, we won't run into anything else. Though I'm not sure that's possible." He said, leaning on a hand and observing the blue-haired boy lying a couple of feet away.

"I don't know, I have a good feeling about this."

Ray grinned, bumping his shoulder into Strike's. "Is that optimism I hear?"

Strike huffed, turning away, but Ray didn't miss the small smile on his face. "Just don't get used to it."

He chuckled. "You should get some sleep, I'll keep watch." Strike stood up and walked over to the spot next to Blu, dropping his bag before sliding to the ground. Ray smiled as he listened to Strike's breathing even out, and eventually slow to normal.

Sitting on the ground, he leaned back against the same stump he'd been sitting on, smiling at his friends. He knew he should be worried, but he wasn't. Whatever happened, they could make it through together.

Chapter 9

↔

Zami groaned, as she opened her eyes to see a blonde with a bright smile that was quite offensive that early in the morning.

"Ray, I swear to God, if you poke me again, I will finish the job. And not the one that Sylvia gave me."

"Oh come on, Zami! Destiny awaits us!"

She groaned again, covering her eyes to protect them from the brightness. And the sun too. "Destiny can go screw itself." He raised an eyebrow at her from his crisscrossed position beside her, his chin resting on his hand.

Grumbling, she sat up. "It's a good thing you're cute." He just grinned, standing and holding out a hand. She took it and stood up. As she flattened out her shirt, she watched as Blu and Ray exclaimed excitedly about the adventure ahead of them. Strike seemed to be the only one with any sense of what you should be like in the morning, with his hair slightly disheveled, and his glare at the others hard enough to make even her shiver a little bit.

Ray's hair and smile were offensively bright, and he seemed to have way too much energy for someone who had pulled an all-nighter. He turned to her.

"You ready?"

"Sure." She held back a yawn as they started walking. And walking. And, she thought sardonically, more walking.

Luckily, or unluckily, she couldn't decide which, all this walking gave her time to think.

With their current pace, and if the prophet actually gave them something useful after this, it wouldn't be ridiculously long until they located the desirable. Had her dad obtained any clues to where it was? What if he had already had it?

She frowned, chewing on her nail. No, if he did, she would know about it. He was extremely arrogant; he would want everyone in the whole world to realize what he had accomplished.

But then there was the whole, her supposed to be a bad guy thing, according to the prophecy. So why was she here right now, helping the very boy she was supposed to have killed, and in the future was destined to kill again? Why was she being trusted to do so? And *why* did everyone think she *wanted* to kill him? The prophecy said some dark person was going to kill the light one and people automatically assume it was her? Well sure, they were kind of the only ones with those powers known to be alive, but still. She didn't really give off "killer" vibes. Maybe killer clumsy, but not an *actual* killer.

And on top of all that, some of her memories had perked back up to the top of her mind. The vibe off that sheriff had given her chills, resurfacing problems from the past. And of course, with that came the little problem that she just could *not* seem to recall anything that had happened from when she was six, to like ten or so. That was just temporary... right? She didn't remember that being a problem a day ago. What had happened between then and now to change something? She bit harder at her nail, trying to push away the welling anxiety in her chest.

What if she permanently couldn't remember anything about that period? Then she frowned. Would that *really* be a bad thing? It was probably just as horrible as the rest of her childhood, so what was the problem?

Well, she supposed the problem was that she couldn't remember the last time she had seen her mom. She couldn't remember how she had died or why. She couldn't remember meeting Elios or her early training, or much of what she had learned.

That was bad. That was really, *really* bad. She hadn't gotten a concussion, right? Nothing hurt, besides some aching in her ankle, and her vision wasn't swimming with dizziness. So why? When did this all happen?

Aware that if she kept on thinking like that, she would only find herself in more trouble, she looked up and stuffed her hands in the straps of her sheaths, not having any pockets to stick them in. She tried to intently focus on the back of Ray's head, attempting to clear any other thoughts in her head. As she came back more and more into reality, she began to notice their conversation.

"I still think she's probably in her own world. She probably doesn't even have a clue what we're talking about." Blu said to the others. She raised her eyebrow as Ray responded.

"No way, she has epic hearing, dude. She's probably listening to everything we're saying right now." They both glanced around, meeting her eyes. Highly amused, she watched Blu pout, and Ray puff his chest out in victory.

"Told you so." He bragged.

Blu frowned even harder if that was possible. "Yeah, yeah, whatever."

As they turned back around she nudged Strike who was beside her. "They do things like that often?"

He shrugged, readjusting his glasses. "I mean I know Blu does, but I haven't known Ray all that long."

She frowned, glancing towards Ray. "Really?" She had thought they had known each other for a considerable amount of time.

Strike nodded. "He only came to the base like two days before you did."

"Wait, seriously?"

"I know, he acts like he's known all of us forever. It's kind of just his personality, I think."

She glanced back at Ray, taking in his slightly tapered hair and crooked smile as he and Blu whispered about something.

"Yeah. Probably." She breathed out sharply, caught up in his sharp jaw line and bright eyes. Strike chuckled beside her as they fell back into a comfortable silence. All previous thoughts were thrown away, her mind only filled with wondering how in the world she hadn't noticed how gorgeous the boy in front of her was.

They spent the rest of the day walking, only stopping when the night had fallen completely, bathing the forest in moonlight. There was something peaceful about the clearing they stopped in, branches bristling in the light breeze and grass waving under their feet. Feeling lighthearted, she dropped her bag and rolled her shoulders, grinning at the others. They seemed to feel it as well, Blu immediately rounding about to tackle an unsuspecting Strike, who let out a loud yelp.

"You look happy." She bit her lip at the ground when she felt a shoulder nudge her own. After a moment she looked up and gave Ray a shy grin.

"Cause I am." He smiled back, seemingly unaffected by any shyness or concern. She turned back to watch as Blu chased Strike, Strike yelling, though it was more giggling than actually angry shouting. They ducked under branches and yelled at each other, smiles wide on their faces as they tracked through the shallow parts of a pond.

"They're very happy too." Ray pointed out as Blu finally caught up to Strike, who looked like he was struggling to run any further.

Really? I can't tell." She replied, feeling more confidence in her snarkiness than anything else. He raised his eyebrow at her, but before he could respond a large splash alerted her attention. She and Ray began to laugh as they spotted a miffed (though still smiling Strike) standing in the water, hair plastered to his forehead.

"BLU!"

Blu had the audacity to look innocent. "Whoops." Zami had to lean on her knees, wheezing, when Strike grabbed Blu's hand and yanked him in, giggling madly. Their smiles practically glowed as they splashed through the water, Strike tossing his now wet glasses carefully onto the grassy shore.

"They're gonna regret getting their shoes wet," Zami remarked, wiping her eyes as she caught her breath.

"Oh, come on!" Ray said, giving her a wild grin. "Have a little fun." She raised her eyebrow as he tossed his jacket to the ground and kicked off his shoes, holding his hand out to her. She rolled her eyes and sighed, kicking off her own shoes and grabbing his hand. She let herself be dragged to the shore, heart warming at the laughs and jostling that filled the otherwise still evening.

He let go of her hand when they made it to the water, wading in until it reached his knees, just flicking against his now rolled up jeans. At his sideways glance, she narrowed her eyes.

"There's no way I'm getting in any further." She said, crossing her arms, though she was afraid her dopey grin didn't help her look any more intimidating.

He shrugged and ran his hand through his hair. "Suit yourself." She rolled her eyes, assuming that he was getting in, and instead glanced to where Strike and Blu were, still splashing and yelling. But what she was least expecting was the arm that encircled her waist and lifted her feet off the ground.

"Ray!" She shrieked, hitting his back as he carried her further into the water. She gasped at how cold it was, staring in shock at Ray's back. She was being carried. Like a sack of potatoes.

Then she was laughing, gripping the back of his shirt as the water got higher and higher. She could hear Blu and Strike laughing along with them as her heart thumped dangerously fast, face flushing madly.

"Ray!" She yelled again, feeling his hands as he gently lifted her off and held her above the water, eyes on her. Her hips were pressed hard against his stomach, and her breath hitched in her throat at the close contact.

"Can I?" She stared at him, the moonlight on his bright eyes and the glinting water that was only at her knees. He was *asking* if it was okay to drop her in the water. Feeling a little breathless, she nodded, letting out a startled giggle as he dropped her, then caught her right when the water reached her shoulders.

"You..." Her voice died in her throat at Ray's mischievous smile and raised eyebrow. She frowned and swished her arm out, splashing him.

He gasped with fake offense. "Wow, how nice to the person who's keeping you from getting your head wet!"

She pouted at him, gripping his shoulders a little harder. "Says the dork who dragged me here in the first place."

"Touché." Then she was underwater, cold shocking her eyes open. When she broke the surface again she glared half-heartedly at Ray, pushing her hair out of her face. Her feet didn't quite touch the bottom so she was left paddling slightly, unable to splash him again without submerging again.

"What?" He said innocently, blinking his stunning eyes at her. "My hand slipped." Instead of responding, she yanked him underwater with her, not willing to let him be the only one who got out of this with some part of his body dry.

When they broke to the surface again she giggled, watching as he rolled his eyes and flipped his hair over, spraying her eyes with water again. She reached up with one hand to wipe the water out of her eyes, paddling with the other one to keep up. Despite their fighting, she felt a hand grip her forearm, helping her stay up.

"That was kinda mean." He complained.

"Sorry," She started, grinning. "My hand slipped." He rolled his eyes and ducked under the water again, successfully splashing her so she couldn't see. That time she wasn't as surprised when hands found her waist, pushing her further out in the water.

The next half-hour was spent with a lot of splashing and yelling, Blu and Strike eventually joining in. When she finally stepped out of the water she was cold but happy. Her skin tingled slightly in every place Ray had touched, a smile permanently plastered across her face.

She was highly amused as Blu used his magic as a blowdryer, successfully removing all moisture from his hair and skin. When he turned and blasted them, she laughed, ducking to avoid wind on her face.

Five minutes later, they were laying on the ground, finally calming down from how much laughing and splashing that had occurred. She didn't think she had ever laughed half that much in her whole life until now.

The night was beautiful once again, and they drifted into a comfortable silence, staring up at the stars. When Strike murmured quietly that he would stay up, she smiled, closing her eyes and falling into a peaceful sleep.

She was sitting on a swing set, staring at a moonlit park.

"Baby, what're you doing here?"

She looked up and her breath hitched. "Mom?"

Her mother smiled, crouching in front of the swing and setting her hands on her knees. "Come on, dinner's ready."

She could only stare, eyes wide as she took in the dark freckles and sparkling hazel eyes in front of her.

"What's wrong, baby?" Her mother frowned at her, taking her hand and squeezing.

"Mom." She repeated in disbelief, reaching out a hand and hesitating. It wasn't real. She would reach out to touch her and her mom would disappear. It would only hurt more. Yet, she still did it anyway. She couldn't help the little bit of hope that her hand would connect with warm skin, feeling a living heartbeat through her fingers.

The moment her hand touched the spot where her mom's shoulders were supposed to be, she was alone again. With downcast eyes, she stared at the spot in front of her, waving a hand through empty air.

She woke up with a shaky breath, opening her slightly wet eyes.

"I want cake." Confused, she looked up. Strike and Blu sat several feet away, facing away from her, Blu leaning back on his hands and Strike leaning on Blu's shoulder.

"Can you think of anything *other* than food?" Strike asked. She watched as Blu looked up, and even though she couldn't see it, she could tell he was grinning at Strike who had an eyebrow raised.

"Actually, yeah, I can." Her heart warmed as Strike gave an unbelieving little scoff but leaned in slightly the same time as Blu did. With a grin, she turned to her other side to give them a little privacy. That brought her gaze to Ray's face, immediately causing butterflies in her stomach.

She struggled to swallow her heart back down her throat as her gaze trailed over the figure beside her. He was a couple of feet away, but close enough that if she wished it, she could easily touch him. When he shifted slightly on his side, and his hair fell over his eyes, she was sure her heart palpitations were on the verge of causing a heart attack. She rolled over to stare at the sky, trying to breathe. Oh no, this was *not* good. Not good at all.

Chapter 10

↔

Ray woke up to the ridiculously bright sun, stabbing through his eyelids and causing him to reach up and throw his hand over his face. When he finally got accustomed to it, he sat up, yawning.

Strike sat on the other side of Zami, leaning back on one hand and tracing the other through Blu's hair. Blu had his head on Strike's lap, legs sprawled out underneath him and hands curled against Strike's legs. Ray grinned at the blank expression on Strike's face as he stared out to the lake, actions completely habitual.

He grinned even harder when Zami shifted slightly, fingers fluttering slightly against the ground. Her hair was still slightly mussed up from the night before, the dry front pieces curling into her cheek and the rest trailing over her shoulder. He would remember every detail of the past night forever, her breathless giggles and shining eyes, to her pouty expression when he dragged her into the water.

It was hard to believe they'd never known each other before a week ago, and he found himself trying to figure out how he had survived that long without her. Now that he had her with him, he couldn't imagine her gone.

Standing up, he stretched his back, wincing at the soreness. Maybe he should try Zami's wall method.

Strike was still mentally checked out, though his hand had stilled in Blu's hair and he was now staring at the boy in his lap instead of the water. Ray was unsure about whether he should get the others up, and after a moment, decided against it, plopping down again. They had enough time... most likely. It had only been a few days.

He spent a while just listening to the loudly chirping birds that had woken up also, and occasionally glancing over to look at the girl beside him, deep in thought about what the prophet wanted. Was it supposed to be a magical object of a sort? That would make the most sense; he wouldn't send them all the way out there to get something he could get easily. Unless the point wasn't for them to get something for him. He had read about stories with things like this; tricks and tests to determine the worth of the person who wanted something from you. He narrowed his eyes at the tree branch in his peripheral vision. That might explain how no one had gotten hold of the desirable so far. But then, what did that mean for them? He'd like to think they were worthy, but how could he know?

"I can practically hear the high-pitch screeching of the wheels in your head turning."

He glanced around to see Zami, sitting up on her elbows and giving him that half skeptical, half amused look. "I suggest plugging your ears then." He responded, receiving an eye roll in return.

"I would, but I'd much prefer to know what you're worrying your pretty head over." He raised his eyebrow as she sat up, brushing off her leggings and looking down at him expectantly.

Sighing, he sat up as well, stretching his arms. "I was just thinking."

She nodded, urging him on. "Thinking...."

"It was just in general." He remarked. "Believe it or not, I do that sometimes."

Zami gave him a "are you serious right now" look. "Oh come on, it can't be nothing. You looked like you were knee-deep into something important."

He frowned, studying the ground. "I was just thinking about how I've read books where people are sent off to get something for someone, and the point ends up not being the item itself, but how and why you get it."

She looked contemplative for a long moment before she spoke up. "So you think it's possible this is a test to see if we should be trusted with critical information?"

He shrugged, picking at a twig. "Maybe."

"I guess we'll just have to watch out. And trust our instincts, they're there for a reason." He nodded, already thinking about what could possibly happen and what they would find at their destination.

They started off nearly half an hour later, ducking under tree branches and trudging through the brush until midday when they decided to stop for a moment to rest. Then it was off again, getting as far as possible until the sky was cloaked in darkness and the sun had passed beyond their vision. It was only probably around one or two more hours until they reached their destination, but they decided against trudging on in the dark where they (with the exception of Zami) would have a disadvantage at anything they had to face.

Zami insisted she would be able to stay up, convincing them that since the moon wasn't nearly as bright tonight, she would be the only one able to see at all times. There was something else in her expression, however, some other reason she didn't want to sleep. And he was determined to figure it out.

By the time Blu and Strike had both fallen asleep, they were in the deepest part of the night, the eeriest hours. From his spot on the ground, he glanced up, only barely able to make out the figures of the others. It had been unsettling being far enough apart to not see if each other were okay, so they had ended up scooting fairly close to one another. If he focused, he was able to see the glint of Zami's eyes and the outline of her body sitting in the moonlight.

Unable to fall asleep anyway, he moved next to her slowly, not wanting to surprise her. She didn't even acknowledge his movement, though he figured it was more due to her being deep in thought than anything else. After a long moment of silence, he felt her drop her head on his shoulder without a word. He wasn't sure what to say, so he didn't, just let the night remain in unbroken silence.

Her hair tickled his neck pleasantly, and he could hear every little breath she took. She was slightly swinging her knees side to side in front of her, occasionally bumping into his leg he had propped his arm on, and he watched the movement for a long time, counting the even rocking. He decided he liked the weight of her head and the way she fiddled with her fingers, staring at the ground as if it held the answers to every question she had.

"I've been thinking about your theory," Zami said, turning to look at him with bright eyes. "I think it's safe to say we shouldn't easily trust what we see. What we perceive may be a trick in itself, no matter how realistic. There are dozens of accounts of prophets having strange connections with the paranormal, the unusual, psychic magic, etcetera."

Ray raised his eyebrow as she talked, listening to every articulated syllable and a little lisp he hadn't noticed before in her s's, t's and h's. "I think," He said, tilting his head slightly with a grin. "That you shouldn't worry so much." She blinked at him in surprise and after a moment turned with a huff, though he didn't miss the little smile on her face.

"I'm not worrying, I'm just.."

"Fretting, concerned... worried?" He offered, faking offense at the small slap she sent at his shoulder.

"You don't worry enough." She pouted back, crossing her arms.

"Cause if you worry too much it'll end up getting in your way of doing great things." He argued, leaning closer on his hand.

"Like killing you." She retorted though some of her confidence seemed to have left her, leaving her a little red in the face.

"Aw, come one." He teased. "There had to other reasons for not wanting to kill me."

She seemed to contemplate it for a moment before shaking her head seriously. "Nope." Then she hesitated before adding, "You do look nice in khakis though."

He laughed, grinning at her flustered but confident words. "I would hope that wasn't the only thing you were focused on."

She shrugged, moving closer as she leaned in, meeting his eyes. "You can't blame me, training must've paid off."

He chuckled again, though he was mostly focused on the green in her eyes, the dusty freckles on her cheekbones and her suggestively lifted eyebrow.

"I'll make sure Aunt Dew knows that." He said, and she smiled widely, reaching up to tug at a chain that he hadn't noticed beneath her collar.

She seemed to notice his gaze and cocked her head slightly. "It's a gift."

He nodded, staring at the small links of the chain. They weren't even the least bit dirty from what he could see, marking its importance. He supposed she hadn't been completely lying about an important necklace back in town.

"Does it have a meaning itself, or is it just special because of who gave it to you?"

She shrugged, pulling it out completely to reveal no locket, just a piece of metal shaped in the form of a heart. "I mean, I don't even remember getting it, what they said when they gave it, or why they did. So I guess, it's just important because it's been with me so long?"

He met her eyes, trying to discern what emotion she was feeling. "Well, sometimes the most important words are the ones not said." He responded as she tucked it back in.

She gave a little snort. "What are you, a prophet?"

"No, an avid reader."

She giggled and shoved his shoulder. "Nerd."

"Hey..." He started, but was cut off again by her statement

"I like nerds."

"Ooooh." He said, nudging her shoulder. "Is it possible that the all great assassin is a nerd herself?"

Zami scoffed and turned away. "In your dreams."

"Yes, please."

And Zami laughed, her eyes crinkling in genuine amusement as her voice filled the air with gentle giggles. "You're cheesy."

He smiled at her, heart leaping. "Good thing you're not lactose intolerant then."

Her laughter dying down, she turned to look at him, visibly swallowing as she tucked a piece of hair behind her ear. "You know most people don't flirt when the fate of the world is in their hands."

He raised his eyebrows and gave her a coy smile. "Maybe that's where they all fail." He remarked, looking up to take in the stars.

"You think flirting makes the line between a failed hero and a successful one?" She asked, leaning back on his shoulder.

"No. I think it makes the difference between a discouraged hero and a happy one."

The next morning he was woken up by Zami, who looked unusually peppy for the early morning, bright-eyed and bushy-tailed, as his Aunt would call it.

"What, you find some magic mushrooms nearby?" Blu asked, turning around looking in a wild circle. Strike looked equally ready to murder Blu, or kiss him until he couldn't breathe. Which Ray supposed wasn't all that unusual.

"No, but..." Zami smiled maniacally. "We're getting closer and closer to finding this stupid desirable!" She bounded off in the direction they were supposed to be going, a bounce in her step.

Sharing an amused look with Strike, he followed after her, though with much less bounding.

It turned out to be only a little over an hour until they found themselves in a large clearing that perfectly matched the spot on the map. Gripping the strap of his bag, he stopped, glancing around at the abrupt, straight edge of the trees, and dark soiled ground that went on for what must have been the size of a large sports field. It almost seemed as if someone had just plucked an evenly spaced chunk of the forest from the ground, leaving behind a bare, dreary spot.

The wind had died down to gentle whistles, leaving them in a perfect silence under the warm sunlight.

"Well darn," Blu said, taking in the area. "You think the prophet knows deforestation is at an all-time high?" Ray didn't answer, trying to figure out why on Ethereal they were standing in this specific spot. There was no visible clue to what they were supposed to be doing, no hints to what spot they needed to look in. After a long moment, he turned to Zami and Strike.

"Any clue?" They both shook their heads, looking equally befuddled. He frowned at the ground, shoulder drooping slightly. Out of all the possibilities, he was least expecting there to be exactly *nothing* there.

"He said we'd know it when we see it," Blu said, seemingly unaffected. "So we wait. It's one of those things that only pops up once we realize something important. There's no rushing that." Ray stared in shock as Blu plopped on the ground, leaning on his hand. Sometimes, he was just a moron. But there were times like these to remind him that Blu was actually extremely bright, acutely aware of every detail surrounding him, despite his oblivious exterior personality. Sylvia knew *exactly* what she was doing sending each of them on this mission.

"Okay, so we wait," Strike responded, dropping down beside Blu and looking around. Ray sighed but followed suit, observing every square inch of their surroundings to see if they missed something obvious. Zami didn't sit down immediately, taking a moment to stare at the sky before dropping down with a defeated sigh.

They spent an awful lot of time wandering around and theorizing, inspecting every bit of knowledge they had about prophets, Zamoth, and magic. By the time the sun had reached high above they were burned out, trying to fathom what possibly the prophet could want.

"I don't get how we're supposed to find this thing," Blu said, kicking his feet up in the air from where he was lying on the ground. "I mean, we don't even know what it is and he just expects us to find it? It's nuts, man."

"The prophet said we would know it when we see it. We just have to be patient." Ray responded, leaning on one of his hands.

Blu groaned. "I don't wanna'."

Strike snorted from where he was sitting. "You never 'wanna' do anything."

"Hey, I have a set schedule for laziness, nothin' wrong with that."

"Except for when, you know, you're trying to keep an evil king from brain-washing the whole world and leaving us to eternal damnation," Zami stated flatly. "Yeah, nothing at all."

Ray raised an eyebrow at Zami who was laying on her stomach, a book open in her hands. She hadn't even looked up while saying that, and it seemed she was somehow still reading while simultaneously being pessimistic. What a talent.

"What're ya' readin' anyway?" Blu asked, sitting up.

Without looking up, she responded, "101 Ways to Kill a Blue-haired Friend Who Won't Shut His Trap."

"That doesn't seem very helpful, for what we're trying to do." Blu pointed out.

"Might be in the future." Ray grinned. Only she could keep the mood lighthearted with a threatening sentence.

"So do you have any clue what the item will be?" Blu asked, still talking despite Zami's extremely open threats.

She sighed, closing the book and sitting up. "Nope."

"Nothing at all?"

"Nope, Nada, Nothing."

"What about you Sun Boy?"

It took a moment for Ray to realize Blu was talking to him, and he hastily responded, "Oh, yeah. Wait, what?" He got some very amused expressions at that.

"I mean, no." He amended, rubbing his neck in embarrassment.

"You have a way with words, dude." Blu teased, as Zami tried to hold in her laughter. Ray turned away, slightly abashed.

"Try to think of the Prophet's words in a different way," Zami suggested, biting her lip. "Maybe he didn't mean what we thought he did."

"He said we have everything we need," Blu informed, still kicking his legs.

"The map." Strike started, sitting a little straighter. "What if that has something to do with it?" Ray frowned and pulled it out of his bag, setting it gently on the ground. It looked just as it had when the prophet first handed it to him; scribbled dark lines and a dark star where they were at.

Zami leaned forward and squinted at it, dark hair falling over her shoulder. After a long moment, she slipped her fingers under the paper and picked it up, then stood with it. He watched in confusion as she held it up in the air, tilting her head slightly.

"Ray, come here." He stood up and leaned over her shoulder, eyes focused on the spot on the bottom of the map, directly under the star.

"Psar tultiem?" He questioned, looking at her in confusion.

"AH!" Ray jumped back, stumbling on his feet as he stared in shock at a woman standing a few feet in front of them. Trying to calm his beating heart, he observed the way she was holding up a gnarled hand, squinty dark eyes peeking out from under bushy white eyebrows. He figured there must've been a small store's worth of jewels on her bony fingers and wrists.

"Phaph." The old woman spat, stretching out her hunched back. "Iss always you kids!"

Ray glanced at the others to assure himself that he was hearing correctly. "Um, uh, sorry?" He responded, not completely sure what was happening.

The woman scoffed, shuffling around and adjusting an awkwardly oversized fur coat. "Let me guess, ol' Edmund sent you?"

"If that's the weird religious dude, with a thing for grapes, yeah." Blu piped in. The lady didn't confirm or deny that option, just shifted around mumbling loudly to herself.

"I told that boy that my magic's not a toy! Test them, my ancient booty!" The woman looked irritated beyond belief as she glared back up at them, narrowing her eyes in skepticism. "His 'heroes' just keep getting younger and younger, don't they! It shouldn't be in my hands to kill a bunch of teens cause they're unworthy."

"Um, excuse me, ma'am." Blu cut in, holding up his own finger. "If you're tired of having to do that, why don't you just give the object away so you never need to protect it again"?"

The woman cackled loudly, bracelets clinging as she waved her hand around. "Oh darling, it's a shame I have to kill you, you're adorable! However," She brushed off her coat and looked back up, eyes glowing with a greenish light. "I said I don't agree with his methods. Not his expectations." Ray stepped back, feeling slightly nervous at her words.

"Now, here's how it goes. I get to practice my magic. And you get to die." Ray ducked as something flew over his head, shoes scuffing up loose soil as he got a grip back on reality. For a moment he thought she had actually missed, until he saw the maniacal grin on her face and heard the unmistakable sound of the ground erupting from behind him. Gulping, he slowly turned around, watching in morbid fascination as dirt rained about their heads, a dark figure emerging from the ground.

"Oh my god!" He whipped around to see a similar column of dust spiraling to his right, Blu having just stumbled out of the way. Another rose on his left, and then another in front of him, where the lady seemed to have disappeared.

"You have *got* to be kidding me right now." Zami breathed as they backed up, all huddling in a circle back to back, facing the open holes in the ground. He nodded in agreement, as the dust cleared, revealing extremely large, ridiculously angry rock *golems*.

"Oh, that's just lovely," Blu said sarcastically, gesturing towards their smoky red eyes. "I've always wanted to be beaten to death by freakin' rocks." If it was any other situation, Ray might've laughed. But alas, they were actually going to be beaten to death by rocks. So he figured it wouldn't look the best on his obituary as a quote; "laughed as he had his head caved in."

"Oh, not just any rocks." The old lady shouted from somewhere out of sight. "*Transforming* ones." As if to prove her point, the one in front of him growled, the air around it whipping aggressively as its growl became a roar, and its hands became claws.

"Wow. A lion. I feel so special." He said, blinking at the beast in disapproval. The golem just roared louder, shaking its grassy mane.

"I like cats," Zami said offhandedly.

"I think it's a problem if you like this one." He responded, shifting slightly as he prepared his magic. He startled again when another ear-splitting roar filled the air. The lion prowled around, swishing its mane and kicking up dirt as its glowing eyes pierced into his very soul.

"I'd say good luck." The woman shouted. "But I really don't care." And the air was filled with sounds of yelling and growling as the golems leaped forward. Ray dodged a pounce with a startled yelp, scuttling around so he was able to watch the lion, which was flicking its tail as it prepared to attack again. He could briefly see the others fighting, but was mostly focused on catching his breath and attempting to figure out what he was supposed to do. Sure, he could continue to dodge, but eventually, he wouldn't have the energy any longer, and the whole point was to *win*. Except, he wasn't really sure how to subdue and kill rocks.

When the lion pounced again, he dodged under it, trying to spot some sort of weak spot. But it immediately whipped back around, and swung its claws so quickly that it managed a hard sideswipe to his stomach. Gasping at the loss of air, he held up his arm against the next one, grabbing its paw and pushing it away as hard as possible. His skin stung a little bit where the claws had caught him, but it didn't affect him much, and he was able to lash out before its next attack, falling down with the creature into a tumble on the ground. Before he could get a good grip on it, however, the rocks began to shift and with a screech, a large bird flew from his grasp, taking flight.

He furrowed his eyebrows at the animal now soaring through the air. Now that was just plain unfair.

Remembering his magic, he pulled his hand back, feeling the familiar weight of a bow appear in his hand. Given the fact that the weapon was more instinctual than physical, the moment he grabbed it with his other hand, a bolt was flying loose. He winced when a sharp thud resounded, followed by a plummeting flash. The heap on the ground was still for a long moment before it shifted again, changing again into its lion form, though one side of its face was crumbling. With a snarl it pounced, further than it had before, and even though he moved in time, the sheer force of its landing was enough to cause the ground to shake, leaving him grasping for balance. Then he was on the ground, a heavy weight on his back. Gasping, he pulled up to his elbows, a sharp stinging in his head.

Grabbing back onto his magic, he used all his strength to turn, stabbing as hard as he could with a magically-formed dagger, into whatever body part he could. He figured he must've met his mark when an ear-splitting scream filled the air. Rolling completely onto his back, he kicked it off and scrambled to his feet.

The golem laid completely unresponsive on the ground, a gaping hole right where its other eye had been, a result of his magic. Taking a deep breath, he turned, eyes widening when a rock flew straight at his face. He held up his arms in defense, shutting his eyes, but blinking in confusion when nothing connected. Glancing up, he found Blu holding his hands up, the rock floating inches from his face.

"Sorry man, al..." Blu cut off as he whipped his hands back around, successfully slamming the rock into another golem's head with a sickening crunch. The golem growled, shifting into a bird in one fluent movement and taking off into the sky.

"Not on my watch, rocky!" Blu called, whipping his hand in a wild downward motion. Ray watched in awe as the bird plummeted, its wings no longer able to push upwards. Before it had the chance to recover, Blu dropped a large rock on it with his magic, leaving it motionless.

"Do they stay like this?" Blu asked him, wiping his hands on his jeans.

Ray glanced back over to the unmoving heap of the lion. "I think so." Remembering the others, he turned around, watching as a startlingly bright crackling strike filled the air, slamming into the ground with a thunderous roar. When the spots cleared from his vision, he was met with the sight of Strike shaking out his hand, looking in distaste at the charred rocks sitting in front of him.

"That's my boyfriend," Blu said happily.

"Ow! Motherf..." Ray whipped around to see Zami holding her stomach, as she staggered forward. The sheer amount of force with which she kicked her golem, which was in the shape of a bear, was enough to make him wince. He watched as she held her hands up, he assumed trying to use her magic, but nothing happened, leaving her defenseless as the bear swiped at her. He moved forward to help, but something pressed against his chest, keeping him from getting any closer.

"You must each prove *yourselves*." The lady's voice echoed through the air.

"But her magic's not working!" He shouted hastily, pushing against the force and watching as she barely dodged another swipe.

"That's not your responsibility." The woman said, sounding just the tiniest bit remorseful. He watched helplessly as Zami attempted to avoid the attacks, her stamina fading with every passing moment. Given the shout from earlier and the way she was holding her stomach, he figured the golem had already landed one hit. And the absence of her normal weapons just concerned him even more.

He yelled when the bear finally made its mark, swiping hard at her leg. It was in almost slow motion that her knee gave out, and as she dropped to the ground, the bear launching itself at her. Then from somewhere came what must've been a last burst of strength, as she lunged out from under it, stumbling up and whipping around, hands flying out. Everything went completely dark for a moment, the only hint to what was happening a beastly roar of fury. Then the shadows faded, revealing Zami standing alone, the golem nowhere in sight.

Her chest heaved, her breathing shaky, and her hands were still held out in defense, eyes on the spot where her enemy was only a moment ago. She slowly looked up and met his eyes, mouth slightly open in shock. Without further thought, he ran, catching her in a concerned hug, stumbling a few feet together before he completely regaining his footing.

"Oh my god." She murmured, voice slightly raspy. He felt her gripping the back of his jacket, heard her slightly pitched breaths, and noted the way she gasped into his shoulder.

"Are you okay?" He asked, not letting go just yet.

She nodded her head in a mute "yes" before murmuring, "You?"

He nodded, feeling a little better. He pulled away a moment later, inspecting every inch of her face. Her eyebrows were slightly scrunched, lips pressed in a tight line as she looked at him, in obvious pain.

"Ah, how sweet." The lady said, sounding a little amused. He turned to see her standing in the middle of the clearing, white hair flitting in the wind. "I wasn't aware that you were actually *the* heroes." Ray swallowed, fingering the back of Zami's shirt in mistrust. "Now, where did you put my little Pancake?"

Ray glanced at Zami in confusion. "Um, what now?"

The woman sighed, gesturing to the three unmoving heaps of rocks. "My Pancake. I see Ketchup, Carrot, and Onion. Now, where's Pancake?" Ray couldn't help but chuckle at the pet names, and then glancing over to Zami, waiting for her to answer where she put "Pancake."

"Ah, uh, well." Zami started, looking guilty. "I actually don't really know."

The woman blinked at Zami for a long moment before swinging her clanging wrists in exasperation. "What do you mean you don't know! 'Iss your power!"

Zami shrugged. "I've never done *that* before. And to be fair, you can't really blame me for not wanting to be killed by a bear-shaped rock."

The woman sighed, running a hand over her face. "Okay, okay. Now, I have to say, overall that was incredibly impressive. You are all excellent individual fighters. The only question is, are you good as a team?" Ray half expected the golems to come back to life and merge or something like that, but nothing like that happened, they just continued to lay on the floor in heaps.

"Oh come on." Blu groaned. "I hate Simon Says." Ray turned to him with a raised brow, along with everyone else. When Blu caught their looks, he flung his hands out, opening his mouth to say something, but instead sending a rock flying straight at the old woman's face. The woman ducked, sending him a glare which caused Blu to let out a nervous giggle.

"Sorry." He squeaked out, tucking his hands into his pockets to keep any further accidents from occurring.

"Worry not, young trouble magnet, I don't do Simon Says. I was thinking something a little more... developing."

Chapter 11

Zami blinked at the woman's words, still trying to process exactly what she wanted.

"Those who are worthy of such power, don't keep secrets." The woman said, eyes piercing her skin as if she could just feel that Zami was keeping a whopper of one.

"So what, you want us to share secrets like a bunch of girls at a sleepover?" Blu asked arms crossed and blue eyebrows raised.

"No, I want you to trust one another. All you have to do is write down a secret that's weighing on your soul. You'll only have to tell if the bag decides."

Zami blinked at the woman in disbelief. "The bag. Some bag will decide if our secrets are juicy enough to tell."

The woman sighed. "No, the bag is a teller of secrets that will affect you in horrible ways. If your secret could tear each of your relationships apart piece by piece, it'll let us know that it's important to say. The more you trust one another, the higher chance it is that you are worthy of wielding such power." Zami's heart sunk as the woman handed her a piece of paper and a pen, looking at her expectantly. Maybe she could write something small, like how she had nightmares, or how she secretly thought Ray was incredibly hot?

"Your *greatest* secret. One you don't want anyone to ever know. That's the point of this." Zami withered under her gaze, hand shaking as she uncapped the pen. The moment the tip brushed the paper she hesitated, trying to calm her fear. Maybe her secret wouldn't even be that important. Of course, she didn't want the others to suffer, but she really didn't think they needed to know what she was writing on the paper. Slowly she scrawled her sentence out, refusing to look at it as she folded it and dropped it in the small bag. The woman then handed them each another slip of paper, explaining before they could ask.

"Once I close this bag, the heaviest secret will appear on that person's paper. I'll have you open it and then," Her eyes flickered over each of them separately. "You tell it." Zami swallowed a lump in her throat as the woman grasped either side of the bag, slowly pulling it in until the sides touched. The moment the cloth joined seemed to mark the looming dread filling her. Deep down, she knew that they were going to find out eventually, that it was better to get out of the way now. But it was still terribly nerve-wracking as the old lady gestured for them to open their papers.

It took her a long time to gather up the courage to open it up, heart sinking even further if possible as she stared at her slanted handwriting in the center of the paper, the dark ink taunting her with each curve of every letter and each scribble from where she had messed up with her shaking hand. She knew the others were looking at her, seeing their empty pages, and seeing her staring at the open paper in defeat.

Well, there went her chance of being the good guy for once.

What would they think? Three words that would forever change the way they saw her. And she had to tell them just for a damned test.

"Just spit it out." The woman suggested, and if Zami wasn't too busy worrying, she would have noticed the genuine concern in the woman's voice as she looked at her. "It makes it easier."

After a moment of being completely silent, she sighed, shoving the paper in her pocket and whipping around to the others.

"Y... yeah." She cleared her throat and pushed back her brain warning her not to say what she was about to. *Just spit it out Zami. No going back now, might as well just get it over with.*

"The reason I'm so close to the King isn't that he likes me." Her voice was surprisingly strong and she swallowed, refusing to look up at the others. "It's because he's my dad." She spat it out, staring at the ground in disbelief that she had just said that. *Well, there goes your chances with the rebellion. They're gonna tell Sylvia, and then Oak, and then I'll be locked up for good and left to wither away in the pits of a cell...*

"I'm sorry."

She whipped her head up and stared in shock at Strike's words. "Wh... what?" She spluttered, blinking at them in surprise.

"It's not your fault he's your father," Ray remarked, face completely serious.

"Yeah, why'd you think we'd be mad?" Blu asked cooly, bouncing on his heels.

She shook violently and laughed in disbelief, running her hand through her hair. "You know, I'm not really sure." She said, heart ridiculously warm in her chest.

"Well, I hate to say it, but..." The woman sighed, waving her hand so the bag disappeared. "I think you passed." Zami gaped at the woman, a grin slowly spreading on her face. "Here." She held a closed hand out to Zami who held out an open palm, watching as the old woman dropped something heavy into her hand. She stared at a small jeweled necklace in confusion.

"It's what he wants. It controls my four golems. Well," She gave Zami a pointed look. "Three." Zami grimaced, looking away. She did feel badly about that, but her aching ribs and stinging leg was enough to keep her from feeling too guilty. Looping the small gold chain around her finger, she clutched the hard-earned jewel in her hand, the edges pricking her skin.

"Now, a small warning, because I think you four actually have potential." The lady looked each of them in the eye. "The prophet may immediately turn on you; he's a man of his own motives. There's no predicting what he'll do with those golems. Watch out." They nodded and she waved. "Good luck, my heroes." Zami held her hands up to protect her eyes from the flurry that kicked up, causing her hair to whip wildly around her face as she gritted her teeth against the unpleasant dirt. When it calmed and she looked up, there was no sign of the lady, golems, or any disturbance in the ground that would signify a fight.

They stood in silence for a long moment before Blu spoke up. "Well, that was entertaining."

Zami snorted at the understatement and winced when it sent a throbbing pain through her chest. She gingerly touched the spot she had been hit, and when she felt the tenderness of it combined with the sting her fingers caused, she knew that one or more of her ribs were broken, others bruised. She had broken enough ribs in her lifetime to recognize the symptoms.

"Zami?"

"Yeah?" She breathed out, trying not to double over when the pain increased. Her adrenaline must've been keeping her up until then.

"You don't look too good." Blu pointed out. She sent him a glare and attempted to stand up straight, blatantly ignoring the pain in her torso.

"Gee, thanks." She slipped the jewel into her pocket and gestured to them. "Come on, I have a prophet to beat up."

She was walking home from school. She had been four at the time, coming home from her first year of grade school. By that time, there had been some complications at home. There always had been, as long as she knew, as long as she remembered. She was often woken up late at night by her parents screaming their lungs out at each other, chairs and glasses being thrown, and walls being punched.

"Mom I'm home." She had called, closing the door behind her.

Silence.

"Mom?"

Then she heard the yelling. Scrambling into the kitchen, she stared in horror at what was in front of her. Her mother on the ground, tears running down her face as her dad hit her again. Blood poured from a deep gash on her head and she could see a broken wine glass on the floor. Zami knew her mother had resorted to drinking. It numbed her from the inside out, but now Zami watched helplessly as her father raised a hand against her mother. He had always been angry, always been discontent, but he had never resorted to physical violence before.

She had yelled, diving in front of her mom only to stumble back from a punch that landed on her face. Scrambling back up, in her father's state of confusion, she had grabbed his hand.

"Daddy, stop!" She gasped, trying to peel his hand out of its fist. Then he pushed and she was sent teetering backward into the wall.

"Don't make me hurt you." He growled, his hand hovering in the air, one jerk away from hitting her hard.

"Dad?" She had asked, trying to understand what was happening. He wouldn't hit her, that's what she had thought. But at the same time, she would've thought he would never hit her mom either. He ignored her.

"Get out of my way before I hurt you."

She shook her head in defiance, struggling to push against his fist, frantic tears streaming down her cheeks. "Don't hurt her!" Please!" She cried out, holding his arm with both hands as his knuckles turned white from strain.

And then her cheek was stinging, and she was staring at the kitchen as he stomped out of the room, slamming the door shut with a thunderous crash. She remembered the throbbing of her cheekbone, the disbelief coursing through her veins that he had intentionally raised a hand against her.

Maybe it was an accident. A one-time thing that would never be addressed. That's what she had thought as she slowly kneeled beside her mom, trying to push the tears in her eyes away,

It wasn't a one-time thing. She learned that every day of the next year. She was accustomed to angry physical fights. And then her mom started to drink more. It started with just some after dinner, or to calm the anxiety of a long day. But then it was all the time, and soon it felt as if she didn't even have a mother.

Kids at school had started picking on her, shoving her in lockers, knocking her books onto the floor, calling her names. But none of it compared to how much her father's words hurt, the bruises that might fade, but would never completely leave her.

She stayed quiet. Didn't bother with defending herself. Why just make it worse, she told herself. Really, it was just an excuse to hide from it. Just acting like nothing was wrong was better than facing your fears. He threatened to hurt her mom even worse if she attempted to tell anyone, tried saying that he was just raising her to be strong. It was almost like he was convincing himself rather than her.

Then there was her, trying to finish her English homework with a shaking hand, glancing up at the clock every minute. Her palms were sweaty, her heart racing. He was going to be home any minute.

He got furious when she hadn't finished her homework after he got home, going into a violent rage. The kids after school had held her up, taunting her. They had begun to pick on her more, now that news of her father's promotion had gotten out. Now that they knew in a short while she would be moving closer to Damrion. To a nice, large capital city.

Later on she would realize they were bitter that she had gotten so "lucky" in having such a famous, successful father. That they were tired of the cooped up, damp air of their small town. And annoyed that she was getting out of it instead of them.

The reason she was so late was that one of the kids had grabbed her bag and tossed it into the creek near the school. She had spent the better part of an hour fishing out each of her books and assignments, and nearly another trying to dry them with her mom's blow dryer.

So now she scribbled hastily on a damp sheet of paper, half-heartedly answering questions and citing the answers. The clock ticked away, and she knew when the door clicked open that it was going to be a long night.

Her dad stomped into the kitchen, dropping his bag on the floor and removing his suit jacket. She tried to not draw attention to herself, hunching in her shoulders and writing furiously.

It would've been better if she could do it in her room, but a dark padlock hung on the doorknob, attached to a chain on the wall, and the only key was the one in her dad's pocket.

"What are you doing?" He asked, voice on the edge of yelling.

"Homework." She managed to get out, avoiding his gaze.

"You're using your left hand." He pointed out, breath on her neck. She nodded mutely, closing her eyes and swallowing roughly. When a hand jerked her wrist upwards, she was forced onto her feet, staring at her father, who was inspecting her left hand. "That's a sign of evil. They're in you."

She shook her head and attempted to pull away, choking on air. "No dad, it's just how some people are born." She said, still attempting to twist out of his grasp. "There's nothing evil in me, I promise." She pleaded with him as his hand tightened and jerked, causing her to lurch forward.

"You lie." He said, pulling her wrist upwards in a painful movement.

"No." She said, crying out as he pulled her wrist beyond its normal mobility. "I promise dad. I'm not. Stop. Please, it hurts." He ignored her, pushing harder. She called out for her mom on the couch, but she was asleep. As always.

"Shh." Her dad soothed, wiping a tear away. "I'm helping you." And then her wrist went numb and she dropped to her knee in seething pain, gripping it. "It's okay kid. You're safe now." She sobbed as her dad left the room, walking into his own room and closing the door. It took a long time to build up the courage to stand and stumble out the door. She knew she had to go to the hospital. But part of her was just telling her to leave. To run and never look back. She didn't. She wasn't brave enough.

Outside, the cold stung her bare arms and feet, making her nose go numb, but she pushed through, knowing the shooting pain in her arm wasn't safe. She needed help.

When she walked in, heads turned and a nurse dropped to her knees, trying to ask her for her name, what happened. She didn't know why she lied then, but she did. She told them it was a bike accident, knowing that was an excuse her dad used whenever someone noticed her injuries.

After they put her in a cast, they kept on asking, over and over, if she needed help. If someone was hurting her. If she needed somewhere to stay. But she shook her head, afraid of what her dad would do to her or her mom. She insisted she was okay, but still let one of the nice ladies walk her back to her house. When nobody opened the door, Zami felt her heart drop. Her dad not being around and the sight of her mother passed out on the couch probably wouldn't help her convince the nurse that everything was fine.

"They're probably asleep." She said, not meeting the nurse's eyes. "I can get in through the window. It's okay."

"Doll, that's not okay. How about you come home with me tonight. We'll drop you off in the morning when I know you'll be safe." The word safe echoed in Zami's head. She was never safe, never would be. But she nodded and let the woman bring her to her house, let her feed her dinner, and tuck her into a large bed. That had been one of the more peaceful nights she could remember.

Zami woke up with a hitch in her side and ragged breath, sitting up quickly and whimpering when it shot pain through her ribs. She struggled to shift to a more comfortable position, wincing at every little movement and leaning on her hand to take the weight off her hips.

She hadn't thought about any of those events since they had happened. She had tucked it far away under all the training, all the schoolbooks she was reading. Yet, as she lay there panting, breathing sharply in pain, her mind was flooded with memories and the ever-present fear that lingered with them.

Since when had her memories been that clear? That neat, that put together? She gripped her sides and briefly wondered if maybe it was the fact that something was changing, shifting in her mind as if it were making room for something bigger. Something more significant.

But then she was thinking again, and her mind was overwhelmed, swarming with everything she had been trying not to think about.

She was helping her father's sworn enemy. The King was going to *kill* her. She was going to be beaten to her last breath, and then there would be nothing left. She would die as a result of his fury and no one would know. No one would care.

She sat up with a gasp, and dug her fingers hard into her skin, ignoring the sting from the skin breaking. What was she going to do? She had to *do* something...

"Zami? What's wrong?" She whipped around to see Blu looking at her quizzically from his spot leaning against a trunk. She couldn't answer. She just shook her head slightly, and then panicked because there were tears stinging her vision, just as they had been that moment years and years ago.

Oh god, she realized she had been subconsciously thinking about going *back*. She pinched her wrist in between her forefinger and thumb, wishing she could be sure what was right. She needed to decide whether she wanted to be on the good side or not, and stick with that choice. Not sit here in an in-between state, thinking constantly of what she should be doing instead of this.

She missed the weight of her knives on her legs, which had disappeared along with "Pancake" the golem. She missed Elios. She missed the stability she had never had as a child.

"I don't know." She gasped and then frowned at the wavering in her voice. She was pathetic. The others would soon realize that too, if they hadn't already, and then she would be kicked out and...

"*Zami.*" She startled when she realized Blu was crouching next to her, eyebrow raised. "We're here. Everything is fine."

She swallowed deeply and stared at the ground, shaking her head in disbelief. It wasn't just *fine*. *Nothing* was just fine. Fine would be her dad not being crazy, her mom not being dead, her not being the daughter of the worst tyrant in history. Fine would be her not panicking every five minutes, not having trouble having fun because she was too distant and scared of relationships. Fine would be anything other than what she was right then.

"You don't believe me, do you?"

She paused at the fact that Blu read her so easily, and then blinked when he settled beside her, close enough that he was almost brushing her leg and arm with his, but far enough that he wasn't.

"You know, if you don't allow yourself to believe that *you* can make decisions yourself, and that not all of them are terrible just because you made them, then you'll never truly be able to feel as if you're doing the right thing." She blinked at him as he met her eyes, lips turned into a soft smile and eyes sparkling with unbridled faith. "We're all giving you an opportunity, and we trust you." He remarked, and her heart thumped in her chest at the fact that he was saying such a thing. "The rest is up to you."

She didn't say anything, and he stayed quiet as she sat there, knees pulled up to her chest and contemplating his words. Making her own decisions and believing in herself? That was much, much easier said than done.

She glanced at Blu and breathed in the optimistic aura that seemed to soften the air around him, lulling her panic into something less painful.

"You're surprisingly good at this." She finally said and expected him to be puzzled at the change in topic. Instead, he just gave her a bright smile, leaning back on his hands.

"Everyone's built for something. It seems I've been built to bring comfort to those in panic." She giggled, and then froze, shocked that she had laughed, just a minute after panicking to the point of tears. "See?" He teased, tilting his head at her. She rolled her eyes, but surprised herself by scooting slightly to allow their shoulders to touch. It felt nice to have the warmth of contact. To have such simple affection, with no strings attached, no worry that any consequence would come of it.

He didn't seem bothered by it, and leaned into the touch. It became silent again, but nowhere near as heavy. The breeze was nearly gone, and at that moment she completely felt detached from who she was, and her past. She felt content with beginning the journey of changing the way she looked at things. Content with what she had now.

She was afraid of sleeping. Scared of what might come of it. But Blu didn't move or complain when they spent the remainder of the night sitting side by side, breathing softly through the night. He just gave her a kind smile, one with no mockery, nor irritation. And for friends like that, she thought that she could continue to push forward and try her best in turn.

Chapter 12

Making their way back to the prophet's town proved to be an easy journey, arriving back at the village in about two days, feeling newly rejuvenated. Ray watched as people bustled through the streets, before turning to Zami.

"It's probably not a good idea to just strut in again, is it?"

She shook her head and sighed. "No, we should hold off until it's late night, when no one will see us."

He nodded in agreement, shifting back a little further out of view from the villagers. They ended up sitting in a small circle for a while, talking in hushed voices until Blu offered to play a game. Ray decided to join, though Zami seemed reluctant to, only caving in when they all pressured her. She smiled shyly though, when he shifted slightly to nudge her shoulder as Blu and Strike argued about what they should play. He was a little worried at how she had been acting after the whole golem incident, what with her occasional winces and the huge secret she had basically been forced to reveal.

He was mostly just concerned about what it meant that her dad was the King. He had heard a lot of rumors about his cruelty, and possible... issues, so what did that imply for Zami?

"How about Never Have I Ever?" Blu suggested enthusiastically. "I love having dirt on my friends!"

Ray shared a mildly concerned look with Zami before shrugging nonchalantly. "I don't have any dirt." He pointed out, but still held up his hands in acceptance. The beginning was mostly just normal party questions, but slowly they turned more and more into personal attacks.

"Never have I ever had a king as my dad," Blu said, grinning evilly at Zami, who narrowed her eyes as she lowered a finger.

"That's a low blow." She said, holding her chin up. "Never have I ever asked to be assassinated." Blu gaped at her in disbelief as Strike reached over to push one of his fingers down since he hadn't already.

"That was one time!" He complained. "You'll pay for that!"

Ray swallowed, trying to keep from grinning. Oh, he had an idea. Up until then, both his and Strike's turns had been fairly gentle, not targeting anyone in particular. That was about to change. When they all looked his way he cleared his throat, pulling a poker face.

"Never have I ever tried to kill a hero." There was a moment of silence before Blu and Strike began to cackle, Zami staring at him, open-mouthed in betrayal.

"I cannot believe you, Ray!" She pouted, whacking him with her now three fingers.

"Well, I suppose if we're playing it that way," Strike started. "Never have I ever nearly been assassinated." Ray gasped at Strike who just grinned, fist-bumping Zami who looked greatly pleased.

The next half an hour was aggressive, teaming up to target the others, Strike and Blu extremely good at scoring against each other since they knew everything about the other's life. The sun had just begun to set when they finished, Ray and Blu losing by a fair amount. Zami and Strike could get *terrifying* when there was a competition.

There was a fair amount of shoving and bickering as they got up and peeked around the trees to view the village streets, which had since emptied.

"How do we know the prophet will be there?" Blu asked, glancing around at them.

"We won't," Zami said with a shrug. "We just have to hope."

Ray thought that was a weird phrase for her to use, considering she was a very "things only happen if you force them to with your fists" type of person, but didn't say anything.

"We'll still want to be quiet." She added, peeking around the tree. "You never know who's watching." Ray nodded and stuffed his hands in his pockets, trying to quiet his footsteps and breathing as much as possible as they stepped into public view. Every crunch of a leaf under their feet seemed ten times louder than normal, setting alarms off in his head.

The trip to the church went quite easily, however, and they ended up standing before the large doors in only five minutes. It was obvious that that was about as lucky as they would get though, when the doorknob stopped about half-way through turning it.

"We could just kick the door down," Blu suggested.

Zami shook her head, nodding her head to the nearby houses. "That would just announce our presence."

Ray frowned at the look on her face, knowing that it was not a good sign. "What?" He sighed heavily, crossing his arms.

"You ever tried sneaking in through a window, hotshot?" He gaped at her, trying to determine whether she was serious or not.

"Ooh, I have!" Blu chirped, looking far too excited about it. Zami looked amused as she trotted around the building, the rest following closely behind. Sure enough, several feet above his head was a small window, one that he wouldn't even *think* about trying to fit through. It was probably just to get some sunlight in the back room, or airflow or something. Not to go *into*.

"Well, I hope you have some experience with windows." He pointed out, arms still crossed. "Cause there's no way any of us are gonna fit through that." She rolled her eyes as she tossed her jacket at Strike, who stumbled to catch it.

"You're lucky you have me." She said, gesturing him and Blu over. Knowing what she was going for, he kneeled, and held his hand out to Blu. Blu seemed skeptical for a long moment, before holding out his hand and crossing it with Ray's.

It wasn't much of a surprise that Zami was easy to lift (not that he had done that before, or anything) and they pulled their hands back away as she pulled herself up on the window with her elbows, kicking her legs out. She disappeared only a moment later, and they hurried around to the door, glancing around to make sure they were still unnoticed.

A few moments later, the door swung open to reveal a slightly disgruntled Zami, cheeks considerably flushed as she ducked her head, avoiding their eyes.

"What's wrong?" Blu asked as Zami coughed, retrieving her jacket from Strike and slipping it back on.

"Um, well..." She bit her lip, cheeks red. "Let's just say I've seen more of the prophet than I *ever* wanted to." Ray raised his eyebrow as Blu let out a soft laugh. "And we may have to wait a little while to talk to him." She gestured to a closed door on the right side of the entrance area. Ray shared a look with the others before walking over and pulling it open, revealing a sleeping prophet on a couch, a large wool blanket draped up to his chin.

"Okay, he's asleep," Blu said, looking at them in confusion. "Let's just wake him."

Zami coughed and turned away, face flaming again. "He's not um, asleep."

Ray stared at her for a long moment before it hit him. "You knocked him out?" He whisper-yelled, flinging his hands out.

Zami held up her hand in defense, still not looking at him. "I was surprised! I'm sorry!" Ray laughed in disbelief, smacking his forehead.

"Reminder," Blu whispered, nudging his rib. "Zami knocks out anyone who gets her flustered."

Ray snorted as they moved back into the entrance area and dropped into one of the seats, beside Blu. Strike and Zami both remained standing, leaning against a couple of seats. After a long moment of silence, Blu spoke up.

"So how big was..."

"BLU!" Zami squealed, shoving her hands at his face to muffle his words. Ray chuckled, secretly liking how she acted when flustered.

"What?" Blu asked, pulling her hands away. "It's an honest question!"

"That you should *not* be asking!" She said, plopping back down on a chair and pulling her knees to her chest.

"I was just curious, you know, what his..."

Zami squeaked again, burying her face in her knees and covering her ears. "LALALALA! Geometry! Onions! Hairless Cats!" Ray raised his eyebrows again, trying to find any correlation between the topics she was blathering on about.

"*What* are you saying?" He asked, highly amused.

Zami popped up again, hands still over her ears. "Things that make me cry." She said, as if that was obvious.

"Oh, I feel you with Geometry." Blu groaned.

"I'm more concerned about the hairless cats." Strike said, looking indeed very concerned.

Zami removed her hands and flung them out, expression shifting into her "I have an opinion and I'm going to share it" face. "They have no fluff! That's like, the best part of a cat!" She exclaimed animatedly, eyes wide. "Without it, they're just poor... naked... potatoes!" Ray laughed this time, enjoying how red she became and how seriously committed to her ideas she was.

"What?" She pouted, crossing her arms. "It's true."

"Yeah yeah, okay. Whatever you say," He quirked his eyebrow and focused on her to see how she would react. "Princess." She stared at him in shock for a long moment before she burying her face in her hands again, attempting to cover her red face.

"Dude, I think you just killed her." Blu pointed out.

"You can't just say things like that!" Zami squeaked, still ducking her head, though she had removed her hands from her face. He knew he wouldn't stop, that she deserved someone to tease her, someone to make sure she understood and believed her worth. And he would gladly take on that position.

"Sorry." He said, clearly not sorry at all. Zami looked up and met his eyes for only a second, before she was sputtering again, turning to bury her face in Strike's shoulder.

Strike looked amused and understanding, reaching around to pat her shoulder in a comforting gesture, before turning to him with a stern look. "I think that's enough flirting for one day, young man."

Ray pretended to be offended, bringing a hand up to his chest. "Who, *me*? What a preposterous claim!" Before Strike could completely tear him apart with his eyes, a pained groan sounded from the other room.

They all shot up and ran to the door, watching as the prophet sat up, rubbing his head with a confused expression. When he saw them, he froze, eyes wandering over each of them in shock.

"You're alive?" He shouted in disbelief, clearly not expecting them to be there right now.

"I hope so," Blu said, reaching down to pat his stomach as if to make sure he was really there. He gave a nod and looked back up. "We're good." The prophet gaped at them before regaining his composure, sitting up completely and getting ready to stand.

"Um, I wouldn't do that if I were you, as Zami is already traumatized enough." Blu pointed out. To Ray's amusement, Zami was already facing the other way, refusing to turn around. The prophet looked down, seemingly only then remembering his current state. Not looking the least bit flustered, he gripped the blanket, keeping it around him as he stood.

"Well, that's what you get for coming back." Ray sighed as the prophet stomped past them, disappearing into the back room where his study was.

"It's safe you know." Ray said, glancing at Zami who hesitantly turned around before dropping the hands that had been over her eyes. She let out a little sigh of relief, rubbing her temple.

"It's times like this I regret having an excellent memory." She groaned, looking deflated. "I'm never gonna' get that image out of my head."

"Just try to get a better picture to focus on." Blu offered.

Zami nodded and turned to him, snapping her fingers. "Ray, take off your shirt."

Ray covered his chest, looking at her cautiously. "You're an unusual girl, you know that?" He found it funny that she got flustered from a mere nickname, but could turn around and ask him something like that only two minutes later. She gave him a mischievous look, making a "give it here" gesture.

"Aw come on, I just want some eye candy!"

Blu popped up beside her, holding his finger up. "I wouldn't mind it either."

Ray sighed and looked towards Strike for some backup, but Strike just shrugged before muttering a small, "Me neither."

Ray stared at them in shock, still protecting his shirt. "You have a boyfriend!" He exclaimed at Strike. Then he turned to Blu and gestured wildly at Strike. "He IS your boyfriend!" They both shrugged and looked at each other before looking back at him.

"We can look at the menu. We just don't order." Blu finally said, completely serious.

Zami snorted, looking extremely pleased with how they were supporting her. He frowned and turned to her. She held her hands up innocently, blinking at him.

"Hey, I'm free to order *whatever* I so wish." Ray smacked his forehead and turned away, praying for the prophet to return quickly.

To his good fortune, the prophet appeared back out the door only a few seconds later, now wearing his normal green robes. He gestured them in and Ray followed, glancing behind to ensure that the others were coming.

It looked almost exactly as before, with messy shelves and stacked books. The prophet stopped at the table, shoving a pile of random objects off of it with an excited gleam in his eyes.

"I assume you have the jewel?" He asked, looking energized despite being knocked out only minutes prior. Ray glanced at Zami who nodded, fishing the little chain out of her pocket.

"Hmm, that's impressive, I have to admit." He held out his hand, but Zami shook her head.

"Information first." She insisted, taking the old lady's caution to heart.

The prophet looked disgruntled, blinking at her in confusion before crossing his arms in defiance. "I can't do that."

Zami shrugged, pulling her hand out and flashing the jewel in her fingers, dangling it in front of him. The prophet's eyes followed its every move, watching it hungrily. Then he shook his head, looking away, though he was still eyeing it out of the corner of his eye.

"No."

Zami sighed, pocketing the jewel. "Well, I guess it's a no-deal then." She gestured out of the room and began to walk out the door, whistling under her breath. Ray followed her, completely trusting that she knew what she was doing. When they stepped back out of the church into the cool air, Blu rounded on her, looking confused.

"What was th..." Zami shushed him, holding up five fingers and counting down. By the time she reached one, the prophet's voice tore through the air.

"Wait! Okay, deal!" Zami grinned widely, winking at Blu before whipping around. Ray, impressed, followed her back inside, where the prophet stood, fiddling with his hands. When they entered again, he shuffled around, grabbing a singular sheet of paper from under a book and shoving it into her hand. When he reached out to grab the jewel, Zami pulled her arm away, holding it out of reach.

"Ah. Ah. Ah." She mocked. "How do we know you're giving us true information?"

The prophet looked about ready to die of anticipation, as he hurried to talk. "I promise! That's what we've gathered so far! That's it! Now, please!" He was getting pathetic now; Ray guessed if Zami pushed him any further, he would be on his knees begging. Zami seemed pleased enough with the response though, and made to hand him the jewel. Before he could grasp it, however, she cracked her fist into his head hard enough for him to crumple to the floor, completely knocked out.

Ray stared at the man on the floor, as she reached down and set the jewel in his hand, wiping his forehead clean of the dirt that had billowed up from the floor. Then she stood up, brushing off her leggings with a satisfied expression on her face.

"What was that for?" He asked, voice coming out a little higher than expected.

She gave him a funny look. "She said not to trust him, so I'm being cautious."

"Why didn't you just take the jewel then?" Blu asked, sounding genuinely curious.

Zami looked offended at that. "I made a deal, and I respect it!"

Ray nodded his head to the unconscious man. "Oh, is that what you call it. *Respect.*"

Zami frowned at him, jabbing her finger at his chest. "I can show *you* some respect."

"Oh, get a room, you two!" Strike complained, rolling his eyes.

A loud clanking alerted them to turn around, meeting with the sight of at least four men in shiny armor, armed with sharp-looking swords.

"And who might you four be?"

Chapter 13

Zami glared at the guard poking her forward with his sword. She could easily slip out of the ropes on her wrists, but these were soldiers of the kingdom they were supposed to be trying to form an alliance with, and she figured they wouldn't be too happy if she hurt any of their guards. However, when his sword poked a little *too* roughly at her back, she whipped around, gripping it in between her hands as she met the guard's eyes.

"I'm *really* trying to be nice right now, but if you move that sword *one tiny bit closer,* I *will* end you." The man looked startled; pleased that she had gotten her point across, she let go and turned back around, ignoring her friends' looks. *They* didn't have to deal with switching sides in the middle of a war. *They* didn't have a stabbing pain course through their body every time they moved their torso. And most of all, they were not going through a mental crisis. Stupid sun boys and their *stupid* nicknames and broad shoulders, and... She growled, clenching her fists. The guards noticeably shifted away, detecting her pure rage.

She let them, because people needed to be more aware that girls could kick your arse too, and she would. If it wasn't for the need to leave a good impression, she would've caved their self-satisfied smirks back into their skulls already.

When she was jerked roughly into a dark carriage, she almost slapped the man, restraining herself with the slightest bit of self-discipline she had left. It was fairly uncomfortable being squished inside with her friends *and* two guards, but she much preferred being squished to Ray's side than being poked by a sharp sword. A guard stood on either side, in front of the doors, not even moving when the carriage began to roll.

She was internally thanking Elios for her training, because the guards had searched them up and down thoroughly and if it weren't for her quick action, they might've taken the paper. Of course, it was considerably uncomfortable tucked in her shirt, but the guards had skipped over that spot when she gave them a dangerous glare.

She blinked back out of her furious thoughts when a shoulder gently rocked into hers, softly pushing them side to side in a rocking motion. How was it he knew exactly what she was feeling at any given moment? The anger slowly dissipated, and though she was still irritated, the feeling of Ray's side pressed softly against hers was enough to calm her nerves. The cool metal of her necklace pressed against her collarbone in a comforting reminder. That she was also thankful that the guards had pass by.

It bothered her greatly that she couldn't remember her mom giving it to her. She just knew it was from her, without any memory as proof. She knew her mother said something important about it, she just didn't know what.

When the carriage gave a sudden jerk, she panicked, realizing she didn't have her hands free to keep from falling forward. She wasn't tall enough to brace herself with just her legs. When she felt Ray shift beside her, she figured he was dealing with the same thing, only to realize he had moved enough that his shoulder was pressed in front of hers, which allowed her to grip his arm with her tied hands. Normally she would've breathed a quick thanks, but the soldiers made her nervous, so she just tucked against him, hoping her action was enough to tell him.

When she saw the position of the sun in the sky from behind one of the soldiers, she realized that they might be in there a while, if they were being taken all the way to the rulers of this kingdom. As the minutes passed, she let her fingers drop to the crook of Ray's elbow, not letting go even when the ride smoothed out. His skin was soft under her fingertips. She had never had skin to skin contact with anyone since she was little, accustomed to primarily fighting and training, so the feel of someone else's skin against hers was pleasing. Especially because it was... well, it was Ray, and that made it even better.

Strike looked mildly disturbed, though that was sort of how he always looked. Blu was acting like this was something he did every day, legs crossed comfortably and bopping his head slightly as if he was listening to music. Even though he wasn't.

Eventually, Strike jabbed an elbow at him, to which Blu responded with an innocent glance. Zami couldn't help but smile when Strike rolled his eyes, but leaned into him, staring at his lap. Blu looked down in confusion, before leaning over and murmuring something to Strike. She didn't miss the smile that spread across Strike's face as Blu pressed a gentle kiss to his cheek. Strike looked up and whispered something in Blu's ear, simultaneously hiding his face in the boy's neck. Blu gave a bright smile before patting his thigh and settling with a slightly worried expression.

She noticed Strike's leg bouncing, along with the little shaky breaths he was taking. She'd had enough panic attacks in her time to recognize the signs. Blu seemed to know exactly what was going on though, pressing his lips to the other's ear and murmuring what she assumed were the words Strike needed to hear. She figured this was one of the worst times to deal with a panic attack, with your hands bound and stuffed in a claustrophobic box.

It was disheartening when she realized that this must happen often enough that Blu knew what exactly what he needed to do, had it down to an art. Watching Strike's throat constricting sent waves over fear through her, triggering an intense fear of her own. She tried to calm herself down before it could get worse, knowing that her panicking would just cause Strike to get worse too. Zami realized she was seeing a reflection of herself. The choking breaths and shaking, paired with the inability to calm down, were like seeing a mirror, her anxieties showing so openly that it caught her off guard.

The idea that no matter how alone she felt, there were other people out there who felt *exactly* what she felt, was eye-opening. Strike could get through his day, peaceful on the outside, no matter what type of panic he was feeling. That meant she could too.

She could tell his panic had faded shortly, about five minutes later, since Strike kept his head calmly on Blu's neck and Blu looked less worried.

The next hour or so passed in complete and utter silence, her legs completely asleep and her eyes starting to droop. The sun had passed noon and was falling again, marking what would soon be half a day that they had been stuck in this horrid contraption. She was lucky she was always dehydrated and didn't have to go.

Around the time the sun began to set, the carriage came to a stop, and she perked up, only to become even more disgruntled when it turned out the soldiers had just switched with some replacements. Sighing, she settled back, glancing at Ray. She did a double-take and then giggled silently. Only he could just fall asleep at a time like this.

She let herself ogle him, taking in his pale eyelashes and sharp jawline. She hadn't met very many teenage boys in her lifetime, but she figured he must've been very popular in school. There was no way people wouldn't notice those stunning eyes and sun-kissed skin. And then there was his irritatingly attractive personality. Now that was unfair. A person should be attractive or funny. Not both. There was no way she would survive being around someone like him when he had both going for him.

His head moved with the bumps in the carriage, and he had his arms loosely crossed across his chest, seemingly unbothered by the ropes around his wrists.

Realizing she had been staring for probably far too long, she tore her gaze away, blinking when she realized both Strike and Blu were asleep. When her eyes complained, wanting to close, she forced them open. They were being transported as *enemies* for God's sake! The next hour passed ridiculously slowly, each minute weighing down her already heavy eyelids. Why was she so sleepy?

Oh right, she remembered, furrowing her eyebrows. She had tried to beat up a pile of rocks a few days ago with her bare hands, and come away a little worse for wear.

Slowly her drowsiness won through, and dropping her head onto her seat-mate's shoulder, she slid off to sleep.

Chapter 14

When Ray awoke, he was alone in a room, illuminated only by a thin strip of light filtered through a glazed window. He scanned the room, taking in the pale white walls, dark gray curtains and matching sheets he was laying in.

The dull pounding in his head had completely faded, and he felt admittedly comfortable. The bed was warm and soft, and he felt relaxed. Though, he noted with a frown, shouldn't he feel more worried, being drug off by this kingdom's soldiers? He shrugged it off. He had never been one to worry, always just gone with whatever happened. So if it had led him here, he supposed he would stay here until he was supposed to leave.

He barely remembered being led into a castle from the carriage, but he briefly remembered looking into a harsh face. That might be cause for concern, but it also made things a ton easier when you were flexible.

Sliding his legs from under the covers, he stood up and stretched his arms above his head, enjoying how strong he felt. After a moment making up his mind, he turned the handle on the door and stepped outside. A long hallway stretched out on either side of him, causing his eyes to narrow in dislike. It could take hours to find your way through a complicated series of hallways.

He slowly padded down the hall, only realizing after a moment that he was barefoot and very alone in an unknown place. Maybe it wasn't such a good idea to go wandering?

Again he just sighed to himself, glancing back at the door beside the one he had walked out of. There was a high chance it would be one of his friends, right?

When he opened the door, he was greeted by the sounds of laughing, which with further investigation, was coming from a very flustered Strike, who in turn looked to be getting tickled by a grinning Blu. He smiled as he listened to Strike's mid-giggle pleas for him to stop, which were bluntly ignored by Blu. In fact, they only seemed to spur him on.

After a minute, Blu finally noticed him leaning on the door, and gave him a big grin, his hands finally leaving the boy beneath him. Ray raised his eyebrow, still smiling.

"Being productive, I see?" Blu didn't even have the decency to look flustered as he leaned back on his hands. Strike, however, was a different story. He was still laying on the bed, chest heaving from trying to take in all the air that he couldn't while laughing. Though, Ray suspected his condition was due to more than the laughing or him walking in on the events.

"He was being too serious. We'll never make it through this if we don't smile sometimes." Blu explained, though the mischievous smirk that he gave Strike told a different story.

"I'm sure he was." He remarked and grinned. They both watched, amused, as a slightly disheveled Strike sat up on the bed. His normally perfect hair was falling into his eyes, and his jacket was slightly crooked and weirdly bunched in a couple of places. He looked extremely happy at that moment, however, which made Ray smile. He was glad they had that effect on one another.

"So, either of you worried about the fact that we're in enemy territory with no clue whether they still hate us or not?"

Blu shrugged. "Not really, I mean we always manage to get out of bad situations." His eyes glittered with mirth. "Plus, I think Zami has the queen convinced. She has a way with words."

Ray raised his eyebrows, crossing his arms across his chest. "What do you mean?"

"Do you remember Sylvia and Oak? Do you really think they would have let any other random person leave on an adventure with their most important asset?"

"I guess that makes sense."

"Yeah, I suppose there's something about snarky, independent girls that appeal to people of power."

"Now that I think about it, she does draw a lot of attention doesn't she?"

"It's in her blood." Ray and Blu both turned to Strike who, at their looks, continued. "Her father was just a normal townsperson when he was younger. Now," Strike gestured to everything around him in comparison to the Dark King's castle. "He's..."

"Powerful." Ray offered, at the same time Blu supplied, "An arse hole." Strike nodded, seemingly immune to Blu's blunt answers.

"Exactly." It was quiet for a moment as all of them let the thought sink in.

"I mean, I can't place it. But there's just... something about her." Strike finally said, and Ray nodded in agreement.

"Her cold, emotionless eyes?" Blu asked, giggling when Strike smacked him with a pillow. "I'm kidding! Kidding!"

"I was thinking along the lines of how confident she usually sounds," Ray remarked, studying a random spot on the wall, lost in thought.

"She does a good job faking when she's nervous, doesn't she?" Blu said seriously this time.

"They say practice makes perfect..." Strike trailed off, leaving them yet again in silence.

After several minutes, Ray started to get fed up, left with only the sound of their breathing in the room. "How long had you guys been with the rebels?" He asked, pulling up a chair and settling backward on it.

"Over two years now," Blu answered, unconsciously picking at his thumb. Strike reached over, gently pushing his hands away from each other. From the way Blu didn't look down, and how casually Strike stopped his nervous habit, Ray figured it happened quite often.

"You guys came at the same time?"

Blu nodded. "Yeah, we lived together, so we left at the same time."

He raised an eyebrow. "You lived together."

Blu rolled his eyes as Strike flushed. "Not in a weird way, dude. My parents fostered Strike when he was three, so he lived with us almost his whole life." Strike nodded, looking slightly embarrassed, and Ray hummed, musing over the new information. No wonder they had been so close.

He peered curiously at how nervous Strike looked. After a moment Ray found out why.

"Yeah, we um... kinda ran away." Blu laughed, rubbing his head.

Ray stared at them, shocked. That wasn't what he had been expecting. "You *what*?"

Blu laughed, though he thought there was a trace of sadness in it. "My parents. They weren't... all that accepting." Ray's heart dropped a bit as he sighed. "They got outraged when they found out about Strike and me. Later, I convinced Strike to join the rebellion and run away with me. Haven't seen them since." Ray felt terrible about his parents, but he couldn't help but grin at their actions. They had done what so many kids couldn't do, standing up to the people who were wronging them. And in such a *Blu* way too.

"So you guys basically big time rebelled, and then joined a *rebellion*."

Blu grinned, already back to his normal cheery self. "If you wanna put it that way, then basically." Then he raised his eyebrows and leaned forward, eyes sparkling with curiosity. "Enough about us, man. What about you? All heroes have a sob story."

Ray laughed at that, giving them a half-hearted shrug. "I mean yeah, but no."

"Yes but no, what?" Ray smiled at the voice behind him as he turned to see Zami standing in the doorway, mischievous grin intact.

"I thought you were gonna' go back to sleep?" Blu asked.

She shrugged as she kicked off her boots and flopped onto the bed beside Strike. "I can't."

"You can't? Or you won't?" Blu asked, giving her a look.

"That's not important. I wanna' hear about tragic life stories; continue if you will." She waved her hand in the air lazily towards him.

"You should ask Blu. His is pretty good."

"I heard it."

"So you were standing behind the door listening?" Blu prodded, looking amused at her honesty.

"Isn't that the definition of an assassin?" They all gave up. She had a point. All eyes turned to Ray, who in return rolled his.

"Fine." Blu beamed and they all quieted, waiting for Ray to start. "My parents and sister joined the rebellion when I was still a kid." He remarked, fiddling with the sleeve of his jacket. "I'm not really sure how it happened, but there was a sneak attack, and well..." He grimaced and studiously ignored the look of shock on the two boys' faces. "I was fairly young, and my brother even younger, and my Aunts quickly took up raising us, so it didn't really affect me that badly. I mean, everyone's had to deal with their fair share of problems, and I lived with mine." He shrugged at himself as the room fell into silence.

None of them gave him that look of sympathy that he had been given so often in his life. And he appreciated that.

"That's rough." Blu finally said. And for some reason, the mix of Blu's awkward excuse of a reply and how serious his story had been, made him chuckle. Maybe letting go was what everyone needed. To let go of everything bad that happened, and to accept that there was more to come, was like letting yourself be free.

"Wow." Strike remarked and Ray turned his gaze to him. Strike noticed his raised eyebrow and shrugged his shoulders. "My story is practically the same as Blu's, since I was so young when they took me in."

"Strike." Blu reprimanded, his eyebrows raised. "We're all telling the truth, you must comply with it."

"Yeah, yeah." He hesitated for a second before ducking his head. "Well... I guess I was bullied a little bit."

"A little?" Blu asked, clearly not letting Strike get away that easily.

"Okay, fine, a lot. People target others who show weakness, act differently. And apparently being skinny and shy was enough of a reason to get shoved into lockers and beaten up by guys who thought you were weird." He sighed, leaning on his hand. "But, Blu stopped that." The look he gave Blu was so full of appreciation and trust that Ray almost felt left out. "Ever since then, I've stuck with him." Blu smiled at him.

"I'm stuck on one thing." Zami said, brows knitted in confusion. "How'd you fit in a locker? Those aren't really made for people over like five three, much less six feet."

"Well, I was actually pretty short for my age most of my childhood. In fact, Blu used to tease me for it." He nudged his friend. "Then I just shot up. I wish you guys could have seen his face when he woke up and I was taller than him."

Blu pouted. "It's not fair. He used to be tiny, and now he's not!" Strike laughed and Blu half-heartedly glared at him, which only spurred Strike to laugh harder.

"Well," Blu started, clearly embarrassed that Strike was laughing at him. "I believe that means we have one more tragic backstory to tell." He pointedly looked at Zami, who was leaning against the wall, having stood up to stretch her legs.

"Trust me. You don't wanna' know."

"That just makes us want to know more," Blu said, leaning forward in anticipation. Zami narrowed her eyes at everyone in the room, giving a big sigh.

"Alright." Everyone was silent, curiosity gnawing their insides. "Well you see, I was born. And then let's see, I went to school and then moved to the castle. Then I sorta' forgot everything. All I know is, I remember coming back to an all-powerful, sadistic father." She looked at them with a smirk of satisfaction on her face.

"Oh come on, Zami!" Blu wailed. "You can't just let us explain everything in full detail and then come up with a half-wit summary of your life"

"There's not much to tell. My father didn't like me, we moved, then he became King. That's it, story of my life right there." Nobody spoke. What were you supposed to say after something like that? 'I'm sorry' didn't quite cut it. The fact that all of the others were able to be so comical about their pasts made it easy to see they had moved on. She hadn't.

"Wait, when we were talking about lockers, you spoke like you had experience with them," Blu remarked, relieving some of the tension in the room. Zami just shrugged.

"Kids didn't like me." She didn't elaborate.

"Um, not trying to pry or anything, but how exactly did anyone bully you? You'd kick their arse."

She smiled genuinely at Blu's question. "I wasn't always able to do that. In fact, the only reason I learned was because I was tired of getting the crap beat out of me."

"I suppose that's a valid reason," Blu answered lamely. "Wait, Ray, did you ever get beaten up by kids at school?"

"Um, not really." He felt sort of bad about that fact, considering two of the others had been.

"Man, kids can really be mean to other kids," Blu said, frowning. "I mean, I know I wasn't the target, but they just targeted the ones they thought were weak."

"It's the way life is." Strike said. "For some reason, shoving people into lockers makes them feel better about themselves."

Zami grinned. "Plus, I doubt Ray would've fit in a locker."

Ray frowned. "I really don't know what you're implying. But I don't like it."

"Well, were you tall?" Blu asked. "I mean you are now, but so is Strike."

He shrugged. "I think I was about average height. But too tall to go in a locker. Not that I ever tried." He hurried to amend, dispelling any questions.

"Just missed the experience." Zami teased.

"And I'd like to keep it that way. Thank you very much."

"I don't know man, if we ever go back to school I might just have to shove you in a locker," Blu said.

"And then I'll shove Blu in a locker," Zami added. "Everyone should get to experience it at least once in their life."

"I'm gonna' pass." Ray said at the same time Blu responded with, "Hell naw." Zami looked ready to say something, but before she had the chance, the door was slamming open.

He startled at the bright green eyes that bore into him, and subconsciously shifted a little closer to the others, as a girl stepped into the room. She looked around twelve, dark hair bobbing just below her ears. He tried not to stare at the ears on her head, black and poking from under her hair.

She didn't say anything, and after a minute of just staring, he glanced at the others to see if they were noticing her too. When he saw Zami holding back giggles, and Blu and Strike chuckling under their breaths, he furrowed his eyebrows.

"Wha..." He was interrupted by someone yelling from down the hall, screaming something about disappearing princesses and the Queen. The girl whisked away in only seconds, and he blinked again. He would've thought she was a hallucination if not for the others laughing.

"Is... uh, anyone gonna'," He pointedly stared at Zami. "Tell me what that was?" She just gave him a sparkly grin, and he gave Blu a thankful look when he answered.

"That was Mindy, aka the princess. She's... a little unusual. She did something similar to all of us when she met us, though she's been especially fascinated with your status for years apparently." Ray raised an eyebrow as Zami pushed off the wall and slapped his shoulder.

"Don't look so morbid! You've got a fan!" He gave her an odd look as Strike stood up, fixing his jacket.

"The Queen plans on seeing us tomorrow morning after she gets out of a council meeting. We should rest. Given her reputation, I'm sure it won't be easy to barter with her."

Ray nodded with a wince. They could only hope the queen would cut them some slack.

Chapter 15

↔

Zami was standing in a large room. It was so dark, and bitterly cold. Even for her, it was far too dark, far too silent. She never liked silence. For her, it had always brought the inevitable.

Then her mom was there, smiling like always. Her eyes were tired and the smell of alcohol masked her pleasant perfume that had once seemed so comforting. Zami tried to call out. Hoping for a response. Anything. But nothing came back and suddenly her mom was gone. Except, as she stood there, hand outstretched, she knew she wasn't alone. She was never alone.

"It's over for you." She tensed at the stare she could feel, harsh on her back. His voice sent her heart reeling in her chest, begging for it to speak no longer. She couldn't even stand his voice as he stepped forward. Closer. "Betraying me, as if I was the one who did you wrong."

When his hand was on her shoulder, she felt as if she were ready to collapse. Her knees shook as she dropped her gaze to the ground, too scared to meet his eyes. Then it shifted away and she flinched.

"I'm waiting."

She woke up with a gasp, unconsciously muttering as she adapted to the fact that she was back to reality. It wasn't real, it was a dream. Then her heart sunk in her chest. But her mom was still dead and her dad was still haunting her dreams. It wasn't over. It would never truly be over. Wasn't she really just waking from one nightmare into another?

She pushed up to her elbows, breathing hard as her eyes adjusted to the darkness around her. Only then did she notice she wasn't alone.

"Ray?" She muttered, her voice trembling.

His eyes searched hers from where he was sitting on the edge of the bed. "A nightmare." It wasn't a question that she could argue with. It was a statement. A searing headache pounded in her head and the only sound in the room was the ragged sound of her unsteady breaths. Silent. It was too quiet. Panic began to rise in her chest.

"Hey, Zami. Everything's alright." She glanced up to see his face, completely serious as he stared at her. It took a couple of minutes for her to recognize it was true, and slowly and surely her heart rate began to stabilize.

The air was calm as she slipped out from under the covers to sit on the edge of the bed with him, again bringing her knees to her chest and wrapping her arms around them.

"You know, one day you'll have to talk about it, right?" He glanced at her out of the corner of his eye and she dropped her gaze to the sheets. "That's the only way to completely overcome your fears. By facing them."

"You sound like the prophecy." She joked, though, her voice came out unusually shaky. His eyes burned into hers when she looked up, but no matter how badly she wanted to look away, she found herself trapped by his gaze.

"We're here for you, you know. You're not alone anymore."

She smiled a smile that she knew wasn't convincing at the least. "You're too kind, you know. Someday someone's going to take advantage of that."

He grinned, leaning back on his hands. "Well, it's a good thing you're here to beat 'em up then."

A warm feeling began to spread through her stomach, only to be quickly dispelled again with a gasp.

"I tried to kill you!" She yelped, getting a raised eyebrow from the boy beside her.

"You just now realized that?" He said, sounding amused.

"Well, no," She started, pressing her forehead against her knees and wrapping her hands around her head. "I just now realized that with a small change of fate, I would've *succeeded.*" Horror filled her mind at the possibilities. What if she had killed him? What would the world be going through right now if she had pressed that knife a little harder? What if...

"Hey. Zami." She glanced at him, knowing perfectly well how pitiful she must've looked right then. "You didn't. That's all that matters right now. That you didn't allow your father's judgment to cloud your mind. You're free now, and you can make your own choices. The day that you decided not to end my life, was the day you subconsciously decided to leave your past behind and start a new one. One with us. One with you, and who you want to be."

A laugh escaped her lips. "You're...." She didn't know what to say. The only words her half-assed excuse of a brain supplied was *incredibly hot.*

He didn't say anything, instead held his arms out. Her heart fluttered at the fact that he was giving her a choice, making sure she was comfortable. And, because she was not dumb, she gladly accepted.

The first thought she had was, "I could get used to this", which was quickly followed by a never-ending stream of what-ifs. Again, panic began to run through her and she felt her lungs constricting. Until she felt his mouth near her ear, whispering a few words that made her brain stop in its tracks.

"Don't think. Just feel."

And she did. She felt the softness of his shirt under her fingertips and pressed against her face. She felt his hands, one curled lightly against her waist and the other grazing her ribs. She could feel the coolness of the sheets under her legs and his hip and thigh pressing lightly against hers as they sat there.

She took a deep breath, enjoying the way his heart thumped so closely to her face. He smelled like the sun, if that was even possible, and like good memories waiting to happen.

And instead of trying to think of things to compare that feeling in her stomach to, or worrying about the fact that she was sitting on a bed in a kingdom she had only ever heard of, she basked just in the feeling of here and now. She focused on the way he breathed, and the feeling of his arms around her. For the first time in a long time, she felt safe and happy. There was no need for worry at that moment, because all of it just faded away. Maybe being around him was exactly what she needed, because when he was holding her like that, there was only *them* and she couldn't focus on anything else.

"How'd you know?" She softly mumbled into his shoulder.

"I felt that something was wrong." He confessed, and she hummed, enjoying the vibration of his voice. At that moment she didn't really care about why he could feel that something was wrong with her from another room. Nor, what that meant. She just cared about how safe and warm she felt.

They stayed like that for what must've been a while, because before she knew it, her mind was slipping into nothingness and she was left with an almost flighty feeling in her body. It wasn't the same as when she purposely separated herself from things, more like her mind felt at ease enough to just let go. Inwardly, she noted the fact that she was getting close to the point where she might do something stupid, like open up to him. She felt *way* too comfortable for this to be a safe road to take. But he was so warm, and she was so drowsy and maybe she could just *not care.*

But like always, her fear kept her restrained. So instead of the explanation, story, or pretty much anything that she owed the boy holding her, she opted for a "thanks" mumbled against his chest. That was okay though. She knew that he would wait for her to open up, so for now, she left everything as it was. Because at least now, it wasn't hopelessness that was holding her back.

"ZAMI!"

Zami woke with a start, yelping as she attempted to sit up in a tangle of sheets that rendered her immobile. Then the world was tipping, and she was staring up at an upside-down Blu, head down on the floor but with knees bent up on the edge of the bed, since her legs were still trapped in the sheets. The chill air of the room sent shivers down her spine, as it chilled the skin that wasn't covered by her leggings and shirt, and a few pieces of stray hair tickled her face.

She wasted no time untangling her legs from the sheets and pulling herself up to stand, before she tackled Blu, pushing him back onto the bed.

He let out a surprised yelp before he started to laugh as she glared from above him. Then, an idea popping up in her head, she pulled off of him, shoving him off the bed to get a taste of his own medicine. She grinned down at a slightly disheveled Blu laying ungracefully on the floor.

Pouting, he sat up. "What was that for?"

"Waking me up."

"Would you've done that if *hot stuff* out there had woken you up?"

"No. Because he wouldn't have woken me up by *yelling* at me."

He seemed to contemplate that for a moment, still laying on the floor. "Yeah, I guess that's true." Standing up he huffed as he caught his image in the mirror across from the bed. "You messed up my hair!" He complained, reaching up to smooth out his obnoxiously loud waves back into their normal state, swept neatly across his forehead with the ends peaking up. There was something about his hair that almost seemed to defy gravity.

"Whoops." She said, standing up and stretching her arms and legs, which gave loud pops in response.

Blu frowned at her, in mid-sweep of his hair. "Do you have the joints of a seventy year-old-woman or something?"

"Don't be ridiculous." She answered, twisting in a way that made her back pop. "It's at least seventy-five."

"That's not disconcerting at all." She just shrugged, unconsciously rubbing her necklace. "You look like you slept better." He noted, catching her off guard enough that she let a blush spread across her face before she was aware of it.

"Um, well, I mean... um, yeah." She managed to get out before she got her heart under control. All she did was hug Ray, so why was thinking about it making her go crazy? She only faintly remembered him leaving before she had fallen asleep, but that didn't matter, she still remembered the exact feeling of excitement and nervousness twisting in her stomach. No wonder people called them "butterflies."

"Oooh, did something happen last night that I wasn't aware of?" He teased, sidling up beside her while wiggling his eyebrows.

She rolled her eyes, shoving his face away. "Don't know what you're talking about."

His eyes widened. "Oh, something definitely happened. You're blushing."

"I do not blush."

"Well either that, or you got a sunburn, and given the fact that you're almost as pale as those sheets, I think we both know the answer to that." Before she could be forced to admit something, the door opened and slammed close again, revealing a terrified looking Ray, who promptly stepped against the wall near the ornate brass door hinges. She grinned. Saved by the person who caused this in the first place. Then, just a moment later, she watched the door open up again to reveal Mindy.

"Have either one of you seen the hero?"

Zami raised her eyebrow at that. "No." She lied.

Mindy narrowed her startling eyes at her. "Are you lying?"

"No." She lied again.

"You know lying to a princess is illegal here, right?"

Zami bit her lip, because she herself was technically a princess. "Uh-huh. Yup."

Mindy scoffed. "Never mind that, you all have to show up in a little while anyway, so I'll find him then." She pulled the door closed and they were quiet as they listened to her receding footsteps.

Then both of them glanced at the boy behind the door. He was currently frowning down at his shirt and brushing some invisible dust off of it. However, before she could make a remark, Blu cut in.

"That's just wrong."

"I know, she's been chasing me around all morning."

"No, your shirt."

Ray frowned. "My shirt?"

"I've never seen you wear a dark color before."

She had to agree that it was slightly absurd, but she couldn't really complain. "You look good in black, sunshine." At that she watched as he flushed, wondering how far the blush traveled down his neck as it disappeared under the collar. She was inwardly thankful that to others, it must look as if she never got flustered, remembering how warm her cheeks had felt the night before. Also to the fact that he got very easily flustered.

"We should probably go wake up Strike," Blu remarked, stepping to the door and opening it. She winked at Ray as she exited, enjoying seeing the red that had just begun to fade quickly return.

"Zami, you're breaking Ray."

"Sorry." She said, not at all sorry. Blu gave her an exasperated sigh that she responded to with a look that said "*you're* trying to tell *me* to cut down the flirting?" Which he grinned at, shrugging and whipping around.

It took a small amount of time to get to the room Strike was in, which no doubt, Blu probably spent the night in as well. He didn't even knock, just slipped through the doorway as she followed carefully, followed by a still slightly pink Ray.

She stopped with the others as Strike came into view, still sleeping peacefully. He was a pretty boy, she noted, as she took in the strands of black hair laying around his head in curls. His face was the most relaxed she had seen except the times he was being hugged by Blu, and little fluttering breaths floated past his slightly parted lips. He was curled on his side, looking incredibly small for someone his height, though given how thin he was she wasn't surprised. He must've been a calm sleeper, since the covers were barely rumpled, and given how neatly they were laying over his sleeping form. Occasionally he would let out a slightly heavier breath, his hand moving a little bit on the covers before stilling again. Yeah. He was pretty.

It didn't pass by her how Blu's breath slightly hitched as his eyes trailed over Strike, with his Adam's apple bobbing as he swallowed. She grinned, nudging his side.

"You scored a pretty one."

Blu's eyes widened before he turned away shyly, brushing his hand through his hair. "Yeah. Yeah, I did." She watched with a warm feeling in her stomach as he walked up and gently shook Strike awake, whispering something she wasn't listening hard enough to hear.

Strike sat up, rubbing his bleary eyes and blinking at Blu, then the rest of them. She giggled when she realized that he needed a few minutes to realize where he was and who he was. She could only imagine how much self-control Blu was using to not just pounce on the boy then and there, given away by the way Blu was avoiding eye contact. Strike looked... soft. If that was a word you could use for a guy with lightning powers.

As Blu tried to wake Strike up to the point of functioning, she felt a gentle nudge against her shoulder.

"Did you sleep well?" She stared up at the boy next to her, trying not to dig too deep into his question. It was obvious what he was asking. She nodded, wincing as she felt the soreness in her neck. It was probably from sleeping crooked.

"What's wrong?" He asked, glancing at her with a furrowed brow.

"Nothing, my neck just hurts a little." She said, reaching up to rub it.

"Maybe it's from looking up too often."

She frowned. Looking up...

"Did you just crack a joke about my height?" She gasped in shock. His answer was a giggle. A *giggle*. The boy beside her, yeah the one who was supposed to save the freakin' world, was giggling at a joke about her height.

She glared at him. "Oh, you are gonna' pay for that."

He grinned at her. "How exactly?"

"Oh, you wanna' test me? I assure you that I didn't spend all that time reading books about fairy princesses and unicorns, Ray."

"Really?" He said, feigning surprise. She glared at him, putting as much fire as she could into her eyes. Another giggle escaped from his lips as he looked away, seemingly biting back something else he was going to say.

In front of them, Strike was now fully awake, standing up from the bed.

"You should probably get changed," Blu said, giving her a playful grin. She grinned back at him.

"Why, you don't think it's appropriate to discuss an alliance with the queen when I'm wearing this?" She gestured at her rumpled day old clothes, feigning offense.

There was no response from him until she felt hands on her back, shoving her towards the door and the sound of a door shutting behind her. Staring at Ray, who had been shoved out of the room at the same time, she half asked, half said,

"I think we just got kicked out."

He snorted beside her, stuffing his hands lazily in his pockets. "I'm not surprised. Blu looked like he was about to have a heart attack if he didn't get Strike alone for a moment."

A laugh escaped her lips as she made her way back down the hall, opening the door of the room she had slept in. "You know, these places have way more guest-ready rooms than the Dark Kingdom did."

He leaned against the door as she rummaged in her bag. "Well, I kinda' doubt your father was one to welcome guests as nicely." He said, surprising her with his bluntness. Not that he wasn't telling the truth.

"Yeah. You're right. He didn't really have *guests.*"

He nodded, eyes scanning over the wall. "Though this is going to come out wrong, everyone we've run into isn't really that bad. I kinda' expected everyone to be like..."

"Eviler?"

"Yeah. From the way I've always been told it, the rebellion was alone. Nobody wanted to help us."

Biting her lip, she responded with something that hadn't even occurred to her until she said it. "It's not that they don't like the rebellion, it's that they're *afraid* to join them. It's much safer to just try and avoid it."

"You think the Demi-human Kingdom might decide to join the rebellion?"

She shrugged. "There's no saying for sure. But, I hope so."

"Yeah, plus they're being extremely nice for someone who hates us."

"Maybe after seeing what the Dark King has been doing, they had a change of heart. Along with that, I think they're having a really hard time staying mad at a couple of kids who didn't even cause what happened."

He smiled at her as she said that. "That and," he flipped his hair dramatically. "I'm irresistible."

She snorted. "Irresistibly stupid."

A pout came across his lips at her words. "Glad to know I'm appreciated."

Rolling her eyes, she shoved him out her door just as Blu had done to them earlier. "Yeah, yeah, you can be appreciated from out there." Then she closed the door, smiling at the little scoff she got from outside the door.

It only took a few minutes to change into new clothes until she let him back in. Then she set off on the adventure to comb her hair, which only ended with a sigh of defeat as she pulled it back into a tangled ponytail. *Maybe I should cut off all my hair.* She thought to herself, feeling impulsive.

When she finished, she glanced over at Ray with a smile. He was laying unceremoniously on the top of the sheets she had pulled up, eyes closed though she doubted he was sleeping. She figured he had just trailed off into his own little world for a little bit, which she had seen happen often.

"Rayyyyyyy." She called, leaning onto the bed.

"Hmmmmm?"

She raised her eyebrow at him. "Did *you* sleep fine?"

He opened his eyes and squinted at her, still laying on the bed and making no move to get up. "Yeah, why?"

"You look sleepy."

"I always look sleepy."

"No, you don't."

"Yes, I do."

"Nope."

"Yeah."

"Nope."

"Yeah."

"Nope."

"Nope."

"Yeah. Wait no!" He said, sitting up and pouting at her. "You tricked me."

"It's called using my brain." She said, tapping her temple.

"I don't know what that is."

"I can tell."

"You're mean."

"Why thank you."

"That's not supposed to be a compliment!"

"I know." She said smugly.

"You're impossible." He groaned, laying back on the bed. She chose to ignore that saying, which had become far more common recently, and instead grabbed one of the pillows and gave him a half-hearted whack with it.

"Ray, we have a queen to see."

"I know."

"Then get up ya' big lump of sunshine!"

"I don't know," he started, glancing at her innocently. "This bed's really comfy."

"That's the point of beds, moron!"

"Well, then I may have to stay a little longer to give it a full review."

"Rayyyyyyy."

"Hmmmmmm."

"Fine." She said, standing up from where she had sat on the bed. "I'll call Mindy in here. She'll get ya' up." She heard a yelp followed by a thump, and turned around to see him in a similar position on the floor that she was in only a short while prior.

"Zamiiiii, you wouldn't." He said, sitting up, still on the floor.

"Oh, I very much would."

He frowned at her and crossed his arms across his chest. "Fine." He huffed, standing up and walking past her. She followed him with her eyes until she had to turn around to grab her pack. Then right as she was turning back, she felt a light shove on her shoulder, causing her to stumble back onto the bed she had just managed to get him out of.

Ray grinned from the door before shutting it and leaving a trail of laughter in his wake, and her, staring at the door in shock. He had pushed her! A playful shove of course, but still.

A warm feeling settling in the pit of her stomach, she made her way to the door with a smirk on her lips. Maybe this wasn't all that bad.

Chapter 16

↔

Ray knocked on the door with a grin on his face, simply happy that everything seemed to be working out so far. It swung open only seconds later to reveal Blu, just as jovial as ever, and Strike behind him, eyes only half-open.

"You guys ready to annoy a Queen? Cause I'm ready to annoy a queen!" Blu called out, pumping his fist in the air and pushing past them to start walking down the hallway. Both he and Zami turned to Strike, who just sighed.

"All I said was, *you're adorable,* and now he's bouncing off the walls." Zami just snorted and walked ahead to follow Blu, as Ray fell into step beside Strike.

"Hey." He greeted.

"Hey." They walked in silence, both wondering how Blu knew where to find the queen.

It turned out, as they found out after five minutes of walking, Blu had no clue where he was going.

"Where are we going?"

Ray stared at him in disbelief. "I don't know! I thought you knew where you were going."

Blu grinned happily. "Nope! No clue whatsoever." A laugh came from the girl beside him, leaving them all staring at her.

"What, I suppose you know where we're going?" Ray asked, trying to sound serious.

Her face changed into its normal smug look as she answered. "Of course I do, what do you take me for, a clueless moron?" She said the last one with no real target, but he was sure who it was pointed at.

"Right. Let's see you lead us then." Ray snarked, unable to keep the grin off his face. Apparently, she was telling the truth, because in a few minutes they found themselves standing at what looked to be the side entrance of the throne room.

"Wait, so if you knew we were going in the wrong direction that whole time, why didn't you stop us?" Blu asked, frowning while somehow still looking overjoyed.

Zami shrugged nonchalantly. "Wanted to see the look on your faces."

"Was it worth it?"

"Every second of it."

"Ah, I see you've all made it here all on your own."

They all froze when they heard the voice. It came from just behind them in a deep drawl, but with an odd undertone that screamed for attention.

"I'm Lev, the queen's personal advisor." Ray nearly did a double-take when he turned around to see the man. At first glance, there wasn't anything odd about the man behind him, with narrow eyes and dark hair. But there was something subtly odd about his eyes and the texture of his skin.

It hit him fairly quickly though, as he flashed back to studying different dynasties across the world in school. It was on a hunch, but as he stared at the lidless green eyes, he fathomed that the queen's advisor was of Naga ancestry.

"If you feel prepared enough, I can take you in." He said cooly, and Ray furrowed his eyebrows at the venom in his voice.

"That would be wonderful, thank you," Zami said, her tone holding just as much snideness as the advisor's. He leered at them as he pushed past them, nose raised haughtily.

"Try not to speak to him if you can avoid it," Zami advised quietly, watching all around with a fiery gaze. "If I know anything from being the daughter of a man head deep in politics, it's that those types of people are bad news."

Blu looked just as upset, his hand laid protectively on Strike's arm. "Why is he mad at us?"

Zami shrugged. "He probably blames our people that a lot of his kind were killed, and the remaining were shunned, by the rest of the Da'raom. Before that, his breed had the highest power, they were even seen as godly. Now that their betrayal is well known, they aren't seen as quite as important." She paused for a moment and her eyes zoned out for a moment. "Trust is hard to build, yet can be broken in only moments."

He didn't have time to contemplate her words, as they were being ushered into the throne room by several annoyed-looking guards.

The throne room was cavernous, complete with soaring ceilings and towering pillars of marble. The floor sparkled in a deep glimmering shade of blue, marked with a strange symbol that lay in the center of the room. On the outskirts of the columns holding up the domed ceiling, stood dozens of guards, arranged evenly in front of windows between each pillar. The door they had come through clearly wasn't the main entrance, considering the large, beautifully polished set of wood doors that shone from off to their right.

However, when his eyes fell to the front of the room on his left, none of that mattered. Sitting on a stone throne with countless tendrils of blue marble, was the most terrifying and stunning woman he had ever seen in his life. Dark hair trailed down her shoulder, and he recognized that hers was the face he hazily remembered from first arriving. Her features were sharp, much like Mindy's, her eyes just as piercing despite the distance. Also, like her daughter, she had black ears curving from around the crown on her head. There was a cat-like quality about her, though not the same way as Mindy. Mindy, he would describe much like a house-cat in the way she moved and acted. This woman was a *wild panther*.

She wore a royal blue robe intertwined with golden accents and pinned at her waist by a thick golden rope. He remembered learning about that, too. In the culture of Da'raom, a woman swore an oath when betrothed, to remain eternally loyal and to never marry again. The minister of the wedding would then bestow the gift of the rope to the wife, who would wear it every waking moment.

That either meant her spouse was busy, or more likely given her current status, that she had suffered a great loss.

"So. I finally get to meet the brats who are going to save the world." She said cooly, her strong voice reverberating throughout the room. Ray gulped. She was almost as scary as Zami in the mornings.

When she finished speaking, a man came out from a door that must've been hidden from sight by the throne. He looked similar to the woman, probably a relative rather than a partner.

In his case, dark hair framed his face which was softer than the woman's, a dark goatee on his chin. He wore the same style robes as the woman, but trousers peaked out from the bottom. They were barefoot, Ray realized, and indeed no shoes were in sight of the two royals. Matching emerald pendants gleamed against their dark skin, both held together by a simple leather strap and laying on their exposed collarbones.

"Now, now, Muradah." His voice was gentle and reassuring. "They are guests, and look at them, they're only children."

The woman sneered, though visibly less coldly this time. More like a facade. "The same children who were sneaking around one of our towns, acting suspiciously."

The man sighed, turning to them. "Welcome, I'm Mayarn, the second in command here." To Ray's left, he could've sworn Zami stiffened a little, though he couldn't be sure. He wasn't sure what to say or do, so he just stood there, expecting Zami, or maybe Blu to say something proper. But it seemed all of them also had the same idea, so the room was filled with an awkward silence.

The man raised an eyebrow at them and Ray realized that they needed to say *something*. Unfortunately everyone else had that same thought simultaneously.

"Nice..." he started.

"We're..." Zami also started.

"Sup?" They all turned to Blu who was standing there with his hands shoved in his pockets.

"What?" Blu asked incredulously, as if he didn't just say 'sup' to the heads of a Kingdom.

"You can't just 'Sup' the royal family, Blu." He and Zami said at the same time, then turning to each other and frowning. Meanwhile, Strike just groaned and buried his face in his hands.

"Just a moment, please," Zami said, giving Muradah and Mayarn a pained smile before grabbing onto his sleeve and what he assumed must be Blu's also. Turning them away from the now slightly confused woman and amused man, Zami gestured as Ray frowned down at her.

"You." She said, pointing at Blu. "Don't say *anything,* you hear me?"

Blu pouted. "Not a squeak?"

"Not even a squeak." Zami agreed, nodding adorably. Then her eyes turned to him. "And you, stop copying me."

Ray frowned. "I'm not copying you, you're copying me."

"I think it's just both..."

"Shut up, Blu." They said at the same time, leading them both to let out exasperated sighs. Ray supposed those who embarrassed themselves together, died together.

"We're gonna die," Zami stated sullenly at the ground.

"Well, if we do, might as well do it with style!" Blu exclaimed loudly enough for his voice to echo down the hall.

Zami sighed, turning around and trying to give the royals her best-winning smile, which in the circumstances, looked more like a grimace to Ray.

"I apologize for that sincerely. I can promise we're overjoyed to meet you." Zami said, sounding official, for someone who had just been scolding them like they were five-year-olds. He looked up as she added a clipped "Your majesties" to the end.

To his surprise, Muradah looked pleased, while Mayarn was still smirking like he was ready to crack up any second. He had to admit, Zami's words were convincing. He himself kind of wanted to thank her. Though he figured he would thank her for not crushing his skull at any time. She had a scary effect on him.

"Of course," Muradah said, almost purring. "You know, I quite like you. I have a feeling you would make a mother proud."

The stiffening in Zami's shoulders was obvious now, and though he doubted the royals could see it, there was pain in her eyes.

"Yeah." Zami responded flatly.

Ray frowned at the answer, though clearly, he wasn't the only one who found it weird, because when he looked around he saw Blu giving him a questioning look. Ray shrugged, conveying the message *"IDK man. I'm not her therapist."* Blu just blinked and looked away.

"So." Muradah started, eyes set on a nervous-looking Zami. "What were you doing in Zamoth?" Ray glanced at Zami and found her eyes on him. He could see her contemplating something, but before he could question it, she was turning back to Muradah and speaking.

"We were looking for information on the first desirable." Out of everything Ray had been expecting, telling the queen about the most sensitive part of their mission was not it.

"Zami!" He gasped.

"*Zami!*" Strike choked.

"We were?" Blu asked.

Ray sent him a look, but froze when Muradah spoke. "Interesting." Ray didn't like the way she said that, nor the gleam she had in her eyes as she studied Zami. "What if just you and I have a little chat?" Muradah purred and Ray stared at her in shock. "You seem to have the hang of the political situation."

Zami's eyes flickered to him and she held his stare for a long moment before speaking. "Of course, your majesty." Ray watched a little anxiously, as the Queen stood and swept across the floor, disappearing behind her throne in a quick motion.

Zami stood there for a long moment, looking undeniably nervous. "Am I supposed to follow her?" Her voice was a pitch higher than normal and she looked a little jittery.

Mayarn smiled. "Yes, please do. Don't worry, she acts all tough but she's really just a big softy."

"I HEARD THAT!" Mayarn's smile didn't waver a bit at her tone.

He watched as Zami slunk slowly toward the room, glancing back at them before ducking inside also.

They heard a door close and the room was again left with an unsettling silence.

"Well, that went well!" Blu remarked from Ray's right, moving to stand where Zami had been.

Ray frowned. "I thought you were supposed to be quiet."

Blu shrugged carelessly. "Whatcha' mean?"

"Not even a squeak," Strike muttered from beside Blu.

Ray chuckled as he watched Blu give Strike a look of betrayal. "You're supposed to be on my side!" Strike turned to hide the smile that was threatening to spread across his face. Ray grinned when he saw the side of his face twitch. Then remembered where they were. Briefly, he felt a little worried, but only until he saw the smile alight on Mayarn's face.

At his glance, Mayarn came closer and gestured at them. "Come with me, we should find a place to sit down."

"You don't have to do that..." Ray started but was cut off with a pat on his shoulder.

"Trust me, women can talk for a *long* time. Even if it's about a war." He winked at him, and with a glance at Blu and Strike, Ray hurried to follow the man in front of him. Behind him, he could hear Blu arguing with Strike, though there was no venom in either voice.

He unashamedly let his eyes wander everywhere as he walked behind Mayarn, taking in the dark walls clad with tapestries depicting a wide variety of subjects. Some showed beautiful forests and ponds, towering cliffs, and dipping valleys. Others revealed hints of unrest, towns with fires burning, soldiers beheading a young peasant girl. One, in particular, caught his eye as they passed through a new hallway. A large portrait hung vertically on the wall, the paints shimmered almost as if they were new.

At the top was an angel, except it wasn't an angel, rather a human who looked like one. Perhaps the bright sun behind the head made it seem that way, or the softness of the eyes. He wasn't sure. The person reached out with a hand towards another, who looked as if they were being depicted as a devil to counter the other's angelic visage. Dark hair swirled around the person's face, eyes hard, background obscured with a dark sky, devoid of a moon. In the center, only their index fingers touched, darkness trickling down the bright one's skin and in return, a bright ray of sunlight shone against the dark one's skin. If he wasn't imagining it, it almost looked as if the connection was sinking into their skin. He absentmindedly rubbed at his forearm, almost able to imagine the burning.

A strong hand clamped down on his shoulder, and Ray just managed to avoid the yelp that threatened to burst out of his throat, before he embarrassed himself.

"Ah, a beautiful painting isn't it? I'm surprised we've kept it after all this time." Mayarn stated.

Ray nodded, ignoring the weird feeling settling in his stomach. As he walked away, he struggled to tear his gaze from the painting. He couldn't shake the feeling that it was trying to tell him something.

He spent the rest of the journey deeply buried in his thoughts. In fact, he was so consumed that he only realized that they were alone in a room when he heard a little protest from Strike. He watched with great amusement, as Blu plopped down onto one of the chairs in the room, huffing and turning away from Strike, who didn't seem at all concerned. He let himself just enjoy watching them bicker like an old married couple, as he let everything that had happened so far sink in.

They already had some of the clues that they had come to obtain. They were currently all in good health, well that is if Zami's normal state could be considered *good*. And so far everything wasn't going that horribly, despite the occasional mishap. Well... more than occasional. But he could live with that.

"You think we're gonna' get in trouble because of what Zami said?" Blu asked and Ray blinked at him before shrugging.

"It's always a possibility, but honestly I have a feeling it's gonna' help us more than hurt."

Strike nodded from his spot beside Blu. "In this case, seeing a group of kids travel across the Kingdoms to try and save the world may get us some slack. Especially since they haven't done anything about it themselves."

"Yeah," Ray replied, brushing his hair from his eyes. "They don't want to be a part of it, so they'll either let us go or suddenly decide to take part in the war. Which means facing the Dark King." The others remained fairly silent after that, the only sound being the occasional shifting in their chairs, or Strike and Blu nudging each other to murmur in the other's ear. He wasn't quite sure how long it had been by the time the door opened and Zami slipped through.

She looked a little pale, but other than that there was nothing visibly wrong with her as she slid into the chair beside him.

"What happened?" Strike finally asked, cutting into the silence of the room.

"She just asked me a bunch of questions." There was a sort of exhaustion in her words that made him raise an eyebrow.

"Like what questions?" Blu shot back, arms crossed over his chest and legs stretched out in front of him.

Zami gave him a look before turning her gaze to her feet. "I don't even know what the purpose was. Just a bunch of questions about the rebellion, and my loyalties, and blah blah blah..."

Ray snorted, leaning in a bit. "Did ya' tell her that you've been part of the rebellion for less than a week?"

She grinned at him. "Nah. That'd be just plain stupid. I took my chance when I saw it."

He took in the mischievous glint in her eyes and gave her a look. "You gonna' tell me what that ambiguous claim means or..."

"Depends." She remarked, eyes wide. "You want to be held liable for any problems that I cause from here on out?"

He blew out a breath and shook his head. "Nah. I'm good."

"Wise choice." Ray hummed in amusement and peered at the others, only to startle at the look Strike was giving Zami.

"What?" She snarked.

Strike just tilted his head. "There's something on your mind that you aren't telling us."

Zami rolled her eyes. "That's called a *secret*. No one is supposed to know about them."

Strike didn't look put off by her words. "Technically secrets can be told. Isn't that what makes them better?"

Zami narrowed her eyes, but there was no anger in them. "Not in my case." Ray raised an eyebrow at that and with the combination of all of their eyes on her, she seemed to crumble slightly. "*Fine.*" She retorted, reaching up to pull at her ponytail.

"I'm just confused... you know?" Ray stared at her, somewhat surprised at her honesty. "If people don't think we're that bad when they meet us, why did they even hate us in the first place? It doesn't make sense! Like why, after all this time, would they suddenly stop to consider that we're just kids trying to do adults' work? Why couldn't they have just avoided the problem in the first place? Plus, none of us are ready to save the world, so why did the stupid prophecy choose a group of kids who are already falling apart?" She let out a little sigh and bunched her fist against her jacket, then continued.

"It's not fair. You guys know that. Ray's family shouldn't have died. Strike's parents shouldn't have left him. Blu's shouldn't have the right to be so judgmental over his choices, that there's nothing wrong with." Her voice wasn't loud or angry or even sad. It was just, really, really tired. "I just hate how unfair everything is for people who deserve more from the world." The room was silent when she finished talking. Ray had to admit that he was a little surprised at her words. Given how well thought through her answer was, and how easily she was able to voice the various repercussions, she must've thought about it a lot.

"It is ironic isn't it?" It was more like Zami was reassuring herself more than anything when she spoke. "That the kids they want to have fix everything, can't even fix themselves?"

"Well, then we don't fix ourselves." Strike replied and Ray looked over at the boy. "We help each other. Isn't that what being a team means? If we want to try and win this we need to understand one simple thing; we don't need to fix anything about ourselves. We need to *grow* from our shortcomings."

"When did you become so wise?" Blu asked from beside Strike, who in return whacked him on the arm.

"I'm trying to be sincere. Something you can't seem to do."

"I can be sincere!" Blu exclaimed, scowling at Strike, though it didn't quite reach his eyes.

They all raised an eyebrow at him, but before he could spew any more nonsense, Mayarn stepped in the room, silencing any conversations happening. He quirked an eyebrow at the silence.

"Talking about saving the world?"

"Of course." He and Zami said at the same time, just as Blu said "Nope."

They all shot him a glare.

"What, I'm just trying to be *sincere*." He exclaimed, sending a sideways glance at Strike who just let out a groan.

"This is gonna' be a loooong war."

Instead of being brought back to the throne room, they found themselves in a small cramped room on the tip-top of one of the towers. It was fairly dark in the room, the only light coming from a cloudy white orb that sat on a little stand in the middle of the room.

Other than that, there wasn't much there, except for curtains hung around the room on the walls, and a few knick-knacks littering the floor, which he was careful not to step on.

"Well, that looks breakable." Zami breathed from beside him, receiving several weird looks from all of them.

"All the more reason for you to stay *away* from it." He said, holding an arm out.

"Ray, are you seriously worried about me breaking that?"

"I can never be sure with you." He could almost feel Zami's eye roll as she reached up to push his arm down.

"I'm not Blu, Ray."

"Hey!" Blu exclaimed. They all snickered at him. "I'm..."

CRASH.

They all froze for a moment, unsure what was happening. Then a boy stumbled through the door, attempting to smile at them. But it seemed something unseen was pushing against him, because as soon as he took another step he tripped, falling ungracefully to the ground with a yelp. Before any of them could help him, however, he was up again, brushing black hair from his face. He looked young, maybe twelve or so, although it was hard to be sure because he was so small. He wore a gray robe that looked like it had been shoved on in seconds, and sneakers that didn't much match the rest of his aesthetic. That was when Ray noticed the ears peeking from under his mop of hair. Not cat ears, but mouse ears.

He scuffled to kick some of the junk on the floor out of the way before shyly looking up at them.

"Sorry 'bout that. I lost track of time." He stated in a voice that was a little raspy, flitting around with nervousness. "Tommy's the name. I... uh, the Majesty told me to see if I could help you with anything."

"I'm Blu." Blu chirped.

"Strike."

"Ray." Silence. Ray nudged the girl beside him.

"Elios." She mumbled.

Tommy frowned. "Your name's Elios?"

Zami seemed to break out of a trance. "Oh, sorry, no, I'm uh...." She trailed off in confusion and Ray stared at her.

"You alright?"

"Ah-ha Zami!" Zami exclaimed.

"Did you just get excited, after remembering your own name?" Blu asked incredulously.

"Yes. No." Zami frowned. "Did I?"

Ray turned to Tommy. "I promise she's not always like this."

Tommy nodded. "Not a problem for me. Unusual is much better than inept." Ray was half surprised and half impressed at his words. "Would you like me to take a look?" Tommy asked, seemingly oblivious at the non-sequitur.

"Look at what?" Blu asked.

Tommy shifted nervously. "Well, I er... I can tell what might happen in the future if we choose to follow through with an alliance."

"You can tell what happens in the future?" Blu inquired, voice rising ecstatically.

"Well um, not necessarily. I can more uh, um, like see some signs to interpret?" Blu glanced at Ray, who shrugged. He couldn't see why it would hurt. "Think of it as a check, to see if you truly mean good." Ray felt Zami nervously shift beside him and subconsciously nudged her.

"Okay." He said, glancing at Zami through the corner of his eyes.

"Just put your hand on the orb." Tommy gestured to Blu and he stepped forward, laying his hand on the orb. From where his fingers touched the orb, wisps of a hot pink swallowed up the inner white of the orb. Tommy looked a little taken aback for a moment.

"What's the color mean?" Blu asked.

"Well," Tommy crouched, examining the orb from every angle. "It's usually the color that best describes someone. A color that suits the way they act and think."

Blu didn't look disturbed by the fact his color was pink. "I do like pink." He said.

Tommy focused intently on the orb, then intoned, "In the future, you'll go through something you never wished to. You'll lose a lot, gain a lot and in the end, you'll settle with peace."

Blu frowned. "That's ambiguous."

Tommy shrugged. "It's an imperfect art." Blu shrugged and stepped away, leaving the orb to fade back into its normal cloudiness. Tommy looked up at them, waiting for the next person. Beside him, Blu gently pushed Strike forward, Strike sending Blu a glare before straightening up and holding his hand up. When his fingers came in contact with the glass, small purple wisps began flowing through the orb. It was a pale purple, an occasional deeper wisp mixed in with the rest.

"You'll learn to speak out when you didn't before, to face your fears. A great mystery will be revealed to you, and a loss will follow." Tommy tilted his head. "You're also destined to do something really great... I think." Ray snorted as Strike stepped back, looking puzzled. Another jumble of words to help them. Yay.

Ray soon felt Blu's hand on his back, pushing him forward. He rolled his eyes, but stepped forward to the orb and set his hand on it. From under his fingertips, a cloud of deep red filled the glass in a second, faster than any of the others. He had to admit he had been expecting yellow of some sort, given that his whole life, he had been compared to the color often perceived as sunlight.

"I see great struggles, a fight with someone you care for greatly. And a disheartening choice." Ray blinked before stepping back, attempting not to explode with questions. What choice? A fight?

Beside him he heard a little sigh, before Zami stepped forward, hesitating slightly again before settling her hand on the orb. It took longer than the rest of them for the color to come out, but when it did, he wasn't that surprised to see a deep, unadulterated black.

Tommy looked a little intimidated by her, before he started speaking, and Ray couldn't really blame him.

"Black. Grace and power." He said nervously, refusing to look up at her. "You're a little scary." Ray watched Zami raise an eyebrow and Tommy scurry to continue. "Uh... sorry, I got distracted. You'll, uh..." he blinked and leaned into the orb, looking confused. "Um, in the future you'll... um, pain?"

Zami frowned from her spot in front of the orb. "In the future, I'll *pain*?"

Tommy gulped. "I can't really tell."

Zami stepped back, and Tommy straightened up from his position staring at the orb. "I don't think your futures show anything to do with a big betrayal to our kingdom." Ray had almost forgotten that was the proposed point of all of this, and he nodded slightly, caught off guard. "I have to go report, I'll be back soon. Just wait here please." Then he was scurrying out the door, another crash following in his wake.

"Well, that was enlightening," Blu remarked sarcastically. Ray had to agree. Now he was just more confused. "I expected you to be like yellow or something, dude."

Ray rubbed his head. "Yeah, so did I." He just sighed, still thinking about what Tommy had said would happen in the future. Who else would he lose?

"You alright, man?" Blu asked, concerned.

"Oh, yeah," he said. "Just confused."

Blu snorted. "At least yours wasn't just *pain*." They all turned to look at the implied person, who was just frowning at the wall. Her hair trailed across her shoulders and a few pieces hung in her face as she bit her lip, focused on something. Blu waved his hand in front of her face.

"Zamiiii." He sang. "Ethereal to Zamiiii."

She glanced up. "Yeah?"

"You look like your brains are gonna' implode."

"Thanks." She said, returning to her zoning. Blu glanced at the others who just shrugged. Who knew what was going in there.

The next thirty minutes or so were spent in relative silence, all glancing at the orb from time to time. Eventually, they managed to break Zami loose from her thoughts, when Blu made a snide comment about how Tommy said she was scary.

"I'm not scary, Blu. I'm just not joy-inducing."

"Really? How about we ask sunshine here?"

Ray looked up in surprise, eyes falling on Zami. "What?"

"Is she scary?" Blu asked, as Zami raised her eyebrow at him and he gulped.

"I mean, it just depends."

"Ray," Blu said.

Ray glanced away. "Okay, maybe a little."

"Ha!" Blu exclaimed, and Ray tried to avoid Zami's eyes. It wasn't his fault that she was terrifying. To his surprise though, Zami just let out a little sigh.

"Yeah, yeah. Okay." They were interrupted by another loud crash and Tommy stumbling back in, slightly flustered.

"What the heck happens out there, man?" Blu asked.

Tommy flushed. "Well, I'm, um, not the most graceful, and the room just out the door..." His eyes flickered around at them. "Never mind, you'll see." He gestured for them to follow him, going out the door opposite from where they arrived.

Sure enough, outside the door, Ray saw the source of the crashes. Stacks of random items, ranging from dolls to hammers, cluttered the space.

"This is the storage room for crafts. It's gotten a little out of hand." As if to prove his point, there was another loud crash. However, when he turned around, it wasn't Tommy. Instead Zami stood behind all of them, a large wooden crate having fallen right in front of her. Her eyes were wide as they flickered over the fallen object, looking positively ruffled.

Blu snorted from beside him. "And here we have an example of a successful assassin." That only made Ray start to laugh, followed by Strike. Zami crossed her arms and glared at them, stepping around the crate and walking towards them.

"You should be glad I didn't succeed. Otherwise," She smirked at him, poking his nose. "not all of us would be here right now." Then she stalked off, triumphant. Blu let out an amused sigh from beside him as Ray reached up to touch his nose.

"That girl is crazy." Then he walked by with Strike, whom Ray hurried to follow.

It turned out they were just being brought back to their rooms; he figured that the queen needed to discuss what was going to happen with them. He hoped they had convinced her to help them, there wasn't much else they could do.

"Hey! Wait, what are you..." Strike yelped from the bed, dissolving into giggles when Blu flopped on top of him.

"There's a whole room to sit in, Blu!" He cried out from beneath the other who just shifted to get comfortable.

"I know." Strike could only huff in response and Ray watched with great amusement as Blu slid off Strike, only to get a pillow shoved in his face.

Blu's muffled voice came from beneath the pillow, which Strike was leaning on with all his weight. Ray couldn't really tell what he was saying, but Strike answered with "Nope."

Blu flung his hands up in a wild torrent of arguing, which wasn't intelligible from under the pillow. Strike just let out a little giggle and another clipped response. Blu's hands slowly dropped, and when he stopped arguing, Strike let out a surprised yelp and let go of the pillow. It fell, revealing a flushed but grinning Blu who, to try and avoid being attacked again, grabbed Strike's wrists and pulled them away from the pillow. Strike just pouted as he glared at Blu.

Behind him, the door opened to reveal Zami, who he had thought been there the whole time. She ignored his questioning look, and he watched her eyes fall on the two on the bed who were now arguing about some useless little thing. Amusement filled her eyes as she looked at them, then it flickered away, replaced with something awfully close to misery. He could have sworn there was some sort of longing in her gaze before it was covered again by her normal smirk.

"I think they're going to sign an alliance." She said, catching him off-guard.

"You've been eavesdropping!" He exclaimed, quiet enough that it wouldn't bother the two love birds on the bed.

She shrugged, not denying it. "I can't help it. An assassin's trained to be one step ahead of everyone else."

A weight sunk into his heart at how easily she called herself an assassin. He knew she didn't want to be known as that; she didn't like killing. Yet, she didn't even bother changing what she called herself. Like she thought fate had already decided what she was.

"What's that look for?" She asked, leaning in front of him.

He found himself longing for a way to help her ease the pain behind her eyes. To pull her out of the miserable feeling of being alone. But he wasn't sure how to. And, he was scared. So he lied to her.

"Nothing." He could tell she didn't believe him but she didn't push it. She stepped back away from him, and he watched her cross her arms across her chest from the corner of his eyes. They were both silent as they watched the boys in front of them, who appeared to be arguing about someone named 'Bryce.'

"Bryce would not hate you." Strike said.

"It depends how badly he's been influenced by my dad."

"But Cyn wouldn't let that pass. You know that she loves you."

"Yes, but what about Andy? Could you imagine if he saw me ever again? He just became the town's new priest; I can't imagine that'd go over well."

"Well, you have Harmony and Daren on your side, they think you're great."

"For how long? They haven't seen me in two years. Strike, I can't just appear out of nowhere."

Strike frowned. "I never said that you had to just appear, I said that maybe after all of this dies down, you should give them a visit to let them know you're okay. At least for the kids?" Strike sounded like he was pleading on the last part.

Blu looked more conflicted than Ray had ever seen him, eyebrows scrunched and eyes downcast. "I'll think about it."

Strike looked up, his eyes catching Ray's. Ray was utterly confused about everything that had just been said. He knew it had something to do with Blu's family, but he had no clue why they were talking so morbidly.

Blu looked up when he saw Strike's shift in attention, and Ray noticed the sadness buried in his expression. His lips, which were almost always in a smile, tipped downward in a frown.

"Oh, hey." He said.

Ray raised an eyebrow at him. "Hey."

"We were, uh, just talking about..."

"His family." Strike cut in, ignoring the scowl he got from Blu. "I'm trying to convince him that after this trip is over, he should check up on his family, you know, in case something happens."

Ray swallowed roughly, and stuffed his hands in his pockets. "Listen to Strike, Blu." Blu looked up at him in disbelief. He spoke before Blu could take him wrong. "I'm not telling you what to do, I'm just reminding you that no matter how bad they were to you, they're still your family. I'm sure they miss you." Blu's face changed as he leaned his head on Strike's shoulder, sighing softly.

"Yeah. I miss them too."

That night was a restless one for Ray. Zami's words from the sitting room flowed endlessly on repeat in his mind, along with his own words to Blu. He hadn't had problems with dwelling on the death of his parents for years. So why, just now, was that all that he could think about?

Knowing he wouldn't be getting much sleep anyway, he didn't even try to rest his mind. Instead he held his hand up and let his magic make patterns on the ceiling and walls, streams of light floating aimlessly through the air.

Then as if he had been punched in the stomach, all of the air was gone from his lungs. He gasped, sitting up and cutting off his magic. However, right when he started to breathe normally again, a wave of nausea hit him.

"Your life, your choice." A pale face with unruly locks flashed through his vision, and he froze. It was hard to tell what was happening, but he was sure of one thing.

The vision was of something real happening right now, and the man he was watching get interrogated was most definitely the prophet. He winced, and pressed his palm to his forehead, as flashes of the man getting yanked to stand up burned into his head.

"I've already given the information away." Ray would've felt impressed by the prophet's calmness, but all he could do was stare in rapt shock, as a gun was cocked to the prophet's head.

Ignoring the gruesome image that flashed through his mind as the trigger was pressed, he stumbled to his feet, ignoring the chill of the air against his bare feet and arms.

He threw the door open and started down the hall, only to come face to face with Blu and Strike, whose eyes were wide with shock.

"What was that?" Blu breathed and Ray shook his head, hand shaking as he gripped at his head, trying to force the searing headache that had developed away.

"Where's Zami?" He gasped through the pain, whipping his head up to look at them. The look on their face was all he needed, before he was sprinting down the hall.

He was aware of the others' footsteps echoing behind him as he skidded to a stop in front of her door. He wasn't sure how, or why, but he just *knew* that something was off.

"What the..." Blu started as he pushed the door open, only to freeze in shock.

"Nice for you to show up." Zami spoke snarkily, but her voice was shaking, and Ray blinked at Lev, the queen's advisor, standing in the center of Zami's room.

"What's going on?" Blu asked, sounding confused. It wasn't hard to decipher that there had been a confrontation, seeing Lev clutching his shoulder with a snarl, or the way Zami's chest was heaving, eyes wide as she stared back at Lev.

Her back was pressed against the wall, and one of her hands was clutching her necklace. There was undeniable fear in her eyes.

"Zami..." He started and her head shot up. He was taken back to when they had found out about her powers, the fear in her eyes now was not unlike back then. "What happened?"

She shook her head breathlessly before speaking, voice almost too soft to hear. "I... I don't know. I couldn't sleep because..." She hesitated before continuing, clearly deciding against saying what had come to her mind. "I couldn't sleep, and he was there, and everything was just chaos. I guess..." She was avoiding his gaze now. "I don't know. I just freaked out. I can't remember anything." It wasn't hard to believe that she was telling the truth, because she looked more terrified than he'd ever seen her, pressed hard into the wall as if it would protect her.

"Don't lie." Lev snarled and Ray stared at him in shock as he started towards Zami, who flinched harshly. "You *attacked* me."

Zami shook her head, mouth slightly open. "N... no I didn't." When Lev stepped closer, Ray started forward.

"Don't touch her."

Lev whipped around to glare at him, eyes narrowed. "She *attacked* me. I have every right to defend myself!" Before they could respond, or say anything to protect Zami, a voice was cutting through the air, sharp and demanding.

"WHAT is going on in here!" Ray jumped and whipped around to see Mayarn standing at the door. His face changed incredibly quickly from annoyed to shocked. "Zami?" He questioned.

Ray furrowed his eyebrows and turned back, heart dropping in his chest when he realized what it looked like. A knife glinted on the floor next to her feet, her eyes wide. Lev was gripping a bloody shoulder in his hand, and a bruise was beginning to form on his cheek. Zami was untouched.

"W... Wait..." She started, and she was glancing around, eyes fearfully flickering over all of them. "I didn't..."

"GUARDS!" Lev was hollering before she could finish, and Ray started forward, only to be pulled back by Mayarn, who was rushing forward himself. For a second, Ray thought that he was going to grab Lev, and realize what had truly happened, but he pushed past the bloodied man and made a beeline straight for Zami.

It was ridiculous to Ray, as several armor-clad people rushed into the room, that they were immediately accusing a teenage girl who looked more terrified of them than anything.

"Mayarn!" Ray growled and Mayarn looked up from where he was, standing in front of Zami. "Don't make ridiculous accusations without proof!" Mayarn looked ready to order the guards on him as well, but then Muradah was there, eyes flaming and everyone fell silent.

"Everyone. Throne room. *Now.*" If it weren't such a serious matter, Ray might've found it funny how they all trudged shamefully into the throne room, sending each other looks. And it ticked him off how a guard was still gripping Zami's wrists behind her back as they pushed her forward, manhandling her in an uncomfortable fashion. But he himself couldn't do much without getting in trouble too.

What didn't make sense to him, was that Lev was walking... or rather *strutting* freely beside them, eyes still narrowed towards Zami. Ahead of them Muradah and Mayarn were whispering harshly to one another, occasionally glancing back at them.

A guard sidled up next to Blu and Strike, but when one tried to crowd him, Ray sent the guard a warning glance. They didn't get any closer.

He was worried about the way Zami was acting, and even more concerned that she seemed on the edge of a breakdown. The unsettled feeling in his stomach was most definitely not his, and he frowned, wondering if it had anything to do with their connection, just as he seemed to have known she was in trouble before.

And then, of course, there was the undeniable confusion in his head as the events of the night swarmed in. Why had he seen the prophet in a vision? Had anyone else seen that as well, or was it some sick, twisted trick of his mind? And what had Lev been doing in Zami's room? Why did he attack her?

When he caught a glance at Muradah's fiery expression, he knew that they would soon be getting answers, whether it was voluntarily or not.

"Now." She started when they were all standing front of her. "What in the world is going on here? And *why* is my advisor bleeding?" Ray peered at Zami, who's eyes were solely on the hands gripping her wrists. After a moment Muradah huffed, glaring at the guard. "Let the child go for lord's sake. Don't you think this is enough to have to handle in one night *without* manhandling her like she's dangerous?"

As the man stepped away, looking rightfully ashamed, it struck Ray that no one there was aware that Zami was his counterpart. That she had magic just as powerful as his, and most likely more dangerous. But, he thought, taking in the suspicion already targeted at Zami, perhaps that was for the best. She already had enough to deal with as it was.

"Zami." Muradah said and she startled, eyes wide as she gingerly rubbed her wrists. "What happened?" Ray was hopeful, because Muradah was hearing her out first, and her eyes were filled with trust. All they needed was Zami to tell them that she hadn't done anything wrong.

"I..." Zami started, voice shaking. "I... don't know. There was so much going on. I saw the prophet and then a gun and I looked up and there was... there was-just-there was-and I was..." Ray blinked as she started to stutter, eyes wide as she looked behind him. When he glanced over and saw Lev, eyes narrowed and glowering at the girl, he furrowed his brow.

"Zami." Muradah remarked, halting her pacing to stop in front of her. "What prophet?" Zami blinked and peered at him before speaking, eyes glazed as if she was on autopilot.

"The one that we went to for information on the desirable. He was being interrogated and then, well..." She furrowed her eyebrows, looking puzzled. "I'm not sure, the vision cut off and then I was fighting and there was a knife and I don't even know what happened." Ray was impressed that she had managed to get out something understandable.

"So, you're saying Lev attacked you?" Muradah asked, and Ray couldn't tell if she was skeptical or irritated. Zami looked conflicted.

"Well I... there's... I can't..."

"Muradah." Ray frowned as Lev spoke, stepping closer to the Queen. "Are you really going to make your verdict on the word of a child? That's blasphemy!"

Ray couldn't help it anymore as he crossed his arms, narrowing his own eyes at the man, before speaking loudly, "Then what were *you* doing in *her* room?" The moment Lev hesitated was enough for the tables to turn, and the suspicion to be flipped onto him.

"Lev?" The Queen asked, as if waiting for his explanation. He spluttered for a brief second before speaking, absolute nonsense that didn't help his case at all.

"I was simply... there's no..." The moment he stepped towards Zami, Muradah was grabbing his arm, practically seething.

"And *why,* prey tell, would you try and *murder* her?"

Lev yanked his arm away and Ray felt the guards shift beside him, ready to move at any moment. "She's clearly got motives and..."

"So you *did* attack her." Muradah growled.

Lev looked shocked, clearly not having realized that he had just given himself away. "But I..."

"He did it." Ray turned at the smooth voice that broke the silence, to find Mindy stalking into the room, Tommy shuffling after her, just as nervous as before.

"Mindy, what are you..." Mayarn started, reaching out to grab her, but Muradah halted him with a hand, eyes bright with something close to pride.

"What have you found?"

Mindy turned to Tommy and pushed him forward, eyes glittering. "Not me. Him, mama. Ask him."

Tommy's eyes widened as all their gazes shifted to him, but then he was speaking rapidly without a moment to let anyone else speak. "I found a sether in his corridor, and I believe it had a spell to connect it to whoever he wished. Which means he could've connected it with the General, given he knew his general location, and used it as a distraction for an assault. That knife in the room was covered in poison, so I fathom his motive would be that Zami was the largest threat to his plotting, and he decided that he needed a way to take her out and distract everyone while he did it." Ray stared at him. And blinked, and stared again. Where in the world did that little head fit all that information?

Ray briefly recalled Zami mentioning the General under the King's rule, a ruthless, cruel man who had become very widely known for his dangerous and devastating attacks. It made sense he supposed; Lev had channeled the vision they saw through the General's eyes as a distraction, while he made his move to kill Zami. Especially considering there was no way the King or his General could know that they'd already found information on the desirables.

"Hmmm." Muradah remarked, seemingly contemplating something. "You're sure about this?" Mindy nudged Tommy, who gave a shaky nod and reached into his robes to pull something out. It was a stone, and by what Ray had gathered in his explanation, a sether, which could allow visions to be shared across a sizable group of people. He briefly recalled learning about it in school.

Muradah took it with a raised eyebrow and then turned to hand it to Mayarn, who settled it in his pocket. "Very good, then. I suppose we'll have to do more investigation, but for now, guards, please take him away."

Lev looked ready to murder, even more so then before, as he was yanked away. And then suddenly, he was lunging forward, and Ray heard yelling over the guards' shoulders, then a thud. Then everything went silent.

Ray slowly looked around the guards and blinked, eyes widening when he realized what had happened. Lev must've made a last attempt to attack Zami, because he was in front of her, eyes wide and fingers reaching for his chest.

He stared at the sword clutched in Zami's shaky hands, and then the empty scabbard at the nearest guard's waist where she must've pulled it from.

She was letting go and jerking back before anyone could react, and then Lev was falling to his knees, mouth open in a silent scream.

He wasn't sure why he reacted so quickly, and the way that he did, but he was rushing to Zami's side without a second thought, grabbing her hands. He didn't care about the blood that lightly speckled them, nor when everyone else overcame their shock and guards were rushing to grab Lev. Ray knew there was no hope for him, as they looped his arms around their shoulders, yanking the weapon out of his chest and hurrying him off. His eyes were already dim and his body was limp. He was gone.

But he didn't focus on that, looking intently instead at the white-faced girl in front of him, who had dealt with more than her fair share of chaos that day.

"I... I killed him." She finally breathed out, and his heart dropped in his chest when he realized what was concerning her. But it wasn't he who spoke to console her first.

"Zami." Muradah said, stepping forward and taking her shoulders in her hands. "You were right to defend yourself and those around you." Ray watched Zami's eyes flicker up to the woman, wide and fearful. Muradah simply gave her a grim smile. "Do not fret, for tomorrow you will be heading back to your rebel base, alliance in hand."

Chapter 17

Zami scrubbed her hands just one more time. Maybe she was getting ridiculous. Maybe it was turning into an obsession, but she couldn't bring herself to care. The feeling she had, when she'd thrust that sword into Lev's chest, was too familiar to be comfortable. All her life she had thought she had never killed anyone before, but now, she wasn't so sure. The weight of being a killer wasn't as heavy as she thought it should be, and the blood on her hands did not feel weird. It felt familiar. And that was what scared her.

She had showered and changed. All the blood was gone. But she could still feel it, see it. Why was it that she was always in the wrong place at the wrong time?

She knew all three of the boys were just outside the door. They had felt safer staying together, something she very much agreed with. She had to compose herself. She had freaked out more than she would like to admit, and now she was trying to make sure that the same thing didn't happen again.

After washing her hands one last time, she slipped out of the bathroom, surprised to see all of the others very much awake. Blu was sitting on the couch against the wall, Strike beside him as always. Ray, however, was standing, right in front of her, though he was facing away.

Poking his back, she muttered, "You're blocking the entrance, dummy."

He turned around and gave her a grin, stepping out of the way so she could get by. She plopped on the edge of the bed, rubbing at the palm of her hand.

They all knew they needed to talk about the serious turn of events. The prophet, her incident, what was going to happen with the alliance. But no one said anything. She couldn't hide her curiosity that well though.

Taking a breath she asked the thing that had been in her mind since the vision. "What... what happened to the prophet?" She hadn't seen what happened after he had been yanked up to stand by the General, because right then, all the chaos in her room had started. But the way everyone ducked their heads and looked down, led her to figure out the answer by herself.

Of course he was dead. Everyone died when her father was involved. It didn't matter who, or why. They were dead. Always.

"What was that man asking for?" Blu asked, breaking Zami from her train of thoughts. "And who the *heck* was that man?"

"Something to do with the desirables most likely." Ray said from his spot, still standing.

She knew they were waiting to see if she had any clue of who the man was though. "He's a general. The General in charge" Something was pushing at her memories, something to do with that man. "Under my fa..." She cut off. She didn't like calling him that. "Under the King."

"Are you okay?" Ray asked, leaning against the wall.

"Yeah, why?"

"Cause you keep on scratching at your hands."

"I'm fine." She swallowed. And scratched her hands one more time before stuffing them under her thighs. Only then did she catch all of their looks. "Fine," she mumbled. "I just don... don't like blood. Ya' know?"

"No offense, but I don't think assassin is the right career choice for you." Blu said.

She snorted, and something about how casual they were acting calmed her down. "You're telling me?"

"Nuh-uh, you're not doing that again." Strike remarked, eyes boring holes in hers.

"Um, doing what?"

"Brushing everything off like it doesn't bother you."

She rolled her eyes, falling back so her back was on the bed. "I don't know what you're talking about."

"Of course you don't." He sighed. She just waved her hand at him, eyes closed. A few minutes later the lights were dimmed and everyone was silent. To an outsider's eye, it would see all of them were asleep. But they all knew there wasn't going to be any of that happening. They were too uptight, nerves getting the best of them.

"Right. Is anyone actually asleep?" Blu asked.

"Nope."

"Nope."

"Nope."

They all sat up, and a lamp was turned on, casting shadows on the wall with a warm glow. When she noticed a small light flickering in the corner, she turned her head to see Ray letting little streams of lights flicker between his fingertips. It seemed he didn't even realize he was doing it.

When she felt a chill, she turned, only to grin when she realized what Blu was doing. Little wispy breezes floated through the air, ruffling their hair and clothes. She quite liked the light chill that rested on her legs, arms and cheeks. It wasn't from fear or loneliness anymore, as it was her friend's magic whipping around the room, drawing giggles from all of them.

"You know, it feels like months have passed already." Blu stated and she nodded, taking in a deep breath. She hadn't been able to breathe well under the pressure of the earlier events, so the fact that air was coming easily again calmed her nerves.

"It's crazy how fast time passes when you're constantly getting attacked, arrested... assassinated."

Zami was positive who Ray was pointing that last one at, and frowned, glancing at him. "Hey, you almost got assassinated too, *sunshine*. Don't be a hypocrite." He stuck his tongue out at her and she scoffed, rolling her eyes. "Real mature for the hero of the world, Ray."

He grinned. "My pleasure."

"So are we gonna talk about... you know, everything that just happened?" Blu asked.

"Nah." She replied, sliding down to press her face into the pillow. She was tired. She was always tired.

"If you're sleepy, you should rest." Ray stated.

She hummed, turning to stare at the ceiling. There was no way she was getting any sleep tonight. "I'm not."

"Really? Cause you look ready to pass out."

She rolled her eyes and pressed her forearm over her head. "I always look like that."

"So you *are* tired?"

She sighed, turning on her side and fiddling with her necklace. "I'm always tired, Ray. I've *been* tired." *For the past fifteen years.* Her mind supplied, and she barely even registered what that meant as she remembered it was her birthday after midnight had passed. A wonderful birthday present it was, she thought, to be nearly killed and then promptly blamed for hurting the attacker. Just brilliant. "Hey Ray?" He hummed and she realized that the others were beginning to fall asleep. "Thanks for helping out earlier. If you hadn't pointed out that he had no business being in my room, they might've thought I was the problem." She blinked when a warm hand slid into hers, heart thumping when she realized he was kneeling next to the bed.

"Always." He stayed like that, leaning against her bed and holding her hand. Even though she might never admit it, that helped her finally fall into an oblivious sleep.

Zami woke up in a groggy haze the next morning, momentarily disoriented before she realized where she was. Something told her it was around noon, which she should've been alarmed at, considering the fact that they were supposed to be leaving for the base that morning, but she just couldn't find it in herself to worry about it.

She found great amusement in the fact that they had all fallen asleep on or around her bed, despite there being other suitable surfaces to rest on. Blu had his head on the other pillow, though he wasn't under the covers. Strike had fallen asleep with his feet near the pillow, and Ray, who was on the other side of her, was sitting on the floor, head buried in his arms which were laying on the bed. His hand was loose in hers still, and she swallowed, gently pulling away.

She sighed as she stared at them, finding it hard to believe she had only known them for less than a couple weeks, when it felt like so much longer.

Slipping out of the covers, she grinned, ruffling Ray's hair as she made her way to the bathroom. It was the first time in a while that she had been the first to wake up, and it felt weirdly refreshing that she still had some energy deep down. The fact that her personality had been created purely on the horrible foundation of her childhood left her a little nervous about losing herself. She wasn't sure who she even was, without the rules that had constrained her whole life.

It was the first time in days that she actually had the energy to comb completely through her hair, and she enjoyed the smoothness of it as she pulled it up again, back into a ponytail. After changing, she slipped back into the room, leaning back against the wall to observe her friends for a moment longer, debating whether or not to wake them up yet. Deciding against it, she made her way to the door, opening it. She wasn't really sure what she was going to be looking for, she just wanted to do something to get her mind off of things.

Halfway down the hallway, that *something* came in the form of a tall, amenable royal. Mayarn smiled at her widely and stopped to talk.

"Where's the rest of the trouble-squad?" He asked her with a relaxed tone, the smile never leaving his face.

"Still in deep slumber." She answered, smiling back even though she didn't much feel like it. Despite his calming aura and genuine smiles, Mayarn still reminded her all too much of her father with the power and confident stance. And even though he acted nothing like him, she couldn't seem to relax around him.

"Well, I'm afraid they may have to wake eventually. We do have a war to fight." The words were teasing and light-hearted. No real accusal in them.

She grinned, even though she knew it didn't reach her eyes. "I'll go get them up if you'd like."

Mayarn chuckled. "Yes, that would likely be better than any of the other options." With a small bow of her head, she whipped around, making her way back into the room. She decided to wake Blu first, partly because he could wake up Strike while she woke Ray, but also partly because he had woken her up the day before.

It wasn't that hard to do, with a few shakes of the shoulder, he was up. Luckily he was good with mornings, and he was immediately bouncing with energy. At her request, he leaned over to awake his not quite as morning-loving partner.

Then she leaned next to Ray, brushing his hair from his eyes.

"Rayyyy." She hummed, poking his shoulder.

He blinked up at her, slightly sleepy. "Hmm?"

"It's past noon."

He jumped up, causing her to stumble back. "What?"

She raised her eyebrow at his reaction. "I *said, it's after noon.*"

He rolled his eyes, pushing his hair back. "I know what you said. It just surprised me." He huffed. "I thought we were supposed to leave in the morning."

She shrugged. "We were. But we didn't."

He frowned at her. "You're not the least bit concerned?"

She shrugged again. "Nope. Why? Should I be?"

"I figured it's a given, since the fate of the world depends on us."

"Nah. It's all good, we do what we do, and what happens, happens." She patted his shoulder, getting a confused look. "If you're so worried, I suggest getting changed as a start."

He mumbled something about her being hopeless as he stalked past her, leaving the room, she assumed, to go get ready. Though she had a feeling no matter what she said, he would stick around. He wasn't the type to give up.

She briefly recalled that Tommy had said something similar about him. And the disappointment that shouldn't have been there at the fact her color was black. Of course it was. She shouldn't have expected anything different.

All of the sudden, all the energy she had woken up with was gone. Everything felt hopeless. With a little sigh, she tucked her hair behind her ears. She just had to pull through, no matter how her past dragged her down; she wouldn't let it keep her from living her life. Even if she felt so tired. Not because of lack of sleep; no, it was a deeper feeling that settled in her bones and the very fibers of her being. It was a tiredness of the soul. And it was getting distressing how often it was there. Some days it was barely noticeable, then some days it just crashed into her. Like today.

Blu and Strike had also left, probably to get changed as well, which meant she was alone. Dropping to a crouch she stared at her hands. Blood. After all this time she had still ended up with someone else's blood on her hands. Why couldn't she just be happy? Where was that feeling from last night? The content? The joy? Gone. Like it had never been there in the first place.

She fell back so she was sitting, and curled her hands into fists that she hit against the sides of her thighs. She had no right to feel as if things were bad for her. Ray had lost his parents and sister when he was just five, and he managed to survive. Blu's parents hated him, and he was managing to find joy in every day. And Strike had been abandoned and bullied horribly by the kids around him. Yet he was still making it through everyday. So why did she feel so hopeless?

Because you're destined to be evil, Zami. Because no matter how hard you try, you can't change fate. In the end your father was right. You'll fail to save the people you love so much. It's inevitable.

She stood up abruptly and glared at the wall. She was fourteen, no, fifteen now. A big girl. She could fight whatever came her way and she would do it without chipping her nails.

Brimming from her self-given pep-talk, Zami turned around and opened the door.

If I can't find a reason to fight, I'll do it out of spite. She told herself. Everyone was always saying to live life fueled by motivation and passion, but she thought she probably deserved a little slack on this one. So, given the fact that she was practically built of spite, she thought she had a pretty fair chance using that to push her forward.

Of course, the second she stepped into the hallway she ran headfirst into an alarmed prophecy boy. The way he reached out to steady her made her heart stutter, and for some reason she flashed back to when she had first met him. That was surely a lovely story to tell friends over a drink.

"So how'd you two meet?"

"Oh, you know, I tried to slice his throat out, just the kind of thing you do."

Lovely.

"You alright there?"

She looked up to his amused expression. "Never been better, sunshine." She patted his shoulder like she had earlier and trotted away, ponytail swishing.

"That's not the way to Blu and Strike's room!" He called.

She whipped around the other way, barely breaking her stride. "I know." And she sauntered down the hall, followed by an amused looking Ray.

"So either you got some really good sleep, or access to some really good drugs." He thought for a moment. "Or both."

"Why can't I just be happy, Ray?" She asked, slowing down so he could fall into step beside her.

"Because you're never just happy."

"Maybe I'm happy that we succeeded at an alliance."

He raised an eyebrow at her. Right. That wasn't super convincing, considering she didn't care much about that sort of thing.

"To be fair, I *was* worried about it last night." He just hummed in response, shoving his hands in his pockets. When they neared the room, they were greeted by shouting that sounded a lot more like laughing. She couldn't quite decipher it, but she caught a little bit.

"Strike! ...not funny!" In return, there was just laughter. Reaching up a hand, she knocked on the door, not sure if she wanted to get stuck in the situation. Strike opened it only a second later. He looked normal enough, his normal jacket and jeans. But he was *crying*. Not sad tears, though. Rather his face was scrunched up in laughter, hand covering his mouth as tears rolled down his cheeks.

Blu wasn't in sight behind him, and after a moment Zami realized he was hiding.

"What is up with you two?" Ray asked from beside her.

Strike tried to elaborate, though it didn't really work considering the fact that he was laughing too hard.

"Blu's just a moron." He finally managed to get out, breathing slightly heavy still. Zami blinked in confusion, but they didn't explain, and Blu just gave an annoyed little scoff before pushing past them and out into the hall.

Strike, still giggling, hurried to catch up with the other boy. He said something brightly, but Blu turned away with a huff. Zami was highly amused when Strike resorted to whispering something breathily in Blu's ear that made him stop cold in his tracks. Blu gave Strike an apprehensive look before rolling his eyes, but linking his arm through the other's.

"What was that about?" Ray asked, looking mildly confused.

She shrugged as she watched them walk away, Strike talking far more animatedly than normal. "You know, I really don't have a clue. Those two are weird." Ray nodded in silent agreement as Blu piped up and yelled something unintelligible.

When they arrived at the entrance of the throne room, they quieted. The Queen may have liked them, but that didn't mean it wasn't possible she would change her mind.

She still remembered when the Queen had asked to talk to her alone. She had been nervous, and honestly a little afraid. But the Queen didn't ask normal interrogation questions like she expected. Instead she bombarded her with questions about their adventure so far, about the desirables, about how long she had known the others. And afterwards she had looked pleased, sending her on her way to go find her friends. Zami had a great appreciation for the chillness of the people here, other than Lev of course; there had been no big problems getting along. Which was good because given her luck, the trip back to the base would probably be a little rougher than it should be.

"Ah! I see you've managed to find the throne room again!" Ray jumped beside her, which after a moment, she realized was because Mayarn had slapped his shoulder hard. People touched his shoulders a lot, she noticed. But then again, she couldn't blame them. He had nice shoulders.

"Yeah, we're ready to leave for the base." Ray replied, reaching up to rub his neck.

"Well then, let's get you going! This world isn't going to save itself!" Mayarn walked forward into the throne room and after a moment Ray followed behind him, then Blu and Strike. For a long moment, she just stared at the floor behind her. Where they had first met Lev. How he had died only a day later.

There was something weird about how it had happened, though. It shouldn't have been that easy to kill him; he should've been more prepared if he truly knew why he was going after her. Someone who managed to keep his subversive plans from the Queen for this long should be cunning and smart. That either meant he messed up, or there was someone else on his side in the kingdom who was the real brains in the operation.

"Zami?" She looked up to see all of them glancing back at her, already in the center of the throne room like they had been the night before. With one more glance back, she stalked forward, sidling up beside Strike.

The Queen was there, and as she began talking about something, Zami zoned out. Who could be close enough to the queen to not get caught, but still have the access to power he or she desired? It would have to be someone who was good at lying, someone who seemed harmless. Her eyes traced across the room, landing on Mayarn.

He was close to the Queen; that would leave him with limited, but plentiful power to pull off a stunt against her. He acted sweet and caring, a good facade for someone hiding his true intentions. Sending someone else close to the Queen in as an assassin would draw all attention away from him. And, he always seemed to be *right* there when needed. But no matter what she thought, it would be impossible to lay plausible blame on the man. In fact, she was sure that he had probably planted the evidence against Lev in his chambers. That meant he felt he was safe, with nothing to hold against him. It was already a stretch to ask the Queen to take her word against Lev. But Mayarn? Even if he was what she assumed, it was impossible; there was no way she would be believed.

Then, she was staring into his deep brown eyes. He held her gaze as she observed him, silently. The glint in his eyes told her that he knew she was onto him, and given the small smile, he also knew that she couldn't do anything about it. She would just have to hope he didn't do anything catastrophic to the kingdom.

"Zami."

She tore her gaze from Mayarn's to look at the Queen. "Yes?"

"I was checking to make sure all of you were prepared to leave."

Zami glanced at Mayarn out of the corner of her eye. The look he was giving her sent shivers down her spine. "Yeah." The Queen was silent. "I mean, of course your Highness." Zami quickly amended, ignoring the looks she was sent by her friends.

"Zami! We cannot have you off guard when you're traveling with such an important message! Your team needs you on-guard and prepared." Zami's stomach settled into a cold feeling. She knew that wasn't what the queen was trying to say, but it was all she could hear. *"Everyone's depending on you."*

"Right, sorry. I was uh," she glanced at Mayarn again. "Just... thinking." She finished lamely.

"Save that brain of yours for when it's necessary. No use tiring yourself out on trivial matters." The Queen commanded.

Zami almost laughed. Oh, if only the Queen knew what she was thinking. Would it be trivial then? But she didn't laugh. This was no laughing matter that she was facing.

"Of course, your Highness." She doubted anyone noticed how much she hated using words like that. Having to call your own father such powerful names all your life meant they carried an unnecessary weight with them. One she wouldn't ever be able to shake.

"Good. Now is there anything else you need before you leave?" Zami's mind was working at full speed. She needed to warn someone. Someone close enough to the Queen that they couldn't get killed, without raising suspicion. Someone she could tell who wouldn't get in trouble, who could watch safely. *Mindy.*

"Actually," Zami started, wincing at the attention brought to her. "Um, can I use the uh, restroom?" She nearly slapped herself at the lame excuse. The restroom? Really, Zami? A whole head of excuses and you chose the restroom one?

The Queen frowned but agreed, so Zami quickly made her way out of the room. Where would Mindy be? Somewhere close to her mother, close enough to spy on them. With a little bit of searching she found her sitting on an armchair in a room close to the throne room. To Zami's surprise, Tommy was also there, and they seemed to be in deep conversation about something serious.

When she slipped into the room and closed the door, the conversation stopped and a pair of unsettling green eyes and nervous gray ones turned to look at her.

"What are you doing here?" Mindy asked, cocking her head. Zami knew that even though she was quirky, she was smart. In fact, the whole *weird* thing was a perfect cover for a very aware princess that no one would suspect an intelligible sentence from. She was someone who could be trusted. However Tommy, no matter how trustworthy, was more at risk of being killed because of knowing. There was no way she could make him risk his life.

"Um. I need to talk to you." They both stared at her. "Like girl stuff, ya' know." Tommy's eyes widened and he stood up.

"I'll just uh, leave ya' to it." Then he scurried out of the room and Zami let out a breath she didn't know she had been holding.

"Girl stuff? Really?"

Zami grinned at Mindy. There was the girl she knew was hiding her full capabilities. "Yeah, actually, I figured you were the safest person to tell this."

Mindy leaned forward. "Tell what?"

And Zami told her. About her observations, her guesses, her worries concerning Mayarn. And Mindy listened. She made a good listener. At the end Mindy sat there, face unreadable.

"So you want me to watch out? Keep an eye out?"

Zami nodded, knowing she needed to return soon. They would get suspicious. "Yeah, your mother trusts you, and in the worst case scenario, you'll have to tell her. She'll listen."

Mindy nodded. "Consider it done."

She breathed out heavily, a weight having been lifted off her chest. "Thank you. I have to go now, good luck." She stood and walked to the door. Hopefully she had prevented something bad from happening for a little while.

"Oh, and human?" Zami turned. "Hold on to the hero. You won't find many like him." She nodded, making her way back to the throne room. When she stepped in she got several weird looks.

"What? I got lost. This place is huge." The Queen laughed, but Mayarn's eyes followed her with an intent not very different to what Lev had looked like only a day before. She hoped gravely that she hadn't endangered Mindy in any way. She couldn't handle another life on her shoulders.

Her friends, however, looked at her suspiciously. They knew her well enough to know she didn't just 'get lost', she *was* an assassin after all. She could tell them later though, once they were out of the castle.

"Well now that our charming young lady has returned, I suppose it's goodbye. Good riddance my heroes. May your magic stay bright, and I say that without irony." Under normal circumstances, Zami might have laughed, but right now she could only feel guilt. They were dragging a whole kingdom into a war that would only lead to many deaths. No one really could *win* in a war. You can't win, when you lose so much more than you gained. So the question was, in this war, how much were they going to lose before they got their freedom? How much would people have to suffer to earn what they should've had in the first place? And how much would her father gain, when he had nothing to lose?

Zami stared into the fire as she twisted a twig in between her thumb and index finger. She knew they probably shouldn't make fires, considering that was like creating a target on your back, but she really couldn't find it in her to care. And neither did the others, apparently.

They had spent the rest of the day and a considerable time after dark traveling. The base they were going to was further than the first one; it would take around three more days to make it there. They hadn't talked much since the castle, all caught up in their own thoughts, and as she sat there, a sick feeling spread in her stomach at the silence. It was too quiet, the only sound being the crackle of the fire and the rustle of the trees.

Her mind began to wander about the similarity between the empty halls of her father's castle in Damrion and the eerie silence that had fallen between the four. The light was dim and the darkness thick, just as in the castle, and she found herself almost anticipating being woken up, to find herself again in the small, dull room she had called home. To find that this whole situation had been nothing more than a horrid figment of her imagination.

In a way, it would make more sense than the reality of the situation.

"You're not alone anymore."

"Leave your past behind and start a new one."

"With us."

She stared at the ground, an unfamiliar feeling fluttering in the pit of her stomach. She had people who cared. She wasn't alone anymore. Nothing that had happened before mattered anymore because she *wasn't* alone. Not anymore.

She glanced up. First at Blu, his bright hair and his bright smile. The way he grinned when he told a joke. The way he leaned back onto a hand when he was comfortable and touched his shoulder to Strike's. The way his eyes closed when he laughed, the way he gestured wildly with his hands when talking.

Then she looked at Strike. His laugh reverberated through the air, his mouth upturned into a grin. His skin contrasted lovely with the bright color of his wolfish eyes. When he laughed, small crinkles formed in the corners of his face and his eyebrows lifted.

Then Ray. His pale eyes glittering in the firelight, and the shadows flickering across his tan skin. His hair glittered in the light, his face turned up in a light smile as he listened to the others. He leaned into a tree, hands resting in his lap. She liked his crooked smile. She liked his expressive eyes and eyebrows. She liked the way his nose crinkled when he laughed, and how he always reached up to run his hand through his hair. She liked how his eyes flickered to her every once in a while, making sure she was fine. She liked how he didn't judge people quickly, and how he believed that everyone had good in them. She liked everything about him.

Then his eyes were on her and she was staring deeply into him. In his eyes, that held so many emotions in the short time she had known him. Worry, joy, fear, grief, love, curiosity, pain. But there was no evil in there, never had been. He was human, oh so very human. And he cared so much about everyone and everything. He was a hero. And he deserved to be recognized as one.

His smile disappeared as he looked at her and in his eyes lay a question.

Are you okay?

She smiled sadly. No. She wasn't okay. She wasn't sure she would ever be. But that *was* okay because as long as they were there, she didn't have to be. And she allowed herself to not be okay. She let herself stand up and walk over to him. She let herself sit beside him, to feel his presence. And when she felt the sadness inside her swallow her up and leave her exhausted, she allowed herself to lay her head on his shoulder. To feel the smoothness of his shirt against her cheek. To feel the heat from the fire and the warmth of his shoulder. And she wasn't about to complain when she felt his arm move around her to keep her from slipping. Or when the fire was put out, and they were left in darkness and silence. Or, when she felt his head lean against hers as she felt herself slip into sleep. Because in that moment, she felt more okay then she had in a long time.

Chapter 18

Ray woke up in a cold sweat, from the first nightmare he'd had in years. He couldn't stop thinking about the prophet. If he'd just been paying even a little more attention, the prophet wouldn't have been killed.

Just something else he could've prevented.

"Ray?"

He looked up. Zami must've taken last watch, as she kicked dirt over the last embers of the fire and came over to settle on the ground beside him. "Yeah?" His voice wavered.

"Nightmare?"

He nodded, trying not to shiver at her unwavering stare. She shifted beside him.

"Was it bad?"

"Nah, I don't even remember most of it."

"That doesn't mean it's any better."

He smiled at her. "I know." He stood up, urgently wanting to stretch his legs. She did as well, and he chuckled when he heard the pops.

"Was it the prophet?"

"Yeah." He watched as she wrapped her arms around her torso, staring at nothing in particular.

"I'm not very good at this comforting thing." She said which made him laugh.

"You don't have to be, I like you just as you are."

She frowned at him. "Stop comforting me! I'm supposed to be comforting *you.*"

"Sorry." He said, smiling at her. They were both silent as he looked at the ground, shuffling his feet.

"You know, there are some things you can't avoid." She said, and he glanced over at her. "You couldn't have known that they were planning to capture the prophet for information on the desirables." She wasn't looking at him, instead rocking on the balls of her feet and staring at the ground. "Your job as a hero isn't to save everyone, Ray. It's to stop what'll kill more of them in the future." Those words sunk deep into him as he processed them. She was right, he couldn't save the people who had been killed already, but he certainly could stop *more* from being killed.

"I think you're better at this then you think."

She gave a small breathless laugh that sounded more miserable than genuinely joyful.

Then after a moment, she looked up at him and he had a rare chance to see the real pain in her eyes before she looked away again. As she looked at him, her smile fell away. She wasn't even trying to hide the fact that she was hurting. But her eyes held a small smile that slowly spread back to her lips as she held her arms out.

He chuckled when he realized she was copying his own actions, to reassure her from when she had a nightmare.

"Trying to win me over, Zames?" The nickname slipped from his lips easily, as if he had said it a million times.

"So what if I am, sunshine?" She said, smirking.

He just rolled his eyes as he stepped into the hug. "Then it's working." He mumbled, getting a laugh.

"Glad my charm isn't failing me just yet." She said against his shoulder. He liked her hugs. The way she bunched her hands into his shirt at his shoulders, as if she was afraid of letting go. He liked the feeling of her breath on his shoulder and her head resting just under his chin. He liked the fact that she was so strong, yet when he laid his hands on her back, he felt as if he needed to do so gently, not wanting to be the one responsible for hurting her.

"Don't think it could if you tried." He said, nearly pumping his fist when he felt her smile against his shoulder.

"I don't know. Would you still find me charming if I beat you up?" Her tone was teasing, but he decided to answer seriously.

"Honestly, yeah."

She snickered quietly. "Never took you for that type of person, sunshine."

"Hmm. I'm not sure what you're saying, but I'm just going to dispel that thought right now."

She snickered again. "Fool."

"Dollop-head."

"Dummy."

"Drama Queen."

"Dork."

"Dweeb"

"Hero-dork."

"Hey! That's not fair." He said, leaning back to see her face.

"Is too."

"Is not."

"Is too."

"Is not."

"Is not."

"Is too. Wait!" He groaned. "I can't believe I fell for that again."

"He who is easily misled, guides a foolish life."

He pouted at her and she grinned at him. "You wound me."

"Whoops."

He narrowed his eyes at her, pulling away enough that they weren't in an awkward half hug. "You don't sound very apologetic."

"That's because I'm not."

He scoffed. "You're not even the least bit afraid of me?"

"Nope. You're too nice." He wasn't really offended by that. He didn't want to be seen as someone to fear. "Now shut up and hug me."

He chuckled as he hugged her again. "Aren't you supposed to be the one comforting me?"

"Are you saying that my hugs aren't comforting?"

"You're impossible."

"So I've been told."

"Those must have been some pretty honest people."

She smacked his shoulder. "If we're too loud, we could wake the others up. Do you really want to travel with a sleep-deprived Strike tomorrow?" He shuddered at the thought and shut his mouth, as he was told. Soon though, something was edging at his mind, and he couldn't help but ask, voice soft and low.

"Doesn't it bother you?" She tilted her head at him and he elaborated. "That in the prophecy, they refuse to see the good in you, that they choose to only focus on your faults and mistakes?" She stared at him for a long time before she responded. But when she did, he felt a little bit of awe at her words.

"Why should it? We're all bad in someone's story." He didn't feel it necessary to say anything more, and they found themselves standing there, sinking into a comfortable silence. He supposed that if she was so aware of the eyes judging her every move, then she must've been aware of the way his eyes seemed stuck on her. But as she pulled away from him to sit again, giving him a grin, he figured that people's attitudes affected her much more than she let on.

The next two days were spectacularly ordinary. They would travel, break at noon, travel and then sleep. The majority of the walking was spent in silence, though with Blu there, some sort of conversation started eventually. By the third day, even Zami was noticeably antsy to get to the base.

"Come on! You have to have some sort of hobby." Blu was getting restless, and this time he had his attention focused solely on getting something out of Zami. Out of the days they had been traveling together, the only person who hadn't talked much about personal things was Zami, which Ray was thoroughly unsurprised about.

"I told you, I didn't have time for a hobby, Blu." Zami answered, stepping over a fallen log. She was taking point this morning without their map in hand; somehow she had their route memorized. How? He supposed he would never know.

Blu pouted as he stepped over the log as well. "So you're telling me the only thing you've ever done is train, learn, and get hurt?"

She looked over her shoulder at them, giving Blu a look that said 'are you serious right now?' "Well, that's vague. I've done much more than that, I just never hung much onto one thing. I was too... distracted most of the time."

"Distracted with training?"

Zami refused to meet their eyes. "Yeah... training."

"For some reason, I'm not convinced." Blu said, crossing his arms in front of his chest as they stopped for a moment.

Zami rolled her eyes, glancing up at the sky. It was getting a little darker, though still early enough that they should be at the base by that night, at least given what Zami told them when they first started walking. Now that he thought about it, this was the most she had talked in the last two days combined. Even Strike had talked more than her.

"You don't have to be." Then she was walking again, occasionally glancing up at the trees.

"I'm getting tired of forests." Blu grumbled, kicking a rock.

"Forests provide cover, that's why the rebel bases are almost always located in them. We're less likely to be noticed traveling in uncharted foliage, than towns with people who are on lookout for a group of rebel teens." Ray said casually, his attention mostly focused on how dark it was getting, with the trees getting closer and closer to one another, choking out the sunlight.

"Okay, encyclopedia."

He ignored Blu, choosing instead to jog up beside Zami. "How are you feeling?" He purposely phrased it as an ambiguous question, to see what she would answer with.

"Peachy." She said without glancing his way.

He frowned, having hoped for something other than sarcasm. "Like a ripe peach, or rotten peach?" That earned him a look. He was surprised to see amusement in her eyes.

"I guess you'll have to determine that for yourself."

"Does that include asking questions?"

"No."

He pouted. "Then how am I supposed to know?"

She grinned at him. "You're not. Women are an enigma, Ray; no man has ever completely deciphered us. So don't waste your time."

"What if I said it wouldn't be a waste of time?"

A wicked grin spread across her face. "Are you trying to make a move on me, Ray?"

He stared at her in shock, a flush creeping onto his face. "What? Wait... I just, was trying, I was..." He spluttered in defeat. Zami just smirked and pushed past him, leaving him standing there in shock. A hand slapped down on his shoulder as he stared at her back.

"Close your mouth dude, don't want to swallow any flies." Blu said, shoving him playfully before following after Zami.

Strike stopped beside him and sighed. "Come on, you can flirt later. We have a statement of alliance and clues to deliver." Then, he too followed the others.

Ray was left in utter bafflement.

The next several hours were silent ones, each of them getting more and more tense as the light coming from the trees dimmed, until finally there was none left. He gave them some light, letting beams of it fall just in front of them so they could see. Not like Zami needed it. Every time she disappeared in the darkness ahead of them, his heart rate went up a little bit. But she was always fine when she came back into the light.

Eventually though, she stopped, gaze leveling on a tree to their right. It was a fairly thin tree compared to most of the others, so he didn't see how it could be hiding a secret entrance or something. Zami didn't say anything, she just kept standing in front of it. When Blu tried to speak, she hushed him, and they stood for a long time in silence. It was an unsettling quiet, no birds chirping, no wind rustling the trees, nothing.

Just as Ray was about to risk Zami's wrath by speaking, a man appeared. He somehow slunk out of the tree, edging sideways, startling all of them except for Zami. He wore earthy browns, with a wave of chestnut hair tied behind his head, and stared at each of them in turn with sparkling emerald eyes. Finally, without a word, he turned around and crouched, laying his palm on the leaf covered ground. Underneath his hand the ground rumbled, disturbingly similar to the way it had when the golems had emerged. But instead of something coming out this time, a tunnel was revealed, the roof just under the tree's trunk and the bottom angled nearly perpendicular to the ground.

"Tunnel." The man said, his voice gravelly as if he hadn't spoken in weeks.

"Um, that's a *hole*, dude." Blu said, wrinkling his nose at it.

"Tunnel." The man repeated, looking like he hadn't heard Blu at all.

"A tunnel is something you walk into man. Not drop into."

"Tunnel." The man repeated relentlessly.

Blu threw his hands up in exasperation. "It's not a tunnel!"

"Tunnel."

"Ughhhhh." Blu groaned, covering his face with his hands. "H-O-L-E. Hole." Blu explained, gesturing to the tunnel that wasn't a tunnel. "Not a tunnel. What's so hard to understand about that?"

"Blu." Zami said, looking greatly amused. "It's a golem. That's how it was able to exit through that tree. It doesn't understand anything you're saying, nor would it be able to answer if it did."

Blu looked irritated, rather than embarrassed, that he had been trying to argue with a golem. "Why would they program it to say something so technically incorrect?" He gestured madly as he spoke.

"Blu. Chill." Ray said, watching as Strike also patted him on the shoulder to calm him down. It was clear he was getting uptight. Blu just huffed and glared at the golem man.

"Right." Zami said, raising her eyebrow at them. "Ray, you go in first."

"Why me?" He asked curiously as he stepped forward, lowering himself and swinging his legs into the hole.

"Cause if something attacks us, you make the best shield."

"Hey!" He exclaimed, just as he was about to release the edge.

She just snickered. Slowly he slid down, clinging on as long as he could before he had to drop. It wasn't a long enough drop to hurt someone who was prepared, but it still caused his heart beat to skyrocket. When his feet touched to ground, he stumbled forward a little, not expecting such an open area.

"Everything alright?" Zami called. He nodded, then yelled back 'yes' when he remembered that they couldn't see him. A second later, Blu was beside him, having nearly fallen when he dropped in. He grumbled as he reached up to fix his hair, looking around the large space. Strike followed a few seconds later, stumbling similarly to the way he had. Then he was also looking around the space in curiosity. When several minutes passed, and Zami hadn't dropped in, he began to worry, only for her to drop in, quite literally, without a single stumble.

It was quite dark, and without a thought he released some light like earlier to allow them to see. The walls stretched out nearly beyond view, even though the ceiling was quite low. To his right another tunnel spiraled from the main room, though this time it was actually a tunnel. Though to his dismay, it looked fairly small.

"Finally, a tunnel!" Blu hollered in excitement.

"Easy enough for you to say." Ray grumbled, glancing into said tunnel. "You're short."

"Aw, man! Sucks for you guys." Blu said, swinging his arm around Zami's shoulders.

Strike frowned beside him. "You're despicable."

Blu just beamed, all anger from earlier gone. He thought for sure Zami was going to say something thoughtful, given the look on her face, but instead she walked towards the tunnel and smirked back at him.

"You should go last this time. You know, in case you get stuck."

He stared after her for the second time that day as she climbed into the tunnel and began to walk, quickly swallowed by the darkness. With a curt 'good luck', Blu followed after her. He shared an exasperated glance with Strike. What considerate friends they had.

With a sigh, he followed Strike into the tunnel, immediately hitting his head on a rock jutting from the ceiling. He yelped, covering his head and attempting to duck under the next one, only to fail miserably. Strike seemed to be having similar luck, considering the little huffs and yelps he was producing. Someone would have to remind him how he was supposed to save the world, when he couldn't make it through a tunnel without hitting his head.

The next ten minutes were spent in a very similar fashion. No matter how much he tried to stay down, there was always something in the way. Whether it was a tree branch to trip on, or an outcropping of the wall that stuck out at an odd angle, something was always in the way. He almost had a heart attack when he temporarily got squished in a thinner section of the tunnel, but he managed to get out, although not without a few cuts and bruises. By the time he finally stepped into a larger room similar to the one before, he doubted he could crouch again even if he tried, given how much his back and neck hurt.

There was no sympathy in Zami's and Blu's eyes as they watched him and Strike rub their heads, wincing as they moved their necks around.

"Um. Well, I have bad news."

He looked to where Zami was gesturing and his stomach dropped.

"You have got to be kidding me." He glared at the tunnel in front of them, similar to the one he had just managed to make it out of.

Strike groaned beside him. "It's not my fault I grew tall!"

"Must suck." Blu sniggered from beside Zami.

"At least I don't have to stand on my tiptoes to get stuff from my locker." Strike said smugly, crossing his arms in front of his chest.

Blu's eyes bugged out. "That's a low blow, man. I'm only a couple inches below average height."

"Couple dozen." Strike mumbled and Ray resisted the urge to laugh.

"Well..." Blu started hotly, getting cut off by Zami.

"Boys. Not right now, you can get out the tension when we're *not* trying to deliver something that could save the world. K?" They both huffed and turned away from one another, but Ray was too focused on what she had just said.

"Did you just use the word 'K' in a real life conversation?"

She narrowed her eyes at him. "Shut up, goal post."

Blu and Strike both laughed as she stepped in the tunnel, again leaving Ray behind in shock.

"Goal post?" He half-asked, half-mumbled to himself as he followed Strike into the tunnel. The only response was laughter.

The second tunnel was almost twice as long as the first. And it had nearly twice the amount of obstacles. When he finally emerged from it with more bruises than he had ever had at one time in his life, and an aching head, he was cursing the genes that made him tall. Beside him, Strike was using a few colorful terms as he nursed an already forming bruise that covered the entirety of his left bicep. When Blu asked how he got it, Strike just threw his hands up and said "I don't even know!" Apparently deciding he had teased him enough, Blu just took Strike's hand gently as a comforting gesture.

It turned out even Blu had acquired a few bruises and cuts from sharp rocks on the wall, leaving Zami as the only one unscathed.

"There were sharp edges everywhere! There was no way you avoided all of them." Blu said as they rested for a minute in the next large area. He dreaded how many tunnels still waited for them.

Zami rolled her eyes at him over her shoulder. "I didn't."

"Whatcha mean, 'I didn't'?"

She avoided their eyes as she straightened up from the wall she had been resting on. He suddenly noticed how pale she looked, and then his eyes trailed to her hand that was pressed hard against her thigh.

"It's nothing. Come on."

He followed her with his eyes as she trudged towards the next tunnel, wobbling slightly when she set weight on her right leg.

A little anxiously, he followed them into yet another tunnel, but quickly his focus was trained mostly on keeping from hitting his head. He seemed to have gotten a little bit better at dodging, because this time he only gained a couple scratches, and only hit his head once when his attention started to wander. Which of course had nothing to do with the girl now walking just in front of him.

This tunnel had been shorter than the first, and to his excitement when they stepped into the next room, there were no other tunnels in sight. Instead, they were greeted with two guards standing in front of a dirt wall.

It seemed they were expecting them, stepping aside to let them pass without a word. With a look at the others, he opened the door set in the wall and walked through, eyes taking in the scene before him. People hurried around, weapons being carted around by a couple of teens, people shouting to hurry up. The smiles that he had seen in the last base had faded into scowls here, and the eyes filled with hope were filled with something else now. Fear.

It was obvious this place was less established then the last one, the majority of the area being covered with tents instead of actual buildings. There also seemed to be far more people than he expected, every extra space being occupied by a tent or bag. A girl around their age was yelling at someone to tend to someone called 'Tessa.' Then she caught sight of them and her shouts died down. She slowly lowered the hands she had been waving in a hurry up gesture, and stared at them from a few yards away.

Her hair was bright pink, with dark roots revealing the natural color as it fell to her shoulders in wild curls. She was a little taller than Blu, and built strongly. With a glance the other way, she jogged up to them.

"Can I help you?"

Ray realized she must've not known who they were, which only made him wonder if anyone other than a select few were aware that they were going after the desirables.

"Do you know where Sylvia is?" Blu asked from his left.

The girl's eyes widened. "Like the second in command, Sylvia?"

"Um," Blu's eyes met his. "Yeah, that'd be the one."

"Well, yeah I do. But," her eyes fell on Zami. "She's busy."

"I'm pretty sure she wouldn't mind taking a moment for this." Zami said and the girl froze for a moment.

"Yeah. You're right, I'll um... just follow me."

Ray gave Zami a questioning look. She just shrugged.

As they walked through the tents, Ray's heart dropped. He saw people bandaging up arms, legs, fingers, even eyes. People were losing body parts because of this. Parts that they would *never* get back. There was fear in everyone's eyes; no one was spared from it. There were kids who looked not much older than Blaze, carrying supplies, bandaging wounds, and sparring with others. This was the result of a war. A war that would only lead to loss for everyone.

For the first time, Blu had nothing to say to lighten the mood, and they walked in a miserable silence. Every scream or cry he heard dug deeper and deeper into his heart.

Kids crying out for their parents, people clutching the spots where a leg no longer was, holding their hands over their ears as if everything was too loud,

A hand slipping into his pulled him away from hearing all the outbursts. Zami looked at him with eyes that said one thing. *Stay strong. You have to stay strong, Ray.* He hadn't realized his eyes were watering, or that he felt so sick. With a shaky breath, he swallowed, willing the emotions to die down. If he wanted to stop all of this, he needed to push down all the things that got in his way. That included the emotions he felt when innocent people were harmed.

Your job as a hero isn't to save everyone, Ray. It's to stop what'll kill more of them in the future.

"She's in there." The girl said, glancing at each one of them again before running off. They were left standing in front of an olive green tent, unsure what to do next. Fortunately, they didn't have to decide, because in that moment a woman stepped out of the tent, yelling something back to the people inside.

"I'm getting it! No need to get your panties in a twist!" She shouted, turning to walk away. The moment the light hit her face, Ray froze. Wavy red hair, shockingly light blue eyes, a crooked smile. When her eyes met his, she froze as well. Suddenly all of the sounds around him were drowned out, all his focus on the person in front of him.

"mond?" She asked.

His heart thumped loudly in his chest as he opened up his mouth to respond. After a second of hesitation the question slipped from his lips.

"Spark?" He choked out. She stared at him, eyes wide as she began to nod her head. Without words, she stepped forward and pulled him into a hug. He wasn't sure what to feel as he trained his eyes on the dirt beneath their feet. His *sister*, the one who was supposed to have died *ten years* ago, was hugging him like he hadn't attended her funeral so long ago.

She pulled away, her hands on his arms as she looked up into his eyes. "You're supposed to be small."

"You... you're supposed to be *dead*."

Then she was laughing, a sound that made people turn around in confusion. A bright omen in a sea of darkness. But she didn't care that she was drawing attention, that those people would regard her as unusual. She never had. Apparently ten years of literal *death* hadn't changed her much.

"Getting our priorities set straight, aren't we?" Her eyes twinkled with the same joyfulness that he remembered.

"I don't understand." He said, unable to tear his gaze away from her. "You were incinerated in that fire years ago! You were *supposed* to be, at least."

Spark smiled her little smile, dimples and all. "Those are some big words for a little boy, Raymond." He gaped at her and she giggled. "Let's get you in to see Syl, and then we'll talk." She shushed him when he began to argue. "Later." Then she was walking away and humming. *Humming.*

Ray followed her with his eyes until he couldn't anymore, various emotions brewing up inside of him. How was he supposed to react? Was he supposed to be sobbing from happiness? Angry at how carefree she was? Grief-stricken?

"Okay, correct me if I'm wrong, but if I saw what I just thought I saw, then the sister that was supposed to be dead a decade ago just appeared out of nowhere and basically just told you to chill?"

Ray tore his eyes from the direction his sister had disappeared in, turning to answer Blu. "Um. Yeah. I guess that's what happened."

"And we've known you for several weeks now, and we're just finding out that 'Ray' *isn't* your full name?"

Ray threw his hands up in exasperation. "My sister that's supposed to be ashes under our feet just *appeared* outta nowhere and you're worried about my *name*?"

Blu shrugged. "It's just kinda weird hearing someone call you Raymond." He shivered as he said it, shaking as if to get the feeling of the name off of his skin.

Ray sighed in defeat. "Right. It's kind of a dumb name. But you shouldn't be the one to judge." He said, crossing his arms and staring at Blu.

Blu frowned. "Why not?"

He stared at him in disbelief. "Your name's a *color*."

Blu's eyes widened, then he started to laugh. "Blu's not my real name! That would be absolutely ridiculous!" He slapped his knee, getting several weird looks from passersby.

Ray frowned. "Then why does everyone call you that?"

Blu, or whatever his name was, shrugged. "Strike started teasingly calling me that since I hate the color, and ever since then it's stuck."

"Wait? Then what's your real name?"

"Oh, my name's Aaron."

Ray stared at him. Zami was staring as well. He glanced over to confirm this answer with Strike, who nodded.

"Aaron." He deadpanned at the bright, loud boy. "Your name is *Aaron*." The simple, professional name didn't match with the boy at all. Even a bit.

Blu didn't seem bothered. "Yeah, what did ya'..."

"YOU'RE BACK!" Blu, or Aaron, or whoever he was, was cut off by an ecstatic Sylvia who tackled him into a hug that nearly caused him to tip over. "When did you get back? Why wasn't I told about this? Are you hurt? What happened?"

"We got back just now." Strike said, smiling at the mop of blue hair peeking out of Sylvia's arms.

"You're crushing me." Blu mumbled, which Sylvia dutifully ignored.

"I have every right to be worried about my boys!" Ray chuckled at the serious look she was sending the boy in her arms, which truthfully, he probably couldn't even see. Blu's muffled complaints were emphasized by hands waving around in his normal expressive way, though Ray was sure no one could tell what he was saying.

When Sylvia finally pulled away, Blu gave a huff, reaching up to fix his hair. He frowned as if he was actually mad, but his eyes told a different story.

Sylvia reached over to give Strike a much more gentle hug, and Ray enjoyed watching her gently ruffle Strike's curls in a loving manner.

Then she was looking at him, narrowing her eyes.

"What?" He asked, still intently thinking about his sister.

"You're not hurt, are you?"

He smiled at her. "Nah, I'm intact."

She grinned at him and then Ray returned the enthusiastic hug he was given. He nearly laughed at Zami's surprised expression when she was given one as well. Unlike the rest of them, however, Sylvia didn't completely let go, instead keeping her hands on Zami's shoulders.

"You're hurt."

Ray blinked at Sylvias' statement. She was hurt? Zami just bit her lip, letting out the overused "I'm fine" excuse. Sylvia just stared at the girl until she let out a little sigh.

"It's just a scratch... I think."

Ray's eyes fell on the hand pressed over the side of her thigh as she lifted it a little to reveal blood staining her palm. There were no tears in her clothes though, which confused him. How'd she get hurt?

"Zami!" Sylvia exclaimed, eyes wide. "That's not fine! If you..."

"Sylvia." Zami interrupted, an exasperated look on her face. "*I'm fine.*"

Sylvia looked like she wanted to argue, but instead she just sighed. "Fine. I'll let this go for now. Come on in." Ray raised an eyebrow at Zami, who just rolled her eyes. "But we're not done talking about this!" Sylvia warned, holding up a finger to Zami to express her authority.

Zami just gave a weak grin as Sylvia stomped back into the tent.

"How'd you even get hurt?" Blu asked, finally pleased with his hair.

Zami shrugged. "I don't know." She hesitated before adding, "I think it's the same injury I got from the golem... I just... don't know *how.*"

Before any of them could make a remark that she had never *told* them she'd been hurt by the golem, she followed Sylvia into the tent. He shared an exasperated look with the others before making his way into the tent as well.

In the center stood a sectioned wooden table that looked as if it could be easily disassembled for convenience. It was littered with maps and papers, though the center was completely cleared out for a large map of the kingdoms, which he guessed were ones engaged in the war. Little red and yellow markers were spread across the map, revealing the locations of the armies. The yellow ones were hopelessly outnumbered by the red, a metaphor to the real battle.

Sylvia was shoving a few of the papers into one pile, trying to clear up a space. When she managed to stack most of them into a messy pile, she looked at each of them sternly. She was acting as a general now, all the traces of her motherly concern wiped from her manner.

"Now, tell me what happened. From the *beginning.*"

Ray spoke before Zami could, predicting that she would try to avoid anything concerning her own health. He told Sylvia everything. Well... *most* of everything. He left out some of the more personal stuff, including the fact that

Zami's father was the King, and all their personal stories they'd shared. Other than that though, with a few helpful comments from Blu, he told her all of what happened. Though he had to admit he went a little quicker than he had too, his mind still on his sister. He *really* wanted to know what had happened, and how she was here.

When he finished, Sylvia was silent for several minutes, contemplating what he had said. However, when she spoke, it wasn't the question he was expecting.

"So you're telling me that you left for information about the first desirable, and came back with not only that, but an alliance with the kingdom that's hated us for decades?" Her tone hinted at a sort of disbelief, and if he wasn't going crazy, perhaps a sort of muffled admiration.

"Yup!" Blu chirped in response. She gave a little shake of her head, rubbing her temple. Beside him, Zami shifted for something in her bag, and after a moment she was holding out the papers of clues, and the letter from Da'raom.

Sylvia took them, ripping open the blue wax sealing the letter envelope. Several minutes of silence passed between them as her eyes trailed over the words. Then she studied the paper itself, tracing her hands over the worn page.

"You guys are unbelievable."

Ray blinked as he joined eyes with Strike, who looked equally confused. "Um... why's that?" He asked curiously.

Sylvia dropped the items on the newly cleared section of the table and stared at all of them in turn. "You don't realize how crazy all this is? You guys knew each other for less than a couple *days* before leaving on this mission. We took a *huge* risk sending her," Sylvia gestured to Zami. "When she had just tried to kill you days prior. We were hanging onto a small thread of hope that we were right about sending you as a team. You were unprepared in every interpretation of the word! And here you show up, not even three weeks later, having done something deemed impossible!"

Sylvia's breathing was labored, eyes twinkling dangerously. "Do you have any idea how worried we were, taking this huge leap of faith, completely blind? We were terrified that Zami, *no offense dear*, might do something to you guys! But here we are, and you're all *acting* like a team!"

Ray was a little concerned as he listened to Sylvia. What was she so angry about? Had they done something they weren't supposed to?

"You four are," Sylvia's expression melted into a smile. "a miracle!" Ray's worry evaporated. She wasn't mad at them, in fact it was quite the opposite. She was ecstatic. It seemed several year's burden had left her body, and when she paced around the room, there was a newfound bounce in her step. "I'm just so proud of all of you!" She squealed, rounding back on them. "Come on, we need to get you all situated! We're gonna' win this war!"

Then they were being led out of the tent by an enthusiastic Sylvia. With an amused glance at Blu, he followed her. She was humming merrily as she walked down the row of tents, stopping to comfort people with encouraging words.

Apparently that was exactly the emotional booster everyone needed, because it seemed as Sylvia made her way through the camp, people began to perk up a little bit. They must really trust her, Ray thought, given how much her mood seemed to be affecting them.

"Oh, wait, I forgot! I'll be right back!" Sylvia called, disappearing before any of them could process what she said. Ray frowned at the spot she had just been standing in.

"Did she just like... vanish?" Blu asked, clearly confused also.

"Ummm, I think so..." He answered uncertainly.

"Look! Seems like we've got some newbies." A smooth voice said from their left. Ray looked over as the speaker moved from beside them to in front, two girls following closely behind her. Her hair was so blonde it seemed white, and pale icy blue eyes peered out from under thin eyebrows in a sort of disinterested manner. The girl to her left was considerably shorter than the girl in front, who was close to his height. The shorter girl was much less noticeable, with dark hair and soft eyes. On the other side stood a girl with bright blue hair and deep violet eyes. Ray had to do a double take at that, given how similar she looked to Blu.

The girl in front looked at each of them smugly, crossing her thin arms and cocking out her hip. Then her face shifted, changing from surprise into a smirk that sent shivers down his spine.

"No way, is that really you?"

He was momentarily confused about who she was talking about, only to feel Zami stiffen beside him. When he looked her way, he was met with the most stress-filled stance he'd ever seen her take, even when she had been fighting. Her shoulders seemed to have subconsciously hunched up, hands curled into fists at her sides. She was completely still, but he could almost hear the gears grinding in her head.

"Still not much of a talker, are we?" The girl smirked, eyes on Zami. "I suppose even several years couldn't change that you're still a wimp." Ray's heart thundered in his chest as he listened to the girl's words. Who was she? And why did she think she had the right to speak to Zami like that? With a glance at Strike and Blu, he caught angry expressions, and it seemed Zami wasn't the only one clenching her fists.

"I don't have time for this, Laci; why don't you go moan and complain about something somewhere else?" Zami replied, seemingly regaining some of her composure. However, the comment had the opposite effect than intended, because instead of getting the message, Laci's eyes sparkled with something new.

"I was mistaken. Apparently even the eternal beatings couldn't get you to shut your mouth."

"I don't think I'm the one who needs to learn to shut their mouth." Zami snapped back, causing Ray to relax a little bit. She could still defend herself.

Laci whistled. "You think with how many times I shoved you into lockers, you would've learned to at least be respectful to me." Ray stiffened again. Shoved her into lockers?

"Yeah well, I've learned that people who need to shove others into lockers to feel better about themselves don't deserve my *respect*." Zami snapped back, venom in her voice. He shivered. He did *not ever* want to be on the receiving end of that.

Laci's laugh was cold and short, more mocking than meaningful. "What are you even doing here? Wasn't your daddy against the rebellion?" But before Zami could say something Laci cut in again. "No, no wait. Let me guess!" She tapped her chin as if in thought, then pointed her finger in an 'ah ha' gesture. "The alcohol finally got to your poor momma's liver? No, no wait. The medics finally took her away! No, no I've got it! Someone finally said something about the bruises!" Laci gave another shrill laugh. "Or, maybe." Her eyes glinted maliciously. "Your dad finally hit her a little too hard!"

Ray's stomach dropped a bit at the implications of her words, and he could see the same thing happening to Blu and Strike out of the corner of his eyes. Zami reached out a hand to hold back Blu, giving him a shake of her head.

"She's not worth it."

He saw the downcast of her eyes though, and knew that Laci had hit a nerve.

"Your mother *was* always a little delicate wasn't she? I doubt it would have taken much, just a hard punch to the wrong part of the head and, poof." Laci spread her hands out in an explosive gesture. "No more mommy."

"Come on, Zami!" Blu groaned from behind her arm. "You can take her! Kick her snooty booty!" Ray couldn't keep a little bit of a smile from his face at Blu's words.

Laci laughed again. "You think she can fight me? I'm sure she very vividly remembers how things like that turned out."

Zami growled. "That's because I was *five* and you were, correct me if I'm wrong, seven."

Blu scoffed. "That's totally unfair, dude. You were probably like four times her size! I mean," Blu gestured at Laci. "Look at you now!"

Laci's eyes widened in anger. "What are you saying?"

"Nothing much. I'm just stating that you're quite a bit, um, *larger* than her."

Laci sneered, stepping forward. Before she could move towards Blu though, Zami grabbed the girls wrist, pulling her down to her own eye level.

"I wouldn't do that if I were you." She hissed acidly and Laci seemed to freeze for a moment. But she quickly pulled her hand away and stepped back with a sneer.

"I'm not scared of you, coward." She growled, though her voice was wavering slightly.

"I'm sure you aren't. Just terrified of making a fool of yourself in front of the only people that can stand you." Zami replied coolly, somehow unshaken, despite the derogatory names. "And resorting to name-calling. That's an all time low for you, *Glacier*."

Laci hissed at the name, glaring at Zami. *"No one* is allowed to call me that."

Zami grinned. "And *no one* is allowed to call me a coward. So I guess we're even." Before Laci could retort, Sylvia clapped a hand on her shoulder from behind, making her freeze.

"Everything all right here, *Glacier?*" Sylvia winked their way as Laci clenched and unclenched her fists. She couldn't fight with Sylvia.

"Of course, I was just on my way." She snipped, pulling away from the grip and pushing right in between Zami and Blu. The other two girls silently ducked in between them, following the steaming girl.

"I'm sorry about her, I would have put her in check a long time ago, but her parents are important figures in the Ice Kingdom, and we really can't afford to lose them as allies." Sylvia explained, sounding exasperated.

"For having ice powers, that girl sure is hot headed." Blu responded, peeling his gaze away from where she had gone. Ray looked at Zami, waiting for a snarky comment, or a response to Blu's, but nothing came. Her eyes cast to the floor, she waved at Blu in a 'whatever' gesture.

"Come on, let's go." Sylvia said, sending a worried glance in Zami's direction before turning and leading them away.

Ray stared at his sister as she plopped down in front of him, while also picking nervously at the left cuff of his shirt sleeve. She smiled at him, eyes sparkling before she hugged him again with a breathy laugh. When she pulled away, she cupped his face with her hands.

"I can't believe you're here! And you're so grown up!"

He reached up to grab her hands and grinned at her. "I could say the same. Though, if I remember correctly, you *used* to be taller than me."

"That's harsh, 'mond'!" She said, still smiling. He just smiled wider. How had he gotten so lucky? So many wonderful people just kept waltzing into his life as of recently. Sylvia, Oak, Blu, Strike, Zami, and now his *dead* sister. He felt a pang in his chest. He might've been having some amazing luck, but Zami... well given the encounter earlier, she wasn't having as good of a time.

"Right. So um, how exactly are you..." Ray gestured to her being *in one piece and very alive* for a lack of a good term.

She sighed. "I figured you'd ask that." She shushed him when he was going to respond. "Just listen, okay? It's kind of a freaky story."

She continued. "That night of the fire, everything was going fantastically. We had actually managed to scout where and how the enemy was going to attack next. We were really excited, because, well we were going to be able to come home to you guys. And then, it just happened *so* fast Raymond, I..." She glanced away for a moment.

"One moment we were packing up, and the next, everything was on fire. And then, well, everything went dark. I had no conscious perception, no senses. Nothing. And then I woke up. For a second I thought I had died; the last thing I remembered was the screaming and the fire. And when I looked around, there were *dragons,* Ray. Like real live, full-sized dragons!" She laughed suddenly, eyes glazing with memories. "And there were people. Really nice people who had saved me and healed me. After I had been awake a couple days, they said I could leave. That was when I noticed something was wrong. Everything had changed, the people, towns, even my body. I hadn't noticed changes in myself at first because I figured it had to do with the effects of healing. But..." She choked and swallowed.

"I... I went to the nearest town and asked someone what day it was. And then the year. Ray... I had been in that place, with no memory, for almost *ten* years. It took months to get here, and oh god, I was so sad. Mom and dad, I knew they were dead. I didn't know about you or Blaze or Laurel or Dew. I couldn't find you. And then I went to their house and it was empty. I was so devastated. I thought that everything was just... crumbling beneath my feet. And then, light came to me. Just *light.* In my dream, Ray. And I thought, it must've been you. You're the only one with that power. And suddenly I was standing in front of that tree that marks the entrance here; it was like a dream, Ray. I don't know how I got there, how I knew I needed to get there. But I did. And now," She gestured around, "I found you, Ray. I found you!" Ray stared at her, mind reeling from her crazy, disjointed story telling. She had been in a coma all this time? How was that even possible? And what about *light*? He hadn't done anything.

"Ray." She said, peering at him.

He swallowed, trying to straighten things out. "I... I..."

"It's okay, I don't expect this'll be easy on you." She patted the hand on his leg. "We'll get through it together though. I promise, I'm here now." He nodded numbly, unable to properly discern what he was feeling. She gave him a sad smile before standing up and holding out a hand. "Come on, let's get you to bed. I'm sure you're pooped!" He gave another nod and followed her through the rows of tents.

He felt so incredibly conflicted. Wouldn't everything be so much simpler if she *had* died? Then he felt guilty for thinking that. It wasn't that he didn't appreciate her coming back, it was just... he had finally gotten over it. And now she was here, and he had no clue how to handle that fact. He had managed to accept that there had been nothing he could've done to prevent her and his parents' death, and now all of his balance was being thrown into question. It was infuriating.

"If you two are doing some hanky panky, you better get decent, cause I'm COMIN' IN!" Spark yelled into the tent they had stopped at. Blu opened the flap with narrowed eyes.

"How dare you think something so slanderous of me." He huffed, and through the open flap, Ray could see Strike rolling his eyes from the floor.

"Yeah, yeah." His sister said, pushing past Blu. Then she leaned in, whispering something into his ear. Blu's face went red as a tomato and he reached up to cover it in embarrassment as Spark walked into the tent with a satisfied smirk. Ray couldn't help but be a little impressed, as he had never seen

Blu so flustered before. When he walked past him with a raised eyebrow, and Blu opened his mouth to say something, he held his hand up.

"You know what? I don't even want to know." Then he walked in the tent, grinning when he saw Strike laying on his stomach, flipping through what looked like a music book, and his sister in the corner, fixing her hair.

For the first time, Blu didn't have a snarky comeback, and instead just walked in and flopped down to sit in front of Strike's legs, his gaze on the ground. From Ray's viewpoint he could see red ears and a flushed neck, which made him grin even wider. Boy did he miss his sister.

"So are you gonna introduce me to your homies, or what?"

Ray frowned at her. "Homies?"

"Yeah, your bros, friends, trouble pals, bi..."

"Spark. I know what 'homies' are."

"Well, then you better get introducing!"

Ray smacked his forehead and slid to the ground beside his sister. "The hyperactive one with obnoxious hair is Blu, the calm one's Strike and..." a big crash resounded outside, followed by yelling. "That would be Zami." A few seconds later, said girl walked in, fuming.

"Who would put a barrel of apples in front of a medical tent! It's called a *medic*! Not a *trip everyone who's just been healed*, because we're a bunch a morons!" She trailed off when she noticed their expressions. "Oh shush, like you don't have any problems."

"I like her." Spark stated from beside him.

"You would." He said, eyes still on Zami as she thumped down beside Blu, quite ungracefully for someone who prided themselves in the art of stealth.

"Did you guys meet at school?"

"No... not really." He responded.

"So how'd you meet?" Spark asked, looking a little confused.

"We met back at the other rebel base." Blu said, leaning back against Strike's legs, Strike having flipped over and sat up. "Well, minus me and him." Blu gestured at Strike. "We've known each other for forever."

"So you weren't at the rebel base when mond' came?" Spark asked Zami, who was picking at the white gauze bandage on her leg.

"No." Zami said, studying her nails.

Spark frowned. "Then how'd you two meet?"

Ray scratched his neck and avoided her gaze, unsure how to answer that in a way that didn't sound incriminating.

"I tried to slice his throat."

Ray gawked at Zami. "Don't you have *any* concerns telling people that?"

"No, why should I?" Zami asked, cocking her head at him in confusion.

"Oh, I don't know!" He threw his hands up in exasperation. "Because people might actually think you're a bad person!"

Zami shrugged."Too late for that. Remember the prophet?" And the demi-humans? And... well pretty much everyone else, ever?"

Ray sighed and slumped down, rubbing his eyes with the palms of his hands. He had never had to deal with both Zami *and* Spark. Only one at a time. Together, they were overwhelming.

"I'm starting to understand why they sent multiple boys on the trip. Cause if there were two of you girls, I don't think we would've survived." Ray mumbled to the floor, receiving a smack from his sister.

"You should be thankful for having such wonderful women in your life!"

"Right. I'm incredibly thankful."

Another smack. "Still just as mouthy as ever, I see."

"It's not me you should worry about, you wouldn't believe the mouth on Blaze."

"Blaze... he's ten now. Right?"

Ray nodded. "Yeah."

"I can't wait to see him! I bet he's so cute!"

He shivered. "No, that kid is so feisty, it's not even funny. And don't get me started on his ketchup fascination."

"Aw, but the feisty ones are always the cutest! And ketchup?"

"You don't wanna know."

"I'm gonna take your advice on this one." Spark stood, stretching her arms above her head. "So you tried to kill him?" She asked, turning to Zami.

Zami shrugged. "Yeah."

"I like you."

Chapter 19

Zami woke up to a white-hot searing pain coursing through her head, prickling down the back of her neck. An aching came from her ribs, lower back and thigh, making her vision spot up. Not wanting to alert anyone, she bit her lip to keep in a cry, and immediately felt her teeth break the skin. Everything hurt, way too much.

As she laid there trying to keep quiet, she tried to give her body reasons why it shouldn't be complaining. There were *little kids* out there in much worse condition than she, adults that had lost so much. A little bit of pain didn't give her a right to take away that medical attention from people who desperately needed it.

When she rolled onto her side, another wave of pain shot through her body, and in that moment she would've probably glared at anyone nearby. If she could open her eyes that was. Stupid, stupid, stupid, human body. You would think God would have cut a little more slack for someone who had such a horrid excuse of a childhood. But nooooooo, it couldn't be that easy, could it?

"Zami."

She sat up abruptly, immediately regretting it and doubling over. "Yeah?" She choked out, her mind too foggy to figure out who was talking.

"What's wrong?"

"Nothing. I'm fine... all fine." Zami lied, her head throbbing harder the more she talked. When a hand touched her shoulder, she involuntarily jumped, unprepared for the contact. Through the spots in her vision she saw red hair, and for a moment she thought it might've been Sylvia, but icy blue eyes stared back at her. The same color eyes she had grown to like so much on someone else.

"Hey, calm down." Spark said, and Zami was sure she was frowning even though she couldn't tell.

"Calm's my middle name." She mumbled, hugging her chest to try and get as far away from the other girl as possible.

"Sure... You want me to get Ray?"

"No, no, it's fine I just..." She trailed off, not sure what to say. *Am in pain? Don't want to be near people right now? Feel really uncomfortable?*

"Okay, I'll come back in a little while. Try to rest."

Zami wasn't sure Spark knew what was happening, but she understood the need to be alone enough to leave her. As soon as Spark was out of the tent, she buried her head in her arms and squeezed her eyes shut. Everything was happening so fast. So many choices of what to do. So many people. So much death. It was too overwhelming.

She took a gasping breath, wincing at the pain it caused in her ribs. Why wasn't healing magic working on her? It did when she was with her father. Nothing made sense. And then there was Laci. Of course, right when she thought she was escaping from her past, that witch just had to waltz back in like the snotty little girl she was. And of course, she was able to do anything she wanted, cause her daddy was someone important. Nothing had changed.

But she wouldn't think about it. She wouldn't. *Just breathe, she* told herself. That was a long time ago, and you're not the same. You won't hold a grudge because that's what bad people do. Good people forgive. Good people forgive. That's right, you tried to kill Ray, and now all these people are welcoming you into their arms. They're giving you a chance and you're not gonna ruin that. Not gonna ruin it. *Not gonna ruin it.*

You were given the biggest choice of your life. To turn around and do what you believe in, rather than what your dad does. And by god you are going to use that. No more little Zami that can't even talk back without regret. You have a voice now. A chance. A chance to use that voice.

Slowly her breath stabilized, and she was back to reality with another painful twist in her ribs. Uncurling herself, she glared at her ribs and held back the urge to yell at them. Stupid delicate bones. She stared blankly at the red soaking through the bandage on her leg. Stupid leg. And she reached back to feel her lower back and lifted it up to see blood on her fingertips. Not enough to be a huge problem, but still blood. Stupid back.

With a groan of pain, she pressed her fingers to her back, trying to figure out the extent of it. Not that bad, just a little reopened scab. She chose to ignore it and instead pressed her bloody fingers to her ribs. At contact, a surge of pain blinded her momentarily before her sight came back in blotches. Yup. Definitely broken.

Standing up, she ignored the pain and instead stomped around in anger. Why? Why why why? Why her? Why now? Just... why? With a growl, she pulled on her boots and tied them, quite angrily. There was a war going on, there was no time for a breakdown.

She grabbed an apple and made herself eat, but she found it incredibly hard to eat more than a couple bites when she bent over with a cough, which only made the pain worse. She ended up leaving it for later with the hope she had eaten enough to help heal her ribs. Dumb ribs. Outside, people bustled around just like the previous day, carrying supplies and such. However, everyone seemed in a much better mood than before, which was quite ironic considering her current situation. She wondered what caused everyone to be so much happier.

"You've emerged! Feeling better?"

Zami stiffened and then forced herself to relax. It was just Spark. "Yeah." She said, trying to keep the response short to reduce the tremble she knew was there. Her voice was slightly croaky, but that much she could blame on just waking up. When she was met with silence she turned around, met with eyes on her, staring as if they could see everything. What was up with Ray's family and their unsettling eyes?

"Hmm." Spark said, breaking her gaze away after a moment. "Come on, the others are over this way." Zami followed her, trying to push the pain off of her expression to hide it from the others. Most likely, they would make a big deal about it.

When they entered the tent, she was met with four pairs of eyes. Emerald green, pale blue, deep violet and honey yellow eyes stared at her as if she was a five-year-old that had just walked into a meeting for adults. She slowly turned her head to check behind her, wondering if someone was behind her. Turning back, she met their eyes and checked one more time. But no one was behind her.

"What are we looking at?" She asked, eyes still searching behind her.

"You."

"Um... is there a reason, or..." She trailed off, looking down to see if there was something off with her appearance.

"You look like crap." Blu said, as if that explained everything that had ever needed explanation.

"Gee, thanks." She answered, rolling her eyes and immediately regretting the pain that shot through her head.

"Anyway," Sylvia started, eyes still on her. "I was telling them that most of the work here was left untranslated, and we aren't sure exactly what language it's in." She gestured to the battered book laying on the table, open to the first page. Zami stepped towards it to get a better look, leaning forward to peer for a couple moments at the scribbles on the page.

"Glarieth, I believe; it was used a long time ago by prophets, which would explain why they had this. Though it doesn't seem they recognized it, does it?" She noted, scanning some of the notes the prophet had made. Unhelpful things like "might mean water", or "grapes", which she greatly doubted had anything to do with the words on the page.

"Where'd you learn that?" Sylvia asked.

"I read a book about it a couple years ago." She muttered, not really paying attention to the others. When there was no response, she glanced up, met with several curious expressions. "What?"

Sylvia shared a glance with Spark before looking back at her. "Did you learn any of the language when studying history?"

Zami shrugged, gaze flickering back to the page, where surprisingly a couple of the words popped out to her. Not all of them, but enough to make sense of the main points. "Sure, I remember a few basic terms. Not a ton though." She said, shrugging.   Sylvia's face lit up and she gave her an excited smile. "You think you could take a look at it for us?" She asked, and Zami felt a weird sense of pleasure run through her veins. She wasn't *ordering* her to do anything, she was *asking* her, giving her a choice.

"Um, yeah, sure." She said cooly, though internally she was celebrating the fact that she was being *helpful* rather than a burden on them.

"Oh, I'm so glad we found you!" Sylvia exclaimed, bounding out of the tent to do whatever Sylvia-like activity she needed to. Zami watched as she left, and even when she had disappeared from view, she kept her eyes on the tent opening. What an unusual lady she was. Lovely, but very, very strange.

"How many languages do you know?" Blu asked incredulously as she slid into the nearest chair, crossing her ankles to keep her legs from shaking like they always did when she sat. Her ribs screamed at her, but she ignored them and instead slid the book towards her, cautiously touching the crinkled pages.

"Fluently, about a half dozen. Other than that, I learned a few scatterings of terms from books in a couple others. Really, it's not that impressive, most assassins are trained to know a lot of information, to blend in." She flipped the paper around, scanning it and trying to discern how much of it she could read before she actually tried to translate any of it. Overall, she only recognized a little over half of it, which she was a little disappointed about, considering she was sure she had read that whole book only about four years ago. No doubt her father would be disappointed; he always expected more from her, because she was his daughter. Like that helped anything.

"Only *half a dozen!*" Blu exclaimed loudly, which surprised her into looking up from the book. "I can barely speak one correctly!"

She snorted, and then winced when she felt the ache in her ribs. "I think that's a personal problem."

Blu pouted and plopped into a chair across from her, wiggling his fingers at Strike in a "come here" gesture. Zami smiled when out of the corner of her eye, she saw Strike roll his eyes, but go sit beside Blu.

After that, she drowned out the conversations happening between the others around her, instead grabbing a sheet of paper and pen. The situation reminded her painfully of when she did schoolwork in her younger days. The paper she was writing on was shifted nearly sideways and on her left side, as she took to copying each line as accurately as she could, keeping blanks in the places she had no clue about. That also annoyed her father, how she wrote sideways and couldn't pay attention to anyone when writing. He had always told her she should be able to multitask, to which she replied that there was technically no such thing, and got a slap as a result. Ah, yes, beautiful memories.

It wasn't that she couldn't hear others when working, it was just too overwhelming to be doing too many things at once. Which was kind of stupid, but that had always been how she had been. Her father had never taken her in to see if there was something wrong with her; he had always been embarrassed that he might have a daughter with issues. Which was also stupid, considering a good chunk of her issues were caused by *him*. Her mother, on the other hand, she wasn't embarrassed. Just... incredibly distracted most of the time.

Zami would've liked to blame it on the alcohol, but there was definitely an underlying problem that was never brought up. It was easier to just believe that it was only because she was drunk. It didn't hurt as much that way, because at least it was blaming something inanimate for not caring enough about her, not her mom. Her mom loved her, and she kept it at that.

She wondered how Elios was doing, whether he was coming up with new theories, and if he still forgot to put away his empty tea cups. She hadn't thought about him a ton, which she felt slightly guilty about. But she had been distracted with all the things that happened recently, for good reason. Her life had literally turned around in the craziest way possible. How was he doing without her there? He had friends, she knew that. Friends his own age, but none like her. They related to each other in many ways, and it seemed her intelligence was closer to his than any of his friends. That alone made them closer to each other than anyone else. He was like the older brother she'd never had.

She wasn't sure how much time had passed when she finally took a moment to look up and crack her knuckles, but she figured it must've been hours. Blu was awake, legs pulled up to his chest, a sleeping Strike on his shoulder. Spark and Ray had left, where to she wasn't sure.

Blu's eyes were glazed over as he stared at his hands on his knee, fingers picking at a hole in his skinny jeans, which were a startling shade of deep purple. He had always had a talent of matching colors that didn't match, this time pairing them with a sort of cream shirt. Strike had a completely different sense of style, with his cuffed blue jeans and the deep grey sweatshirt she had never seen him without. They complemented each other quite nicely she thought, looking so at home with one another.

With a sigh, she glanced back down at the paper with the translation. She had mostly finished, with quite disheartening results. It seemed that even translated, it was still nearly impossible to understand. Like the prophet had warned, it was all jumbles of poetry, riddles and figurative language. Her head hurt too much to try and understand any of it just then, and when she realized she could barely read the paper because the words blurred together, she pushed it away and laid her head on her arms in defeat. Her ribs still stung, and her leg throbbed along with her head. Sure, she had been through a significant amount of pain in her life, but she was always healed soon after. This seemed to be here permanently, considering the healing was only make it better for a little while.

Taking deep breaths, she attempted to relax her muscles and just rest for a moment. She would just close her eyes for a moment, and in a couple minutes she would be up, ready for some big brain time. Just close her eyes for a second... just one second she thought. And as soon as she closed her eyes, she was fast asleep.

When she woke up, her head felt slightly fuzzy and muddled, and she felt unusually warm and cozy. The table was sturdy against her arms, and there was a strangely comforting weight against her shoulders and back. As she breathed in, a familiar scent flooded her nostrils, and she searched her mind for where she remembered it from. Warm and fresh. Some sort of mint, and a hint of a woodsy undertone. It smelled like... Ray. She frowned and lifted up a finger to her shoulder, coming in contact with smooth leather. Her heartbeat quickened involuntarily. The weight on her back was his jacket.

She buried her face back into her arms and bit her lip, feeling her face heat up. Why must something so simple have such a large effect on her? It was utterly ridiculous how stupid she felt when she thought of him. It'd been less than a month since she had met him! This was ridiculous behavior! But lord, was it nice to have something so lovely, to feel something so wonderful. Something to cherish amidst everything she hated.

With a bubbly warmth in the pit of her stomach, she peeked out from her arms. Blu and Strike were gone, no one visible in her range of sight. Relaxing back into her arms, she snuggled further into the jacket and closed her eyes. In only a couple minutes her mind was slowly fading into sleep again, but right as she felt herself begin to nod off, a loud yell came from outside.

"I can't believe it! That's crazy!" That was Spark, sounding extra exuberant. A laugh followed it as they walked into the tent, which she knew well enough was Ray's. "That kid is a troublemaker! He must've gotten it from you."

"No way! That's definitely you!" Ray argued, and she could almost see his fake pout.

"Considering that neither of you are his parents, I think it's fair to say it's not either of you." Blu said. She hadn't realized he had walked in as well.

"Shut up, shorty." Spark answered and she heard a little whack.

"Hey! That counts as assault!"

"Not if there's no witnesses." She said smugly.

"That's just harsh! Ray, why aren't you doing anything about this? It's *your* undead sister!"

"I'm gonna stay out of this." Ray answered from across the table. Blu and Spark continued to bicker for a moment before Spark rushed out to go find Sylvia, leaving the tent fairly quiet. She heard the ungraceful plop of Blu falling into a chair to her left, and again she peeked out of her arms. Ray was sitting in the seat Blu had been in earlier, feet kicked up on the table in a surprisingly bold gesture, for him. He held the paper she had written in his left hand, eyes scanning it. He twirled a pen in his other, flipping it through his long fingers in a way she could've only hoped to mimic. Sure, she was mostly coordinated, but only with a lot of practice. He seemed to have it down as an art, twisting the pencil around each of his fingers back and forth over and over again. His jacket was unsurprisingly absent from his figure, leaving him in his usual white shirt.

Now though, she got an eyeful of skin that she wouldn't normally be able to be distracted by. She liked the sharp angle of his wrist and the curve of his forearm. And of course there was his collarbone. She *really* liked his collarbone.

She knew it was a bit weird, how she noticed the littlest things, but those were the most enjoyable things to look at. To know you knew so many little details about someone. The relaxed slope of his shoulders, the line of his neck into his jaw. The little piece of hair that curled above his ear and the flickering of his eyes in the limited light coming from the little globe of fire in the center of the table. There was another thing his eyes looked good in; firelight.

To her surprise and enjoyment, he was wearing *black* jeans, which she liked quite a lot. She wasn't sure how, but he managed to look older than he was, but boyish at the same time. It must've been the innocent glint of his eye, and the little crooked smirks. She figured if you didn't look to closely, he could've passed for several years older than he was, with his height and stature. He must've had *really* good looking parents, considering how good looking everyone in the family was.

Then she found herself thinking of how strong he must be, to be in fine shape after all this time what with all that had happened. He inspired her to push her past away, and think only about what was yet to come. And he, hopefully, would be in her future as well.

Blu looked pretty much the same as the last time she had been awake, minus Strike on his shoulder, which hinted that it hadn't been that long since she fell asleep. Blu looked incredibly bored, picking yet again at his jeans and seemingly glaring at the nearest town on the map. She wondered where Strike was; she didn't think she had ever seen them apart for long.

Deciding that she had spent a little too much time pretending to be asleep, she sat up and smoothed her hair back, frowning when she felt a lump. Reaching behind her cautiously so the jacket didn't fall off her shoulders, she pulled her hair out and rubbed her scalp where her hair had been pinned. Maybe that was part of where the headaches were coming from.

"And finally, she awakens." Blu announced as she continued to fix the part in her hair. Choosing to ignore him, she yawned and uncurled her legs from the position they'd been in for a while. Ray had looked up from the paper and when she glanced up, she was met with his stare.

"You doing fine?" He asked, tilting his head at her in a way that made her heart flutter.

She turned away, flushing. "Y... yeah I'm fi... fine." Wow. Real smooth Zami. Real smooth.

"Yeah, cause you sound *real* fine." Blu said, giving her a look that said all too much.

"Shut up, shorty." She teased, grinning when he frowned.

"But I'm taller than you." He muttered.

"Doesn't matter."

"What do you mean! I'm at least three inches taller than you! If not more!"

"So?"

Blu groaned, pressing his forehead to the table. "Well you're..." He trailed off, trying to find something that would insult her. "What even are you insulted by?"

"Nothing. I'm a flexible person." She answered, biting her lip.

"Hmmmmm, I'll just have to ask Miss Ice Queen out there. She seems to know what gets on your nerves."

She gaped at him. "You wouldn't. That's a new low, even for you."

Blu looked victorious as he leaned back in the chair. "Let's see... getting called short doesn't bother you. What about..." His head shot up to reveal a huge grin. Her stomach dropped.

"What about what?" She asked, voice coming out a little more shrill than normal.

"Cutie."

"I am *not* cute." She said, glaring at him with all the fire she could muster.

"Aw, would you look at that! Cute little Zami getting mad!"

She growled at him, shoving her hair out of her face. "This cute little girl could kick your arse."

Blu cooed at her, laughing when she threw a pen at him. "Little wittle Zami getting cwanky!"

"Real mature, you two." Ray said, and she turned around to level a glower at him. He just gave her a heart-stopping grin, pushing his hair from his forehead.

"Shut up, goal-post." She said, ignoring her heart.

"Only for you, cutie."

She stared at him in shock as he just winked at her, turning back to the paper. "Oh no, you didn't."

"Oh yes," He looked back at her, completely serious. "I did." She would've normally had some witty remark, but the seriousness in his eyes made her freeze. Before she could recover enough to make a retort, he slid the paper back over to her.

"Any of this make sense to you?" He asked, nodding to the paper and shifting so he was sitting like a normal person.

She shook her head with a sigh, reaching forward to grab one of the pencils on top of the map. "I have some theories, it just might take some serious evaluating."

"You're back!"

Zami raised her eyebrows as she watched Blu tackle an unsuspecting Strike. With a few stumbles back to get on balance, Strike gave Blu a shy smile.

"I was only gone for a few minutes."

"I know!" Blu chirped from Strike's arms. Strike sent her a questioning look and she shrugged at him in a "it's your boyfriend" gesture.

With a little bit of resistance, Strike managed to sit down beside her, Blu settling beside him with a pleased expression on his face.

"You look much more comfy." Strike remarked, eyes flickering from her back to her face. She coughed with embarrassment and refused to look up at the boy in front of her, even though she could feel his gaze. It was his fault, after all.

Deciding to focus on the paper, she scanned her eyes over the words she had neatly printed across the page. Tracing one of the terms with the tip of the pencil, she ghosted possibilities under it. What did it mean?

"You're left-handed?" Blu asked offhandedly. Confused, she glanced at her hand. She was using her left hand. She quickly switched the pencil to her right and looked away, abashed.

"Naturally, yeah." She said, feeling slightly nervous.

"Then why don't you use it?" Blu asked, and when she looked, everyone's eyes were on her. There was no avoiding the question here.

"Oh, um... my uh," She felt her leg start to bounce. "My dad thought it was unnatural." The silence made her heart leap in her throat and she reached up to tuck her hair, then decided against it. She liked the curtain of privacy it created.

"Well, that's just hypocritical, isn't it? He's allowed to use his right hand since it's natural, why wouldn't you be able to use your left since that's natural for you?"

She looked up in surprise at Blu. "Um, I mean y... yeah, I suppose." She said, unprepared for that type of answer. Then her eyes lit up and she sat up in excitement, remembering something. "Though, it does have some perks." She reached over for a different piece of paper and grabbed another pencil in her left hand. Settling on a simple sentence, she wrote the first half with her right hand and the other with her left, grinning up at the others. "I can write twice as fast!" She explained excitedly.

When she looked up she was met with three very amused expressions and a raised eyebrow.

"What?" She asked, confused by their reactions.

"Nothing." Ray said, eyes twinkling. "It's just nice to see you so happy about something."

"Can you draw like that too?" Blu asked, leaning over Strike to see the paper.

Zami nodded enthusiastically. "When I got older and real stubborn, I started practicing things with both. My mentor, Elios, was alway really confused at how fast I could write something. When he found out why, he laughed. It was great." She said, smiling at the memory. And like that, any sadness she had been feeling evaporated as she thought of all the nice times with Elios.

"Who's Elios?" Blu asked, and she tapped the table with her pencil as she giggled.

"He's this wonderful genius back at the castle, got three times the brains as anybody you'll meet. You should've seen some of his inventions! And he didn't even have magic!" She threw her hands up as she told them about him, feeling slightly giddy. "It was all science and math. The King put him in charge of teaching me, since I wasn't in school anymore. He's the best thing in that castle. You know, maybe I should convince him to take over. I'm sure he would make a wonderful King." She added thoughtfully, stroking her chin.

"You realize that would require being able to get your dad out of power first?" Blu said.

"That's a good point. We'll have to kill him first." She said, thinking of how she would be able to do that.

Blu snorted in amazement. "You really hate him."

She shrugged, glancing at him. "Hate's a strong word.Though I suppose it is proper in this situation." Before anything could be said in response to her statement, Sylvia walked into the room, Spark close behind.

"Ah! Our lovely assassin awakes!" Sylvia sent her a blinding smile as she walked around the table to stand on her left. "Now, I know we're trying to plan something critical for the war, but first we need to get something out of the way." Sylvia took a deep breath and met each of their eyes separately. "Technically, we need to assign each of you a guardian. Like an *adult*." Zami saw Blu open his mouth, but Sylvia quickly continued. "I know, I know. You've done things most adults haven't accomplished. It's not my rule though; we need an adult to go for legal reasons. I think we all have a tendency to forget you're still children."

"Now, I had already arranged to be legal guardian for you two," She gestured to Blu and Strike.

Spark stepped up behind Ray and ruffled his hair. "And, I'm technically allowed to be yours." Ray looked ecstatic as he looked up from the chair at his sister.

"Yes, we would normally say it's your Aunts, but since they're so far away, it's easier to have Spark, who's right here, take guardianship."

Everyone's eyes shifted to Zami, who wasn't paying attention in the least bit. When it was silent for an uncomfortable length of time, she looked up.

"What?"

Sylvia sighed and gave her an exasperated but affectionate smile. "Do you have anyone to take guardianship of you? We would normally just have one of us do it, but technically living relatives are supposed to first."

"Nope." Zami answered.

"Father?"

"Evil." She responded, ignoring the looks she got from the others.

"Mother?"

"I mean, you can try. It might be kind of difficult though." Zami said, crossing her ankles to keep her leg from bouncing.

"Where is she?"

"Six feet under, in Damrion." She answered, staring at her fingernails.

Sylvia gave another sigh. "Older siblings?"

"Not that I'm aware of."

"Aunts? Uncles?"

"No clue. Probably either dead, or evil."

"Older cousins?"

Zami frowned at the table. She briefly remembered some teenage boy. "No." She lied, not wanting to deal with tracking down an old memory.

"Oh, come on! Grandparents?"

"N..." Zami froze, very distinctly remembering an angry old woman.

"So, yes?" Sylvia asked, eyes boring a whole into her head.

"Might be dead." Zami muttered. "Not *evil*, as such."

"Do you think she might be alive?" Sylvia asked, clearly relieved that they might've found someone.

"Likely. She's too stubborn to die."

"And she's not against the rebellion?"

"I doubt it. She hates my father, wouldn't want to share a house with him, much less an opinion."

"So what's wrong with her?"

Zami sighed and stared at her translation on the table. "Nothing really. She just doesn't really like me all that much. Or my parents."

"Great! Let's go!" Sylvia exclaimed, bounding out of the tent.

"She does realize that my Grandma lives clear across another Kingdom... right?" She asked, glancing around at her friend's faces.

"I'm sure she has a plan!" Spark exclaimed, dragging Ray up from his seat and pulling him out of the tent. He stumbled after her with a surprised look on his face that made her laugh. As she followed Blu and Strike, who were following the others, she pulled her hair up again, a little nervous about going to her grandma, who she hadn't seen in a decade. It wasn't that her grandma was a bad person, in fact she was her mother's mom, so Zami wasn't all that worried from that angle. It was the fact that she could be very... blunt. She wasn't afraid to share her opinions and tell others what she thought of them, which was a good trait to have in general. Just not when you're talking to the second in command of the rebellion, and some of the only friends she had ever had.

No, definitely not good.

When they caught up with Sylvia, she was talking to a man with a bright pink mohawk, and about a thousand visible piercings.

"Of course!" He answered in response to whatever Sylvia had asked. His voice was high and cheery, and he looked like the type of person to offer drugs to little kids in the middle of a funeral. "Anything for you, sweetie!"

Sylvia turned to them with a big smile. "Leon can make the portals." She exclaimed, gesturing her forward. "Just think about the place you remember best, closest to your grandmother." Zami nodded and tried to picture her grandma's house, only to come up blank. Frowning, she conjured the image of the supermarket across the street, which she remembered much more prominently than the house, for some reason.

"Right, here we go!" Leon said and she opened her eyes to see a portal similar to the one she had walked out of not so long ago, at the start of the adventure that would change her forever. And with a deep breath, she stepped through, preparing to deal with her only reasonably safe relative.

Chapter 20

↔

Ray watched as Blu and Strike stumbled out of the portal, Blu whooping and Strike clutching his stomach, face pale. It was an unusual experience, feeling like you're falling and then ending upright in another place. The portal was some sort of warped mix of colors, swirling yellows, blues and greens.

He watched in amusement as Zami, who one would think would be graceful, stumbled out with a curse that he was sure her grandmother would not approve of, holding onto her stomach and a slightly green face. He wasn't sure whether she had forgot she was still wearing his jacket, or just didn't care, but he hoped she wouldn't take it off for a while. She looked adorable. The sleeves hung past her fingertips and the hem fell mid-thigh. She hadn't zipped it up, but he noticed she must've slipped her arms into the sleeves when he hadn't noticed, since he had only laid it over her shoulders while she had been asleep.

"Um, I don't think this is a house." Blu said and Ray glanced around. They were in the middle of a store, several clothing racks in rows around them.

Zami just huffed a breath and walked away. "Come on, we shouldn't go out the front. It'll raise suspicion."

With a glance at his sister, who just shrugged, he followed Zami through the store. Several rows of food ran horizontally across most of the store, providing a blockade from the clerk's eyes in the front. Zami walked to the back of the store, stopping at a door in between rows of meat coolers against the back wall. He watched with a raised eyebrow as she grabbed a pin from her hair and stuck it in the lock, wondering how many times she had done that in the past. Within a second, it clicked open, and she strolled through the door casually. He followed Blu and Strike as they walked through the door beside her, ending up outside in a winter wonderland. Snow covered everything, and small snowflakes trailed leisurely down from the clouds, settling on the ground. It was ethereal, seeing trees covered in icicles and most of the snow left undisturbed by footsteps. He had only seen snow a couple times in his life, so he drilled the memory into his mind.

They trudged through the snow behind Zami, who looked like she was freezing. He supposed she did have it worse than the rest of them. His sister and Sylvia both had a warming power that helped in keeping their body temperature up, and his power did the same when necessary. Strike seemed to be somewhat similar, which made sense, and Blu looked like he was immune to it. Zami looked miserable, as she shuffled through the snow, her cheeks and nose turning red from the biting wind.

"Why'd you remember a shop?" Blu asked, twirling around in the snow and hopping like a little kid.

"I... I got mugged there a c... couple times." Zami chattered out, the 'S' in her sentence coming out slightly garbled. She stared at the ground, crossing her arms against her chest. Ray frowned. Mugged?

"Wait, how old were you? I thought you left for the castle when you were like, five?" Blu asked, having stopped twirling and now looking concerned.

Zami shrugged. "This place re... really s... sucks."

Ray glanced around, only now noticing the stragglers on each corner, smoking and scowling. He supposed it was a bad environment for a lone adult, let alone a five year old girl.

He saw Sylvia and Spark's surprised expressions out of the corner of his eye and he frowned down at his shoes. Zami didn't deserve this. He looked up when she stopped after turning a corner and walking past several houses, staring up at a small house with a wooden porch and wind chimes.

Zami turned on her heel and looked at each of them sternly. "I'm warning you now, most of what she says is bull crap. She's very, very strongly opinionated, and that includes about most people. So don't take anything she says to heart." She turned back around and walked up the steps, knocking twice on the door.

Sharing a look with his sister, they slowly stepped up onto the porch, unsure how to act upon what she just said.

The door in front of them swung open to reveal a small, pouty faced woman. Grey hair was pulled into a bun and despite her age, she stood up perfectly straight at about Zami's height. Which wasn't very imposing.

Her face seemed to be turned in a permanent scowl, and her hazel eyes stared at each of them in disapproval before landing on Zami.

"Zami Wayz!" She cried out, staring in shock at the girl. "What are you doing here?" She pronounced each word with a thick accent, slurring the 'ayz' in Wayz.

"Hey, nana." Zami answered, seemingly unperturbed by the greeting.

"Hey! What do you mean, 'hey'?" Her grandmother yelled. "You haven't shown your face in ten years, and all I get is 'hey'?" She glowered at Zami, then turned her head. "Rando! Get your fine self out here and look who decided to show up!" A man lumbered into view, a cane in hand. He must've been Zami's grandpa, considering the balding hair and hunched back. His smile was sweet though, unlike the woman's, and his eyes sparkled as he looked at Zami.

"Ah Zami, you've grown so much."

Zami smiled lightly and her grandmother gave her another glare before resting her eyes on him.

"And you are..." She asked, eyes still narrowed.

"Oh, uh, Ray." He startled.

She frowned at him. "Your name is oh uh Ray?"

"No." He said quickly, holding out his hand. "I'm Raymond..." He trailed off, unsure whether it was required to share more than that.

She seemed pleased enough with that though, and took his hand with a firm handshake. "See that Zami Wayz?" Her grandmother turned to look at Zami who just looked tired. "That's called manners. Get some." Zami sighed and closed her eyes as her head drooped to her chest. "Now, are you going to introduce me to the rest of these lovely people or am I going to have to spank you?"

Zami looked slightly alarmed at that and whipped her head around. "This is S... Spark, S... Sylvia, S... s... Strike and Blu. You've already met Ray." She gestured to each of them in turn, her teeth chattering. He hadn't realized how many of their names started with 's' before, and he sent a sympathetic glance to Zami who was prone to stutter on the consonant.

Her grandmother studied each of the younger people, with blatant disregard for Sylvia. When her eyes reached him, he stiffened, concerned about sending the right impression. But when her eyes met his, there wasn't any hostility or hatred. In fact, the level of concern in her eyes was more alarming than anything else.

Her grandmother stared at him sadly for a long moment before looking away. "Please come in." Ray stayed behind as the others walked through the door, each sending him a worried look. At his sister's curious look, he shrugged. He had no clue what the old lady was thinking.

He was left with Zami on the porch, who looked perfectly composed, contrary to the previous two minutes. She gave him her signature grin as she straightened up and walked through the door.

"Come on, sunshine." She said, stopping when he didn't respond. For a long moment she searched his eyes and her playful gaze softened. "You didn't do anything. I promise." She gave him a genuine smile before walking away, and he walked in, closing the door behind him, feeling a little bit better.

The house was warm and cozy, walls covered in framed photos and tapestries. To his left was a large study, bookshelves stuffed with uneven stacks of books pressed against each wall. Instead of a desk or anything of that sort, there was a large bright purple couch with various knitted blankets thrown over it, pillows on the floor from where they'd been knocked off. To his right, he could briefly see a large dining table covered in a bright tablecloth as he walked by. In front of them were several more brightly covered couches, with what seemed to be more blankets and pillows with mismatching patterns. A hallway to his left probably led to the bedroom, he guessed, and he grinned when he caught sight of a fluffy cat hopping onto one of the couches. Talk about a crazy cat lady.

The others were crowded into a kitchen, the sink cluttered with unwashed dishes. It was a well lived-in house.

When he heard a squeal, he whipped around in surprise, only to be met with the sight of Zami scooping up the fluffy cat from earlier and rocking it like a baby in her arms.

"Osiris is still here!" She exclaimed in excitement and he watched in amusement as the cat just snuggled into her, purrs rivaling Blu's snores. The cat, Osiris, seemed pleased enough with Zami, and she let out a giggle that made his heart thump, cooing at the cat.

"You're not supposed to hold cats like that, Zami Wayz!" Her grandmother exclaimed, waving a dish towel around. "They don't like it!"

"Seems to me like he doesn't mind." Zami cooly responded, only rocking Osiris harder. "You didn't forget me, did you? No, you remembered me cause I'm your *favorite* Wayz. Isn't that right?" She giggled when the cat let out a little 'mroop' and pressed a kiss to his fluffy forehead.

"If you keep swinging him like that, he's not going to *be able* to remember you! Because he'll be DEAD!" Her grandmother yelled as the rest of them watched in amusement.

"Oh shush." Zami said to the cat. "Don't listen to that cranky old woman. Someone tied their knickers too tight." She continued to sway the cat as her grandmother let out an exasperated sigh.

"I swear to the lord, we need a miracle to make that girl listen."

Zami ignored her, instead grinning up at the others. She looked undeniably happy with the cat in her arms.

"So I'm guessing you didn't just come for a friendly visit. Considering you haven't done that in *ten years.*" Her grandmother said. She pointedly glared at Zami, who was too busy cuddling the cat to care, or notice.

"Yes. We have to ask about something to do with Zami's guardianship." Sylvia said.

"Right. This was bound to happen." Zami's grandma waved at her husband. "How about you show the rest of them to the living room, while this lady and Zami and I talk."

Ray watched as Zami's grandmother opened the back door and gestured for Sylvia and Zami to follow her.

Zami turned to him before leaving. "Hold out your arms." He held out his arms in confusion and watched in shock as she slid the cat into them with a glint in her eyes. "You're welcome." Then she stalked off after her grandmother. The cat stared up at him in confusion, and he raised his eyebrows at it. If he wasn't going crazy, it raised its own back. Then with what seemed to be acceptance, it just laid back in his arms, purring again.

Zami's grandfather chuckled from beside him. "That girl is a handful. Lovely, but a handful." He hobbled over to the couch and Ray followed, sitting beside his sister, who looked very amused at the cat now laying in his lap. He couldn't help but reach down and scratch its chin, smiling when it closed its eyes and nudged into his hand.

"She always loved that cat. Too bad her parents wouldn't let her get one. I think it would've been good for her." Rando said, eyes on the cat in Ray's lap. "Now tell me, who are all of you?" Ray turned to his sister, unsure what to say.

"We're with the rebellion." Spark said, giving the old man a smile.

Rando's eyes widened in surprise. "Zami's gotten herself mixed up in the rebellion?"

"Yeah." Blu answered from beside him, where he was playing with one of Strike's hands. "Is it that surprising?"

Rando shook his head. "No. It's just, her father was a very pro-monarch politician. I'm happy she managed not to be too affected. After what happened to her mother, we didn't know what she was doing, or where she was. We accepted the fact that we might never see her again."

"Wait, so are you her mom's dad?" Blu asked. "Or dad's?"

Rando smiled sadly. "Her mother is my daughter. Amazing woman. Poor choices." He sighed. "Choices that affected Zami."

"No offense, but why didn't her mother just leave him if he was mean?" Blu questioned.

"She refused to. Insisted that he loved her, that he wasn't doing anything wrong. It was her choice really, and we couldn't get her out of it. But if we had known he was hurting Zami too, we would've done something." Ray's heart nearly stopped at that. He was *hurting* Zami? "That's our biggest regret. Not getting her out of there when she needed to be protected." Rando met each of their eyes with a sort of grim realization.

"She does a good job hiding it, doesn't she? You had no clue."

Ray shook his head in disbelief. Sure, he had guessed her father had been mean and that she had been neglected. Heck, based on what Laci had said, he guessed that he hurt her mother. But never her. Not *her*.

"And here she is, dragging herself out of her parents' mess. She's strong. So very strong. The question is," He looked up. "Is she strong enough?" Rando stood up. "I'm going to go get some water, would any of you like anything?" They all shook their heads as he shuffled away. Ray could see his own emotions echoed in the others faces. Concern, disbelief, anger, pretty much everything. He couldn't believe someone would do that.

"I should've noticed. Back in the tent this morning, she jumped when I touched her unwarned." Spark said.

"Remember how she acted with Mayarn and Lev?" Strike breathed.

"That's why she felt so conflicted when she killed Lev." Blu added in.

"She had bruises." Ray said in shock, putting the pieces together. "Bruises when we first met. They were..." Spark touched his shoulder and he trailed off.

"Oh god." Blu exclaimed. "Remember how she flinched when Leon came near her?" Sure enough, he remembered the slight flinch as he had set his hand on her shoulder to bring them there. Ray stared at Osiris, who seemed to be catching onto the mood as he had stopped purring.

"Please don't beat yourselves up about it. It was happening for a long time before you met." Rando said, settling back down with a glass of water. "Plus, I think she's doing okay. Even when she was younger, she wasn't nearly this energetic."

As if to prove his point, they heard a little yell and Zami was sliding through the door with a big smile. When she saw their faces, her smile slowly faded and she stared at them, worry etched into her face.

"Wh..." She started, only to be cut off by her grandmother.

"ZAMI!"

"I'M GETTING IT!" She yelled back, glancing at them one more time before disappearing into the hallway. After a moment she came back with a book and then she was gone again.

"Her grandmother really loves her." Rando said, smiling gently at the door.

"Really? It doesn't sound like it." Blu said, frowning at the man.

Rando laughed and took a sip of his water. "It's a love-hate relationship. They're too similar to get along like you all likely do with her." He glanced at Ray. "Some of you more than others."

Ray coughed and turned away, feeling the cat give an annoyed 'mroop' at his sudden movement. Out of the corner of his eye, he could see Rando wink at Blu, who gave a little laugh.

"Would you like to see pictures of Zami when she was little? We only have up to about five, but I think you might enjoy seeing them." Ray nearly laughed. No matter in what situation, they were still very much grandparents. And everyone knew grandparents thought their grandchildren were little angels.

"Ooh yes, blackmail!" Blu exclaimed in excitement.

As Rando stood to get something from the other room, Strike nudged Blu. "Some friend you are."

Blu pulled an innocent face, which didn't look the least bit innocent. "Whatever do you mean, my fair-haired, Strike-at-my-heart?"

Strike narrowed his eyes at Blu. "I thought we agreed on *not* using our pet names as puns."

"Of course, our love hits me like lightning." Blu said, dodging a smack. "You know..." He said, grabbing Strike's wrists. "You're just *striking* in this light."

Strike groaned, pulling his wrists out and covering his face. "If you don't shut up, I'm breaking up with you."

"That's quite... shocking." Blu giggled madly as Strike whipped him on the head. Then Strike froze for a second, face completely serious.

"You really *breeze* through those puns."

Blu's mouth dropped open in shock and his eyes bugged out. Then he was smiling widely, as he tackled Strike into a hug.

"This is why I love you!" He exclaimed and Strike laughed.

"Don't get used to it."

"The puns, or loving you?"

"Depends."

"On what?"

"How high you are on Zami's hit-list."

"Hit-list?" Blu exclaimed, pulling away from Strike. Ray watched them, smiling. They may be cheesy, but that was better than not being in love. He could imagine them years from now, still madly in love, making puns and fighting over useless things. *But by then*, he thought, grinning, *There'll be a ring involved.*

Before Strike had the chance to elaborate about Zami's hit list, Rando appeared again, beaming.

"This one holds the best ones!"

There were multiple meanings behind those words, Ray was sure, but he didn't have long to contemplate it before Rando was gesturing them all towards him.

Ray leaned over the back of the couch, watching as Rando opened up the book. The first picture was of him and his wife holding a baby, a beautiful young woman standing beside them, arm around Zami's grandma and eyes staring lovingly at the bundle in their arms. Another picture showed the same woman holding the baby in a white bed, looking tired but happy. The resemblance between her and Zami was uncanny. Dark silky hair, shining hazel eyes, a small nose and long lashes. Even her smile looked exactly like Zami's. Baby Zami was small and happy. A toothy, or rather, a gummy grin, spread across her little face, eyes sparkling with mischief.

"She was such a happy baby." Rando said, tracing his fingers over the picture. "She looks so much like her mother now. It's unbelievable." He flipped the page to reveal Zami, in what seemed to be a year later, with a small label scribbled beneath the paper. *'First Birthday'*

She had an evil glint in her eyes, one that was still there today. Her hair had grown quite a bit and her smile was malicious in her mother's arms. A couple other pictures showed her playing with toys, laughing in her mother's arms, asleep on Rando's chest. There was no sign of her dad.

Then there was two year old Zami, showing an incredible skill for reading at that age, while balancing on the edge of the couch. One picture showed her mother mid-lunge to protect her, as Zami stared at her innocently from high up on a counter.

"She was so smart already. Nearly gave her mother a few heart-attacks though."

Ray chuckled. That sounded like Zami.

Then there she was another year later, looking every bit independent. She wasn't smiling anymore, but instead, grinning in a way that no three year old should be able to. She stood behind a card house, with a proud look on her little face.

The next picture was her with her arms crossed, eyes focused on Rando, who was dancing in a silly way. Her face was scrunched up in obvious judgement, looking too serious for the bright yellow sundress they had put her in.

"She acted like she was a decade older than she was. She was a very independent three-year old." Rando laughed as he flipped the page. Then there was a four year old Zami, eyes averted from the camera. The previous grin on her face had transformed into more of a wince, and she gripped her sides, looking extremely worried. The picture next to that showed her in a similar stance, except her left wrist was in a deep blue cast. She wore darker clothes than before, and her jacket and pants covered more skin.

"They insisted it was a bike accident. Went too fast down the street and landed wrong on her wrist. Up to this day, that's the last picture we had of her." Rando said, trailing off.

"I never even owned a bike." Ray turned to see Zami standing beside him, eyes on the picture. "I mean, if you're gonna lie about something like that, at least come up with a justifiable one." She sighed, shaking her head. "I honestly don't know how he even managed to get into politics. Dumb as a brick, that man."

To his surprise, Rando laughed, reaching around to pat her arm. "Ever the optimist, I see."

"Says the man who's sharing depressing stories about me with the friends I met barely a month ago." She responded with a smirk.

"I'm glad to see you again."

Zami smiled sadly, and he couldn't help but think that in that moment, she looked quite like the picture from when she was four. Yes, she was older, and so much had changed. But at the same time, nothing had changed at all. Except now he knew why she wrapped her arms around herself, why she had a hard time looking men in the eyes, why she had such terrible nightmares. He knew. And that made all the difference.

"Anyway, if you're done ruining my reputation, I believe we've come to an agreement with the papers. Sylvia and Marcia are signing it off right now."

As if to prove her words, her grandmother, who they now finally knew was named Marcia, stomped back into the room. Sylvia was behind her, holding a paper and looking triumphant.

As Marcia passed Zami, she growled. "You better not die until I go. That's far too much paperwork for an old woman with arthritis."

"I'll keep that in mind." Zami responded, amusement sparkling in her eyes. Then she leaned over to him and he tilted his head so he could hear her. "Remind me again, what's the easiest way to get away with murder?" She whispered.

He raised his eyebrow at her. "Come again?"

"I HEARD THAT, ZAMI WAYZ!"

"So you can hear me from across the house, but signing three pages because your granddaughter needs it is too much to ask?"

Marcia didn't respond to that, whether because she didn't hear her, or chose to ignore it, he wasn't sure. Zami mumbled something that sounded an awful lot like "horse face" and stuck her tongue out in the direction of her grandmother.

Ray couldn't help but let out a chuckle at the sight, and Zami turned to look at him.

"Have something to say, *goal post*?"

He glanced around, seeing the others had disappeared to go talk to Sylvia, and gave her a grin. "Actually, yeah I do."

She frowned at him and huffed a breath. "What?"

To his surprise, it wasn't hostile or defensive, more nervous than anything. He realized she must be worried that he was going to say something about what he had just found out. With his heart thumping, he reached out and pulled her into him, grinning at the little "umph" she let out.

"You're really cute." He felt her stiffen in surprise but after a moment she relaxed into him.

"You know what? I'm gonna let that slide, just this once." She nuzzled her head against his neck, arms tightening around his waist. He shifted his weight from one foot to another, rocking side to side in small motions that made her giggle. After a minute or so he stopped, standing still and listening to her even breaths.

"You're not gonna' like... ask me about what my grandpa told you?" She sounded nervous again, and with a soft smile he pulled back, keeping his hands on her shoulders.

"You know what, Zames? No, I'm not. You can tell us whatever you want, whenever you want. We're not here to judge you or force you to do something you don't want to. We're here so when you need it, you *have* someone to talk to." He searched her eyes which were opened wide. "That's what friends are for. That's what it means to care about someone."

She stared at him for a long moment before turning away and tucking a loose strand of hair behind her ear. "Do you suddenly become a poet when you're around me?"

He knew what she was doing, and reached forward to grab her hand. No words were needed when she met his gaze, and for a long moment he was sure she was going to make another sarcastic comment. Then her resolve crumbled and her gaze fell to the ground.

"I... I'm just so confused Ray. I had no one. And now..." she gestured to the space around them, looking both sad and worried. "I have more than I ever expected." Her voice was quiet, a sure sign that she really *was* trying to hold back a whole bunch of emotions.

"Then how about you use that. Use the fact that you have people to lean on, people to talk to." He stared at her for a long moment before adding "And to help beat your dad to a pulp." To his relief, she laughed, still looking down, but like maybe everything was going to turn out fine.

"You've got your priorities straight." She teased, nudging his arm with her shoulder. "I like that in a man."

He laughed, linking his arm through hers. "Come on, 'miss priorities' we've got to go set something straight with the others."

"To be fair, I don't think there's anything *straight* about Blu's and Strike's priorities."

"Touché." He said as she dragged him to where the others were, seemingly in a very graphic discussion about the ways Zami could die while they were on a mission.

"Oh! oh!" Blu called. "Don't forget defenestration!"

"Should I be concerned about your extensive knowledge and vocabulary of ways to die, when you don't even know the word 'toad'?" Strike asked.

"They're just overweight frogs!" Blue exclaimed overzealously. "I don't get why we feel the need to have a billion different words for the SAME THING!"

"Yet you know several different methods of drowning people." Strike deadpanned. "And a word for just about everything you could do to kill someone."

Blu scoffed. "Come on man! Cut me some slack will ya'? I promised myself that if I didn't do something great by sixteen, then I was gonna become a serial killer. I've just been getting prepared."

"Wait, how old are you again?" Ray asked, slightly alarmed.

"So anyway." Sylvia cut in, interrupting Blu's answer. "I believe Zami now has an actual guardian. So that means we can go on the next mission whenever we figure out the riddles."

"Wait, those papers you were holding are riddles?" Blu asked. "I thought it was just a bunch of letters."

"Come on, let's get out of here." Strike said, pulling Blu out the door. Ray grinned as he heard the startled yelp and then, "What the heck, Strike!"

"Sorry about him, he can be quite... eccentric." Sylvia said.

"Eccentric is better than hard-headed." Marcia said, and they all turned to glance at the implied person with said personality trait. Zami just averted her eyes, looking up somewhere on the ceiling and cracking her knuckles.

When they didn't look away, she shrugged. "Emotions and murder don't go well together." She pointed out. He supposed she had a point.

Marcia huffed an impatient breath. "It was nice meeting you all. Now shoo!"

Ray laughed as he stepped out of the house and made his way over to Blu and Strike. They both stood under a big pine tree, shuffling their feet in the snow and talking with little wisps of breath that showed in the cold. They had one arm curled around each other, grinning like a newly married couple.

"Hey." He said, stuffing his hands in his pockets, more out of habit than coldness.

They both smiled at him as he turned to face the same way as them. Sylvia and his sister had just stepped off the porch, in deep conversation about something. He watched as the door opened again, this time with Zami and her grandparents. Marcia said something that caused Zami to smile sadly, then Rando said something else that made her laugh. He watched as Rando gave her a big hug and Zami returned it. He had never really seen her hug someone else, as even Sylvia's hugs had been too brief, and he wondered if she hunched her shoulders that much when he hugged her. Then Rando patted her on the shoulder and said something before walking into the house, leaving Zami and her grandmother.

Marcia said something, a long reprimand he supposed, by Zami's nods and Marcia's grim expression. They stood there for a long moment before Marcia grabbed both of Zami's shoulders and pulled her into an awkward, but loving hug. It was short, but somehow it held enough feeling that he could feel the waves of multiple emotions rolling off of them. Then Marcia walked back into the house and closed the door, leaving Zami standing alone on the porch. She didn't move for a long moment, rocking onto the balls of her feet and clutching her arms around herself. As she walked down the steps, she kept her expression fairly neutral, until something white flew through the air and her hand whipped out, somehow catching the snowball in mid-flight. Ray looked around to see Blu, arm outstretched, looking miffed.

"Hey! That's not fair!" Then he yelped, ducking behind Strike, who looked thoroughly betrayed. But the snowball never hit either of them; instead, he felt it slam into his chest, sending a chill down his body. He looked up in shock to Zami, who was trying to look innocent.

"Whoops. I must've missed."

He raised an eyebrow at her. "I'm *sure* you did." He reached down and scooped up some snow, catching Blu doing the same thing. Zami let out a giggle before running away to duck behind a couple trees. He watched his sister join her, and he suddenly became very worried that two of the most dangerous women in his life were plotting against him.

"Truce?" Blu offered to him.

"Truce."

Ray smiled as he observed the people around the bonfire. Most he didn't know; he recognized the pink-haired girl from when they first arrived, and he had seen some of the others walking around. Everyone talked in hushed voices among their groups, and he was reminded of high school, with all the cliques.

To his right sat Blu and Strike, both looking very content. Blu was leaning against one of the crates that had been dragged out for sitting, Strike settled between his legs, leaning back against his chest. His head rested on Blu's shoulder, and Blu had his hands lazily wrapped around him, Strike's hands laced in his. He almost thought they were asleep, until he watched Strike mumble something to Blu, whose response made him smile and snuggle further into the other.

He glanced to his left and watched Zami slide against the crate beside his to sit down, bringing her legs up to her chest. She had removed his jacket, which he supposed was likely because it was wet from all the snow. Though that was mostly his fault, considering he had been the only one who had managed to hit her. She didn't look miffed though, in fact the first time he managed to get her on the leg, she gave him a beaming smile. Blu had been quite irritated that Ray and Zami were the only ones who could hit each other, while he was getting pelted regularly. Perks of having their type of magic, he supposed.

She had now donned a thick grey turtleneck sweater that suited her incredibly well, along with her normal black leggings and boots. Though she was pretty much completely dry, he could see the slight dampness of her hair, where he had 'accidentally' hit her in the back of the head. Needless to say, she took revenge very seriously.

He watched as she brought her hand up to her mouth, chewing on her index finger in a nervous habit. She had a lot of those, now that he thought about it. Though, he supposed that happened when you were constantly nervous. Her right foot tapped the floor in an even pattern of triplets and she tucked an invisible piece of hair behind her ear. Occasionally her hand trailed down to the bandage on her thigh and then she would wince, bringing her hands up to her ribs.

"Hey, Zames?"

She looked up. "Yeah?"

"Was that the only injury that still hurts?" He asked, eyes on the white gauze on her leg. The pause she had before she responded was all the answer he needed. "Did you get the other ones looked at?" He asked, trying to gauge an answer from her reaction.

She looked away guiltily. "They aren't that bad. Just some bruising."

He sighed. "Fine. But promise if it gets worse, you'll get it checked."

"Yeah, yeah, whatever." She leaned over so her head was on his shoulder and he smiled, shifting slightly to make her more comfortable.

"Whatever." He mocked. She grinned, wrapping her arms around her legs. But truthfully, in that moment, he was feeling much more than just "whatever".

Chapter 21

↔

Zami stared at her neat writing lined across the page. It didn't make sense. It was like someone had taken a riddle and jumbled the words into a random order. She shifted forward on the seat. Okay, so what if it was just a scrambled riddle? How would you solve that?

Leaning forward, she reached to grab a pen off of the table. She placed a new sheet of paper next to the other, which was slightly crumpled from everyone looking at it and trying to decipher it. The words converged in her mind, possible combinations floating in and out of conscious thought. She let her instincts take over and began to reorder the words, sticking to a basic rhyming pattern. It was a long shot, but at least it was something.

She didn't know how much time she spent hunched over the paper, trying to make sense of it, but after the eleventh time re-writing she sat back, eyes widening as she read it.

With the rise of the sun my peak will show
Under bellowing mountains
Where secrets grow

I only open to the portal of the past
You must find your key
To that of which you lacked

In me is
What you desire to have
But proceed with caution
Even the dove gets mad

When you find me look
In the rivers eye
Where the rest of this clue
There will reside

She slammed her head down onto the table with a frustrated groan. She had been sure she had been getting somewhere, when she thought about it being an anagram. It seemed no matter what she did, it was still rubbish.

"You good?" Strike asked in amusement from the seat across from her. Blu and Ray had gone off to sleep, at least she had assumed, and Strike and her being night owls had stayed up. He sat curled up, as much as he could with his long legs, reading what seemed to be a thriller novel.

"I need to hit something." She groaned, slamming the side of her fist into the table.

"As long as that something's not me, go ham."

Sitting up, she studied Strike, who was smiling at her with something close to affection. His dark curls fell across his brow and his yellow eyes glinted warmly in the firelight.

"Are you giving me permission to whoop your boyfriend's arse?"

"You always have permission to whoop my boyfriend's arse."

"I'll keep that in mind." She mumbled, dropping her head to the table again.

"Just take a walk. Look at it with fresh eyes." He offered.

"Why can't you look at it?"

"I'm rubbish at riddles."

With a sigh, she stood up and pushed in the chair. She mentally noted to always listen to Strike's advice, because as soon as she stepped into the chilly air, all her anger dissipated. She really needed to learn to control her temper before she did something rash.

Careful of people passing by, she skirted the edges of the camp, observing everyone in it. She watched as a girl grabbed a boy's arm and pulled him over to a table with a book on it, pointing *something out to him.* Then something clicked into place.

The four desirables were symbols of War, Peace, Hate and Love. No one knows for sure where any are located, and we can only assume that they're still there.

Doves were a symbol for peace. Right? Her heart thumped in her chest as she hurried back to the tent. Maybe her latest version wasn't wrong!

She ignored Strike's startled jump when she stormed back into the tent, instead beelining straight for the paper she had been scribbling on.

Even the dove gets mad

What you desire to have

She couldn't help a smile spreading across her face. Every minute she was getting more and more certain that this was what they were supposed to be looking at.

"The walk help?" Strike asked, sounding amused.

"Yes!" She exclaimed in excitement, shoving the paper over to him. "Look!"

He set down his book, leaning over to read the paper. "Well that's an ambiguous riddle." He offered lamely, looking up at her. She just waited to see if he would connect anything. After a long moment of rereading it he sighed. "I give. What's so important about this?"

She grabbed the paper and read the two lines out to him. *"Even the dove gets mad. What you desire to have."*

She sighed at his blank expression. "One of the desirables is peace, right?" He nodded. "What's a common symbol for peace?" She watched triumphantly as understanding dawned on him.

"A dove."

"Exactly!"

"And it says what we desire to have." He added, standing to look at the paper again.

"Yeah!' She squealed in excitement.

"You did it!" He said, turning to look at her in admiration.

She nodded with a big grin. "I did it."

"I'll get Sylvia." He said, grabbing his sneakers from the floor and pulling them on as he hopped out of the tent.

Only seconds later, Sylvia was bounding in, red hair flying. It was obvious she had still been up, considering her daytime clothes and alert expression.

Zami bounced on the balls of her feet as Sylvia read the paper, catching on quicker than Strike had.

"This is it!" Sylvia exclaimed, giving Zami a proud grin. "You got it!"

She smiled shyly, feeling ecstatic that she had done something so good.

Before Sylvia could say anything else, a loud yell came from outside, followed by a shout and a startled cry. She shared a concerned glance with Sylvia, sprinting out of the tent behind her. As she ran through the crowded tents, the shouting got louder and louder, and eventually two figures came into view.

She wasn't even surprised to identify one as Laci, screaming at the pink haired girl from earlier who was on the ground. Holly and Rip, her two friends, stood on either side of her, cocking their hips and frowning.

"WHAT THE HECK!"

"Hey! Hey!" Sylvia called, stepping between the two. "What's going on?"

"She pushed me!" Laci yelled, holding her shoulder like she had been burned. Sylvia looked irritated.

"Are you sure it wasn't an accident?"

"Why would it be!" Laci complained and Zami couldn't help but roll her eyes. Nearly ten years and nothing had changed.

"Calm down." Sylvia said. "You're not hurt!" But Laci's eyes had already found hers, and she was no longer interested in the girl on the ground.

"What are you staring at, loser!"

Zami let out an exasperated sigh as Laci stormed forward, leaning closer than she was comfortable with. She tried to push down the panic that arose in the all too familiar situation. Except now, she wasn't going to stand for this crap.

"If it makes you feel better to make a big deal out of something that's not a big deal, get mad at me all you want." She answered calmly, watching Sylvia slowly back up from where she had been about to step in. It was important that she handle this calmly, both to create the right reputation and as a role model. The people here didn't know who she was yet, but once they did, she had to project a good face, to be known as someone trustworthy.

"You little brat! You haven't changed at all."

Zami wrinkled her nose when she felt a little bit of spit fly from Laci's sneer. She opted not to say anything, knowing that everything she said would just be used against her. Everything seemed to go in slow motion, as she watched Laci raise her hand and heard Sylvia and Strike both yell. Then she felt a sharp sting on her cheek, and she found herself staring at the kids to her right. Slowly, she turned her head back to stare at Laci, maintaining eye contact as she reached up to the corner of her mouth and drew her fingers away to reveal blood.

She was staring at her dad in her house. His glare was piercing and her cheek stung from where he had slapped her. Panic filled her body and everyone of her instincts told her to flee. She couldn't be here again, she couldn't.

"I said, WHERE IS YOUR MOTHER?" He screamed, stepping uncomfortably close to her. She couldn't help but shake, fear building in her gut. Her body refused to respond. He growled and she was barely able to register what happened, before she was on the floor, gripping her stomach.

"She... she's at th... the store." She mumbled out between a cough.

"What did I tell you about that stupid stutter? Stop it! People are going to think you're messed up!" He yelled, grabbing her shirt and pulling her up. "And everyone knows that *I* am not the father of..."

"What's going on? What are you doing?"

Zami blinked back into reality to see Laci, looking at her in disgust and fear. When she turned around, she was met with a terrified Sylvia and concerned Strike.

"Zami!" Strike yelled. "Stop!"

She looked down to see rapidly moving tendrils snaking across the ground, curling around people's feet and wisping into the air. Everyone looked absolutely terrified, which only caused her to panic more.

"I can't!" She yelled back, voice coming out slightly strangled, as she tried and failed to will the darkness back in. It just kept spreading. All she could see was her father, his angry glowering and physical abuse. She tried to tell her power *no*, to please stop, she couldn't hurt anyone else, but it didn't listen. The ringing became incessant in her ears and she squeezed her eyes shut, gripping her head with her hands. She couldn't think straight, couldn't fix what was happening. It was too much. Too much for her to handle. Too much.

She could hear screaming, and feel the unsettling darkness settling in the air. It wasn't even necessary to look, to know that everything was pitch black. People's startled yells and terrified shrieks were enough. Amongst all the chaos, she could hear her name being called, but she couldn't call back. Couldn't seem to get her mouth to open.

Then, all at once, everything was better. The ringing disappeared along with her father's face. After a long moment, when her senses returned to normal, she realized she was being held tightly in someone's arms. It was so silent that she could hear Ray's heartbeat, but she didn't even bother opening her eyes to see the expressions she would be met with. Fear, disgust, and disappointment. No, she'd much rather just stay standing there, face buried in his chest and soaking in the feeling of calm she had when he held her.

"What happened?" Ray's voice was filled with an edge she'd never heard before, and it seemed like he wasn't even asking a question. More like demanding an answer.

Laci began to say something in a shrill tone, most likely a lie, but Sylvia drowned out her voice with her own.

"We came out to see Laci yelling at Sydney, and then she just started yelling at Zami. *Unprovoked.*" Sylvia sounded angrier than they had ever seen her as she continued. "She *hit* her." Zami could feel the waves of unsettled anger rolling off of the boy in front of her, and for the sake of the alliance, she opted to step in before he could do anything to Laci. No matter how badly she would like to see that.

"It's fine. I was just surprised, and lost control." She said, pulling away from Ray and trying to put on her normal poker face. She was unprepared, however, for the faces she was met with; ones of sympathy, concern, protectiveness. She had been expecting fear and loathing, but she wasn't prepared for this response.

She felt her resolve falter as she realized *why* they looked like that at in response to someone hitting her. They knew the world dissolved into memories of her father, the moment Laci raised her hand. All of her plans to act like everything was fine seemed to crumble beneath her feet as she stared at the crowd of people surrounding them. She felt like she was five again, standing helplessly in front of a bunch of older, meaner kids. She couldn't handle this, not again. It was all too familiar.

Knowing what was bound to happen with the new wave of panic coursing through her, she backed up, the kids behind her spreading out. With one last glance at the others, she ran. She didn't know where she was running, but she did, not noticing when she made her way through the base and out of the tunnel, finding herself in the forest again. Not caring about the ache in her legs and chest as she stumbled through the scratchy bushes, ignoring the startled yells from the guards.

When she finally stopped, her throat burned and her legs ached even more. Barely able to take another step, she stumbled to the ground, pressing her back against a tree. *It's alright*, she told herself. *You're alone now. You can't hurt anyone, and they can't see you anymore.*

With a shaky sigh, she stared at the ground, trying to take deep, calming breaths. But the panicked hyperventilation wouldn't stop, and her breath got caught in her throat as tears began to well in her eyes. She couldn't cry now, not over something so stupid. Not after she had managed not to for so long.

But the tears came anyway, in hot streams down her cheeks, landing on her legs. She hadn't cried in so long it felt almost like a relief, like tension was flowing out of her with each tear. So she let her body shake with deep, wracking sobs that sounded pathetic, even to herself. She buried her face in her knees and covered her head with her arms, squeezing her eyes shut against the slightly damp cloth. She found herself unconsciously rocking back and forth in a manner meant to be soothing. But the tears didn't stop after a minute or ten or even thirty. They just kept coming, and coming, and she thought in that moment, that she had never felt so alone.

She cried herself to sleep that night, despair filling her. Because right then it felt like no matter who she met, no matter what she did, the empty feeling in her chest would never, ever go away again.

Chapter 22

Ray held the paper like he was paying attention, but in reality he could only focus on one thing. Zami hadn't come back that night, or the next morning, all day, or last night. Now it was evening the next day, marking almost two days that she had been gone. He could tell it was affecting the others' moods too; Blu, Strike, Spark, even Sylvia. All of them were terrified for her and what she was going through right now. He hadn't realized how close they had become, how tightly dependent they were on each other. And now the person who seemed to make everything feel better, more light-hearted, was gone. And they had no clue what she was doing, how she was, and where she was.

He felt like he was over-reacting, but the last time someone had left him, they had never come back. So now, he couldn't help but panic a little about whether she was okay or not. He was trying to keep it together though, considering everyone at the camp was now aware of who he and Zami were, and what they were meant to do. Every step he took, he was being watched, judged for his character and the hopes of the rebellion. He reminded himself that he had been practicing his whole life for this. It wasn't a surprise; he knew people were going to be watching his every move. So he just did things like always, trying to keep his cool every time he saw Laci, and holding Blu back from doing anything to her as well. Although one part of his mind urged him to beat the crap out of her, he knew that was not the right thing to do. That's not what a gentleman would do, no matter how horrible the person.

Sometimes he wished he wasn't a gentleman.

"Ray! Ray! Have you been paying any attention to what I've been saying?"

He blinked at Sylvia who was standing in front of him with a cocked hip. "Um... yes." He lied.

"Fine. Then what did I just say?"

"Fine. Then what did I just say?" He answered, blinking up at her with as much innocence as he could feign.

"No! Before that!" She said, narrowing her eyes at him.

"Um... I believe you said, and I quote. 'Ray! Ray! Have you been paying any attention to what I was saying?'" He said, raising his voice to her octave. He was rewarded with a smack to the head with a book. "Ow!" He yelped, rubbing his head, not really in pain. "What was that for?"

"Ray! You're supposed to save the world, you can not afford to be daydreaming about Zami!"

He frowned at her. "I wasn't daydreaming. I was thinking."

She rolled her eyes. "I'm sure you were. Thinking about kissing."

He gaped at her bluntness, feeling his face redden. "Sylvia!" He exclaimed, trying to ignore the rambunctious laughter coming from Blu and Strike. She whistled, looking up at the ceiling, like she hadn't done anything. However, it was only when she began talking again, that he realized she had been trying to lighten up the mood and joke a little bit. Glancing around, he thought it must have worked, because everyone seemed a little more relaxed then before.

"So tomorrow, you'll leave in the portal to your childhood homes to find that 'key' from the riddle. You'll need to sort through your memories, for something big from your youth. Something that caused a major difference in your life. Find it, and return. We only have three days before Leon leaves and won't be around to create portals, so if you don't want to do a bunch more walking, you'll need to get this done quickly."

Ray nodded along with the others. They had all talked and decided that the word "key" in the riddle must be something that had changed their lives. Something important that symbolized a new beginning.

"Oh, and remember, only you four need to find something. Since you three and Zami are the ones we believe are central to the riddle. However," Sylvia raised her finger up. "There will be a few others joining you on the journey." She turned back to a board filled with pinned papers. "Now, shoo."

Ray sighed, standing up and grabbing his jacket.

"What about Zami?" Blu asked and Ray froze, waiting for the answer.

"She'll come when she comes." Sylvia said, and he knew that was the end of the conversation. With a deep breath, he pulled his jacket on and zipped it up, stuffing his hands in his pockets. She would come back... right? He would like to say he knew for sure that she was, but he didn't even know that much about her. Heck, he didn't know that she was abused to that level until a couple days ago.

He watched as Strike and Blu walked off, arm and arm, deep in conversation. His sister was gone too, having left on a scouting mission. She had hugged him tightly before leaving, insisting that she would be fine. He sure hoped so, he had just gotten her back in his life.

Unsure what to do, he shuffled down the rows of tents for a while, barely paying attention to what was going on around him. It felt weirdly *wrong* to just be doing nothing.

Keeping his head down, he eventually made his way back to the tent he had been sharing with Blu and Strike. When he slipped in, he was met with the sweet sight of Strike laying on his back, reading a book, with Blu's head on his stomach. Blu was blabbering about some random facts and theories, and Strike nodded when appropriate, not actually seeming to pay attention. With a smile at the two of them and a wave at Blu, he grabbed his backpack and slung it over his shoulder.

"If Sylvia asks, I'm taking a walk." He said, not waiting to hear their responses before walking out of the tent again. It was fairly easy to slip by the guards, who seemed not to care about people going out as much as in. Once in the camp, there was an easier exit to use, so in a few minutes he was standing in the familiar dark forest. He hadn't tried to reach out to Zami for the pure respect of her privacy. If she needed time she could have it. But that didn't keep him from walking around, both to clear his head and keep an eye out.

Nothing unusual happened, so he just ended up walking around, breathing in the fresh air, deep in thought for nearly an hour before he realized that he should probably get back. With one more longing look back at the trees, he returned to the base.

When he walked in, Blu was asleep already, and Strike's hand dropped from where it had been in Blu's hair down to his stomach. Strike's book laid open on his chest, and Ray watched as his eyes flutter closed. He sighed in amusement, reaching down and picking up the book, setting it down closed beside the two. He decided against covering them with a blanket, because there was no comfortable way to do it when they were in such a position, and slipped off his shoes and jacket, laying down, head on his pack.

That night his dreams were filled with scary possibilities of where Zami was and whether she was hurt. Around three in the morning, he woke up in a cold sweat, and even though he laid back down after a moment, he knew he wasn't going to be getting any more sleep that night.

Despite his hopes, Zami didn't show up the next morning either. He half-heartedly ate an apple, as Sylvia reminded Blu that he couldn't afford to get distracted when they went home. "Get the object and get out" was the objective. Luckily for them, both Strike and Blu should be able to find their objects in one place, since Strike lived there for so much of his life.

With a sigh, he stood and tossed out the apple core, grabbing his jacket since he wasn't sure how cold it would be where they were going.

The answer turned out to be *way* too hot.

"How did you guys live here?" Ray panted, peeling his shirt from where it was sticking to his chest. They had only walked through the portal about three minutes ago, and he already felt unbearably hot, hair plastered to his forehead and sweat running down his back.

"It's not *that* hot, dude." Blu said, looking amused at his suffering. Neither he nor Strike seemed to have been having an issue with the temperature.

"Says you." He said, pushing his hair back. "It has to be at least a thousand degrees right now."

"Actually, it's only Ninety-three." Came a statement from right behind them.

Ray jumped in surprise as Blu and Strike both let out a startled yelp. Then Ray froze. There was only one person in the whole wide world who could sneak up on him like that.

Sure enough, there she was, standing in all her Zami-like glory, playful smirk still intact. She looked exactly as she had a couple days ago, before she had run away.

"Where the wazzocks did you come from?" Blu yelped, holding his chest and breathing heavily.

"My mom, I hope." She responded, eyes everywhere but on them.

"Yeah, yeah, okay whatever." Blu said. "Let's go."

Ray followed him, studying the house they were walking up to. It was tall and good size, maybe three stories high and well kept.

"Who's your daddy?" He murmured and Zami snorted beside him.

Blu sent him a look before clearing his throat and straightening his shirt. "Just be warned, if you meet my dad or brother, they aren't mean. Just... snotty."

"His dad's the mayor." Strike whispered to them as Blu knocked. That made a lot of sense he supposed.

A yell came from behind the door, before it opened to reveal a young woman, all bright blue hair and violet eyes. She was wearing an odd mix of plaid pajama pants and a mustard yellow blouse.

"BLU!" She shrieked, tackling him into a hug and drawing a muffled yelp from Blu. When she pulled away, she was bouncing up and down on her feet and he could almost feel her energy vibrating in the air. Definitely Blu's sister.

"Hey, Cyn." Blu said, grinning at her.

"Aw, you haven't grown since you left." She cooed, ruffling his hair. "Strike!" She yelled, spotting the boy. Her mouth dropped open in surprise as she stared at him. "You've grown like a foot!"

Strike laughed and ducked his head shyly. "Hi Cynthia."

She galloped over to him and gave him a hug so hard that Ray could see him wince. "What are you doing here?" She asked, a little loudly for a normal talking voice. Well, there was another thing she had in common with Blu.

"I have to find something..." Blu said, glancing off into the distance.

"Well, you better be quick, Andy's coming home in about an hour."

"We will be." Blu said, grinning madly.

"Oh, everyone's going to be so happy to see you!" She squealed, walking back into the house as she talked. Ray raised his eyebrow and followed behind Blu and Strike. He watched as Strike leaned over to whisper something in Blu's ear, which caused Blu to giggle and say something back. Strike swung at his head in response, though it was more affectionate than anything, and Blu ducked with a laugh.

The halls on either side of them held picture after picture of the family, which seemed to be fairly large. To his surprise, Blu was still in all of them, and Ray couldn't help but laugh when he saw a picture of Blu and Strike years ago. Sure enough, Strike had been considerably shorter than Blu at a time, and in the picture Blu seemed to be trying to teach Strike to skateboard. They must've been only ten in the photo. Pre-teen Strike looked absolutely terrified, standing on the board and holding onto Blu's shoulder with both hands. Blu was mid-laugh, his blue hair shorter than it was now, and his face scrunched up. It was obvious even in a photo how connected they were, how much they loved each other.

He didn't have time to look at many other pictures before they broke into a large room, a staircase spiraling to their left and a large open kitchen on their right. Blu went straight for the staircase, bounding up it with surprising dexterity.

"It's a wonder he hasn't fallen off of it, after so many years of being so careless." Cynthia sighed. "That boy has broken so many bones we could make a house out of all the casts he's needed." Ray grinned, unable to even say he was surprised. Blu seemed the sort to get in such situations.

A woman walked out of a room next to the staircase, freezing when she saw them. Her hair was also blue, tied up in a messy bun. She looked exhausted, with dark circles under her eyes. In her arms was a baby, resting on her hips, a little bald head resting on her shoulder.

"Cynthia..." She began, blinking at them. Then her eyes landed on Strike who was still with them, and something flashed through her eyes. "Strike. You've grown so much. What..." Her voice broke and he watched as she handed the baby to Cynthia before stepping forward and gathering Strike in a hug. "Where's Blu? Did something happen? Wh..."

"Blu's fine." Strike said with a smile. "He's actua..."

"GOT IT!"

"-lly right there." Strike finished as Blu jumped over the banister and landed on the floor, beaming.

"Blu! How many times have I told you not to do that!" His mother reprimanded, cocking her hip and pointing her finger at him. You could get hurt!"

"Sorry." Blu said, trying, and failing, to look sorry. His mother just sighed, running her hand over her face. "Come here, baby." Blu walked up to his mother and she hugged him too, rocking back and forth slightly, face buried in his hair as she stroked his head. Then she frowned. "You are going to sit your cute butt down and explain everything that's happened since you left. Oh, you are in *so* much trouble!" She gripped his ear and dragged him into the kitchen, eliciting several yelps from Blu.

Cynthia laughed as they heard Blu's mother's voice echoing through the halls, as she shoved him into a kitchen chair.

"That boy's a trouble magnet." She rocked the baby on her hip and he gave an excited babble. "This is Bryce."

Ray smiled at the baby's vibrant eyes and gummy grin, raising an eyebrow when he heard a little intake of breath from beside him.

"Oh, he's so *cute!*" Zami squealed, eyes sparkling. The baby seemed to like her and reached out a pudgy arm to grab her.

Cynthia laughed. "You can hold him if you'd like."

Zami's eyes widened. "Can I?" She breathed.

Ray watched, slightly amused, as Cynthia slid Bryce into Zami's arms. The baby stared at Zami for a long moment before jabbering loudly and grabbing her shirt. Something rushed through Ray when Zami giggled, cooing at the baby and swaying a little bit.

"Hold on, I'm going to go tell Daren and Harmony that Blu's here." Cynthia said, rushing up the stairs.

"I didn't know you liked babies so much, Zami." Strike remarked, seemingly amused.

"Of course I do!" Zami said, grinning at Bryce. "Who wouldn't. Isn't that right? You're just so lovable and chubby!" She lifted the baby and he squealed happily as she brought him down and up again.

"STRIKE!" Two voices shrieked simultaneously, followed by the thudding of feet across the floor as two young kids beelined straight for Strike. They both had dark hair and eyes, seemingly around four or five.

Strike laughed as they attacked his legs, reaching down to ruffle their hair. "Hey guys."

"Where have you been?"

"Why are you so tall?"

"Where's Blu?"

"Why's there a stranger holding Bryce?"

"Who are they?"

"BLU!" They both shrieked, galloping away to where Blu had just come back into the room.

Blu let out a 'umph' as they tackled him. "Hey!" He yelled, more playfully than mad. "Watch your elbows!"

Harmony dragged Blu down by his sleeve and Daren leaned over. "I think someone is robbing our house." He whisper-yelled, loud enough for everyone to hear him. They both pointed at Ray and Zami in an accusing manner.

Blu just laughed. "Nah, the only thing they're here to rob is my dignity. That's Ray and Zami. They're my friends." Daren and Harmony both straightened up and fixed their wide eyes on them.

"I'm Daren Alexander Scott."

"I'm Harmony Grace Scott."

"Oh, um, I'm Ray." He said, holding his hand out. They both narrowed their eyes at him.

"We require full names." Harmony said.

"You know, it's just business." Daren explained, completely serious.

Ray bit back a laugh and tried to fix his facial expression. "Well, in that case, I'm Raymond Coreon." The twins nodded and each shook two of his fingers. When they turned to Zami, she sighed, shifting the baby to one hip and holding out her hand.

"Zami Wayz." She said and the twins both shook her hand as well.

"You will make wonderful parents one day." Harmony said and Ray choked on air, doubling over in a coughing fit. He felt Strike pat his back as he tried to take in a normal breath, face red.

"Thanks... I guess." He heard Zami say, sounding slightly flustered as well. Then they both bounded away, yelling to their mother about being hungry.

"They can be a little bit of a handful." Blu added, unhelpfully.

"Gee, thanks for warning us." Ray said in a raspy breath, rubbing his throat.

"To be fair, they are *my* family, even if we're not all blood related." Blu said.

"Touché." He responded, raising his eyebrow at Bryce in Zami's arms, who seemed to be staring deep into his soul. After an uncomfortably long moment of staring, he leaned over to Strike, not taking his eyes off the baby. "I think the baby is trying to determine my net worth."

Strike just patted his shoulder. "Sleep with one eye open."

Ray frowned as Strike walked away, up the stairs. "Thanks." He sarcastically mumbled, watching Zami give Bryce back to Cynthia, not without a little bit of cooing before walking over to him.

"Shall we go find what treasure lies just beyond those stairs?" She asked, linking her arm through his.

He sighed. "If we must."

Chapter 23

Zami took in every detail as she walked up the stairs; the wood banister, carpeted stairs (no doubt because of the children, as well as Blu), the pictures that seemed to cover each wall. Pictures of them laughing, of them serious, of them playing. Exactly what a loving family was supposed to look like. She inferred from the fact that Blu was so easily allowed in the house, and no pictures were taken down, that his mother held authority over his dad in the house. Which meant, as long as his dad and brother didn't come home, everything would go smoothly.

The halls were similarly lined, and she drifted in the direction where she could hear voices. No amount of expectation, however, could prepare her for Blu's room. It was just... so... bright. Everything single object in his room held more pigmentation then she had been aware was possible. His walls were a startlingly bright shade of pink, the bedsheets a weird mix of green and purple. Again, like always, he somehow managed to pull off pairing colors together that should've never even been in close proximity to each other.

The bed sat in the center of the room, an open door to its left revealing a wardrobe that definitely belonged to Blu. Bright skinny jeans, dorky T-shirts with puns on them, and of course, what would he be without a bunch of cardigans? And was that... a *scarf*? She shook her head in exasperated awe at the blunt message of all his clothing. He was so loud and ridiculous. But, she mused, that was what made him so wonderful to be around.

She had to admit, however, that she loved the little things about the sense of style people had, which showed the type of person you were dealing with. Like, she had never seen Blu wearing *normally* colored pants, and she wouldn't want to change that for anything. The perfectly white sneakers that he wore seemed to be the one little sign of his neatness.

She glanced at Ray, who was currently raising his eyebrow at something Blu was saying to him about primary and complementary colors. She liked his simple style, jeans and plain shirts with his light brown leather jacket that she was still curious about. She frowned when he ran his fingers through his hair.

Stupid boys and their impeccable selves.

"Are you sure that's it?"

"Of course!" Blu said in response to Ray's question. "Is nail polish *not* the most important thing in your life?"

"Can't say it is." Ray responded, mouth quirked in a smile.

"Uncultured swine." Blu remarked, flopping down on the desk chair to the right of the bed and kicking his feet up on the desk. Zami watched in amusement as he opened a bottle of nail polish and began to paint his nails.

"I'm going to go look in my room to see if there's anything." Strike sighed, sounding exasperated.

"I'll go with ya'." She said, feeling a need to get out of the *too* mismatched and *too* bright room. When Ray started to leave, she pushed him onto the bed, grinning at his startled look. "You should stay. Maybe you'll get a free manicure." The look on Ray's face was well worth it, as she slipped out of the room.

When she stepped into the room that Strike had gone into, she let out a little sigh of relief. "This is much better." The room was way more modest as far as colors go, the brightest color being the regular white of the walls. He had pale lilac sheets on the bed and a few pictures hung up on the walls, showing the family. The room size and set-up were identical to Blu's, but the closet was open to reveal much more pale and light-colored clothing, and there were even a few potted plants on the dresser across from the bed. His desk had a line of books across the back that looked well taken care of.

"I know, right." Strike grinned, shuffling through the drawers of his dresser. "I almost never purposely went into his room. It gives me a headache."

"It's very... him." She said, studying the books.

Strike laughed in response, gently brushing the plants with a finger. "Someone must've been watering them." He said, and she glanced his way.

"They care about you." She replied, hoping that was what he needed to hear. She must've gotten it right, because he gave her a smile.

"Yeah, they do." He frowned and steepled his fingers to his chin. "Now, what would be super important to me?" She watched as he looked under the bed, in drawers, flipped through books. After nearly ten minutes he sighed. "I don't know."

"Is there something, like," she bit her lip, deep in thought. "Someone gave you? Your birth parents? Blu?" Something flashed across his face for a moment.

"Well, yeah. Blu gave me this..." as he picked up a picture depicting them on the beach. He frowned. "No, I don't think that's it."

She sighed, doing a full take of the room. "Did you make something? Spend a lot of time on a hobby or something of the sort?" This time the expression that came across his face was that of realization.

"Yeah!" He said, crouching and opening the drawer on his desk, pulling out a small notebook. "We, uh, made a lot of music." He looked sort of abashed and she smiled.

"Don't be embarrassed, I'm sure it's a lot better than you thought." She watched as he flipped through it, looking like he was reliving a lot of good memories. "Do you play something?" She asked, looking around again to see if she had missed an instrument.

Strike looked abashed again as he shifted slightly. "Um, well I *can* play some, but this was like..."

"You sing?" She asked, feeling slightly awed.

Strike ducked his head, though he was smiling. "Yeah."

"That's amazing!" She said, completely truthful. "Though," She flung her arm around his shoulders. "Now I have more to use as blackmail."

He laughed, and she felt happy when she realized he was completely comfortable with her being there. "You're as bad as Blu."

She gaped at him, acting hurt. "That's just harsh, Strikey poo."

"Sure, *Zames*."

She narrowed her eyes at him. "I would hurt you right now, but I don't want to mess up your gorgeous hair."

"I appreciate the concern for my hair." He responded with a smile.

She nodded, waltzing out of the room. "Let's fetch our boys, shall we?"

Strike grinned, pulling the door closed beside him and following her back to the other room, notebook in hand.

They were greeted with a startled yelp, followed by, "I *will* hurt you, Blu!" They heard a large crash and another yell, this time by Blu.

"You wouldn't hurt a fly! You're too nice!"

There was a loud thud and another yelp. With a sigh, Zami pushed the door open, raising her eyebrows at the two boys in front of her. They both looked up at her, looking equally parts guilty and miffed. They were both on the floor, Ray hunched against the bed and Blu's head against the wall across from the bed. One of Blu's arms was pushing at Ray's foot which was awfully close to his face. Ray was holding one of Blu's ankles down, their legs tangled in a way that she wasn't sure she was capable of mimicking on purpose. Their hair was disheveled, along with messy shirts and Ray's jacket falling off his waist where he had tied it.

She turned on her heel, and followed Strike back out, who seemed to have made the same decision. She heard Blu and Ray yell from inside, Blu yelling Strike's name and Ray yelling hers, and there was some bickering inside before they both stumbled out of the room, eyes narrowed at each other.

After a long moment, she asked the question she was sure Strike was wondering as well.

"What were you doing?"

"Nothing." They both answered, far too fast, and in synch, to be nothing.

She raised her eyebrow at them and gave a little sigh, pinching the bridge of her nose. "You two are going to be the end of me."

"What'd we do?" Blu asked in exasperation. "It's just some brotherly messing around." He punched Ray in the shoulder and Ray sent him a look.

"That." Strike said. "That, right there."

Ray and Blu both looked at each other, confused. "What?" They both asked at the same time, sending each other a glare.

"That!" Strike said, cocking his hip. "You two are so aggressive with each other!"

Zami sighed when Blu and Ray both pulled their "I'm completely and utterly innocent" faces. "Come on now, we've got what we needed." She said, making her way back down the stairs. She chose to ignore the blatant shoving happening behind her, and the quiet bickering, and instead focused on Blu's family sitting downstairs.

Cynthia was holding Bryce, as Blu's mother watched over Darren and Harmony, who were eating something. Something pinged in her chest as she hung back, watching Blu and Strike hug all of them, laughing and smiling. She missed her mom a lot.

She stumbled when she felt someone bump her, and frowned in Ray's direction, as he just whistled and stared up at the ceiling.

"You're just feeling ornery today, aren't you?" She remarked, raising an eyebrow at him.

He had the audacity to give her an innocent look. "Whatever do you mean?" He asked, bumping her hip again.

She frowned, though she was secretly glad for the distraction. "I think you perfectly well know what I mean." She said, bumping his hip back.

"Nope." He answered, stuffing his hands in his pockets. "I'm completely innocent."

"Innocent of being innocent." She mumbled.

"What?"

"Nothing." She answered sweetly.

"Are you trying to dupe me, Zames?"

"Why would I ever do that?" She answered, looking up at him innocently.

"I don't know..." He grinned in a way that made her heart pound a little faster in her chest. "Cause you're intimidated?"

She huffed, crossing her arms over her chest. "Like I ever would be." She caught her breath when she felt him move a little closer, enough that she could smell the familiar minty scent that surrounded him.

He just hummed and she let out a little breath, trying to force the blush off of her face.

"You're horrible." She muttered, leaning back a little so her shoulder brushed his chest.

"You're horribler." He answered.

"You're horriblest."

"That's not a word."

"Neither is horribler."

He didn't answer, but she felt him lean into the touch.

"Touché."

"Lets go!" Blu yelled from the door. "Remember, world to save and all that!" He called, and Zami rolled her eyes, following Ray to the door. After shaking hands with the adults, they were back out in the heat.

"Man, I'm so glad today was the day both Andy and my dad were working." Blu said cheerily, grabbing Strike's hand and skipping to the spot where the portal would show up. After waiting only a few minutes, the portal appeared again, and with a little internal pep talk, Zami stepped through it, trying to hold in the nauseous feeling as she stepped back into the rebel base.

Standing right there waiting for them was Sylvia, a glare on her face. After a moment, Zami realized she was the object of the glare, and sunk into herself.

"Where in Ethereal did you come from?" Sylvia asked, stomping up to her.

Zami chuckled nervously. "Um, the portal?"

"You know perfectly well what I mean!" Sylvia demanded, eyes glowing.

"Okay, fine, I kinda' ran off. But, I did learn something important, soooo..." She gave Sylvia a pleading look.

"Whatever." Sylvia began to walk away, before whipping back around. "But don't think you can continue getting away with it."

"Don't worry, I will." She muttered under her breath and Ray snorted. They followed Sylvia back to the command tent and Zami stared at the map, recalling what she had seen.

"There's a small force hiding out just beyond these cliffs near Da'raom." She said, pointing to the place on the map. "I'd say around fifty men, all armored and well-armed. None with visible magic marks, and none were using it." She looked up to see the others' faces and frowned. "I wasn't just sulking all that time. I figured since I was out there, I could take a look around."

"Taking a look around is not the same thing as traveling a dozen miles, Zami!" Blu exclaimed.

"Oh, calm your horses." She turned back to the map. "And there was another army, the bigger one you were already aware of. But it's moving towards here." She pointed at a spot on the map. "Not here."

Sylvia stared at her for a long time before stepping forward and studying the spot. "You're absolutely positive?"

"Completely." She said, tucking a piece of hair behind her ear.

"Okay." Sylvia said, sighing and running her hands through her hair. "You guys decide where to go next for your special keys."

Zami nodded and turned around, met with three gazes. "What?"

"Well, my house was kinda' destroyed, and we've already visited Blu's and Strike's, sooooo..." Ray said, arms crossed.

"Your house was destroyed?" She asked slightly alarmed, thinking about the house she had seen at the start of their journey.

"No, not *that* one." He explained. "The one my parents owned."

"Well that clears it up quite nicely." She snarked, raising an eyebrow at him. "I think you're forgetting that no matter how long it seems we've known each other, it's barely been a month."

"I'm well aware of that!" He responded, narrowing his eyes at her. "I'm simply try..."

"WAR! DESTINY! PROPHECY!" Blu yelled, throwing his hands up in the air and waltzing out of the tent. "LET'S GO!"

Strike looked tired as he walked out of the tent, rubbing his temple with his fingers. "You guys are going to kill me."

"I'm so confused." Ray muttered as he followed Strike.

"What a bunch of morons." She sighed, rolling her shoulders before following them.

Chapter 24

↔

Ray glanced back as Zami sauntered past him and up to Leon, then took a deep breath before closing her eyes. This time, she seemed more prepared, and he looked ahead again in fascination as the portal appeared. This one looked quite different than the others, rougher and darker.

"What's up with the pit of hell?" Blu asked, voicing Ray's thoughts, though a little more bluntly.

Leon just shrugged. "The portal does what it does based on the traveler's memories of the place."

"Just hurry up you three, I'd rather get this done before my dad ends the world." Zami sassed, cocking a hip. Even with her eyes closed, she did a good job at glaring.

"Okay, okay!" Blu exclaimed, grabbing Strike's hand and walking into the portal. Ray followed him, silently thanking whatever great power out there that he was blessed with a strong stomach.

When his vision cleared, he found himself in a small, simple bedroom. The bed against the far wall had normal grey sheets, with a bump at the top indicating a pillow underneath. Next to the head was a bookshelf, with neat rows of textbooks, as well as non-fiction books with titles like *History of Nuin* and *Evolution of The Brain* lining the three shelves. A layer of dust covered every surface.

"Ah, I forgot how drab and lifeless this place was." Zami said, crouching to examine the bookshelf and then standing to trace her fingers across the sheets. Ray half expected Blu to say something making fun of her sense of style or lack of color, but he was only met with slightly crestfallen faces. He heard the sound of a door sliding and glanced over to see her pushing the closet door open to reveal a dresser of the same cherry wood as the other furniture in the room, and a row of uniforms. Navy blue, tan, white and black shirts and skirts hung in order of color and style, slightly dusty, but undisturbed.

"You had to wear a uniform to school?" Blu started, sounding thoroughly offended.

Zami turned, raising an eyebrow at him. "Um, yes?"

"Uniforms repress a sense of individuality and personality!" Blu stated, placing his hands on his hips. "It's just cruel to raise kids making them wear certain things. Cruel."

Zami snorted, looking in each of the drawers. "I'm pretty sure my 'repressed sense of individuality' was the least of my concerns at the time." She said in amusement, closing the closet door when she couldn't seem to find what she was after.   "I don't think we're gonna' find anything in here." She said, glancing distastefully around the room. He watched her reach to open the door behind them, only for it to be locked. "Oh right, I completely forgot about this." She said, ushering them back. "I'd move if I were you."

Ray moved. Turned out that was a good idea, because Zami backed up and then took a couple quick steps before kicking forward harshly. The door crashed into the floor with a resounding thud, which echoed from the now revealed hallway, then she looked over her shoulder with a glint in her eyes.

"I've always wanted to do that." She remarked before stepping over the debris and into the hallway.

"Uniforms." Blu muttered as he followed her, clearly still caught up in the idea that she had been required to wear them. "Who makes kids wear freakin' *uniforms*?"

Strike sighed from beside him and Ray gave a sympathetic nod. "Me too man. Me too."

Across the hall was another doorway, but Zami ignored that, moving down the hall towards a living room area. A grey couch was up against the wall under a window, and bookshelves covered the wall shared with her bedroom, lined with very similar books. The room was open to a kitchen area, and the front door was straight across from the couch, with another room next to that with more bookshelves and a large desk against the back wall. Plaques and certificates hung perfectly spaced above the shelves, showing business awards, personal recognitions and such. Overall the house looked absolutely perfect, but that was exactly the problem. Parents with kids just didn't have perfect houses. Where were the family portraits? The toys? The scribbled drawings that parents hung up on their fridge? It was all missing, and somehow that made the place feel haunted and empty, devoid of all the homeyness it should've had.

"Why hasn't it been emptied and sold?" Blu asked, peering around.

Zami shrugged. "He must've never got rid of it. I don't know why, though. It wasn't like we liked living here together." He didn't miss the long look she gave the couch, or her avoidance of the kitchen, but there was nothing except her normal expression on her face. He couldn't tell what she was thinking or feeling right then.

"I guess there's no fighting it." She said, pursing her lips and taking a deep breath. He watched as she turned back around, and disappeared into the room across from hers. Through the open door, he could just make out a bed and row of shelves, but he didn't make a move to follow her, not wanting to invade her privacy.

"Man, this place is depressing." Blu said, wrinkling his nose at the couch. "You can just smell the misery." Ray didn't respond, just glanced in Zami's direction, feeling slightly concerned for how she was feeling. If they could physically sense the misery, what was she feeling?

Only a second later, Zami walked out, avoiding their eyes, arms crossed against her chest.

"Got it. Let's go." Ray shared a look with Strike before following her back into her room. As if on schedule, which it was, a portal appeared again, in the same place. Without a glance back at them, Zami waltzed back into it and vanished from view.

"That was snappy." Sylvia remarked as they stepped out.

"Told you it would be." Zami responded, giving her a signature grin.

"Of course." Sylvia said, smiling. "So it's just Ray left?" He rubbed his neck when everyone turned to glance at him, and shrugged.

"I really don't know." He said truthfully and Sylvia nodded.

"Okay, how about you guys just rest for a bit and we'll see if you come up with something. Remember," she said, placing a hand on his shoulder. "Something that symbolizes a significant part of your life, that changed you forever in a way, no matter how small." He swallowed and nodded in understanding. With a pat on his shoulder she walked by, striking up a conversation with a couple young adults.

"Well. I'm gonna' go sleep until the world ends." Zami informed them before turning on her heel and disappearing into the rows of tents.

"I'm going to also." Strike added, grabbing Blu's wrist and dragging him in the opposite direction.

Ray stared after them, feeling slightly unimportant.

"Did your homies just abandon you?"

He sighed in defeat and glanced around to his sister walking up to him. "I think they did."

"That's rough."

He pouted slightly in the direction Zami had gone.

"Hey dork. I need to talk to you about something."

"If it's how hot the guys are around here, I don't wanna' know." He received a small smack to the back of the head. "Hey!" He complained, frowning at her and rubbing his head. "It's a reasonable condition!"

"I'm serious, mond'." With a glance at her face he realized she was, indeed, serious.

"Right, okay." He responded. "Let's take a walk."

They spent nearly ten minutes in complete silence, him shuffling his feet slightly as he walked, keeping his hands in his jacket pockets.

Eventually though, Spark whipped around to stop him. "I, uh, when they found me, they apparently found something else." She grabbed something from her pocket and held it out in her palm so he could see. His heart thumped loudly in his chest as he stared at the two, all too familiar, golden bands in her hand. "I figured you might want to have dad's for a while, just you know, as a comfort thing. When we see Aunt Dew and Laurel we can talk about where they should go." He swallowed the lump in his throat as he gently picked up the bigger ring and turned it in his fingers.

"Yeah, yeah, I would love that." He choked out, ducking his head. After a moment to compose himself he looked up again, meeting his sister's eyes.

"I love you, dork." She said, ruffling his hair.

"Love you too."

She gave him a dimpled smile before walking off again and he sighed, looking down at the ring again. Something important, something significant. He grinned at the ring, closed his hand around it. He had just found his key.

He had found Sylvia and told her, causing her to squeal in excitement, before ordering him to get some rest since that meant they could leave tomorrow. So now he slipped into the tent he knew Zami was in, equally hoping she was asleep so she could rest, and that she was awake so he could warn her. And to be honest, he just wanted to talk with her.

When he walked in, he was met with the sight of her laying down, not even under a blanket, head propped on a bag. One of her arms was thrown over her eyes, crook of her elbow against her nose and the other tapped a rhythm on her stomach. Unable to resist the opportunity, he slowly walked up and crouched beside her, reaching out a hand. With a grin he poked her side and she gave a startled yelp, jumping up. He was a little stunned when he was shoved on the ground, but was quick to laugh when she seemed to realize it was him. She sighed, letting go of his collar and flopping back down again.

"Stop laughing! It's not funny!" She yelled, sounding more tired than actually mad. He just laughed harder, receiving a half-hearted smack to his chest, which in retrospect should've made him stop, but only made him laugh harder.

"Rayyyyy." She drawled, slightly pouty. The cute face she was making and the pretty mess of her slightly bed-headed hair made him freeze. Her bright eyes were slightly hazy as she stared at him through half-lidded eyes, glancing out beneath her lashes. From the close proximity, he could see every freckle, every flushed part of her cheeks and nose, her slightly chapped lips as she bit them and the webs of green in her eyes.

"Yeah?" He murmured, finding his gaze locked onto her lips as they parted slightly with a breath. He could see the flutter of her eyes as they trailed down and the gradually spreading flush that spread across her face and neck. She seemed to subconsciously reach up and finger the necklace around her neck, gripping the heart. He didn't focus much on that, however, as much as the little breaths she was taking as he leaned a little closer, watching her eyes flutter closed. He could feel his heart leaping out of his chest as she leaned in too, and he shut his eyes as he felt her lips hovering near his.

"NO WAY!"

Ray jumped and then frowned at the direction the yell had come from outside the tent.

"I swear to god, if it's that annoying ass bi..." Zami started.

"Zami!" He exclaimed, surprised at her language. She gave him a glare but before she could finish her thought, the yelling outside caught their attention.

"OF COURSE! MY FATHER'S ORDERS!"

With a sigh, he pulled himself to standing, reaching out a hand. Zami took it and he couldn't help but notice the tingle that spread against his hand when her fingers touched his palm. Instead of letting go though, she traced her fingers along his, looking up at him.

"Since when did you wear a ring?"

He smiled gently at her observance. "Spark gave it to me. It's my key."

Her eyes widened in surprise. "Wait, that means..."

"We can leave tomorrow." He finished for her, enjoying the way her eyes lit up.

"Really?" She asked, slightly shyly.

"Really."

"Oh my god, this is so exciting Ray!"

His breath hitched in his throat at the use of his name, but he smiled at the excited girl in front of him. "Yeah, it is."

"THAT'S NOT RIGHT!"

Ray sighed, smile fading, having forgotten about the yelling. "Right. Let's go see what troubles are stirring." He said, a little nervous because of what occurred last time Laci had gotten in a fight.

As always, Zami seemed to read his mind and reached up to boop his nose. "I'll be fine, hot stuff. I've got you here." Then with a sparkle in her eyes and a blood-rushing grin, she walked out of the tent, leaving him staring after her for a long moment before remembering that he should probably *do* something. With a love-stricken grin on his face, he followed her, knowing perfectly well he looked far too happy to pass it off as just a normal good mood.

His mood faltered a little bit, however, when he realized the two yelling at each other included not only Laci, but also Blu. Strike was wincing slightly as he stared at the two yelling back and forth, and Zami was standing next to him, looking furious.

"What's happening?" He whispered to Strike as he sidled up on the other side.

"Turns out Laci has to go with us, because her father demanded it, and Blu is not too happy about it. Not that any of us are."

Ray frowned at the tall, pale blonde fighting with Blu. Why her?

"None of us want you there!" Blu argued, arms crossed over his chest and a hip cocked to the side.

"No, *you* don't want me there! I'm sure the hero would be ecstatic!"

Ray snorted, ducking his head and trying to cover it with a cough. However, it was inevitable that he would be noticed, considering the look Blu sent his way.

"What do you say, *hero?*" Blu asked mockingly, though it clearly wasn't geared towards him. The way Laci eyes bugged out of her head, and the way her jaw dropped, suggested she had *not* been expecting that.

"*You're* the hero? But you... your friends with that!" She spat, pointing to Zami. "A hero wouldn't be friends with her!"

"You're right." He responded, ignoring his friends' stares of shock. "You don't have to be a *hero* to know the difference between someone who's a good person and someone who has their foot up their ass." After a moment of frozen shock, Laci began to splutter, face turning red. Everyone else was laughing, hard.

"How dare you! You can't just..."

"Actually, yes he can." Zami responded cooly, and the air abruptly seemed to drop a dozen degrees. "Whatever role you believe you play in this war, no matter who your daddy is, Ray is a hundred times more valuable than you. It's time you realize you're *not* in charge anymore, *Glacier.*"

"My..." Laci began, sounding furious.

"War hurts everyone, and time doesn't just *stop* because you're a princess. Death spares no one, not you, not me, not the holiest being in the world. Because in death's eyes," Zami's eyes darkened dangerously. "Everyone is equal."

Laci growled, stepping close to Zami. "Who the hell do you think you are? Why do you have the right to patronize me? You're not the hero!"

Zami grinned. "You're right, I'm not. Which means I can do this." She pulled back her fist and Laci gasped.

"Good people don't hit other people!" She cried out, stepping back.

"Well newsflash," Zami's eyes flashed as she stepped forward. "I'm not *all* good." Ray winced at the crunch of Laci's nose and the startled cry she let out as she stumbled backwards, hands flying up to grab at her face.

Zami flipped her hair over her shoulder and cracked her knuckles, a wicked grin spreading across her face. "So you better get prepared *princess*, cause last time I checked, your daddy's not going to be there to protect you." Laci looked terrified, and mortified, as she scrambled away, sprinting away through the crowd of people that had flocked close by.

Zami glanced up at the crowd and frowned. "There's a war going on people! A war!" They all quickly dispersed, whispering amongst themselves and sending Zami looks. Most were a mix of terror and admiration. After a long moment, Zami turned around, eyes still slightly glowing. She whisked past them without a word and he watched helplessly as she disappeared again.

So much for a good mood.

Chapter 25

↔

Zami stared into the not so dark darkness of the tent, frowning at nothing in particular. Spark's light breaths were the only sounds other than the distant murmurs of people already up and about. She hadn't fallen asleep the night before at all, knowing all too well that it would just result in nightmares. She didn't want yet another person to be aware of her troubles.

Her knuckles were tingling, mostly just from the memory of punching Laci. If someone asked, she would say it was to show her that she wasn't invincible, and even though that was some of it, most of it was her desire to *not* be seen as a weak little kid anymore. She couldn't deny the rush of power it gave her, to feel like she *was* strong, was powerful.

But then with that came the fear. A fear that she had *liked* hitting her. She liked it! And that scared the crap out of her.

Sitting up with a glare at her hand, she pulled on her boots and stumbled up, pushing into the large fire lit cavern. Most people were still asleep, given the early hour of the morning, and usually she would be happily asleep dreaming about sunshine and a bright-eyed boy, but instead she found herself shuffling to the headquarters tent. No one was in it and she sighed, plopping down into one of the chairs and staring at the maps on the table.

New yellow markers were covering it, though there were still more of the red ones. She had to admit, her father was smart. He was one of the first to openly accept non-magics into his armies, and even though the rebels weren't against those without magic, he had gained the loyalty of thousands and thousands of people by doing so first.

She pulled her legs to her chest and chewed on the side of her thumb. In only a couple hours, they would be trying to find one of the most important pieces of magic on Ethereal, with only themselves and their magic to count on. What if someone died? What would she do with herself if she lost Blu or Strike or Ray? The only friends she had ever known were some of the most at-risk people in the world. She was tired of grieving.

But her mom was hovering in her head; she could almost see her, feel her. The token her mother had never earned sat in her pocket, practically burning a hole. Her mom had never even *been* capable of sobriety for a full year, but Zami still remembered how excited she had been at the prospect of giving it to her. She never did though, and now she was using it as a *key* to her past. A reminder of what she had been through.

She could feel her mother telling her that she was her own person, that she could choose what she did. That was the problem. Why, after all this time, was she still hesitating? Why couldn't she stop thinking about her mom, and Lev, and the prophet? They weren't here, they were all dead. But somehow they *were* there, resting their heads on her shoulders and weighing her down.

Their blood was on her hands, their ghosts haunting her, reminding her of how horrible she was. Hitting Laci, just like her father hit her. How was she any better than him? Killing people, hitting people, what was next? Abandoning those who needed her, hurting them, and leaving them helpless and broken?

It was only a matter of time before her past caught up with her. Only so long until karma got her.

You didn't kill me. That's all that matters right now. Ray's words echoed in her head, drowning out her doubts.

That you didn't allow your father's judgment to cloud your mind. You're free now, and you can make your own choices.

She remembered every word he had whispered, every bit of seriousness in his expression.

The day that you decided not to end my life, was the day you subconsciously decided to leave your past behind and start a new one. One with us. One with you, and who you want to be.

How had she gotten so lucky after all this time? She didn't deserve him, or his sweet words, or his stunning eyes or... anything. Yet, he was here. And he hadn't left her, and he wasn't going to any time soon.

A sense of calm fell over her when she remembered his arms around her, his teasing, the gentle touches and caring nature. A smile flickered across her lips when she remembered yesterday. How surprised she had been and how secretly amazing his laughs made her feel. And then his eyes were on hers and she realized how close they had been. If it hadn't been for Laci, she would've just had the first kiss of her life, with the only person she wanted it to be with. But she was too happy to care about that, instead thinking about the fact that she had years and years and years left. She had time, and she planned on spending every moment of it with him.

"Couldn't sleep?" Zami smiled at Blu as he ungracefully flopped onto the chair across from her, studying his nails.

"You could say that." She breathed, all her bad thoughts gone.

"Too busy thinking about the adventure? Or perhaps," he wiggled his blue eyebrows suggestively. "Something far more endearing?"

"I guess you'll never know." She replied, still seeing only her vision of the future.

"Oh no, I definitely know from that look. Don't tell me, you're falling for our very own, resident sunshine-boy?"

"Oh," She responded with a roll of her eyes. "Is that what's happening? I couldn't have known, I just can't look at him without smiling, love every part of him and want to have a future with him." She waved her hand in the air sarcastically. "Isn't that what having friends means?"

Blu laughed, looking pleased. "At least you're very aware. It would be so annoying watching you guys take forever to realize you like each other."

Zami ignored the teasing, but his words made her heart thump a little faster than before.

"Well, I might've already had him if it wasn't for that snooty long-nosed..." She waved her hands around, remembering Ray's shock at her cussing. "Girl." She mumbled, frowning at the table.

"Competition?" Blu asked curiously.

"Oh no, more like interruption." She responded, rolling her eyes.

"Ooooooh!" Blu squealed, leaning forward. "What was interrupted?"

"None of your business!" She exclaimed, sticking her tongue out at him and leaning back in her chair. "But," She added at Blu's pout. "I bet you're well aware what tends to happen between two people with the hots for each other when they're alone in a tent."

Blu didn't even have the decency to act flustered at her accusatory comment, instead just shrugging. "Sometimes I can't help myself."

"I'm sure." She responded, raising her eyebrow at him.

"Oh, I see we have two early birds!" Sylvia interrupted from the entrance of the tent. "I assume you're discussing possible destinations for the location of the first desirable."

"Definitely." They both lied, trying not to laugh when they made eye contact.

"Hmmm." Sylvia said, looking skeptical. "In a half hour or so, I suggest getting the others up; you'll want to get there early enough to be back at a safe time." Zami nodded, trying to keep a straight face. With a sigh, Sylvia disappeared again and as soon as she vanished from sight, she and Blu began to laugh.

"You think she heard us?" Blu choked out, wiping his eyes.

"Most assuredly." She answered through her own tears and Blu wheezed, laying his head on the table and slamming his fist down on the table through his fits of laughter. That made her laugh harder, which made him laugh harder, so it took nearly ten minutes for them to finally calm down enough to have a normal conversation. They spent most of the time talking about how cute the other boys were, laughing at each other's comments. She was especially amused at the last one.

"My boyfriend has a *really* nice butt."

"TMI, Blu."

"What! You can't tell me you haven't noticed."

"Can't say I've stared at your boyfriend's butt."

"That's fair."

Other than that, they didn't do much during those thirty minutes. By the end of the time they both got up and practically skipped arm and arm to the tent, trying to shush each other's giggles, which only caused more to come. However, when they entered, they both immediately sobered up, focused on their respective affections.

She stared at Ray in all of his sleepy glory, hair ruffled against his jacket that he was using for a pillow, and shirt slightly wrinkled in some places. He was laying on his side, arms curled up in front of him and one leg shifted slightly higher than the other. With his and Strike's long legs, Zami wondered how Blu even fit in the small tent also, even with the two curled up into themselves.

Crouching, she decided against doing anything unpleasant, and instead gently shook his shoulder. She briefly had deja vu to nearly a month ago, when she had woken him up in the forest. Oh how far they had come.

"Rayyyyy." She murmured, heart fluttering when he mumbled and turned over, facing her. "Rayyyyyyy." She tried again. This time his eyes fluttered open and he looked at her in confusion before remembering life in general.

"Yeah?" He asked groggily, sitting up and blinking at her.

"We've got a desirable to find, remember?"

He yawned in response, running his hand through his hair. "Right." She watched affectionately as he grabbed his bag, still looking sleepy and slipped on his shoes and jacket.

Strike was in a similar state, though he looked a little more annoyed at having to wake up as he tied his shoes. Soon though, they were both up and considerably more awake as they walked out to where Leon was standing. Sylvia was waiting there along with Laci, who looked miffed, and Spark, who looked just as excited as always.

Sylvia started, "Now, none of us have been to this place we're looking for, but we chose the closest location we know, so it should only take a couple hours to get there. The portal will open back up by midnight, and if you aren't ready by then, you'll have to find your way back on foot since Leon has to leave tonight. Stay safe. Get the desirable and get out. Be prepared for tricks and dangerous tasks." They all nodded and Sylvia hugged each of them, minus Laci, before stepping back and nodding to Leon, who placed a hand on her shoulder. The portal opened up next to Sylvia, looking similar to a sunrise.

"Goodbye, and good luck. May your magic always stay bright."

Zami swallowed. Suddenly everything was so much more serious now. There was so much on the line. She watched as Spark and Laci walked into the portal, and with a glance back at the base, she stepped through, trying to ignore the nausea that swept over her.

They stepped into a large empty field, overgrown grass brushing against her knees. In the distance she could see a thick forest, and the small peak of a mountain revealed by the slowly rising sun.

"What makes Sylvia so sure this place is it?" Blu asked, looking around.

"Well, the peaks looking like it said in the riddle as the sun rises for one, plus the town got its name from the way the blowing wind makes it sound like the mountains are bellowing." She responded, crossing her arms.

"What about the whole 'secrets grow'?"

"This is where the last hero killed the dark girl. One of the biggest secrets to this day. How did it happen, and why?"

"Lovely."

"Tell me about it." She responded distastefully.

"Well! Let's go!" Spark exclaimed, bouncing on her feet as she made her way down the trail. Zami sighed, readjusting her bag before following her.

The way to the mountain was surprisingly uneventful, the peace before the storm she decided, and they made it to the edge of the forest in barely an hour. It was fairly hot by then and she uncomfortably shifted, disliking the dampness of her hands and the sweat dripping down her back. The others looked considerably warm too, and Laci being an ice elementalist, looked like she disapproved of every puddle of mud and the bugs swarming around them in the heat. Zami secretly enjoyed how miserable she looked, although she wouldn't say that out loud.

When they finally made it to the edge of the mountain, it was about mid-morning, and all of them except for Laci were dripping with sweat.

"You'd think if people wanted the world to be saved, they'd make it easier on us." Blu panted, lifting his hands and causing a chilly breeze to sweep past them. She was glad for the slight distraction from the heat and closed her eyes against the wind, grateful that they had Blu.

"Not if the same magic can kill millions of people." Strike commented.

"Good point."

Zami stared at the rocky edges sloping up to meet the top of the mountain, thousands of feet above them.

"So... what exactly are we *supposed* to do with *this?*" Laci asked, gesturing to the mountain. Zami shrugged, thinking of what they could be looking for. A door? An opening? A random object laying haphazardly thrown on the very top of the mountain? A depressed, very very old man who had been waiting for them on the peak for too long?

"Well, it said it opens to the 'portal of the past'" She quoted, glancing at her pocket. "Maybe it has something to do with the keys?" She watched the others pull out their objects and she slipped the coin out of her pocket. Not to her surprise, nothing happened, and she let out a sigh.

"Try touching the mountain with our objects out." Spark suggested. Zami glanced at the others and pressed her other palm to the rock wall beside her.

She stumbled forward in surprise when her hand connected with nothing, and scrambled to catch herself before she fell. When she looked up, she was in a dark tunnel, extending beyond her visibility. She looked back around to find herself facing the others, still outside. They all stared at her for a long moment before Blu stepped forward with fist held out, straight into the tunnel.

"Wicked." He said, looking around. Strike and Ray did the same thing, both staying silent, but observing the dark walls and stretch of tunnel.

She looked forward again just in time to see Spark walk forward, only to slam straight into an invisible barrier and stumble back with a few colorful curses.

"Guess it only works for those with their keys." Blu said, looking a little too excited at the fact that Laci wouldn't be able to join them. Laci looked irritated, but through the barrier they couldn't hear what she was yelling. Spark pointed to a ring on her fingers, staring at Ray who nodded and mouthed something along the lines of *Love you too* and *I will*.

That was when Zami realized she wasn't holding her token anymore. Frowning, she glanced at the others, finding them empty-handed as well. She couldn't help the obvious disappointment that she had lost it, but reminded herself that if she could go so many years without it, it clearly wasn't that significant.

She still remembered making it for her mom, how excited she had been, how *proud* she had been of her mom. How happy she had been with the thought that her mom would *be* sober and stay so. Shaking herself from her thoughts, she looked up, staring at the foreboding path before them, feeling a chill in her bones.

"Ray, can't you use your light?" Blu asked and she turned to them.

He shook his head, looking concerned. "Not working."

Zami froze, and for the first time in a while she felt *afraid*. She couldn't feel her power, and by the looks on Blu and Strike's faces, neither could they. No weapons, no magic. They were defenseless.

"Zami, you can still see through the dark... right?" Blu asked, sounding slightly scared.

She swallowed deeply, trying not to let the fear consume her. "No." And she hated it. She hated the dark. It was stupid, since her magic was darkness, but she couldn't handle not being able to see.

Welcome, my young heroes.

Zami froze, wildly searching for the voice.

The challenge begins.

The open space connecting them to the others, and the sunlight, closed, drowning them in darkness.

"What challenge?" She squeaked out, only able to see black. There was no answer, only a cold breeze whispering against her back that made her shiver.

"Excuse me?" Blu called from beside her. "Mr. Ominous voice?"

Again, there was no answer.

"Come on, let's go." She heard Ray say.

"Here."

She felt what must've been Blu's hand grab hers, and figured the others were doing the same. She took careful steps as they walked down the tunnel in a linked line, shivering at every little creepy sound. Occasionally a voice would whisper in her ear, and she knew the others heard it too by the little gasps.

"Leave now."

"Watch out for the dove."

"You'll die here, just like me."

"They betrayed me. They did."

They were sad, haunted whispers. Echoes of voices. Some sounded young, some female, some male. All of them had one clear message: Danger.

When something cold brushed against her neck, she jumped, heart leaping out of her chest. It didn't happen again though, and she tried to focus her attention on walking with even steps and listening to the breathing from the others.

It seemed like forever when the voice spoke again, causing all of them to have a mini heart attack.

Look for the clue.

Only a minute later, they were met with the end of the tunnel and a lit lantern hanging from the ceiling, revealing a large map painted on a smooth section of the wall. It showed every current kingdom and province in the world, each one labeled neatly and accurately. Which meant it couldn't have been painted very long ago, since so much had changed since her father came into power.

"Um, what clue?" Blu asked, letting go of her hand.

She frowned, thinking back to the riddle. "Look in the river's eye, where the rest of this clue there will reside."

Ray leaned forward at her words, studying the map. "It's a trick, right? The 'eye' in the river. Like the actual letter 'I'."

"Given the past of this riddle and the weird voice, everything is probably a trick." She said, staring at the bright paints.

Ray reached forward, brushing his fingers against one of the labels, and the room was filled with an ear-splitting screech. She shut her eyes and pressed her hands to her ears to try and muffle the noise, but the screech rattled her bones, sinking into her core, and she felt her eyes widening at the sudden *strength* that rushed through her.

She felt incredibly strong, like nothing could knock her down. Blinking, she glanced over at the others, shocked by the distress on Blu's face and the determination on Strike's. However, the most horrifying was Ray. He looked *terrifying*. Sure, she had seen him mad, but she had never seen anything quite like him now with blazing eyes and gritted teeth. His shoulders were squared and fists clenched.

But as soon as it started it was over, and they all blinked several times, while Blu's shoulders pulled up, Strike's normal quizzical expression returned, and Ray's shoulders and jaw relaxed again.

"What was that?" Blu asked, sounding like his normal snarky self again.

"I don't know." Ray said. "But, it worked." She looked up to where he was gesturing to the now open room before them.

"Damn, what did you do man?"

"I pressed the 'I'."

"How'd you know which river it meant?"

"I didn't."

"So you just based a decision that could have ruined everything on a guess?" Blu asked incredulously.

"Basically."

Good job, you've made it past the first round. The voice said.

"What was *that* all about?" Blu shouted, staring at the ceiling. This time, the voice responded.

Your least used, yet most necessary emotions, of course.

Blu looked about as confused as she felt. "Why?"

To better understand yourself. In order to deserve magic of such great ability, you must prove yourself.

"What do you mean pr...

All is fine, my friends. You will understand in due time. Now please, unless you're giving up, move on.

Blu grumbled something that sounded awfully disrespectful, but waltzed into the next room with purpose. With a little smile fueled by the fact that Blu was still Blu, she followed him, looking around the room. When Strike and Ray walked through, the wall slammed shut, startling her yet again.

Now. Welcome to the real challenge.

Chapter 26

↔

Ray felt a chill crawl down his spine at the words. The air crackled with random voices, familiar voices. His sister, his parents, his aunts, little brother, teachers and friends. Then it stopped abruptly, and he was staring at a pale mist that floated through the air around them in a blanket.

The past is an interesting thing isn't it? Not quite here, but always here at the same time. It has a funny way of catching up with you.

At that, the light flickered, plunging them into darkness for a long moment before flickering back on. He heard a little gasp from Blu and blinked, opening his mouth to question his fiend, only to be interrupted.

Aaron Scott. Quite the optimist aren't we? Let's see... rejected... hated... fell in love. A pretty classic love story, huh?

Ray was confused. What was the voice doing, analyzing how classical their pasts were?

*Ah, now you **have** been hiding something! I just wonder, how would you feel if they knew everything?*

"What do you m..." Blu started, but the voice interrupted him.

All is fine my friend, just sit back and watch the show.

Ray stared in fascination as the mist formed a thin veil in front of them and colors began to appear on it, revealing a picture. There was Blu's mom, younger, less tired looking and holding a small bundle. A young Cynthia played with baby Blu, wiggling her fingers over his face, as a young boy sat in the background, coloring with his dad.

You had a happy beginning, a healthy family that loved you more than anything in the world, and would do anything for you.

Then they were in the hospital and the mother was crying as she talked to the doctor, her husband next to her, holding her hand.

You were far too young to be affected by what happened, but sometimes you catch yourself wondering what it would've been like if your sister had come out as healthy as you. Unfortunately, your twin was lost. However, it wasn't for nothing; without those events you would've never met Strike.

There was Blu, around two or three years of age, standing in the hallway of their home as his mother walked through the door, with none other than what must've been toddler Strike. There they were, avoiding each other at first, Strike hiding behind the woman's legs. But then the image showed them beginning to get along, the blossoming buds of friendship.

Strike and you became inseparable, two halves of a whole.

There were both of them, standing in front of a big building bustling with kids. Strike looked absolutely terrified, and Blu, well, looked like Blu. He slung an arm around Strike's shoulder, urging him forward, and together they walked into the school.

The next one showed Blu messing around and accidentally blowing a whole wall down with his powers, and his parents patting his shoulders as he bounced in excitement.

In the next one, a several years older Blu was walking down the hall and turned the corner just in time to see a kid shoving Strike into a wall. The kid ran away before Blu could do anything, and he instead reached down to help Strike up, giving him a hug and telling him something that made him smile.

Then there they were, walking in a park and laughing about something as his parents played with the younger kids in a playground area.

Visions passed of them taking walks, talking late at night, doing homework together and playing games flashed in the mist, and in each one they were older and older. It stopped at one though, letting it play out completely. Blu looked to be humming as he strutted down the hall, probably around ten or eleven, waving at some kids as he passed. The smile was wiped from his face though, when he saw a small crowd in the hallway. He pushed through to see what the commotion was about, only to be met with the sight of a mean-looking older kid holding the collar of Strike's shirt as he shoved him into a locker. Tears were running down Strike's face and a little bit of blood trickled down from beneath his hair, indicating it wasn't the first hit. Then Blu was yelling at the boy, pulling his hands away and grabbing Strike away from him.

You had felt horrible when you realized you had missed the blatant fact that he was being bullied right under your nose. So you tried to make sure it never happened again, using your likability as leverage to keep the kids away from him.

Blu was smiling gently as he sat beside a less frightened Strike, who was holding an ice pack to his head. The tears were dry on his cheeks, though his eyes still looked wet, but he was smiling.

And everything calmed down again; you were happy and so was Strike. But one day you just started feeling... off. You tried to fight it, but no matter what you did, the feeling overwhelmed you. You were tired, unmovable, unsure what was going on.

There was Blu, looking blanker than Ray had ever seen him, shuffling his feet as he walked through the halls. People said things to him, greeted him, but he seemed to barely register it, eyes glazed over. Then he was laying in bed, the room dark and staring at nothing in particular.

Ray watched him struggle to continue schoolwork, and keep up basic things like hygiene. It seemed to take him forever to wake up each morning, and then all day it looked as if he was ready to just get back in bed again.

*Strike noticed though, he knew something was wrong. And **he** ended up helping **you** this time.*

Blu opened his door to see Strike, who rushed to say something. And then they were sitting on his bed and Blu was talking, looking extremely distressed. Then Strike was hugging him, whispering something in his ear.

Soon after, Blu was sitting in a chair in a clinic as a man with blonde hair asked him questions. Then his mom was signing a paper at the front and Blu was holding what looked like a medicine bottle.

That night Blu sat on his bed, staring at the bottle, uncertainty in his eyes. But Strike was there, and he smiled at him, ruffling his hair. And Blu took a pill.

It was nearly a year later, and Strike and Blu were racing down the halls, Blu yelling something back at Strike, who was falling behind. They both had wild smiles on their faces as Blu stopped and Strike caught up, panting for breath. Blu said something that looked a lot like "loser" and Strike pouted at him, shoving his book bag into his hands and tilting his chin upwards in a "peasant, get on my level" manner before strutting off. Blu ran after him and nearly knocked him over with a slap on the back. Strike then smacked him on the back of the head.

Then they were both lying on Strike's bed, Strike reading a book and Blu blathering about something as Strike nodded along. Blu reached over and pushed the book out of Strike's hands as he sat up, leaning forward. Strike turned around to complain, but before he could, Blu was kissing him. Then he was kissing him back, the book long forgotten somewhere on the floor. The moment was broken though, as they pulled apart looking up at the doorway in shock and surprise.

But of course your perfect, righteous older brother walked by just in time to see something that should've been a private, special moment for just the two of you.

There was Blu's dad, yelling at him and knocking over a chair, as his mother tried to get him to stop in the background, and Blu clenching his fist, glaring at him.

Then he was in church, standing in the front during service, ducking his head and clenching his jaw. When Strike walked in, everyone whipped around and Blu lifted his head, staring at him with furrowed brows. However, only seconds later, he was pulling away from the minister's touch and stalking down the aisle. Without a glance back at his father, he grabbed Strike's hand and pulled him out of the door.

He pulled him through the street, finally stopping in a secluded alleyway far away from the church and shoving him against the wall. Strike looked surprised when Blu kissed him again, but quickly melted into it, curling his fingers against Blu's neck.

That night Blu and Strike snuck out of the house with one bag of belongings each, and disappeared off into the town, hand in hand with bright smiles. Then they were standing in front of Sylvia, standing tall and proud as they shook her hand.

The next scene showed Blu and Strike both circling each other in what looked like the training arena in the first rebel base. Strike looked extremely nervous, his fists loosely clenched in front of him as he watched Blu.

It flashed into what must've been later that night, Strike pouting at Blu from the bed where he was holding an ice pack to his shoulder. Blu rolled his eyes and said something to him that made Strike look away with a huff. Blu reached forward and grabbed his hand, pulling him up and dragging him out the door. Strike looked like he was complaining as he was pulled through the night, but there was a smile on his face. His eyes were bright when Blu stopped in the middle of the field and said something to him with a mischievous grin on his face. They spent a while talking as they practiced their stance and moves but eventually it dissolved into both of them laying on the ground, giggling madly. Strike reached over and grabbed Blu's shirt, pulling him up and saying something with a shy smile. Blu laughed, hugging Strike for a long moment before pulling back and kissing him again, pushing him back to the ground.

The next set of scenes flashed quickly before them, training, studying, laughing, kissing, talking late at night as everyone slept. There was a hauntingly lovely feeling to the scenes which made Ray's heart throb. A couple of them showed them yelling at each other, breaking down into tears, but very soon after they would apologize and then everything would be fine again.

Then a very familiar scene popped up, of the two of them fighting in the field. It was weird to see himself in Blu's eyes, stepping into the arena with confusion laced into his expression. Blu slung his arm around Ray's shoulders, gesturing to Strike and himself and leading him up the hill.

The following scenes were familiar, messing around in the training court, laughing over dinner and teasing each other mercilessly. However, if he thought seeing himself was weird, it was even weirder seeing Zami in Blu's eyes. There was something that stood out about her eyes in Blu's vision, a sorrow he hadn't quite seen. It only took him a moment to realize Blu must've been connecting his own feelings to the ones she had.

Familiar scenes of them went by in the forest, in the church and everything else flashed in the mist, almost too fast to make out. It slowed back down though at Da'raom with the whole Lev incident, and the chaos that ensued.

The rest of the time passed by incredibly fast as they came back to the base and went to each of their houses, only slowing a moment to show Blu with his family, laughing again and then him and Blu arguing in his room. Only when it flashed to the current time, with them standing in the dark room, did the voice speak again.

So all these years, your happiness hasn't even been real, has it? Artificial smiles and laughs from those little pills you have to take, since you can't even be happy by yourself. Pretty lame isn't it?

"Will you just shut up!" Strike yelled angrily, frowning at the wall. "There's nothing lame about his medication!"

"Plus," Blu cut in, looking surprisingly pleased. "I haven't taken any in months."   The voice didn't speak again for a long moment, but when it did, it sounded almost happy.

Well, I must congratulate you, young man. You've passed.

Blu looked confused.

"Um, I passed what exactly?"

The lights flashed again, and this time Strike was the one who let out a startled yelp before the lights flashed back. Strike was still beside them, though he looked a little surprised as the mist shifted in front of them to create a different picture.

In it was Strike being ushered into a building by someone, their face too cloudy to recognize. They signed a paper, and hugged little Strike, before rushing off and leaving him alone with the lady.

You never knew why you were just given away, why your parents decided to just leave you. You never knew their names, barely even remember their faces. And you disliked it in that child care facility, didn't you? Too loud, too gross, everyone was unpleasant.

Strike was probably around three, sitting on a bed and frowning at a couple boys horsing around the room, shoving each other and yelling.

Didn't have to wait too long though, did you? When a couple heart-broken parents stumbled into the building, wanting to adopt.

There were Blu's parents, walking into the room. None of the kids noticed at first, too caught up in their activities, while Strike focused on a book. Eventually the boys began to take notice and stared up at the adults, except for Strike, who was too absorbed to notice. Blu's mother whispered something to her husband, eyes fixed on Strike.

You know they chose you simply because you looked the most miserable there, because they wanted to help a kid, and you were the one who needed it the most.

They urged Strike into the house and through the door, trying to make him feel comfortable. The visions showed something similar to Blu's, at first them avoiding each other, but then them getting along and forging a bond.

There was Strike, looking absolutely petrified as they stepped into the school. His tension lessened though, when Blu slung an arm around his shoulders and walked in with him.

He was walking out of a classroom, accidentally bumping into a random kid and apologizing profusely. But the kid growled at him, shoving him backwards. That was when Blu walked around the corner and ran to him, eyebrows furrowed at the other boy.

Strike avoided kids in the hallway, keeping his head down as he walked and only brightening up when Blu found him. More bittersweet images flashed in the mist, similar to Blu's. Doing homework in the library, attempting to play a game with a ball, laughing as they huddled under a fort in the dark, sharing scary stories and giggling at the absurdity of each other.

There was them learning about his magic, Strike jumping in excitement as he learned that he had magic also and Blu giving him a big hug, smiling.

Occasionally, there would be one in between the others already shown from Blu's view, of Strike being shoved by another kid, being teased, sometimes even getting hit. Ray's heart hurt when he watched one kid shove him inside a locker, leaving him alone until someone found him. Then one identical to Blu's showed up, of him being slammed against the locker and tears running down his face.

He was sitting on the bed with an ice pack on his head as Blu talked to him, a smile shining through the drying tears.

The next one was Strike frowning as Blu gave him a curt nod, walking down the hall and ignoring everyone else. Of Blu avoiding doing things with him, refusing to go mess around or to study together. Strike looked concerned as he watched Blu's behavior, and eventually they watched as he slipped into a public library, scanning the sections before coming upon the book he wanted. That night he stayed up, reading under the blankets with a flashlight, eyes wide.

He knocked on Blu's door, saying something to him with furrowed eyebrows and a worried smile. Then as with Blu's vision, they were speaking, Strike listening to his struggles intently. He waited outside the office while Blu was talking to the doctor, biting his nails. And the scene where he reassured Blu showed up, almost identical to the earlier version.

Then they were in the library and Blu was fast asleep, head on the table and his textbook open beside him. Strike smiled, reaching over and ruffling his hair before turning back to his own book.

The next scene was familiar, down the last detail. Strike laying down and reading as Blu talked, Blu pushing the book from his hands and kissing him. Both of them looking up in surprise at the doorway where Blu's older brother was standing.

You felt horrible. Blu's father and brother hated him after that; he was forced to go to church to change himself, and he hated it. You felt like it was all your fault.

Strike was standing beyond the door as their father yelled at Blu, looking crestfallen. He spent that night laying in bed, staring up at the ceiling with a lost look in his eyes. The next day he got up and walked to the church, pushing through the doors and immediately drawing all attention to himself. Then Blu was dragging him out of the building and down the street, and kissing him in the alleyway.

The next visions were nearly the same as Blu's also, them sneaking out, meeting Sylvia, training, and messing around. There were fights, and them making up, studying, meeting new people and so on. Eventually it all led to the very same scene of him walking out of the room in the rebel base and meeting them.

You still blame yourself, don't you? That if you just simply hadn't kissed him back, or maybe hadn't sat there that day, anything really, he could've still had a good relationship with his family. You wouldn't have run away, and he could've been living a life not so full of danger.

Strike was frozen for a long moment before he spoke, and even though his voice shook slightly, the message was clear.

"Kissing him wasn't the issue, his parents were."

But sometimes, don't you feel just a little bit guilty? A little bit bad for taking away everything from him just so you could have him?

This time, Strike looked torn and unsure what to say.

"Well he shouldn't, because I wouldn't change a thing that happened." Blu said, which caused the voice to laugh.

Quite defensive of each other, aren't we? Though, I shouldn't expect anything else. Love is a strong thing.

Ray gasped when something stung his skin, blinking madly as it faded into the mist again. Then it was changing to form a different picture.

It was absurd to see a little version of himself, something he had only seen in pictures. Yet there in front of him was himself, about a year old probably, and a young Spark cradling him on the couch, giggling madly. His breath caught when his mother and father appeared, both smiling brightly as his mother scooped him up and stuck her tongue out at Spark before running away. Spark jumped on their dad's back and yelled something, pumping her fist in her air as he charged into the kitchen to get to him and his mother.

Then he was about a year older, watching as his sister pulled a backpack over her shoulder and waved before leaving out the door. His mother cooed at him, bopping his nose as she opened a book to read to him. The mist swirled again to reveal a four year old version of himself at the entrance of the school, his mother smothering him with kisses as he pushed her away, even though he was smiling. There was him playing with other kids, zoning out in class, tripping as he tried to kick a ball, doing things with his family. Then he was watching his mother walk in the door with a little bundle, his Aunts next to him and Spark, who had been waiting. The vision showed all of them laughing and playing games through the night to celebrate Blaze's birth.

There was the time they found out about his magic, when he accidentally nearly blinded them. They were all so happy, ruffling his hair and saying things like 'our little hero' and 'I always knew you would change the world.'

He had to swallow to hold back from yelling out, when he saw the all too familiar scene of his parents and sister walking out the door for the last time; he could almost hear their voices as they said they would be back soon. He continued going to school, moving into his Aunt's house, playing with friends and his little brother. And then the inevitable came, him waking up to voices, running out only to see his Aunts sobbing as they talked to a tall man at the door. The next visions flashed by, almost as they had in his memory, him and his family in all black as they stood in a cemetery, staring at a gravestone with no bodies underneath it. Then him crying into his Aunts' shoulders as a barely one year old Blaze stared at them in confusion from their arms.

It cut to nearly three years later, a nine year old version of him walking with a little four year old Blaze, backpacks on their backs. To his embarrassment, there were even the times he woke up crying from nightmares in the middle of the night, staring into the darkness of his room helplessly.

The scenes flashed by, celebrating birthdays, helping Blaze with his homework, shoving him playfully as they walked to school. It showed him sitting in class, only half-focusing as his eyes drooped shut and sitting up only to fall over onto the floor when the bell rang. The class laughed and one of his friends, Riley, reached out to help him up as he rubbed his head.

There was even the time when Blaze broke his ankle from falling off a tree that he had told him not to climb. Him carrying Blaze on his back as he made his way to the house and him waiting in the doctor's office for them to put Blaze's foot into a cast. His heart throbbed when he saw the time he taught Blaze how to play football, picking him up and throwing him over his shoulders like the football, and earning a lot of screaming and laughing. There was him telling off some kids who were messing with Blaze, and bringing him to get ice cream afterwards to make him smile.

In the next one, he was thirteen and it was Valentine's Day. He was walking with his friends who were shoving each other and giggling about girls. Then it was later in the day and he was eating lunch with his friends when a girl came up to him, blushing madly. He remembered how badly he felt when he rejected her, and the one after, then others after that. He just... couldn't seem to be interested in them at the time, no matter what his friends said he should do.

But then there he was, being dragged into a high school party about a year later, his friends jostling him and joking about how he could 'get some love'. He rolled his eyes and shook his head, peeling off as they went off to mess around and instead standing by a group to act like he was listening to a story someone was telling. He remembered how someone had come up and grabbed his hand to drag him away, and then he was in another room, being kissed by a girl he didn't know. He remembered the way he tried telling her to get off as she kissed him, gently pushing her away and trying to say 'no thank you.' She was insistent, trying to push him back and to tell him 'it's fine, you'll enjoy it', but he shook his head madly and only when she wouldn't stop did he push her away and sprint out of the room as fast as he could. That night he walked back to the house, walking through the front door with a frown on his face. When he saw his brother's concerned expression, he quickly smiled, shoving his head and plopping down beside him to help him with his math homework.

Then he was walking down stairs, barely awake, only to nearly fall over when everyone surprised him. That was an amazing fifteenth birthday, eating a homemade carrot cake and going to the park to play with Blaze. The next ones were basic things, him looking quizzically at a page of geometry homework and staying up past midnight to finish a language essay he'd been procrastinating on. Him being asked to play in the football team and refusing, since he greatly disliked the idea of spending so much time throwing a ball or hitting people, instead of doing things with his brother and friends.

Then he got the letter for the rebellion. And his Aunts were glowing as he packed a bag. It showed him that night, not so long ago, tossing and turning in his bed and then waking up a mess the next morning when he was supposed to leave. He was hugging his Aunts and brother before he walked out the door, leaving for what he thought at the time might've been for good.

There was him meeting Sylvia, and then walking out of the door to meet Blu and Strike. Then he was standing under Zami's blade, chest heaving as it pressed into his neck. And Sylvia was talking to her, trying to convince her not to kill him. He hadn't seen how terrified she looked, considering he had been facing the other way, but now there was no mistaking the fear and uncertainty in her eyes as she looked between him and Sylvia. And there was him, watching as Zami stood before the council, arms crossed and looking intimidating. Most of the visions flashed by fast, but it slowed enough to show a couple important things. Him hugging her in the dark, having a pillow fight, setting his jacket over her shoulders as she slept.

It also showed him seeing Spark and staring at her in shock, them hugging, her giving him the ring.

His heart nearly leaped from his chest when their time alone in the tent came up, showing him surprising her and her shoving him with a yelp. Then her pouting gorgeously at him, glancing up from beneath her lashes. And somehow even seeing it in the vision caused butterflies in his chest, watching as he leaned forward and she closed her eyes. But then they both jumped, glaring up at the entrance of the tent.

"You almost kissed!" Blu yelled, reminding Ray that they were indeed in a random dark room in the middle of nowhere.

"That's what you're worrying about?" He said, staring at Blu in disbelief.

My, Raymond. You don't have many regrets or overall fears do you?

He frowned at the voice's choice of words. "Why would I?"

There was a time when you felt like your family's deaths were your fault, right? After all, most of the reason they decided to go to the base was because of your magic and future. But you don't feel that way anymore. Interesting.

There was an almost curious tone to the statement, which was quite odd considering the circumstances. Ray found himself frowning.

"You know, sometimes people do something called 'getting over it' instead of, you know, like hiding out in mountains for dozens of years just to scare some kids who've had the fate of the world thrown on their shoulders." He responded, narrowing his eyes at the wall.

OOOh. Imposing. The voice teased, laughing. *This is only just the beginning for you, my young hero, I wouldn't hold your breath. Now, I do believe we have someone else's mind to look into.*

"Can I take a rain check?" Zami asked, raising her hand like you would as a student in a classroom.

I'm afraid not, young Zami. Your past is far too interesting to just ignore. After all, the point of all this is to show you that no matter what, you can't escape who you are.

The mist swirled aggressively, and even though Zami didn't yell like the rest of them, he could hear her sharp intake of breath as an image began to appear.

He stared at the vision in the mist with great interest, which he felt kind of bad about, but he also didn't know that much about her past. He couldn't help his peaked interest.

There was Zami's mother, just like in the pictures at her grandparents, holding a little Zami. Except in the middle of a cuddle, she looked up at someone not in the vision, her smile disappearing along with the rocking motion. She gently set Zami down and pressed a kiss to her forehead before walking away in the direction of the voice.

That one faded away to another one, showing Zami at probably two or so, sitting on the couch and frowning, her eyes downcast. The object of her distress, or more like two objects, came into the frame, her parents yelling at each other, in what looked to be a really loud argument. Her father was a handsome man, tall with dark hair and eyes, and broad shoulders. From seeing her mom, he had assumed she looked most like her, but the resemblance between her and her father was also there. A strong set jaw, the eyebrow lift, the facial expressions. Zami was like a perfect mix in between them, mostly her mom's looks, with her father's expressions.

He was brought back to focus on the vision when her dad knocked over a chair and her mother backed up in fear. Zami hopped off the couch and ran to her mom, saying something to her dad with a wild look in her eyes. Her father stared at her for a long moment before backing up and stomping away.

The next one showed Zami standing in what looked like an office, her father talking to another person and signing something. She looked about four, though her behavior copied that of someone much older. Then she was in a classroom with a bunch of far older kids, bent over a paper and writing. It showed her getting along mostly fine with other kids, eating lunch with them, making them laugh. Despite the scenes of her parents screaming at each other, she seemed to be getting along mostly fine.

But he could tell there was something wrong, when the mist began to darken at the edges and a little Zami walked in the house, dropping her bag and yelling out something. Something made her freeze and her eyes opened wide before she ran skidding down the hall and into the kitchen. He felt slightly queasy as he watched the scene unfold. Her mom on the floor, arms around her head as Zami's dad hit her. He could only guess what had happened, based off of the shattered wine glass and her blood mixing with the liquid. Zami yelled, running to her dad and trying to keep him from hitting her again. Then he screamed something at her, slapping her across the face. He stomped out of the room, leaving Zami standing there in shock, slowly reaching to touch the already reddening skin. But she snapped out of it quickly, dropping to her knees and trying to shove some of the broken glass out from beneath her mom's head and shoulders. He could see the name 'mom' on her lips as she tried to wipe away the blood.

It then shifted to Zami doing homework at the counter, occasionally glancing at the now clean floor. She jumped when her dad stormed in, trying not to look up and to act like she was focused on the work. But when her father slammed a hand down on the table, she looked up, breathing heavily from fear. He roughly grabbed her left wrist, gesturing to the paper on the table and the pencil that had dropped from her fingers. She looked terrified, trying to pull away, but he just held her tighter until she gave up. Ray stared at the mist in shock when he connected the dots of what was about to happen to an earlier conversation with Zami.

"You're left-handed?"

"Naturally, yeah."

"Then why don't you use it?"

"Oh, um... my uh, my dad thought it was unnatural."

"They insisted it was a bike accident."

"I never even owned a bike."

Then her dad was yelling at her and she was trying to pull from his grasp again, tears running down her face. To his horror when the vision widened, her mother was laying on the couch, fast asleep with a bottle of wine next to her. Zami yelled, clearly trying to call for her, but she didn't wake up, only shifted slightly in her sleep. He twisted his hand slightly and she cried out, body trying to move the same way as her arm. Bile rose in his throat as he watched her dad twist her wrist away from the rest of her body, and he could almost hear a snap through the screen as her dad let go and she dropped to the floor, gripping her wrist.

The next one was her at school again, except kids began to shove her in the hallways. It started out with mocking, then shoving, and eventually more. Then the unmistakable figure of Laci appeared, younger, yet just as snooty. She shoved Zami against a locker, snarling something and opening the nearest empty locker and then shoving her into it. Zami yelled, slamming the door with her fists, but everyone else just laughed and walked away. She spent the whole night in there, shivering and trying to stop the bleeding from a deep scratch on her arm. The next morning, a janitor found her and she stumbled out, trying to leave. But the man grabbed her arm and crouched, trying to say something to her. She shook her head in fear but he gently pulled her to the principal's office, walking in and pointing to her as he said something.

You begged them to forget it, pleaded for them to not bother your parents to come get you.

There was her saying something with wild gestures and tears in her eyes. But only a little while later her dad walked in the office, fuming. He exchanged a word with the other men before roughly gripping Zami's shoulder and steering her out.

In the end, it all just made it worse. No one did a thing about the bullying, just passing it off as 'messing around' in hopes to maintain the school's reputation. And your dad was furious with you.

The next set of visions flashed by rapidly, her dad hitting her again and again, everyday, kids at school hitting her too and her mother in a constant drunken sleep. He got the answer to why her bedroom door had been locked when the vision showed her dad installing a padlock on it.

The next one showed her dad telling her something as she stared at the lines of boxes on the floor, and then her shoving some clothes into a bag before being ushered out the door. And the next thing he knew, they were living in a castle. She looked even more miserable, if that was possible, walking around in dark gloomy hallways and sleeping in a too-dark room.

All the sudden the mist darkened and the vision faltered, eventually cutting off completely.

Ah, yes, and on top of all of that, you have no clue what happened for more than four years of your life. All you knew when your memories came back, was that you had powers, and you acted like you didn't, and your mother was as dead as could be. You don't know how, don't know why, don't know anything...

The vision flickered back to life and revealed a much older Zami, probably eleven or twelve, training with other assassins, practicing with real knives. None of the other people seemed to hold back either, no matter how much older or bigger they were. But Zami looked like she knew what she was doing, in fact almost no one landed a punch on her.

Then she was talking to someone, a young man that was probably eighteen or so, grinning the first real grin he had seen in the vision since she was a baby, as the young man tried to explain some complicated graph on the board. He had roughed up brown hair and thick glasses that prevented any real interpretation of what his eye color might be.

Again the visions quickened, her dad still beating her, her training until late at night, learning from the friendly man. The next years seemed to pass by in a blur, all blending together until she looked like she did now. She was sparring intently with a big man with a scarred face, but Elios startled her, and she was fuming as she gripped a red nose.

Then she was standing in front of her dad as he told her something that made her eyes widen in surprise.

Then he gave you the order to kill the prophecy kid.

And then there was the scene he had seen in his vision, her holding the knife to his throat and staring between him and Sylvia in hesitation. Then she dropped it and the visions flashed to them leaving the rebel base.

Their travels flashed similarly across the screen, slowing similar ones as his, him hugging her in the dark, teasing each other, her breathless laughs. And again he felt butterflies in his stomach as the tent scene popped up, showing him startling her and then their almost-kiss before the yell.

When it finally flashed to them standing right there in the mountain, and the mist cut off, they fell into a heavy silence. Ray tried not to fix his stare on the girl next to him, because he knew it would only make her feel worse, but he couldn't help but glance at her. Who couldn't after seeing such things?

So we have four messed up kids standing here in an attempt to save the world? What are you supposed to do in this big huge world? You're just kids, so why are you the ones who have to do this?

The answer is simple. Adults want you to fix their mistakes, everything they ruin is now your responsibility to fix. Dumping all the responsibility on a group of teens who have trouble enough functioning on a day to day basis doesn't seem like a worthy thing to do, does it? So the real question I have for you is, why?

Why are you here trying to save the same world that messed you up so badly? Why are you risking everything you have, just to help people who don't even trust you enough to let you make the decisions?

They remained silent, heads spinning as they processed the words. It was ridiculous what they were being expected to accomplish, what adults couldn't accomplish themselves. So why were they doing it? Why weren't they just trying to live their lives like normal teenagers?

"Because we can."

Ray glanced at Zami, doing a double-take at the amount of anger laced in her expression.

"And because we live in this world too, and want to make it better."

Somehow those few words seemed to resonate through the room, leaving him speechless. They weren't particularly powerful words, nor did she say them with a special voice like the prophet. The thing that left him speechless was that after everything that people did to her, after all her suffering and the horrible influence of her father, she still believed in doing the right thing. She still believed in helping people, even when they wouldn't help her.

Well, that's surprising. The voice said, sounding a little more repressed than before. *You were the last one I expected to say something so... good.*

Zami opened her mouth to say something, but across the room a door opened, one that he hadn't noticed before. He couldn't quite tell what was behind it, but there was something that was telling him to walk towards it, that he *needed* to go in there.

"That's it." Zami said, eyes locked on the door. He nodded, and before he knew what was happening, he found himself walking towards it, the others close behind him.

And without a second thought, he stepped through the doorway.

Chapter 27

↔

Zami stared raptly at the pedestal in the center of the room, supporting a small figure on top that was hard to discern, due to a bright glow and uncertain shape. The room was fairly large, and overall, incredibly empty, their footsteps echoing in the open space. Only when she registered a snoring sound did she notice the girl asleep on a bench next to the desirable. It was clear she was supposed to be a guard, though she didn't seem to be doing too much guarding right then.

She walked up to girl, and in sympathy for the fact that she would probably get in a lot of trouble if she failed in her guard duty, decided to wake her up. She didn't try very to be gentle, however, as she was tired and annoyed at the events of the last few hours. So she may, or may not have shoved her off of the bench, which did successfully wake the girl up. The girl yelped as she fell, and quickly scrambled back up to standing, adjusting her robes.

She looked up after nearly a minute of shuffling in her robes, freezing when she saw Zami. "What? Don't judge me, I had a rough night of sleep. Patrick wouldn't shut up." A loud squawk filled the air as a brightly colored parrot soared through the air and landed on the girl's shoulder.

"Don't judge! Don't judge!" It squawked loudly, widely flapping its wings.

Zami suppressed a laugh and held up her hands in surrender. "Don't worry, I'm not judging."

"Good!" The girl exclaimed, flicking short dark hair over her shoulder and squinting at her with bright blue eyes. She looked about thirteen or so, with almond shaped eyes and pouty lips. "I suppose you're here to take the bright thingy?"

"Um, yeah, the bright thing." She copied, biting her lip to keep herself from laughing.

"What! It's not like I ever get told anything! It's always, we'll tell you when your older, Spring! You don't need to know, Spring!" She glanced behind her, taking notice of the others, and her frown deepened. "Well whatever, go ahead."

"Um, no offense, but aren't you supposed to be like... protecting it?" Blu asked quizzically, and Zami nodded. There was no way after that creepy hallway, ominous voice, hurtful memories and patronizing questions they would just be *handed* the desirable. What was so hard about getting it that all of the others had failed?

"Well, technically!" The girl threw her hands up in the air and aimed her yelling to the floor. "No one would be coming right now!" She mocked. "Don't worry Spring, no one's gonna be here and we'll only be gone for a couple days! Well would you look at this," She gestured at them widely. "That doesn't seem like NO ONE, MA!"

Zami snorted and tried to cover it up by coughing, far too amused to not laugh.

"No one! No one!" The bird chirped and Zami lost it. She laughed, stumbling backwards to keep her balance and gripping her stomach. Tears sprung from her eyes and she could almost feel everyone looking at her in confusion. But it was just so ridiculous! This whole time, everything they'd done, when the only people who helped them were the ones supposed to be against them. It was all just incredibly ironic!

"Zames? You good?"

She nodded from her hunched over position, wiping tears from her eyes and glancing back up at them.

"I think she's finally lost it." She heard Blu whisper to Strike and Ray, and she shot him a glare, though she was still giddy.

"So how do we know you're not trying to trick us?" She asked, slightly out of breath as she looked back to Spring.

Spring shrugged, reaching up and stroking Patrick's head. "You don't." Zami liked that answer. "Though, I would be careful. No one's touched the glowing thing in years, but last time I heard about it, I think something bad happens when the wrong person touches it."

"Well, that's kind of ambiguous." Blu said sarcastically and received a smack from Strike.

"Any way to know who should touch it?" She asked, examining the desirable. She couldn't make out a shape, or a way to grab it. The light seemed to resonate from the center of it, sending a soft thrumming into the air around it. Something about it made her feel calm, some sort of warm feeling spreading in her chest. "Do you feel that?" She breathed, glancing at the others. They all nodded, eyes focused on it.

"It's the peace desirable." Ray observed, eyes slightly glowing.

She nodded, trying to figure out what they needed to do. "The dove gets mad." She quoted, turning back to the others. "It keeps on repeating that, the riddle, the voices, it must have some significance."

"Well the dove is the symbol of peace." Strike said.

"But why would the peace desirable get mad?" Ray asked.

"And how?" Blu asked, frowning.

She shrugged, trying to think. Who needed to touch it? Was there even a clue to who needed to, or was it just a wild guess? She went over everything the voice said, trying to discern any clues, anything that hinted to who was supposed to touch it.

"Blu..." She started, staring at him.

"Um, yeah?"

"He chose to show your past first, there must be some reason for that..."

"Peace." Ray cut in, straightening up. "Blu, what changed your life the most?" Zami blinked at him, understanding dawning on her. It was Strike who said it, however.

"Peace. He came to peace with who he was!"

Zami grinned, her heart racing. The others looked excited as well, all staring at Blu. Blu's eyes widened as he looked at them.

"So I'm supposed to touch the bright thingy?" He asked, waving his hands around to make a sphere shape in the air.

"Yes!" She exclaimed, along with the others. Before Blu could make a move though, a yell filled the room. Standing on the other side of the room were three women, fierce looks on their faces and thick swords in their hands. They froze for a long moment, but as soon as Zami saw the muscles in their arms twitch, she yelled.

"BLU!"

All at once he lunged forward and grabbed the light as the woman in front yelled, charging forward. But they stopped when Blu picked it up, and it instantly shifted into a small stone carving of a dove.

The room was silent until one of the women spoke, voice seething with anger. "You picked it up!" She yelled, looking around wildly as if waiting for something to happen. She stormed forward, but Spring grabbed her arm.

"Nothing's happening, Ma. That means he's *supposed* to have it."

Blu was holding the stone as far away from him as possible, looking disturbed. "Was something supposed to happen?" He squeaked, eyes still on the dove as if it would jump up and bite his head off.

Before the woman could respond, yet another yell filled the air, this time from the entrance. They slowly turned around, coming face to face with a group she recognized. They were assassins she'd trained with back with her father.

"You've gotta be joking!" Blu yelled, and Zami guessed if he hadn't been holding the desirable he would be gesturing madly. "Can't we kill each other someplace else?"

However, the invaders wasted no time, and before she knew what was happening she was ducking under a fireball. "Hold a grudge much?" She mumbled underneath her breath as metal clanging filled the air and various dangerous magic whizzed through the air. She could feel her hair standing on edge from the sparkling electricity filling the room and the whoosh of water putting out fire.

It was hard to tell what was going on as she kicked a guy hard in the stomach, trying to locate her friends. When a sword was swung at her face though, and nearly took out a chunk of her head, she slowly turned around to focus on her adversary. When he swung again, she didn't hesitate, calling on her magic the only way she could. She didn't even register the weapon in her hand, just swung it at the man as hard as possible. She couldn't afford to avoid killing someone when there was so much on the line. Whipping around, she jumped back to avoid another fireball from another attacker, pushing Spring out of harm's way as well. Anger boiled in her bones as she realized that he had fully meant to kill the young girl. With a growl, she attacked him, not even bothering to give him a chance before she struck the weapon of darkness deep into his stomach.

She felt panic consume her, however, when her magic flickered away from her hands, remembering that it was just as unreliable as learning to walk was to a toddler. With a yell, she reached up to protect her face from another sword, only to realize it hadn't connected. She looked up to see Ray twisting the man's arm and grabbing the sword before it hit the floor, swinging it back and twirling it around so he was gripping the blade, then slamming the hilt hard into the man's head.

"NO!"

Zami whipped around to see Spring's mom yelling at something happening on the other side of the room. She slowly turned, met with the sight of an unknown man holding the desirable high above his head in triumph. The celebration was short however, when a deep rumbling filled the cavern and everyone froze, staring at the opening to the room.

Then before anyone could say anything, the wall crashed down and a flood of water crashed in the room. She was barely able to take a breath before it hit her hard, the crashing force of it hitting the other wall and filling her ears with noise, as she tried to push against the water, her lungs quickly running out of air.

Slowly though, before she succumbed, the water lowered, leaving her disoriented and wet. When she managed to blink the water from her eyes, she looked around to see crumbling walls, water flowing out of many new cracks to the outside.

Moonlight shone on the rubble, highlighting the still standing figures of the three women and Spring, and the bodies laying on the ground, unmoving. From what she could tell, the bodies were all soldiers of the King. A hand grabbed hers and she turned to see a wet, but alive Ray standing there, relief on his face. The air slowly calmed as they realized everything was fine, Spring huddling with the other women.

Then her stomach tightened and she whipped around to face Ray who had just come the same realization.

"Where's Blu and Strike?"